THE LAST SNOWFALL

THE LAST SNOWFALL

Copyright © 2023 Justine Castellon

Paperback ISBN 979-8-9883810-5-1 / ASIN B0CKRMYC7D
Ebook ISBN 979-8-9883810-3-7 / ASIN B0CKPR4Q4H

Printed in 2023

Published in the United States of America

By Brandbureau Consulting LLC
Cheyenne, WY 82001

Book design by Aina Robeniol

For Carlos, Luis & Julia

Download Spotify Reading Playlist at bit.ly / TLS-Playlist curated by Mike Dee.

1

With sleep still clinging to my eyelids, I found myself cocooned in the coziness of our bedroom. Beyond the penthouse windows, New York City was in the icy clutches of a pre-dawn December morning. Despite being wrapped up in the warmth of our modern heater, I couldn't help but shiver as I glimpsed the frosty cityscape. Winter was here, its arrival as silent and unannounced as a thief in the night.

Our bed, a vast cloud of comfy goodness, was a mess of ruffled white sheets — telltale signs of a good night's kip. My gaze drifted to a shadowy corner where Salem, my stubborn black fur ball, was curled up tighter than a Danish pastry, his soft purrs composing a soothing morning symphony in the tranquil silence.

My eyes landed on the dreamy face sleeping next to me — Richard, deep in Dreamland. Carefully, I traced his lips with my fingertips, soaking up the warmth of his sleepy exhale. A hint of a smile danced at the corners of his mouth, as if my touch had tickled a happy nerve in his slumber.

I could spend hours studying that face and never get bored. His jawline could have been chiseled by Michelangelo himself, and his dark, tousled hair only added to his boyish charm. Hidden behind closed lids were his stormy blue-grey eyes, so intense they could give the dawning city skyline a run for its money.

This handsome man beside me wasn't merely a Hollywood and British heartthrob; he was a human hurricane that set box offices, TV ratings, and endorsement deals ablaze. But his looks? That was just the tip of the iceberg. Richard was as brainy as he was beautiful, with a love for books that matched mine and possessing an understanding of art that would make any art scholar green with envy. This combination of brawn and brains had me head over heels, irrevocably and passionately in love with him.

So there I was, taking a trip down memory lane, thinking about our first date — talk about an unexpected plot twist! We were supposed to be at this big shindig celebrating the wrap-up of *Back In Time* (a pretty snazzy TV series now airing on ABC, with yours truly as the scriptwriter, thank you very much). But instead, it turned into an impromptu matchmaking session. Who would've thought?

The next day, Richard, being the charming devil he is, surprised me with the first edition of Jane Austen's *Pride and Prejudice*. I mean, come on! How am I supposed to resist a man who knows his classics? That book now sits pretty in our home library downstairs, rubbing spines with other first editions that Richard has hoarded over the years.

Fast forward a year, and we're still together, riding this emotional rollercoaster they call love. We've had our share of highs, lows, loop-de-loops, and everything in between. We've weathered everything from shared laughter and hushed whispers to facing the heartbreak of losing our pregnancy. And through every twist and turn, our bond has only gotten stronger, like superglue on steroids.

As I lay there, watching Richard sleeping beside me, a wave of gratitude hit me like a ton of bricks. Despite the whirlwind of city life and the crazy world of showbiz, we've managed to create our own little sanctuary. Sure, we've had our fair share of trials, but the laughter, love, and unwavering support made every bump in the road worth it. Life with Richard? Now, that's a script I'd write any day!

I nuzzled into Richard's hair with a sigh that could've rivaled the wind outside. His scent wrapped around me like a *Snuggie*, a comforting blend of his cologne and something uniquely him. He stirred, reaching out for me in his sleep. I planted a soft smooch on his lips and whispered, "Go back to sleep, my love." Even in his slumber, he smiled and drifted off again.

* * *

I picked up Richard's crumpled white shirt from the pile of clothes on the floor and wrapped it around my naked body. Donning Richard's shirt, which, let's face it, looked good on me in a post-sex moment, I walked over to the mirror and gave myself the once-over. Standing at a not-too-shabby five feet seven inches, my body and long legs were toned from regular yoga. My skin wasn't the typical New Yorker's alabaster complexion — it was a delicious caramel, courtesy of my Filipino dad and American mom.

My facial features were like a cocktail of East and West — Mom's high cheekbones and sharp nose, complemented by Dad's rich brown eyes. I often wished I got my mother's eyes, which were green with specks of grey. My hair, a cascade of chocolate waves, tumbled to my shoulders while my bangs played peek-a-boo with my forehead. My teeth, as straight as a ruler and as white as fresh snow, were the crowning glory of my teenage years spent in braces. You could say I was like a human United Nations, a blend of the best bits from both sides of the globe.

Despite being 28, people often mistook me for someone in their early thirties. My best friend Erin joked that I was trying to level up to Richard, who, at 44, still had the charm and looks of a thirty-something heartthrob.

One last glance in the mirror, I couldn't help but smirk. I could just imagine how Richard would react if he woke up seeing me wearing his shirt, which always drove him mad with desire. With a wink at my reflection, I tiptoed over to the window.

Outside, Mother Nature was putting on a show. Snowflakes were falling like confetti, each a tiny work of art, turning the city into a giant snow globe. It was like watching a ballet, only with snowflakes instead of ballerinas. They twirled and pirouetted in the air before settling down on the windowsill, creating a frosty masterpiece that sparkled under the glow of the streetlights.

My breath fogged up the glass as I peered outside. The streetlights cast a soft glow on the pavement below, illuminating the otherwise deserted streets. New York City, the city that never sleeps, had hit the snooze button. The usual soundtrack of honking taxis and wailing sirens had been replaced by the soft whispers of the wind and the crunch-crunch-crunch of boots in the snow. Watching the city morph into a winter wonderland, I felt a wave of peace wash over me. This was our little slice of heaven amidst the concrete jungle, and as long as we had each other, we could weather any blizzard.

Curled up on our white couch, so plush it could double as a cloud, I was completely engrossed in the snow show happening outside. The city was slowly waking up, its usually vibrant palette replaced by shades of white. The city of technicolor dreams was now a black-and-white postcard, a picture-perfect moment of serenity.

All of a sudden, I felt something plop onto my lap. Salem. And he promptly began his morning grooming routine. Afterward, he gazed at me and blinked his yellow eyes — his way of kissing me. Then he turned toward the window, his ears dancing at the sight of the snowfall. He let out a tiny meow, sounding as disappointed as if saying, 'I hate it here.' I scratched his ear and replied, "I know you can't enjoy your usual outdoor activities today. Too chilly for your daily shenanigans."

We sat together, watching as the city woke up from its slumber. I could almost hear the sound of muffled laughter and chatter floating up to us. The miniature-like people emerged from their warm apartments, bundled up in coats and scarves, their breath visible in the chilly air — a gentle reminder of the life buzzing below. The snow continued to fall, blanketing the streets and rooftops in a pristine layer of white. It seemed as though the city had been granted a fresh start — a clean slate on which to write the next chapter of its story.

Throughout the day, the cityscape will change. The pristine sheet of snow will quickly be marked by endless footprints and tire tracks, like an artist's canvas coming alive with each brushstroke. But at this moment, up in our penthouse with Salem on my lap and Richard in our bed, it was as if New York City had hit the reset button, its usual hustle-bustle giving way to a moment of calm.

A feeling of warmth spread through me as I thought about the change in seasons. Each one came with its own set of surprises. What would spring bring? Or summer? Or fall? The mystery of the four seasons made me feel like a kid on Christmas Eve.

After one last look at the snowy spectacle outside, I returned to our bed as Salem followed. The choice between the aroma of coffee and a hot plate breakfast or snuggling back into Richard's arms was more challenging than picking a favorite pizza topping. While the latter seemed more appealing and was definitely my ultimate choice, I also knew that going back to bed meant not wanting to get up... just staying within Richard's arms. But adulting called, and I had to answer.

As I stroked Salem's soft fur, I whispered, "Keep an eye on Richard while I'm gone, okay?" Salem gave me a look that seemed to say, '*Why would I do that? That fellow is the reason why my life is so miserable now!*' before jumping off my lap and strutting off to find Leticia, our housekeeper, and make her day a little more... interesting.

I stood from the bed and covered Richard's naked body with a blanket. His peaceful face made me smile; a silent promise of love awaited me when I returned. As I shut the door behind me, I couldn't help but feel grateful for the life we've built — a little piece of paradise amidst the city jungle, filled with love, laughter, of course, and a dash of feline drama.

———

As I walked into the dining room, I could sense the tension, so thick you could cut it with a butter knife. There was Salem, the feline prince of drama, perched on the windowsill like a jilted lover in a soap opera. His tail flicked back and forth like a metronome set to agitated while his eyes, as yellow as a pumpkin soup, stared longingly at the winter wonderland outside.

I knew he was missing our old neighborhood on 89th Street, particularly Charlie and Victoria Sung, who owned the flower shop downstairs but also fed him treats. Before we moved in with Richard, Salem was the king of his little jungle, chasing butterflies and climbing trees like they were going out of style. But ever since we moved into this swanky penthouse on the Upper East Side, his wild adventures had been reduced to epic naps and occasional cloud-watching sessions from the window.

Across the room, Leticia, our housekeeper and resident cat skeptic, was busy giving our kitchen shelves a thorough dust-busting workout. The furrow in her brow was deeper than the Grand Canyon as she tried to ignore Salem's theatrical sighs and longing glances.

"Salem, for Pete's sake, knock off the drama!" Leticia finally snapped as Salem let out a meow that could shatter glass. Watching them — my brooding cat and our equally grumpy housekeeper — was like watching a sitcom. Funny and endearing but also a stark reminder of Salem's struggle to adjust to his new life.

"Leticia, let's cut him some slack," I said, jumping to Salem's defense. "The poor guy is just having a tough time adjusting."

Leticia let out a sigh that made Salem's dramatic sighs look like amateur hour. She put her duster down, disappeared into the kitchen, and re-emerged with a plate piled high with bacon, eggs, toast, and roasted tomatoes. "Alright, I get it," she conceded, "but he needs to understand that this is home now. No more sulking."

As she set the breakfast plate before me and filled my glass with fresh orange juice, my stomach did a happy dance. Leticia was right. We needed to help Salem stop dwelling on the past and start enjoying his present.

I walked over to Salem, giving him a comforting scratch behind his ears. "Hey," I whispered, "I know you miss our old digs, but we've got to roll with the punches here. You'll grow to love this place, pinky promise."

Salem looked up at me, his big, yellow eyes full of hope and confusion. He purred softly, but the sadness still lingered.

"Maybe we could make things a bit more comfortable for him," I suggested to Leticia as I returned to my seat. "How about a new cat tree, which we can put at the promenade on the kitchen side, or some toys to keep him entertained?"

She mulled over my idea for a moment before nodding. "That might work. I'll pick something up when I go grocery shopping later."

With that, Leticia returned to her chores, and I went back to consoling Salem before returning to my breakfast. I knew it would take time for him to settle in, but I was ready to move mountains to make him feel at home. And who knows? Maybe one day, Leticia would crack a smile when Salem struts into a room.

Richard emerged from our room upstairs, looking like a Greek god on a casual Tuesday. The sunlight transformed into his personal spotlight, his hair still damp from the shower. The droplets glistened as they caught the morning light. I paused for a moment, unable to resist admiring how handsome he looked.

"Mmm... good morning, beautiful," he drawled, his voice smoother than a Barry White track. He leaned in to kiss me, his lips soft against mine. They tasted of mint and carried a heavenly scent that made my heart race.

"What did I miss?" Richard asked, his blue-grey eyes twinkling with mischief. He glanced between Salem and Leticia, picking up on the frosty vibes quicker than a weatherman. At the sound of Richard's voice, Salem's ears perked up, and he turned to face us. His yellow eyes narrowed as he hissed at Richard, seemingly holding him responsible for all the changes and upheavals in his life.

"Salem's been grumbling again," I explained with a sigh. "He's missing the Sungs and their endless supply of treats."

Richard's eyebrows shot up to his hairline at the mention of our treat-hoarding neighbors. His gaze landed on Salem, who responded with a hiss that screamed, *'You're dead to me, human.'*

"Yikes, tough crowd," Richard quipped, raising his hands defensively, feigning shock at Salem's reaction. "Didn't know I was playing the villain here."

* * *

I laughed at his dramatics, grateful for the comic relief. "Don't take it personally, Richard. Salem is just being... Salem."

Leticia joined in, her voice laced with amusement. "Just give him some space. He'll come around... eventually." She punctuated her words by popping more bacon and tomatoes into the oven, filling the room with the mouthwatering aroma of breakfast.

Richard ran a hand through his tousled hair, looking thoughtful. "It's funny," he mused, "I managed to win over you and even your parents, but Salem? That cat is a tougher nut to crack." His face showed an exaggerated apologetic look, and I burst into laughter.

As Leticia placed a plate of steaming breakfast in front of Richard, he turned back to me. "So, what's on your to-do list today?" He was off filming duty and planning a trip to London to renew his US work visa, which was set to expire in a few weeks. He hadn't asked me to tag along, knowing that London and I had a complicated history after my harrowing kidnapping incident last year.

"Well, it's Tuesday, so I have a management meeting at the office, and later, I'm meeting with a tech firm to discuss our new expansion into film production," I told him, sipping my coffee. "Want to play the supportive boyfriend?"

Richard flashed a charming smile but shook his head. "Darling, as much as I'd love to, I don't want anyone to think I'm guarding the lady boss," he said with a playful smirk.

I rolled my eyes, chuckling. "Oh, please! As if the entire universe isn't already aware that you're sleeping with the lady boss," I retorted, unable to hide my amusement.

Richard joined in my laughter, his eyes filled with mischief. "True, but no need to rub it in their faces. I still don't want to make your colleagues uncomfortable. Plus, I trust you can handle everything on your own — you're a powerhouse. But how about dinner tonight?"

I stood up, planting a quick smooch on his lips. "Sounds perfect. Jeffrey can play chauffeur for you, and I'll stick with the twin goons," I teased, referring to our bouncer-like security detail, Chen and Arthur.

"Do you need me to guard the shower, darling?" Richard winked, his grin cheeky.

"Dream on, Richard. I'm running late!" I called out, leaving him laughing and cooing at Salem, "Now, I see where you get your attitude from, buddy."

2

Stepping out of the sleek black town car, I plunged into the pulsating heart of Manhattan. The skyscrapers were like lofty giants, stretching their necks to kiss the sky. And among them, my father's newly remodeled building stood tall and proud. This was the nerve center of the US and European expansion of his global real estate empire, and now, it housed the new headquarters for my publishing and film production company.

I took a deep breath, feeling a surge of excitement and anticipation course through my veins. My heels clicked against the pavement as I approached the grand entrance, the sound echoing through the busy streets. The sun glinted off the glass facade, casting a warm glow on my face. I couldn't help but smile — this was the beginning of a new chapter, and I was ready to embrace it with open arms.

Chen and Arthur, the formidable twin goons, moved in perfect synchrony as they followed closely behind me. They're not actually twins — both Asians who dressed exactly the same as Tommy Lee Jones and Will Smith in *Men In Black*. Their poker faces and bulging muscles screamed, "Don't mess with us!" They were now officially my bodyguards, assigned by my father to ensure my safety. In addition to them was Jeffrey, employed by Richard, who always had my six.

Before I discovered I wasn't just a regular Jane but actually an heiress to Daddy Warbucks, Chen and Arthur had been my secret guardian angels since my university days. Back then, I was blissfully oblivious to my VIP status and happily living in la-la land. It wasn't until last year, while working as a screenwriter for the TV series *Back In Time*, that our paths crossed again. That's where I bumped into Richard, the smoldering lead actor who turned out to be more than just a pretty face.

Once upon a time, I was just a girl next door, sharing a cramped apartment with my furball, barely scraping by. Now? Well, let's just say things have changed quite a bit. There were moments when I yearned for the old days — the freedom to walk down the street or hop on a subway without the fear of being papped.

Sure, I missed the simplicity of my past, but I'd be lying if I said this new chapter didn't have its own perks. Making my way across the marble-floored lobby, I felt the weight of my new world settle on my shoulders. I wasn't just an ordinary girl anymore — I was Oliver Ortega's sole heir and a budding powerhouse in my own right. And so, the adventure begins...

Stepping through the revolving doors, I caught my reflection doing a little dance on the glossy marble walls. My long, wavy brown hair framed my face, accentuating my high cheekbones and brown eyes. I looked more American than Asian, a unique blend of my heritage. Today, I opted for a tailored navy blue pantsuit, exuding an air of confidence and professionalism. The fabric hugged my figure just right, making me feel powerful and elegant. I accessorized with a delicate gold necklace that lay gently against my collarbone, matching earrings that sparkled in the light, and the four-seasons Tiffany charm bracelet Richard gave me.

The lobby was abuzz with activity, but as I walked in, there was a noticeable shift in the atmosphere.

"Good morning, Ms. Ortega," chimed one of the receptionists, sounding like a star-struck fan. I'm still trying to acclimate myself to being addressed as Ortega. I was Hope Williams for 27 years, proudly bearing my mother's family name. But last year, in an unexpected twist, both my parents decided that it was time for me to adopt my father's last name. This ensured no one would question my place in the world and aligned my identity with the name emblazoned across every facet of Ortega's Holdings.

* * *

Meanwhile, the private security guards, who probably moonlight as bouncers at some swanky nightclub, were busy playing 'Elevator Traffic Control.' They were making sure no one dared to invade my personal space by sharing an elevator ride with me. I mean, come on! It's not like I've got cooties or something. I really don't mind rubbing elbows with other humans in an elevator. Heck, I've survived riding the subway for decades, so packed you could smell what the guy next to you had for breakfast!

As I strutted across the lobby, I could feel a million eyes on me, their gazes bouncing off my invisible shield of determination and poise. My father had built an empire, and now it was my turn to make my own mark on the world.

I stepped into the elevator, and Chen pressed the button for the top floor. The ascent was smooth, and the panoramic views of Manhattan took my breath away. When the doors finally slid open, I was greeted by the familiar sight of my office.

"Good morning, Ms. Hope!" Hillary, my secretary, was someone in the executive office assigned to assist me and do some heavy lifting in my administrative functions. "Here's your coffee, soya milk, half sugar." She handed me the usual Starbucks coffee on the go.

Hillary was a blond, petite woman, very energetic and capable of working magic on logistics. "You have a management meeting at 11 AM, which I already canceled because your father's secretary informed me that he wants to see you at lunch. Ms. Yumi will join you at the meeting with Star Communications at 3 PM. Jenna Huey called and asked for a return call. I will dial her number as soon as you're settled. Do you want me to close your schedule for today?" She asked, her pen poised over the day planner.

"Yes, please. And pencil in my dinner with Richard," I said as we walked into my office. "Oh, and can you ring him up and give him a hand with the table booking?"

"Of course, Ms. Hope! I'll take care of it right away," she chirped back, flashing me a grin that could outshine the sun.

* * *

"You're a star, Hillary!" I exclaimed as I took a sip from the paper cup. Hillary was a walking, talking efficiency machine, I swear. As she left to make the arrangements, I settled into my chair and prepared myself for the day ahead.

It may be where I worked but my office served as a sanctuary, reflecting my personality and passion for the creative arts. Floor-to-ceiling windows bathed the room in natural light, showcasing the rich mahogany bookshelves filled with my extensive collection of novels and scripts. Framed movie posters and original artwork from some of my favorite films and authors adorned the walls, including the promotional poster of Richard dressed in 1920s attire for *Back In Time*. "Hello there, handsome," I whispered to the framed poster.

In the cozy nook, a neat stack of my very own novel, both paperback and hardcover editions of *Fleeting Embers*, were proudly displayed. This is my pride and joy — this baby of mine was more than just ink on paper, it was a gut-wrenching saga of love and loss, a poignant reminder of the fleeting nature of joy. *Fleeting Embers* painted the lives of two young hearts, Sarah and Martin, who found a haven in each other amidst the whirlwind of their personal battles. The backdrop? An idyllic, postcard-perfect town that added its own charm to their story.

Flashback to last year, I remember the sting of reality as I pitched this novel to an array of agents and publishers. They didn't want my novel; they wanted me. More specifically, they wanted an autobiography — a tell-all tale of my life with Richard, or rather, Richard's life with me. It felt like a punch to the gut, but then, Astral Ink came to the rescue. They saw the potential in my novel, published it, and voila! A successful launch!

During my book launch, after months of separation, Richard surprised me and returned to New York. In front of the press and guests, he slipped my engagement ring back onto my finger, and from that moment forward, he never let me go. Every time I glance at *Fleeting Embers*, it serves as a sweet reminder. Despite owning a publishing and film company, at heart, I will always be Hope Williams, the writer.

* * *

At the heart of the room, a sleek glass desk symbolized my aspirations and the work I still had to accomplish. A plush, high-backed white leather chair beckoned me, inviting me to immerse myself in the realm of storytelling and imagination.

The office phone rang, and I switched it to speaker mode. It was Jenna. "I didn't call your mobile because I know Richard's in town, Esperanza. I don't want to intrude," she said, skipping any pleasantries and diving straight to the point — typical Jenna.

Jenna Huey, a bestselling author known for her romantic fiction, was my boss once. I was privileged to work as a book editor and character developer for her novels. Things took an exciting turn when one of her books, *Back In Time*, was selected for a TV series adaptation. This opportunity propelled me into the world of screenplay writing. My career took an unexpected turn, and suddenly, I was thrust into the glitzy world of screenplay writing, and boy, was it a wild ride!

And the best part? Jenna and I hit it off somewhere along the line of plot twists and character arcs. We went from sharing professional critiques to sharing inside jokes and going on café hunts. Yes, you heard it right - I became pals with THE Jenna Huey. Crazy, huh? But hey, that's just how the cookie crumbles in the writing world!

"You know you can always reach out to me, whether Richard's around or not," I replied.

"Anyway, I'm calling to pitch Season 2 of *Back In Time*," she announced.

I paused, confused. "But, Jenna, we're already committed through Book 3, right?"

"That was during your father's time, when he was the producer. Now that you're in charge, I thought it proper to pitch it again," she asserted.

I laughed. "Come on, I wrote the script. It's done. You just need to work on the production timeline. Besides, Season 1 is rating well as we speak.".

"Aren't you going to head the production for Season 2?"

* * *

"Jenna, I want to focus on screenwriting. That's where my interest lies," I clarified.

"Esperanza, you never change. You're still my favorite girl, with better clothes and a handsome fiancé now," she laughed.

I smiled, glancing at the silver-framed photo of Richard and me on my desk — a candid shot he'd posted on my Instagram account and our very first photo together. We weren't even a couple then, but we already looked so happy. Returning to the present, I told Jenna we'd have lunch the following day before saying our goodbyes.

I ended the call just as Hillary slipped into my office, reminding me about my lunch meeting with my father. "I've already notified Arthur and Chen to meet you in the lobby," she informed me. "And don't forget about your four o'clock meeting with the tech firm."

"Thanks, Hillary," I said as I collected my phone and bag, preparing to meet my father.

———

As I stepped into the lavish Manhattan restaurant, I immediately spotted my father, Oliver Ortega. He was comfortably seated by a window, looking every bit the influential figure in his customary dark pinstripe suit. A handsome man of 50, his Filipino-Chinese lineage lent him a unique charm. His 5'11" frame was topped with hair that was a handsome blend of dark and salt-and-pepper shades, while his intense brown eyes held an allure few could resist. He had a natural ability to be the center of attention, even when he wasn't consciously making an effort. I strolled over and claimed the seat opposite him, eager to catch up and discuss our plans.

"Hope, sweetheart! You look absolutely stunning," he exclaimed, his eyes sparkling with delight as he kissed my cheek affectionately. "How does life treat you these days?"

"Busy but good," I replied, smiling. "The Quill Quest Publishing is taking off."

* * *

Our waiter approached, and we quickly ordered a delicate lobster bisque for me and a hearty steak for my father. We both opted for glasses of rich, velvety Bordeaux, knowing it would perfectly complement our meals.

The sommelier filled both our glasses. As we savored our wine, my father dove straight into business talk. "Tell me more about your publishing firm," he asked, reclining in his chair. "Are you planning to expand?"

"Dad, you've seen the reports. You're aware of everything happening at my firm. Our updates go to the executive committee, and I'm certain they relay everything to you," I replied, idly spinning my wine glass.

"I do. But I want to hear it from you," my father insisted.

"Okay!" I nodded eagerly. "Dad, we're contemplating diversifying into other media. We're exploring film, television, and even podcasts. The opportunities are limitless!" I told him about my meeting with a tech company about developing an app for writers all over the world to pitch their books or scripts without needing to travel to Hollywood in Los Angeles.

"An app for writers to present their work without traveling? That's an excellent idea, Hope. It'll create numerous opportunities for undiscovered talent."

I grinned, a wave of pride washing over me. "Precisely. We aim to provide a platform as accessible as possible for creative minds to showcase their stories to the world. With the right guidance and support, we might just discover the next bestseller or blockbuster hit."

My father nodded, impressed by the concept. "And how do you plan to monetize this app? Will users need to pay a subscription fee, or will you rely on advertising revenue?"

"We're still working out the details," I admitted, "but we're considering a freemium model. Basic access would be free, while premium features like personalized feedback and priority pitching would come at a cost.

We believe this approach will strike the right balance between accessibility and profitability."

My father's eyes sparkled with excitement. "That's fantastic, Hope. I always knew you had a keen eye for business. It's in your blood."

Our food arrived, and we eagerly dug in. The lobster bisque was divine, its creamy texture and hint of sherry made my taste buds dance. My father appeared equally delighted with his perfectly cooked steak, accompanied by a mouthwatering peppercorn sauce.

Pausing between bites, he asked, "How do you plan to manage all these projects? It's quite a lot to take on."

I thought for a moment before responding. "We intend to hire more staff and partner with other creative agencies. Having a strong team in place is crucial for supporting our growth."

Dad nodded, taking a sip of his Bordeaux. "True. And what about financing? Expanding into new territories can be expensive."

"We're casting a wide net," I responded with an air of assurance. "We've entertained overtures from potential investors while simultaneously considering the route of crowdfunding campaigns. I'm confident that we'll secure the necessary funds."

"I want Ortega's Holdings to retain majority ownership. If necessary, only offer a 20% stake to outside investors," he instructed. "Maintain as much family control over the business as possible and limit outsider involvement to a minimum."

"Dad, you've already poured so much into this. This venture is a small fish in your vast sea of holdings – it barely makes a ripple, let alone a significant contribution. At least not yet! I'm so excited about our future but I don't want to impose on you, especially now that my firm is finally out of the red," I asserted with pride.

"All the more reason for me to invest further in you," he pronounced with conviction.

* * *

"Thanks, Dad. By the way, how long are you in town?" I asked, dabbing my lips with the linen napkin from my lap. My father was primarily based in Manila and Singapore, where our main headquarters were situated.

"I'm jetting off to London on Wednesday. I've heard Richard is heading there this week; he could accompany me. It's high time I spent some quality time with my future son-in-law," he remarked with a smile, then promptly followed up with, "When is the wedding date?"

"That sounds like a great plan!" I replied. "As for the wedding, we're still in the process of finalizing the date."

He savored the final bite of his steak before remarking, "You know, your mother never ceases to inquire about it."

The revelation that my parents were in consistent contact took me by surprise. When my father left New York to oversee their businesses, I was just two years old. My mother was so heartbroken, she severed all ties with him. However, after my heartwarming reunion with Dad last year, she found it in her heart to forgive him. Mom now led a contented life with my stepdad Steve in sunny California, while Dad remained a bachelor. "Dad, when Mom broached the subject, she actually wanted you to discuss it with me," I explained, rolling my eyes playfully.

He responded with a hearty chuckle. "I'm aware of that." He seemed to hold onto a thought momentarily before choosing instead to say, "Your mother appears genuinely happy with her life now, and that fills me with joy."

Reaching across the table, I gently clasped his hand and asked, "Do you still have feelings for Mom?"

"I never stopped loving her. But ensuring her happiness has always been my foremost concern. Seeing her find it with Steve is more than I could have ever hoped for," he confessed, returning the squeeze on my hand.

Then, without missing a beat, he deftly steered the conversation in a new direction. "Hope, I understand this is a delicate matter, but we need to address it. Regardless of your choice, I will respect it." He paused for effect before proceeding, "You are my only heir. I feel a certain unease at the thought of you not presenting Richard with a prenuptial agreement."

"I'm still unsure about the best way to broach that subject," I admitted, fiddling with my wine glass. "Richard had already dismissed his prenup agreement before your re-entry into my life and all that came with it. He did note that my circumstances are significantly different now and recommended that I formulate a prenuptial agreement to safeguard myself — not just from him, but from any potential threats."

"Hmm... I've never questioned his intentions. I've seen the depth of his love for you and how he almost lost his mind when we couldn't locate you." Dad's voice faded as if he wished to erase the last phrase, a painful echo of my traumatic experience at the hands of Richard's ex-wife. We both sank into a contemplative silence.

During the previous summer in London, I had uncovered Richard's disturbing past — how Emilia Grant, a celebrated fashion icon in Britain, had emotionally tormented him. Instinctively, my hands cradled my stomach. At that time, I was 20 weeks into my pregnancy when Emilia abducted and tortured me. I miscarried my baby — my precious little bean. Sensing my shift in mood, my father gave my hand a reassuring squeeze, reminding me that I was safe now and Emilia was behind bars.

"Are you still keeping your old apartment?" He asked, steering the conversation away from my haunting memories of London.

"Yes, I can't bring myself to let it go. That place was a part of my identity," I confessed.

"Well, that's good news. Because I've asked Yumi to negotiate for the purchase and renovation of the building to provide better homes for the tenants," he declared.

"Oh my God, Dad!" I exclaimed. "The Sungs will be thrilled!"

* * *

Once our plates were cleared, we ordered a delectable chocolate soufflé to share. As we relished the warm, molten dessert, my father lifted his glass.

"To the future of your publishing and media enterprise," he proposed a toast, his eyes sparkling with pride. "May it continue to scale new heights."

I tapped my glass against his, brimming with excitement and gratitude. "Thank you, Dad. Your support has been indispensable."

As we finished off our dessert, we exchanged our farewells. I was set to return to my office while he was chauffeured to his subsequent meeting outside New York City. As I watched him stride towards his car, I couldn't help but feel an overwhelming sense of gratitude for having reconnected with him and getting to know him as my father. More than two decades of separation may have been a formidable gap, but we were both committed to bridging that chasm. I took a deep breath and allowed Chen to usher me into the back seat.

————

I exited the conference room promptly at 6 PM, leaving Yumi and the rest of my project core team to finalize the details with the tech firm. As I stepped into the hallway, my eyes widened in disbelief — there he was, Richard Collins, the Hollywood heartthrob and the love of my life, right in the middle of the floor lobby. He casually unbuttoned his navy blue suit jacket, revealing an immaculate white shirt underneath as he emerged from the elevator. The moment he appeared, the entire space seemed to brighten as if illuminated by a thousand stars. Every woman on the floor blushed or giggled, stealing glances at him from their desks while trying to maintain composure.

I approached him, my heart pounding with excitement. His eyes sparkled as he caught sight of me. "There you are, darling. Are you ready for our dinner date?" Richard asked, his voice smooth as silk. He leaned in and gently kissed my lips, causing my heart to race faster.

"Almost. Just give me a moment," I replied, sounding calm and collected as we walked toward my office together.

* * *

"Good evening, Mr. Collins. Can I get you anything, like water or coffee?" Hillary greeted him warmly.

"There she is, the superwoman! Thank you for helping me with the reservation. But don't worry, I'm all set," he replied, offering her a charming wink that likely sent her heart fluttering.

I allowed Richard to explore my office as I quickly retreated to the bathroom to change out of my business suit and into my exquisite Vivienne Westwood black pencil dress – the perfect outfit for a night out. The dress featured a flattering, structured bodice that beautifully accentuated my curves, while a tastefully plunging neckline added a touch of allure without being overly revealing. The classic cap sleeves provided just enough coverage for a chic and polished appearance. Falling just below my knee, the dress exuded timeless refinement. A hidden zipper closure at the back ensured a seamless and secure fit.

As I fumbled with the zipper, Richard appeared behind me. His strong hands gently intervened, effortlessly zipping me up. "You look absolutely stunning, darling," he whispered into my ear, our eyes meeting in the mirror, sending shivers down my spine. Richard's blue-grey eyes seemed to transform into a mesmerizing smoky grey shade. Suddenly, he unzipped my dress and let it fall above my waist. His breath was hot as he pulled down my black lace bra to expose my breast. He cupped them, and my nipples hardened at his touch. His gaze from the mirror never left mine. He held my eyes as if taunting me to watch him make love to me. He pinched my nipples and pulled them gently, and I cried from a frenzy.

"Oh, Richard…" I murmured. He planted one last kiss on the back of my neck — a real toe-curler. Then, with a sigh that sounded like a deflating balloon, he fixed my bra and zipped up my dress. Talk about a party pooper, right?

"Later, my darling. As much as I want to take you now, I look forward to having those legs wrapped around me," he whispered, his warm breath sending shivers down my neck, creating a familiar longing. He then gently turned me around, and our eyes locked for a brief moment, filled with an intensity that took my breath away. Richard pressed his lips against mine, kissing me with a tender and fierce passion as if our souls were merging instantly.

I could feel my heart pounding against my chest, the rhythm echoing through my entire being, overwhelming me with excitement and vulnerability. Overcome by the intensity of our connection, I rested my head on his chest, seeking solace in the steady rhythm of his heartbeat. The warmth emanating from his body enveloped me, providing comfort and reassurance.

Richard held me tightly, his strong arms wrapping around me like a protective shield, making me feel secure and loved. As we stood there, wrapped in each other's arms, it felt as though time itself had come to a standstill, allowing us to savor this precious moment before embarking on the night ahead.

Hand in hand, we walked out of my office, leaving the starstruck employees behind, their eyes glued to us as we made our way through the room. As we prepared to step outside into the cold winter night, Richard assisted me with my long coat. Once outdoors, despite the chill, I barely noticed it as Richard's arm wrapped protectively around me, providing a warm shield.

Richard pulled me closer as we approached the posh restaurant, our breaths visible in the frosty air. "I've been looking forward to this all week, Hope. I can't wait to spend the evening with you."

"Me too, Richard," I said, my heart swelling with happiness.

And with that, we entered the restaurant, ready to enjoy a magical evening together, away from the admiring glances and giggles that had filled my office just moments before.

3

SATURDAY.

Today, we marked the day when we would finally make pivotal decisions for our wedding. At the very least, we aimed to settle on critical details such as the date and venue, enabling us to engage wedding planners who could handle the remaining logistics. As I stepped into the living room, excitement surged through me. The sweet aroma of freshly brewed coffee filled our penthouse apartment while sunlight streamed through the windows. The melted snow outside cast a warm glow upon us as we lounged on the plush white couch, surrounded by stacks of bridal magazines and wedding planning books.

"Let's kick things off by picking a date," I suggested, my eyes glinting eagerly. "How about December 15th? The festive decorations create an enchanting atmosphere."

Richard nodded approvingly. "That sounds splendid, darling. I'm looking forward to the day I get to call you my wife." He slid closer to me and lovingly tucked a few stray strands of hair behind my ear.

We shared an affectionate gaze before plunging into the next agenda – the wedding entourage. I had always envisioned having my nearest and dearest by my side on my special day. I retrieved a notepad and began to scribble down names.

"Let's see, for my bridal party, I'd like Jenna to serve as my maid of honor. As for the bridesmaids, I'm leaning towards Jane, Lizzie, and of course, Brittany, who's been quite keen to be involved,".I said, glancing at Richard for his affirmation. Jane and Lizzie were my friends and former roommates from university, while Brittany Ginger was Richard's co-star in *Back In Time*. She was the first to witness our whirlwind romance; since then, we've become close friends.

"That sounds like a strong lineup, darling. As for my groomsmen, I'm considering Tom, Jack, and Robin. I want Henry to stand as my best man." Henry was Richard's son from a previous marriage. He also happened to be a friend of mine. At 25 years old, he was closer in age to me than Richard was. As for Tom and Jack, they were yet to cross paths with me. Robin, however, was a familiar face; he was the director of our current TV series.

With the entourage settled, we moved on to the most crucial detail — the location. Both Richard and I were avid readers, and our shared love for literature held great significance in our lives. It seemed only fitting that we chose a venue that represented this passion.

"Richard, I've thought about it a lot. When Carrie Bradshaw planned her wedding with Mr. Big, I dreamed of having something similar," I said, but before I could continue, Richard interrupted me. "Who are Carrie Bradshaw and Mr. Big?" He asked with a puzzled expression.

I laughed heartily. "For someone who's into Hollywood, you're unfamiliar with these two? *Sex and the City*, remember?" I raised my eyebrows.

"Ah, I see," he responded with a smirk.

"Come on, Richard! It's impossible that you missed such a popular TV series," I argued.

His laughter echoed, "Of course I know, darling. I was merely joking." He flashed me that smile, the one that never failed to melt my heart.

"So I would love to have our wedding at the New York Public Library. It's such a stunning and historic place, symbolizing our love for books and reading," I said, my eyes imploring.

* * *

Richard's face brightened at the suggestion. "That's a fantastic idea! Look who's excited now. I thought you just wanted to wed at the registrar's office?" He teased.

Before I could counter his teasing, my phone rang – it was Yumi. I put her on speaker. "Yumi, you're on speaker. Richard is with me."

"Well, good!" Yumi was my father's right-hand woman and often guided me in business and, occasionally, my personal life. "Our PR department just informed me that *Vogue* wants to feature you as the Winter Bride."

"What?! Yumi, I can't. I don't want to. I want my wedding to be intimate. I don't want to turn this into a circus!" I protested, glancing at Richard, who was already smiling, knowing how much this situation was beginning to torment me.

"This will give *Back In Time* excellent publicity and boost your reputation as the new production and publishing lady boss. Plus, it could skyrocket the sales of your book. Don't you want that?" Yumi countered. "Richard, help me out here."

"Yumi, this might be a bit overwhelming for Hope. Perhaps we should cut her some slack; this isn't the world she's accustomed to," Richard suggested.

"Well, it is now — given that she's about to marry you and she is Oliver's daughter. She has a role to play," Yumi retorted. She had a knack for pushing her agenda to benefit the business, even if it meant overshadowing the joy of my impending wedding. "What's so daunting about posing for a few photos in designer outfits? Millions of women would jump at such an opportunity for their weddings."

"But we both know that she's not just any woman; she's one in a million," Richard responded calmly, enveloping me in his arms to offer comfort. I shot Richard a pout, to which he responded with a smile, revealing his flawless white teeth.

"We need this publicity for our new project, Hope. Trust me when I say

I know what I'm doing. Our PR head will reach out to you shortly," Yumi said with an air of finality. Then, as if a lightbulb flashed in her mind, she added, "Oh, and I've just sent a new script to your email. I'd like you to review it; it's promising. You might want to consider getting James King on board for it. His current movie is on the top chart and the list of nominees for Oscar."

"Would you like to decide on our wedding cake as well?" I asked sarcastically, and Richard chuckled at my cheekiness.

"If you can send the cake samples to my office, I can do it," she replied, a tinge of amusement in her tone. Yumi was really good at winning arguments and getting her way. I rolled my eyes and ended the call.

"This isn't bad, darling. I'd also love for my bride to grace a fashion magazine for our wedding, and on their website, too! Millions of people will see my girl. But if you don't want it, I can make Yumi squash that," he said, kissing my lips.

What I cherished most about Richard was his ability to lift my spirits. So, if he desired to have me in the magazine feature, so be it.

"I will do it, Richard, but on one condition," I declared.

"Anything, my darling," he replied, embracing me tightly against his chest.

"I want George and Catherine at our wedding," I whispered, my voice trembling slightly. I knew that this request was not an easy one for Richard. He still held his mother responsible for what happened to me in London.

He hesitated, his voice tinged with a mixture of sadness and anger. "You're asking too much."

"She is still your mother, and I want her to like me. This is our chance to extend an olive branch," I reasoned, gazing into his eyes. "It's a monumental day for their only child — in the same way, I want to be a part of our children's weddings someday. I don't want to deprive her of that, Richard."

* * *

Richard remained silent, but he tenderly kissed my forehead. Though he didn't give me an answer, I felt confident that he would eventually invite his parents.

With the date, entourage, and location settled, we eagerly delved into other aspects of our wedding, discussing catering, music, and floral arrangements. The room hummed with excitement and joy as our dream wedding slowly came to life. As we planned, I couldn't help but feel that our love story was indeed one for the ages.

4

As I stepped into the hallowed sanctuary of the Vivienne Westwood flagship store, tucked away on 14 East 55th Street, I was greeted by an ethereal ambiance. The air was a fragrant cocktail of delicate vanilla sweetness laced with the robust scent of cedarwood. A magnificent crystal chandelier hung from the lofty ceiling, bathing the room in a soft, inviting glow. Mirrors and plush velvet furnishings adorned the space, punctuated by accents of gilded opulence.

In such a splendid setting, one might expect me to be surrounded by my bridesmaids, but that is not the case today. Instead, in today's fitting for the photo shoot, my companions were Yumi, Ave, the seasoned fashion editor from *Vogue*, and his digital counterpart, Carol. Together, they had carefully handpicked three stunning designs for a feature in the coveted pages of *Vogue*, one of which would grace me on my upcoming wedding day. This clever marketing ploy was intended to stoke my excitement and strengthen the bond between the magazine and my father's flourishing business empire. Although I found the entire situation somewhat unpalatable, Yumi reassured me that it would enhance the prestige of our publishing house and the TV series it sponsored. Then, of course, there was Richard, the man I was set to marry in what was shaping up to be the season's social event.

When I shuffled onto that platform, all decked out in the first design, I felt like a deer caught in the headlights. Their excited stares were bouncing back at me from that floor-to-ceiling mirror — and let me tell you, it was huge! My heart was doing this weird thing, sort of like a drumroll, matching their expectations beat for beat. This was more than just saying 'yes' to a dress; it was like going on a treasure hunt inside my own soul.

I mean, think about it. It wasn't just about finding a fancy dress that wouldn't make me look like a marshmallow. No, siree! This was about digging up a piece of myself — unearthing a fragment of the woman I was blossoming into. It was like looking for Waldo in a crowd, except the crowd was my life, and Waldo was the woman I was becoming — only a lot less stripey. So there I was, standing in front of that gigantic mirror, about to play a game of 'finders keepers' with my own identity. Talk about a weird Wednesday, am I right?

The first gown I tried on was a stunning blend of silk and lace, an ode to romanticism, complete with cascading ruffles. The bodice was form-fitting, embellished with intricate beading that danced under the soft lighting. The dress flowed into a full skirt that seemed to whisper fairy-tale endings and forever love. As the cool silk caressed my skin, I was transported back to my childhood dreams of being a princess. But, as I studied my reflection, the young woman gazing back seemed utterly overwhelmed by the dress's grandeur. I yearned for a dress that reflected who I had grown to become, not the princess I once dreamt of being.

Ever the professional, Ave captured the moment on his iPhone, scribbling notes as he observed. "Pull hair up to emphasize her graceful neck; it enhances the intricacy of the bodice," he instructed the two girls flanking him, presumably members of the styling team.

With a hint of amusement playing on her lips, Ave asked Yumi, "Doesn't she look like Cinderella on the verge of marrying her Prince Charming?"

"Or perhaps someone attending a high school prom," Yumi countered, her expression a mysterious blend of intrigue and indifference.

In the cocoon of the Vivienne Westwood dressing room, I was gently extricated from the confines of the first gown and guided into the second. This creation was a sleek, satin number that whispered modern elegance. The neckline plunged daringly low, meeting a thigh-high slit that promised just the right amount of scandal.

* * *

The fabric embraced every curve of my body, amplifying my femininity. There was an undeniable allure to the dress, a bold statement of sensuality that was impossible to ignore. But as I twirled around to face my audience, their wide-eyed, 'deer-in-the-headlights' expressions told me that maybe, just maybe, it was a smidge too racy for a wedding.

I mean, sure, I was a woman head over heels in love, but that didn't mean I wanted to channel my inner Jessica Rabbit on my big day.

"Do I really have to wear this one for the photo shoot?" I asked, my voice wobbling with uncertainty. It was like I was a kid again, asking Mom if I really had to eat my broccoli.

Ave, always the pragmatic editor, replied, "Yes, Hope. It's part of the deal with Vivienne Westwood. These gowns are like the fashion world's best-kept secrets, not yet unveiled to the public. You'll be the first to strut them for *Vogue*."

Well, when he put it that way, it did sound kind of cool. Besides, who am I to argue with fashion?

As the satin gown was replaced by the third, something shifted. This masterpiece, a symphony of tulle and organza, sang to me. The off-shoulder design was adorned with intricate floral embroidery, striking a harmonious balance between whimsical charm and understated sophistication. The skirt billowed out like a cloud around me, lending an ethereal quality to my reflection.

As I twirled before the mirror, I caught a spark in my own eyes. This was it. This was the dress. It wasn't merely beautiful; it was a mirror to my soul — equal parts playful and refined, dreamy yet grounded.

Stepping down from the platform, a wave of emotions washed over me. Excitement mingled with relief, but there was a profound sense of clarity above all else. I was no longer just Hope, the bride-to-be adrift in a sea of white gowns. I was Hope Williams-Ortega, a woman standing at the threshold of a new chapter, ready to leap into the future with unbridled enthusiasm.

* * *

Yumi's smile, radiant and genuine, confirmed my decision. At that moment, I knew with absolute certainty — this gown was destined for me.

———

I felt like a lone ranger in the weeks leading up to my wedding. Dad and Richard had flown off to London — Dad to play Monopoly with our European expansion, while Richard busied himself with his working visa and a string of promotional tours across Europe — I was already yearning for him. My mother was similarly entangled in her work commitments. However, despite her bossy pants persona, I found solace in the fact that Yumi decided to stay put in New York, overseeing our North American expansion.

So, in moments like today, stuck in this godforsaken photoshoot for *Vogue*'s Winter Bride edition, at least I wasn't alone in the city. I was grateful to have company. As I stepped into the enormous canvas tent, temporarily transformed into a bustling studio for the day, I was immediately enveloped by a sea of expectant faces. Beauty stylists, brandishing their brushes as if they were magic wands, and fashion editors, sporting enigmatic smiles, bustled around the space. Their eyes sparkled with an intoxicating blend of enthusiasm and anticipation, mirroring the electrifying atmosphere. I was teetering on the edge of an extraordinary metamorphosis: soon, I would personify the epitome of a Vivienne Westwood exclusive bride for *Vogue*'s most coveted bridal edition.

"I adore your hair, Hope. It's still untouched by colorings and chemicals," Marianne, the head stylist, remarked as she began to work on my locks. A vibrant redhead with a personality as fiery as her hair color, Marianne held sway over the room with an unwavering air of confidence. With the finesse of a seasoned expert, she started taming my hair, artfully weaving it into an elaborate updo that epitomized elegance and sophistication.

Beside Marianne stood the makeup artist, a gentle soul named Luca, ready to work his magic on my face. His hands, as soft as his understanding gaze, fluttered over my skin. His brushes waltzed across my features, skillfully highlighting aspects I hadn't even realized possessed such allure. As I snuck a peek at my reflection, I was greeted by an unfamiliar image. The woman peering back at me was a version of myself I had only ever encountered in my wildest dreams.

The place was buzzing like a bee on a sugar rush, with a swarm of production assistants zipping around, their fingers practically tap-dancing over their camera phones. They were religiously documenting every product and brand that had the honor of gracing my hair and face. These behind-the-scenes shots, capturing the nitty-gritty of the makeover process, would later play a starring role in the advertising and editorial campaign — talk about fifteen minutes of fame!

Amid this crazy twister of activity, I felt a strange sense of calm sneaking up on me, like a cat on tiptoes. Here I was, an introvert about to star in a fashion editorial with a gazillion photographers glued on me. It was like being the main course at a buffet; all the forks were out! But right there in the heart of this madhouse, I found a surprising pocket of peace. Imagine finding a quiet corner in a rock concert — that's what it felt like!

I was as ready as a racehorse at the starting gate for my transformation, all set to blossom into the Vivienne Westwood bride. It was like I was about to turn from Cinderella's pre-fairy godmother wench to Cinderella's post-fairy godmother princess, without the pumpkins and mice.

As the flurry of activity began to subside, I found myself stepping into the pièce de résistance of this transformation journey — a jaw-droppingly gorgeous Vivienne Westwood gown. The dress was a thing of beauty, a dazzling mix of classic elegance and cutting-edge creativity, a mirror image of the legendary designer herself. Despite my inherent shyness and penchant for solitude, the thrill that surged through me was intoxicating.

Like a champagne cork, a gasp popped out of me when one of the fashion editors opened the Cartier jewelry case. A diamond necklace and matching drop earrings were snuggled within its velvety confines, so breathtaking that they'd put a crown jewel to shame. Their facets winked cheekily under the unforgiving studio lights. "Oh, sweet lord of bling!" I squealed as my fingers traced each jewel, probably leaving smudges of awe on them.

With a gentleness that made butterflies look clumsy, Marianne placed the diamond necklace and earrings on me. "Hope," she whispered, her eyes wide with wonder, as if she was looking at a unicorn, "You look absolutely breathtaking." I shot her a small, grateful smile, touched by her words. And just like that, Cinderella was ready for the ball!

With help from the production assistants, I stepped out of the tent and took a short but oh-so-grand walk to the dreamy Bethesda Terrace in Central Park. You know, the one famous for its quiet winter mornings that make you feel like you're in a snow globe? The paths were all tucked under a blanket of snow, and the trees were decked out in frosty finery. It was a peaceful picture, a world away from the organized chaos of a *Vogue* photo shoot. Talk about a tale of two cities!

As we stepped onto the terrace, the morning air gave us a brisk, cheeky kiss on the face. The photographers, already deep in their zone like wizards working their magic, were busy tweaking their equipment. And the light guys were scurrying around, bending and twisting reflectors like they were doing yoga, all to catch the morning light in its soft, glowing best. It was like watching a ballet, only with more camera flashes and less tutus!

Antoine, the principal photographer and a celebrated artist in his own right, approached me. His French accent lent an exotic lilt to his words, "Hope, we're going to start with some solo shots."

I nodded, stepping into the spotlight as directed. The rhythmic shutter of the camera became my heartbeat, capturing every subtle shift of emotion, every fluid movement. I tried to channel my inner model, desperate to do justice to the exquisite ensemble I was privileged to wear. Yet, amidst the glamour and glitz, I couldn't shake off my old self. Beneath the layers of couture and diamonds, I was still Hope Williams, a writer. My place should be in the editorial corner, writing this piece instead of this girl, modeling for one of the sought-after fashion brands in the world.

* * *

The next act of this carefully choreographed dance commenced with introducing the ring-bearer, an endearing 7-year-old cherub named Christopher. His role was to stand by my side, a delightful deviation from the conventional groom setup. His broad, innocent eyes gazed up at me with a mix of awe and curiosity. I couldn't help but crouch down to his level, whispering words of encouragement, "We're going to turn this into a fun game, okay?" A shy smile tugged at his lips as he gave an enthusiastic nod in response.

"Alright, Hope, Christopher, let's get you ready for the shot," Antoine directed, his voice firm yet comforting. "A subtle smile, keep it enigmatic. And Christopher, gently hold onto a part of Hope's dress as if you're her gallant little escort."

With each click of the shutter, a moment was immortalized, a story told. Every gesture, every flicker of emotion, was captured with surgical precision. The scene felt dreamlike, like I had stepped into a narrative that was not my own. Yet as I glanced around at the bustling crew — the stylists fussing over minute details, photographers engrossed in their craft, and the endearing boy beside me — I felt a wave of excitement envelop me.

Now, I'm a private person by nature — like a hermit crab but without the shell. I grew up in the shadows. And even though I was engaged to a guy who lived under Hollywood's spotlight like a well-tanned lizard under a sun lamp, my shy bone usually steered me clear of the public eye. But today, right smack in the middle of a magazine photo shoot whirlwind, all dolled up in one of the most exquisite bridal collections, I discovered a newfound appreciation for stepping out of my comfort zone.

Life, I realized, was about evolution, growing, and sometimes, striking a pose against the peaceful backdrop of Central Park on a nippy winter morning, creating magic for a *Vogue* photo shoot while trying not to freeze your toes off.

So, here's to stepping out of my comfort zone and into the limelight, one high-heeled step at a time!

5

I stood in front of our bathroom mirror, rhythmically brushing my teeth. My gaze was held captive by the sight of Richard stepping into the shower. He had returned late last night from London, and we had made a pact to play house since Leticia had taken a brief sabbatical to visit her family in Mexico. As my eyes flickered to the glass shower door, I watched the steam twirl around him, crafting an enigmatic veil that obscured his robust, athletic silhouette. Despite the months we'd shared together, I found myself still gasping at the sight of his finely sculpted body — a tribute to his unwavering commitment to fitness.

Suddenly, the sound of water splashing filled the room like a waterfall's lullaby, pulling me into a state of peaceful anticipation. But just as I was about to start daydreaming, my attention was swiftly drawn to the ringing phone on the bedside table, its shrill melody shattering the moment's tranquility.

"Darling, can you get that?" Richard's voice echoed from the bathroom, muffled by the cascading shower water.

Pulling myself away from my own personal peep show while putting on a moisturizer, I tiptoed out of the bathroom, my bare feet whispering against the plush carpet. I reached for his phone, perched on our antique oak bedside table. The screen fluttered awake, displaying Peter's name, his London-based agent. Without hesitation, I swiped to answer, "Hello?"

"Hope! It's Peter," the voice on the other end crackled excitedly. "Is

Richard there? I have a piece of incredible news that'll knock his socks off!"

A grin spread across my face, its edges tingling with anticipation. "He's in the shower. What's the news, Peter?" Clutching the phone, I strolled back into the bathroom, leaning against the cool, tiled wall. I called out over the sound of the running water, "Richard, it's Peter. He says he has something to share."

His reply bounced cheerfully off the tiled walls, barely audible over the shower, "Could you take a message for me, darling?"

"Did you get that, Peter?" I asked, still holding the phone close. My heart fluttered with anticipation, eager to hear Peter's news.

"Richard has been asked to reprise the role of Steve McQueen in *The Getaway*!" Peter's voice oozed excitement, the news carrying through the speaker.

An involuntary shriek of delight surged from my chest, ricocheting off the walls and filling the room with a tangible wave of joy. Richard, now wrapped in a plush towel with another draped over his damp, tousled hair, emerged from the bathroom. Water droplets trailed after him, splashing onto the floor. "What? What happened? What's the good news?" His voice was thick with curiosity, eyes gleaming with anticipation.

I held up the phone, my heart pounding with excitement. "Peter just shared that they want you to reprise Steve McQueen in *The Getaway*!"

Richard stood frozen, openmouthed, the towel clenched tightly in his hand. "Are you serious?"

"I wouldn't joke about something like this, Richard," I replied, my voice brimming with pride. "Peter says the role is yours."

His eyes sparkled, disbelief mingling with delight. He strode over, grasping the phone from me. "Peter, it's Richard. Fill me in."

As Richard listened, his face lit up like a Christmas tree. A wide grin stretched across his face, his eyes twinkling with renewed enthusiasm. His voice filled the room, firm and filled with resolve. "Absolutely, Peter. I appreciate you bringing this to me. I can't wait to dive in."

Then, a flicker of worry danced across Richard's face, causing my heart to skip. "I see. Let me talk this over with Hope before we confirm," he said, his tone tinged with concern.

A hint of unease settled in the pit of my stomach. I watched Richard intently as he listened to Peter, his brows furrowed in deep thought. Finally, he ended the call, and I couldn't help but voice my concern.

"Richard, this is the role of a lifetime. Why do I get the feeling that you're having second thoughts about accepting it?"

He moved towards me, his damp towel clinging to his body. Wrapping me in a warm embrace, he confessed, "Darling, this film will star me opposite Ingrid Simon."

My arms instinctively wound around him, holding him close as I searched his eyes for answers. "So? What does that have to do with anything?" I asked, my voice laced with curiosity and a touch of insecurity.

"Hmm... sometimes I forget that you're not the type to dwell on celebrity background," Richard admitted, his gaze fixed on mine, a hint of regret shadowing his features.

Tension coiled within me, and worry etched itself onto my brow. "Now I'm starting to feel slightly concerned," I admitted, my voice softening with vulnerability.

"Ingrid and I, we had a... complicated history. It was nothing serious, though," he said, his expression apologetic. His eyes met mine, an uncertain look crossing his face.

"You slept with her," I stated flatly. It wasn't a question.

"Yes, but we both agreed it was nothing serious," he said quickly.

* * *

I detached myself from his embrace, crossing my arms over my chest, "I sense there's more to the story," I replied.

Richard cupped my face, "Around the time of filming, she developed feelings for me and wanted more than I was willing to give. She didn't take it well."

"Should I be worried?" I asked him. A mix of emotions welled inside me — a tinge of jealousy, insecurity, and a sense of protectiveness for my relationship with Richard. "Does she still have feelings for you? And you?"

Richard's grip on me tightened as if to reassure me. "No, darling. We both moved on long ago. But sometimes history has a way of resurfacing, like how the press will play this. I want to make sure we're prepared for any potential complications."

"I've seen the remake of *The Getaway* with Alec Baldwin and Kim Basinger. The scenes are quite intimate, Richard," I whispered, unable to hide my concern.

"I understand your worries, darling. As much as I want this role, if you're uncomfortable with it, I won't take it," he promised, brushing his thumb across my lips before pulling me into a deep, comforting kiss.

When we finally broke apart, I rested my head on his chest and murmured. "I'm a big girl, Richard. I can handle it." I knew I was lying to myself. But I was willing to put aside my fears for Richard and his career.

"My darling, you're the only woman in my life now. If I work with Ingrid, it will be strictly professional," he reassured me.

As Richard's words hung in the air between us, I found myself drawn into the intensity of his gaze. His eyes, usually so warm and inviting, now bore a new quality: a fierce determination that both thrilled and terrified me... well, in an exciting way. Without breaking eye contact, his hand, warm and steady, cupped my cheek, pulling me closer. I could feel the warmth radiating off him, the scent of his aftershave mingling with his shower's fresh, clean smell. My heart pounded against my ribs, each beat echoing the anticipation that thrummed through my veins.

Slowly, almost hesitantly, he leaned in. His other hand slid around my waist, pulling me flushed against him. Every fiber of my being was hyper-aware of his proximity, of the solid strength of his body against mine. We simply stood there for a moment, locked in a silent understanding.

Then, his lips met mine.

It was a soft, lingering kiss filled with the promise of unspoken words and hidden desires. His lips moved against mine with a tenderness that belied his earlier intensity, his touch gentle yet firm. His fingers traced patterns on my back, the subtle pressure anchoring me to the present moment.

I responded in kind, my hands tangling in his damp hair, pulling him closer. The world around us seemed to fade away, leaving only the two of us lost in the intimacy of our shared connection. Every worry and doubt was swept away in the tide of emotions that surged within me.

When we finally broke apart, I was breathless, my mind spinning with the intensity of what had just transpired. Yet, as I looked up at Richard, his expression was one of calm certainty. In his eyes, I saw the promise of tomorrow, a future where we would face any challenge together.

Richard scooped me up in his arms with a mischievous glint in his eyes. I let out a startled yelp, clutching onto his shoulders as he carried me towards the bathroom.

"Richard!" I protested with a laugh, swatting his chest lightly. "You're impossible!"

He merely grinned at me, his eyes twinkling with unspoken delight. His grip on me was firm yet gentle, a silent promise that he wouldn't let me fall.

He set me down as we entered the bathroom, but not before pulling me closer. The shower room was steam-filled, and the mirror fogged over from the heat. Richard turned the shower knob, and a soft patter of warm water began to fill the room.

He looked at me, his gaze softening. His fingers brushed away a stray lock of hair from my face, tucking it behind her ear. "I want you," his voice barely above a whisper.

I looked into his eyes, my heart pounding in my chest. More than anything, I wanted this—wanted him.

Suddenly, he tugged me into the shower with him. Warm water showered over us, soaking my night dress. But neither of us paid any attention to the cascading water. We were absorbed in each other's presence, lost in our shared world.

We held each other under the comforting spray, sharing a moment as intimate as it was breathtaking. Richard gently removed my drenched clothes. "Darling, you're so beautiful," he whispered. At that moment, the rest of the world disappeared. It was just Richard and me, two souls intertwined in a timeless dance.

6

The second I nudged the door of Purple Apron open, nostalgia hit me like a truck. This wasn't just any bakery, tucked away in my old stomping grounds on 89th Street. Oh no, this was a vault of memories that would make even the toughest cookie (pun intended) go soft. My close friend Erin had turned her crazy love for baking into a full-blown business here and stepping back into its cozy, beckoning embrace felt like coming home from a trip that had lasted way too long.

This little gem is hands down one of my favorite spots in New York City. Especially when the 'Closed' sign goes up, Erin and Mavi, our yogi friend, take over the squeaky-clean kitchen. It's just us girls doing our thing with beers and pizzas or sometimes classing it up with wine and tapas. Back when I was scraping by, this place was my lifeline. Heck, at one point, I even worked the counter to scrape together some extra dough for rent.

Purple Apron, along with the Sungs' Victoria's Bloom—this cute little flower shop in my old apartment building—were my safe spaces. They made the neighborhood feel like home, only cooler. But I've been a stranger since the big move to the Upper East Side and the grind of work. Tonight, though, with Richard off playing movie star in Australia and our house echoing with silence instead of his laughter, I was glad to be back in this old comfortable place.

And so, there I was, stepping back into Erin's cozy bakery, a place that smelled as if heaven had opened up a divine patisserie. The intoxicating scent of freshly baked bread mingling with the tantalizing aroma of sweet pastries, and just a hint of robust coffee, wafted through the air. It wrapped around me like a long-lost friend, a scent so mouth-watering it could make your knees go weak, and your stomach perform a jubilant jig.

The heady scent of fresh bread and sinful pastries hung in the air, mingling with the comforting aroma of brewing coffee. That tasty cocktail of smells yanked me right out of my daydreaming. Erin, the ever-gracious hostess, welcomed me with a smile brighter than a thousand suns. Her eyes sparkled with the kind of warmth and familiarity that only comes from years of friendship.

Erin, always the bubbly hostess, greeted me with a smile brighter than the midday sun, "Look who we have here... the bride-to-be!" She hollered, expertly removing her apron and hair net, freeing her cascading auburn hair. She enveloped me in a bear hug that was as warm and comforting as the seductive smells wafting from her bakery. "Well, aren't you lucky to have lured you all the way from your posh Upper East Side!"

"Erin, you have no idea how much I've missed this place," I confessed, returning her hug with equal fervor. "The house feels like a haunted mansion. Richard dashed off to Sydney this morning for another shoot."

"Oh, you poor thing!" She cooed, lifting my chin and looking into my eyes, "Well, you've come to the right place, baby girl! Time to put some meat on those bones." She gave my arm a playful pinch as if she were measuring my 'skinny index.'

Weaving our way through the symphony of clinking dishes, laughter, and chatter that filled the bakery, we made our way to our sacred haven—the sprawling kitchen at the back. This was our fortress of solitude, our bat cave, where over countless cups of steaming coffee, peals of laughter, and heartfelt conversations, we'd shared life's joys and sorrows, all under the comforting aroma of Erin's scrumptious culinary masterpieces. My squad, my partners in crime, were already there, huddled in every corner, groaning under the weight of cupcakes, cookies, and all manner of sugary delights.

* * *

There they were—my college friends — Florence, Jane, and Lizzie! I practically barreled into them, "Holy cannoli! You guys are here! It's been forever!" We held each other in a bear hug that could rival Erin's. Jane even shed a few happy tears as we basked in the warmth of our reunion. I shot Erin a grateful look and mouthed 'Thank you'. She had gone out of her way to rally my old gang for this special gathering.

"Look who finally decided to show up," Charlie Sung ribbed, his eyes twinkling with the kind of warmth and familiarity that only comes from years of shared memories. As soon as I extricated myself from the group hug, I beelined for Charlie, an old friend who felt more like an uncle. Hot on his heels were his daughter Victoria and my erstwhile neighbor Sara who lived with her boyfriend Matt on the 7th floor. I pulled both girls into a group hug.

"Alright, enough with the chit chat," Erin interjected, brandishing a notepad and pen like a battle-hardened general. "We've got a wedding to plan."

I took a deep breath, feeling a whirlwind of emotions. Excitement. Fear. Anticipation. I was about to embark on a new chapter of my life, and this motley crew of friends was my compass, my rock, my ride-or-die squad.

We flopped onto those same ol' aluminum bar stools that knew our butts all too well. Erin went to work, pouring us a couple of cups of the good stuff—freshly brewed coffee. That rich, dark magic flowed into my cup, steam dancing upwards in mesmerizing spirals. She slid a plate my way, loaded with a delicious array of her latest oven-baked masterpieces.

"Mavi's gonna pop in any minute now," Erin shared, punctuating her update with a swig of her own joe. "Word on the street is, she's got herself a serious beau."

"No way! What happened to her 'I'll die a virgin' pledge?" I asked. I was dead serious, but Erin lost it. She started laughing so hard I thought she'd fall off her stool. Pretty soon, we were all giggling right along with her. This was classic us—poking fun at Mavi's oh-so-serious approach to life... when she wasn't around, of course.

* * *

Sure enough, as I savored a bite of a succulent raspberry tart, the door swung open to reveal Mavi. Our trusty yoga instructor and all-around good egg, Mavi was like a shot of espresso—always buzzing with positive vibes, the total opposite of Erin and me, who always expect bad things to happen to people. Tagging along behind her was a couple so engrossed in their phones they were practically tripping over each other, their giggles adding a dollop of cheer to the bakery's usual soundscape.

As they got closer, I recognized the unmistakable mug of Tess O'Brian — Erin's vivacious cousin. This young heiress, barely out of her twenties, was the proud owner of the building housing Mavi's Yoga Place. With her long, wavy chestnut locks flowing down her back and her boho-chic getup, Tess was the poster child for the 'bohemian heiress' style. Sticking to her like glue was a tall, muscular man with sun-kissed skin that screamed beach bum. His feet were covered with cannabis-design socks under a pair of Birkenstock slippers, showcasing his affinity for natural living. His thick beard and long hair, stylishly tied in a man-bun, added to his captivating aura.

"Hey, isn't that Tess?" I quizzed Erin, squinting to make sure I wasn't seeing things. "I thought she was off gallivanting in Greece?"

"Nah, she actually went to India," Erin whispered back.

"Ah, that explains the hunky plus-one!" I chuckled, nodding towards Mr. Yoga Instructor.

"Hopey! You're here!" Tess practically shrieked, her eyes lighting up like a pair of disco balls. "I mean, look at you! About to be married to Richard Collins and hobnobbing with the under-30 billionaire crowd. You're practically a celebrity!"

"Tess, you gotta stop believing everything you read online," I chided, leaning in for our customary double-cheek smooch.

She let out a hearty laugh, her eyes sparkling with mischief. "Yeah, I guess you're right. Oh, by the way, meet Zaldy. He's my pal and the newest addition to Mavi's yoga squad." She yanked Zaldy into our little huddle.

"Hey there, Hope," Zaldy said, sticking out his hand. "Mavi and Tess have been singing your praises."

As I shook his hand—firm as a rock, just like you'd expect from a yoga buff—I quipped, "I hope they stuck to the PG-rated stuff."

"And look who's graced us with her presence—hello, Upper East Sider!" Mavi chimed in, doing her best *Gossip Girl* impression. She wrapped me in one of her signature bear hugs. "I've missed you, girlfriend. How's life in Nanny central?" Mavi always refers to this part of New York City, because you couldn't swing a designer purse around without hitting a nanny. Seriously, they're everywhere in this neighborhood!

"I've missed you too, Mavi. And honestly, I really miss the studio," I confessed, returning her embrace. The sense of belonging I had always felt at Mavi's studio washed over me, reminding me of the tranquility that yoga had introduced into my life.

"Anyone in the mood for coffee? There's a freshly brewed pot over there, along with some homemade cookies and tarts," Erin announced, filling my cup with a fresh batch of aromatic coffee and passing another to Mavi.

"Look at the dynamic duo at work," Mavi quipped, nodding towards Tess and Zaldy. They were hunched over a phone, heads practically bonking together as they giggled at whatever was on the screen. "Doing their favorite thing—stirring the pot with Twitter celebs. A hobby that usually ends with them up to their eyeballs in trouble."

Caught in the act, Tess and Zaldy glanced up, their faces bathed in the glow of their digital mischief. Their laughter bounced around the room, spreading like a contagious case of giggles. The sight of their genuine friendship had me grinning from ear to ear.

Suddenly, Erin's eyes zeroed in on something. She strutted over to Tess who was holding a half-chomped protein bar and Erin snatched it in disgust and held it up like Exhibit A in a courtroom drama. "Tess, you're rolling in money, yet here you are, munching on expired food!" she teased, her tone all mock outrage.

Tess threw her head back and laughed, the sound rich and full of life. "Oh, Erin, you, of all people, should know that expiration dates are mere suggestions!"

Zaldy joined in, his eyes twinkling with mischief. "Besides, everyone knows the best things in life don't have an expiration date – laughter, friendship, and, yes, trolling Twitter celebrities! Only gossip grows stale with time."

Laughter erupted in the room, bouncing around like a hyperactive toddler and etching itself into the very fabric of the place. I realized how precious these moments were as I joined the collective laugh.

"Hope, we've got a teensy-weensy situation," Tess announced, her eyes glued to her phone, her lips curling with a hint of mischief.

"And what would that be?" I asked, my curiosity piqued.

"Well, the rumor mill's in overdrive. These digital tabloids say your dear hubby-to-be Richard is rekindling an old flame with ex-lover Ingrid Simon for the remake of *The Getaway*," she dished, her eyebrows arching higher with each word, relishing the juicy gossip.

"Oh, that old chestnut. Richard was on the fence about taking the role, worried it might stir the unnecessary drama. But I encouraged him to go for it because it's his dream project," I said, my gaze dropping to my coffee cup as I swirled the contents absently.

"Alright, time for a little digital deep-dive," Lizzie declared, her fingers already dancing across the screen of her phone with the grace of a seasoned pianist.

"No, no, no!" I protested, waving my hands in front of me like I was trying to ward off an evil spirit. "I don't need to know anything more about Ingrid Simon. This isn't a spy movie, Lizzie!"

But as usual, Lizzie paid my protests no mind. She was like a bloodhound on a scent. Once she got her teeth into something, there was no shaking her loose.

"Wowzers! Seems like our girl Ingrid is quite smitten with Richard," she announced, her eyes wide with excitement. "Listen to this—she gave an interview saying they're planning to get hitched, and that she's met his son."

"Henry?" I asked, my heart sinking faster than the Titanic.

"Hope, you need to get on the blower to Henry and verify this," Victoria insisted, her voice firm and uncompromising.

"I most certainly will not!" I retorted, crossing my arms over my chest. "And, Lizzie, for the love of all things holy, would you stop snooping around her life?"

"But it's always wise to know your enemy, Hope," Lizzie countered, her eyes still glued to her phone. "Oh, and here's another juicy tidbit from a gossip column. Apparently, Richard was utterly enchanted by Ingrid's beauty. He was quoted saying, 'Ingrid has one of the most beautiful faces in the industry, and I can't wait to spend more time with her.'"

Her voice trailed off as she finally looked up and saw the worry etched on my face.

"Guys, those are just rumors!" Erin interjected, coming to my rescue.

Mavi, always the voice of reason, chimed in, "Hope, you and Richard are going to be married soon, and I'm certain he loves you far too much even to give Ingrid a second glance."

Tess, ever the drama queen, lived for a good gossip session and had a knack for seeing the glass half empty—much like her cousin Erin. "But did you see the previous remake? Alec Baldwin and Kim Basinger reignited my teenage sexual fantasies! Hot stuff!"

"Wow, Tess, way to boost my confidence," I shot back, laying the sarcasm on thick.

Her teasing grin morphed into a comforting smile. "Oh, Hope, I didn't mean it would happen in real life. It's just a movie. And besides, Ingrid's pushing 40. She's got nothing on Richard's vibrant, twenty-something bride-to-be."

Zaldy, always the voice of reason, said, "And don't sweat it, Hope. If this juicy tidbit hits Twitter, we'll be your online knights in shining armor. We'll be there to defend your honor."

"That's no longer the 'bird app,' Elon Musk has rebranded it to 'X,'" Sara said, correcting Zaldy.

He scoffed, "What a nonsensical move. So now, instead of tweeting, do we say, 'I X'ed it?'"

Jane said, "Twitter's got one of the most kickass brand identities in the biz. I mean, come on, words like tweet, bird, and retweet are all part of this epic branding story."

"I reckon Musk's mainly eyeing that juicy user base. He'll likely fiddle with the algorithms to give a leg up to certain businesses. Game the algorithms, game the sales, and voila, you've got the dough," I mused.

"Jeez, Hope, you're starting to sound like one of those bigwig corporate honchos. Is that a British accent I'm detecting?" Florence teased, her eyebrows wiggling comically.

"Well, Erin, my dear, I believe I am one of the guys in suits now, remember?" I fired back, laying the faux British accent on thick. "Living with a Brit does leave its mark on you, you know... like saying 'lift' instead of 'elevator', or mimicking Richard's oh-so-posh pronunciation of 'vitamins' as 'veetamins.'" Our laughter echoed through the room as we pictured the scene. "Thank heavens Richard has figured out to say 'panties' instead of 'knickers'... otherwise, I'd feel positively ancient!"

"Can just picture Richard cooing, 'Darling, would you mind terribly removing your knickers'... That's about as romantic as a wet sock!" More laughter erupted, filling the room with our shared mirth.

* * *

"But seriously, don't worry too much about Richard and Ingrid. That man is head over heels for you," Jane comforted me.

"I know. I'm trying not to let it get to me. But I do miss him terribly," I confessed, leaning my head on her shoulder.

"We've got your back, always," she reassured me.

Our sentimental moment was abruptly interrupted by raucous laughter from Tess and Zaldy.

"You are incorrigible, Tess!" Zaldy exclaimed, shaking his head in disbelief. Turning towards us, he explained, "Her mom asked her to buy a gift for her sister's nephew. They bought a Lego set, and Tess removed five pieces so the kid won't be able to finish it!"

"Holy cow, Tess!" Mavi burst out laughing.

"I have to admit, that's something I might do too," I confessed, joining in the laughter.

"Group hug, my fellow mischief makers and evil sisters," Tess declared, pulling us all into a warm, comforting circle.

As we dove headfirst into the whirlwind of wedding planning, I felt a wave of gratitude wash over me. This wasn't just some run-of-the-mill wedding hullabaloo. This was about friendship, love, and support. This was about embarking on a wild new adventure with my motley crew of misfits. This was about finding joy in the chaos, the shared belly laughs, and the endless debates over cake flavors and flower arrangements that sounded more like UN peace negotiations.

We unanimously decided that Erin couldn't be one of my bridesmaids because, well, who would want to be distracted from their masterpiece? It's like asking Michelangelo to paint the Sistine Chapel while juggling bowling balls.

"I have one job that day — the cake," she declared, her eyes gleaming with determination. "And you bet your sweet bippy I'm going to knock it out of the park!"

So, there it was—my wedding day shaping up to be an event packed with laughter, love, and a whole lot of frosting. And honestly? I wouldn't have it any other way.

In the midst of it all, I realized that I wasn't just planning a wedding. I was building memories. And as I looked around at my friends, their faces lit up with enthusiasm and love, I knew these were moments I would cherish forever.

"Alright, ladies," I said, raising a cupcake in a toast. "To friendship, love, and the most unforgettable wedding ever!"

And with that, we dug into our pastries, our laughter echoing through the bakery. It was the perfect start to my wedding journey. And though I didn't know what lay ahead, I knew I had the best team on my side. Bring it on, world!

While everyone was busy demolishing the cupcakes like a pack of starving hyenas, good ol' Charlie decided to break the silence. "Alright, Hopey," he began, leaning back in his chair with a grin that could give the Cheshire cat a run for his money. "You see, I've been around the block a time or two, maybe even three. And if there's one thing I know about this crazy thing called marriage, it's this—it's like a good, hearty sandwich."

I blinked at him, "A sandwich?"

"Absolutely!" He exclaimed, slapping the table for emphasis. "Think about it. You've got your bread—that's your foundation. That's trust, respect, all that jazz. Then you've got your fillings—that's the fun stuff. Shared dreams, adventures, belly laughs at 2 AM. because someone snorted in their sleep."

"And the cheese?" I asked, playing along.

"The cheese," he chuckled, "That's the love, Hopey. It holds everything together. But here's the kicker—it can get a bit melty and messy sometimes. But that's okay! Because at the end of the day, it's still cheese, and it's still delicious."

I couldn't help but laugh. Trust Charlie to turn marriage advice into a food analogy.

He leaned forward, his eyes softening, "But seriously, Hope. Marriage isn't always going to be a walk in Central Park. There will be times when you'll want to throw your sandwich at the wall. But remember, every squabble, every challenge, it's just another ingredient in your sandwich. And I have no doubt that you and Richard are going to make one heck of a tasty sandwich."

With that, he raised his coffee mug in a toast, "To Hope, our soon-to-be bride. May your life be filled with lots of love, laughter, and sandwiches."

And with that send-off, I knew I was ready to step into this new chapter, armed with the wisdom of my dear friend Charlie, and a newfound appreciation for sandwiches.

This crew was indeed something else—a delightful mix of laughter, company, and just the right amount of chaos. As I stood there, surrounded by these like-minded souls, I found myself wondering how my upcoming adventure as Richard's wife might shake up these precious dynamics. But then it hit me — the secret to dealing with the uncertainty of the future is to savor the present fully. And right here, right now, wrapped in the warmth of friendship in a place that felt like home, I couldn't have wished for anything more.

7

As I stood here outside the luxurious suite at The Mark, the enormity of tomorrow's event hit me — the big day. My heart pounded with a mix of anticipation and anxiety, — not just at the prospect of seeing my mother again, but also at the impending meeting of two families — mine and Richard's. I lifted my hand and knocked gently on the glossy mahogany door, the sound echoing like a lone heartbeat in the quiet hallway.

Slowly, the door creaked open, revealing an interior that was all about indulgence, bathed in a soft, dreamy light. It was a perfect blend of sleek modernism and timeless class. Plush velvet sofas, their rich colors reminding me of juicy plums, were artistically scattered across the room. Shiny marble countertops added a dash of flair, and the floor-to-ceiling windows showed off a killer view of the city skyline, each skyscraper a tribute to human ingenuity.

In the middle of this luxury stood Mom, looking as radiant as ever. Her blond hair tumbled down her shoulders in a waterfall of golden curls, each strand catching the sunlight from the windows and turning it into a halo of light. Her green eyes, specked with little grey flecks, twinkled with a kind of excitement that was both infectious and a tad scary.

"Hope, my sweet girl!" she cried out, her voice overflowing with happiness as she pulled me into a bear hug. "I've missed you terribly."

"I've missed you too, Mom," I replied, my voice muffled against the soft fabric of her blouse as I returned her hug.

* * *

The suite screamed luxury, and I hoped that would compensate for the lack of personal touch. My mother was expecting me to house her in our home, but I decided to put her in the hotel where Richard's parents were also booked. "What do you think of the suite, Mom? Comfy enough?" I asked, trying to keep my voice from wavering.

Mom looked around, her eyes wide with awe, but there was a touch of longing in them. "It's lovely, Hope. But I would have loved to bunk with you," she admitted, reaching out to cradle my face in her hands.

Her touch was warm and familiar, a soothing balm against my guilt. "I know, Mom. I wish you could have, too. But considering Richard's parents are also staying here, I didn't want them to feel slighted," I admitted, hoping she would understand the precarious balance we were trying to maintain.

She studied me then, her gaze soft but piercing. "You look anxious, sweetheart. Those eyebags are becoming noticeable. Is everything all right?"

Her perceptiveness caught me off guard, and I hesitated before answering. "Work is piling up on my desk... plus this wedding preparation," I said as I took her hands on mine. To divert the topic off me, I asked, "Steve called me last night and apologized for not being able to attend my wedding due to an emergency at work. I hope everything is alright." There was a dual significance to my statement — I was concerned not only about his work situation but also about the state of his relationship with my mom.

A shadow passed over her face briefly before she forced a smile. "Yes, he had an unexpected business trip," she explained. "But don't worry, everything is fine, and he said he'll try to catch up, if he can."

I felt a strange mix of relief and guilt. Don't get me wrong, I'd come to adore my stepfather, but having both my parents walking me down the aisle felt like slipping into a comfy pair of old jeans.

As if reading my thoughts, Mom gave my hands a comforting squeeze. "I can see that secret little happy dance you're doing in your head,

Hope," she said, her lips curling up into a knowing smile. "And you know what? That's perfectly fine. Your dad and I... we'll be right there with you, just like we always have."

Her words were like a soothing balm on my jittery heart, oozing with understanding and acceptance. Amidst the whirlwind of wedding prep and family drama, I knew I could always count on Mom's love and presence as my safe haven.

We plopped down on the squishy king-sized bed, the silky white fabric feeling like a giant, comforting marshmallow beneath us. Mom's hands engulfed mine, her touch as warm and soothing as a mug of hot cocoa on a frosty day. "So, how are you feeling about tying the knot with Mr. Hollywood tomorrow?" she asked, genuine curiosity lacing her voice.

A dreamy smile spread across my face, my gaze getting lost in the cityscape beyond the windows. "It's surreal, Mom. I mean, I'm head over heels for Richard, but never in a million years did I see myself saying 'I do' to someone who's got his own Wikipedia page. I always pictured my life as low-key and drama-free."

Mom gave my hands a comforting squeeze, like she was trying to squish the doubts out of me. "Remember, Hope, he's not just some celebrity. He's the man who makes your heart flutter. Don't let the glitz and glam cloud your feelings for him."

A tsunami of doubt crashed over me, making my voice do the jitterbug. "Am I rushing this too soon? I mean, he's my first go at this 'serious relationship' thing. What if this doesn't work out?"

My mother tightened her grip on my hands, her gaze soft yet resolute. "Sweetheart, I know you love Richard — it's clear as day. I saw how much you suffered when things were rocky between you two. Yes, life isn't perfect. There will be times when you and Richard clash, and there will be nights filled with tears. But you'll weather those storms because you love each other. Life may never be perfect, but together, you can make it beautiful." Her smile was nostalgic as if she was reminiscing about her own journey with her own love stories.

"But what if he gets bored with me? He's always in the company of stunning women who'd give anything to be with him." I thought of Ingrid and all the other beautiful women in his world.

"You're selling yourself short, sweetheart. In this relationship, you're not just the bait; you're the whole fishing kit," she said, trying to boost my confidence. "Which brings us to the elephant in the room... have you both signed your prenuptial agreements?"

"That's the thing, Mom. Richard never drew up any papers for me to sign. He claimed his love for me came before he knew about our family's wealth. What he owns is solely his so he can decide on that on his own, while my finances are a bit more complicated. My assets are linked with the family business and managed by the board. It's not wholly mine," I clarified.

"That does make sense..."

"I know it doesn't feel right, Mom," I said. "I truly wish I could be as open with Richard as he is with me when it comes to sharing our finances. However, my situation is quite complex. I'm still trying to grasp the intricacies of things like stock shares and their values. Dad mentioned securing some personal assets, like properties and substantial trust funds, but I haven't had the time to fully comprehend them. I'm still acclimating from my simpler, old life."

My mother raised a hand, signaling for me to pause. "Richard is correct; your financial situation is complicated. The assets you'll inherit come from your father and generations before him. You didn't create that wealth from scratch, so sharing it with someone else, even a spouse, wouldn't be fair. Richard, however, amassed his fortune on his own."

"Mom, I bet Richard's parents don't see it that way," I retorted, unable to shake off the nagging worry in my gut.

"Let Richard handle his parents," she suggested, her smile radiating warmth and reassurance. "You've got enough on your plate as your wedding day is tomorrow. Now, what should I wear to this dinner with your future in-laws?" That's my mom for you, always knowing how I feel and precisely what to do to lighten my load.

* * *

I glanced down at my own ensemble, a sleek black Dior dress that hugged my figure just right. Then, my gaze drifted toward my mother's suitcase, a treasure trove of potential outfits.

"Let's see what my stunning mother has packed in those bags," I suggested, dusting the clouds off my mind. "And if nothing catches our eye, we can always indulge in some last-minute retail therapy," I said, a playful lilt in my voice.

"I'm sure I packed something suitable for meeting the Collinses," she said, her tone confident. But there was a hint of excitement in her eyes at the prospect of possibly shopping together for a new outfit. She glanced at me and smiled, "Your father always dresses well."

Recalling my previous conversation with Dad about his affection for my mother, I couldn't help but grin at their playful, emotional tug-of-war. "Hmm... are you dressing up for him or the Collinses?" I teased.

"Esperanza Williams Ortega! Enough of that... you're not a 6-year-old playing cupid anymore," she retorted firmly, yet her voice had a touch of amusement.

We laughed together, like old-school friends. In that instant, I felt grateful for my mother's company. I knew that no matter how intimidating the future appeared, I would find solace in her presence. She was like a beacon in turbulent waters, guiding me safely through each obstacle. With this reassuring thought, I experienced a surge of renewed strength and resolve, prepared to tackle whatever came next.

———

As we stepped into The Mark Restaurant, we made quite the mother-daughter duo in our outfits. There I was, sporting a black sleeveless dinner dress — a near reflection of my dark hair and eyes, while my mom stunned in an emerald green strapless number that mirrored her green eyes and beautifully offset her blond locks. A few heads turned our way; we almost looked identical but in our own unique styles.

The grandeur of the place struck me like a wave. Illuminated by the soft glow of crystal chandeliers suspended from lofty ceilings, the entire room was elegant. The polished marble floors reflected the light, adding to the brilliance of the setting. Plush velvet chairs, dark as midnight, encircled dining tables adorned with crisp white tablecloths, creating a stark and beautiful contrast. A mouthwatering medley of gourmet aromas swirled in the air, intertwined with the heady scent of fine, aged wine.

Mom and I made our way to our table, where Richard and his parents, George and Catherine, were already chatting with my dad. Seeing Dad with Catherine brought back memories of our initial meeting in Amsterdam. It was a meeting where Catherine, along with Richard's ex-wife Emilia, had invited themselves to join our meeting with Dad and Yumi. That was the occasion when both women attempted to pressure Richard into securing a prenuptial agreement, under the pretense that I didn't have any financial assets of my own. At that time, Dad was just an employer — a producer who wanted to dine with his biggest star, Richard. Unbeknownst to me, he had financed the film production just to bring me on board. During that dinner, Dad came to my defense and declared that I was indeed wealthy, his sole heir. The rest, as they say, is history.

Like clockwork, the gentlemen got up from their seats — sticking to old-school manners like glue — proof of their refined upbringing.

Richard, decked out in his tailored black suit, was all shades of Mr. Dapper. His eyes sparkled with a joy that screamed, 'I'm head over heels' — it kindled a cozy fire in my heart. I looked at my dad, who exuded an aura of serene calm, his steady-as-a-rock presence acting as my lifebuoy in these pre-wedding jitters feelings I found myself in.

"Hello, darling," Richard greeted me warmly, his voice as soothing as a lullaby, "You're looking absolutely stunning." His arms naturally wrapped around my waist, pulling me into a fiery embrace that set off a wave of warmth within me. Turning to my mom, he added, "Debbie, you're breathtaking." A kiss on her cheek followed his compliment. She was indeed radiant, her emerald dress highlighting her figure and making her green eyes twinkle with delight. My dad, playing the perfect gentleman, greeted her with a gentle kiss on her hand.

* * *

Next, I greeted Richard's parents. I gave them a peck on their cheeks — because, manners. "George, Catherine," I acknowledged them. Catherine, drop-dead gorgeous but colder than an ice cube, gave me the once-over with icy blue eyes that could freeze a volcano. On the flip side, George was charm personified. His warm smile and friendly vibe melted away any initial jitters I had.

"Ah, Hope! One of my favorite people in the world," George greeted me enthusiastically, his voice full of genuine warmth. "Come, give this old chap a bear hug." I obliged, wrapping my arms around him. The tight hug he reciprocated was a comforting blanket, reminding me that we were all family despite the grand setting and serious discussions.

"Debbie Williams, meet my parents, George and Catherine Collins," Richard introduced my mom formally.

"It's wonderful to finally meet you both," My mom cheerfully extended her hands to George and planted a peck on Catherine's cheek.

"Likewise, Debbie," Catherine managed to say formally, keeping it cool as a cucumber.

"Now I can see where Hope got her killer looks," George clasped my mom's hand, sparking a round of chuckles from our group.

Just then, a waiter appeared at our table, his demeanor as refined as the silver tray he carried. He presented us with menus, each one leather-bound, hinting at the culinary adventures that awaited us. Alongside them was an extensive wine list, a comprehensive guide to the world's finest vineyards. We unanimously chose a bottle of Château Margaux, its reputation for rich, velvety flavors promising to enhance the gourmet dishes we had ordered.

My eyes meandered around the room, sneakily scanning faces, hoping to spot a familiar one. Sensing my unease, Richard leaned in closer, his voice barely louder than a whisper. "Henry will be here soon. He got snagged by an urgent suit alteration."

Just as he wrapped up his sentence, Catherine switched gears and turned the conversation to me, "How's the wedding planning coming along?"

"So far, so good. No big hiccups yet. Fingers crossed, it stays that way till tomorrow," I replied. "The wedding planners are on top of their game and won't let me stress over even the tiniest details." I glanced at Richard and added, "All thanks to your hefty checkbook."

"You didn't chip in at all?" My mom queried.

"I wouldn't let her. But she's taken care of the honeymoon, and I'm still in the dark about where we're going," Richard spilled.

"That's my surprise. I won't spill the beans until we're there," I said, a smug grin plastered on my face.

"In accordance with the English tradition where the bride's family funds the wedding ceremonies, I arranged to cover all the costs, including the honeymoon," Dad said. "However, these two are determined to defy the norms of two different countries," he added, glancing directly at Mom as if to assure her that he had fulfilled his homework.

Catherine cleared her throat and steered the conversation onto a more contentious path. "So, have you two settled your prenuptial agreements?" she posed, her intense gaze locked on me as she delicately sipped her wine.

Richard's reply was swift and unyielding. "Mother, that matter is between Hope and me." His tone was frigid, mirroring his icy relationship with his mother.

Undeterred, Catherine pressed on. "Richard, I spoke with Raphael. You haven't drafted any prenups, but you signed the one Hope presented." Her words were a thinly veiled challenge.

A sigh escaped Richard's lips as he ran his fingers through his hair, a telltale sign of his mounting frustration and barely controlled temper. "Mother..."

* * *

Before he could continue, I reached out and gently rested my hand on his. My pleading eyes implored him for peace. I yearned for a simple family lunch without legal jargon and monetary negotiations.

Amid the tense standoff, my father cleared his throat, commanding our attention. Unexpectedly, he slid a leather folio with the Ortega Holding logo embossed on it towards Richard. "This was intended as a wedding gift. But since we're all gathered here, it seems like the right moment."

Richard cautiously opened the folio. Inside were pages of a board resolution, assigning several shares under his name as part of the Board of Directors. "One seat on the board, Richard, complete with voting rights," my father declared.

The offer seemed to catch Richard by surprise. "Thank you, Oliver. I'm overwhelmed by your generosity. But this isn't necessary. I assure you, Hope will be well provided for. My earnings are wisely invested." His earnest grin served as proof of his sincerity.

However, my father wasn't one to back down easily. "I know that, Richard. That's why I trust you with Hope's future." His gaze shifted to Richard's parents. "The idea of a prenup on Hope's side was mine. Hope already has a voting seat. While she has significant personal assets, the majority are tied up in holding companies, managed by the board and senior officers. It's a complex arrangement."

I cleared my throat, "Let me clarify this. My dad has always given me autonomy in these matters. Whatever decisions I make, he will support." I paused, carefully considering my next words. "My father and grandfather, and the generations before them, built the company holdings. I didn't have a hand in it, so it's not my right to share it with anyone, including my spouse. But my shares in the holdings including my board seat and voting right will be passed on to our children. Hence, they will carry the name Ortega-Collins so that no one can question their birthright." My father looked at me with pride. Then I continued, "As for Richard's assets, although they become shared property after the wedding, they will be passed on to Henry and his siblings."

* * *

"Darling, we've been over this countless times," Richard gently took my hand and kissed it, then turned to my father. "Oliver," Richard started, his tone respectful, "I fell in love with Hope before she became an Ortega. And I would marry her with or without the fanfare." His warm and sincere smile was the perfect conclusion to the evening's discussions.

"I know you do, Richard," my father acknowledged, his gaze steady. "There's also a pressing matter why I decided to put you on board. The future of business does indeed lie in media and entertainment. Retail, real estate, and even tech — they're all being shaped by the influence of the media. I desire to harness this power, to control it. This is a smart move. That's why the most significant expansion is happening within Hope's company — publishing and film production. The plan is to branch out into newscasting and social media. It is the logical next step."

George, a man more inclined to listen than to speak, but brimming with wisdom, voiced his approval. "That's quite an impressive plan, Oliver!" His tone carried a hint of genuine admiration. "This generation is so different from ours; it's quite a challenge for me to keep up."

Oliver nodded appreciatively at George's words, his gaze shifting toward Richard. "It is the future, George. And I believe that Richard can play a crucial role in realizing this vision." He turned fully towards Richard, his voice firm yet gentle, his demeanor serious. "Richard, our company is on the cusp of global expansion, particularly in the domains of media and entertainment. You and Hope are the best people to spearhead this venture. I wouldn't extend this offer if I didn't have absolute faith in your abilities."

My mother, ever the voice of reason, added her thoughts to the discussion. "Richard, you don't need to abandon your passion for acting and filmmaking. You can continue acting, directing, and making money out of it while also attending board meetings, contributing your ideas, and participating in major decisions. After all, you understand this craft better than half the people in the boardroom."

I broke the silence that had fallen over our table. "Richard, there's no need for an immediate answer. You don't have to say yes or no now," I said, my voice barely above a whisper. "But I want you to know how thrilled I would be to make business decisions moving forward, knowing that you got my back and you're supporting me every step of the way."

Richard turned to me, his eyes softening as he picked up my hand, bringing it to his lips. "Always am, always will," he vowed, his voice a soothing murmur. The warmth of his breath against my skin sent a shiver down my spine, a silent promise of unwavering support and enduring love.

Despite Catherine's typically frosty demeanor, her tone softened, "Hope, I was never against Richard's sharing everything with you. My only concern was to protect Henry's interests."

Instinctively, I reached across the table and touched Catherine's, "I understand that your intentions have always been for Henry. I'm grateful that you're supportive of this. He will always be Richard's firstborn, and he's my friend. I wouldn't let anything happen to him."

She nodded, then turned her gaze to Richard. A hush fell over the table as everyone absorbed the conversation. Pride welled up within me, both for Richard and myself. This was more than just a wedding now; it was about forging a future together - a future rife with challenges, growth opportunities, and shared dreams.

Suddenly, a clatter on the restaurant floor broke the silence. A familiar voice echoed across the room, tinged with a hint of apology. "Sorry, I'm late. It took longer than I thought it would." It was Henry.

I barely recognized him at first glance. His usually flowing blond hair had been trimmed short, giving him a striking resemblance to his father. The only difference was their hair color — Henry's golden locks were a stark contrast to his father's dark mane.

Leaping from my seat, I threw my arms around his neck, my fingers brushing against his newly cropped hair. "Oh. My. God! You look so handsome!"

* * *

Henry's boyish grin widened at my reaction. "What do you think? I'm not quite used to it yet," he confessed, a playful glint in his eyes.

"I won't miss that long hair now that I see you with this shorter version." My words were punctuated with a giggle, my excitement barely contained.

Following our exchange, Henry made his way around the table, greeting each family member. He embraced his father warmly, planted affectionate kisses on his grandparents' cheeks, and shook my father's hand with respect. He didn't forget to shower my mother with his charm, eliciting a radiant smile from her.

"You look absolutely dashing, Henry!" My mother complimented, her eyes twinkling with maternal pride.

In a playful turn, Henry pointed toward my mother and asked me, "Who is she, your sister?" His question, absurd as it was, sent ripples of laughter around the table, even coaxing a rare chuckle from the usually stoic Catherine.

As Henry nestled in his seat between his father and grandmother, Mom asked how Richard and I had met. "So, Richard, Hope already told me how you met. She told me you met on set. But I want to hear your version. Do writers often cross paths with the leading stars?" she queried.

"Sometimes, we do hand scripts to them," I replied before Richard could.

"Actually, our first encounter was quite memorable," Richard said, chuckling. "She tripped over her own feet and spilled her drink all over me during the initial film meet-up party. I'll never forget those eyes and red cheeks... she looked as if she had just committed a crime and was about to be carted off to prison!"

"My word! That sounds just like Hope," my mom interjected, laughing.

"I was terrified because I was living on a modest writer's salary, and I'd ruined his expensive shirt!" I defended myself.

"I searched for you everywhere, but I couldn't find you," he said, tracing my cheekbone with his fingers.

"I hid somewhere, googling you," I confessed.

"From that moment, I simply couldn't get her out of my mind, so I told myself I had to see her again. When Robin invited the entire production crew for a nightcap, I invited myself along," he admitted.

"I had no idea!" I beamed from ear to ear.

"Then, after a couple of beers and some coaxing, she was persuaded to perform on stage," Richard continued.

"You're joking! She has terrible stage fright, Richard!" My mother protested. "Numerous times, she would feign illness to avoid her piano recitals."

"Debbie, she played the piano beautifully that night... and her voice when she sings... I was hooked right then and there," Richard added.

We all chuckled at the exchange of stories. As the conversation wound down, Dad gently tapped his wine glass. The sound echoed across the table, drawing everyone's attention to him. He stood up, a mischievous twinkle in his eye as he raised his glass. "A toast," he announced, his voice firm and authoritative.

"To Hope and Richard, may your future be as bright and promising as the stars above. May your love for each other continue to grow, nurturing you and guiding you through life's journey."

We raised our glasses in unison, the room filled with the soft clink of crystal. The Château Margaux in our glasses shimmered under the soft lights, its rich aroma filling the air.

The Mark Restaurant was known for its world-class menu; tonight, it did not disappoint. The first course was a warm shrimp salad, the succulent shrimps seasoned perfectly and paired with a light, tangy dressing. The freshness of the ingredients was evident in every bite, the flavors subtly innovative yet comforting.

Next came the lamb chops, cooked to perfection and served with a side of grilled vegetables. Each bite was a symphony of flavors, the tender meat melting in our mouths.

The pièce de résistance of the meal was the lobster. It was a sight to behold and served whole and bathed in a buttery sauce. The sweetness of the lobster meat, coupled with the sauce's richness, was an indulgence worth every bite.

With an unexpected curiosity, Catherine shifted the conversation. "I hear Americans are quite traditional about bridal showers. Is yours going to be any different?"

"Just a small gathering of close friends and former colleagues in my old apartment," I replied, casually scooping up the last of my chocolate sundae. "Nothing grand, just a simple pajama party, a few drinks, and colorful stories."

Henry, never one to let an opportunity for teasing pass, chimed in with a gleeful cheer. "Too bad, we're gearing up for a wild stag party!"

"Henry," I warned, my tone firm but playful, "there better not be any strippers at your father's party. If there are, I promise to make your life miserable from the moment I say 'I do'!"

"Of course, no strippers," he retorted, a mischievous twinkle in his eye. "Just a couple of models."

I shot a mock, exasperated look at Richard, who quickly came to my rescue. "Darling, those days are long gone since the day I met you," he assured me, punctuating his promise with a passionate kiss that drew amused glances from the rest of the table.

Seeking to steer the conversation to safer waters, my mother turned to Catherine and George. "Would you like me to show you around MOMA or The Met?" she offered.

* * *

Catherine, thawing noticeably towards my mother, responded with interest. "I believe some pieces are currently on loan from Amsterdam; we could check them out."

"Why don't you two enjoy your museum tours while I take George to the office?" Oliver suggested. His offer was met with an enthusiastic nod from George.

Richard slid his arms around my waist as we began to prepare for our respective afternoon outings. His whisper, coupled with the warmth of his breath against my ear, sent a shiver down my spine. "So, I won't get to see you tonight, or what's hidden beneath this sexy little black dress?"

"I'm afraid you'll have to wait until our honeymoon, my love," I whispered back, a seductive undertone coloring my words, causing his eyes to light up with anticipation.

Planting another tender kiss on my lips, he smiled. "Then I'll see you tomorrow."

"And I'll be the one in the white dress," I promised, returning his smile with one of my own.

8

In the heart of a city that never sleeps, the day was nothing short of enchanting. It was the day I married Richard at the majestic New York Public Library — known for its architectural grandeur and literary history, and for two book lovers, our chosen sanctuary. A place usually echoing with hushed whispers and the rustle of book pages transformed into a haven of love for us. The library's renowned marble decor, which could house countless guests, was adorned lavishly, reflecting our unique love story.

Its grandeur and elegance were adorned with cascades of white tulips, ivory roses, and blue hydrangeas, reflecting the color scheme beautifully. Delicate sprigs of baby's breath and touches of greenery added texture and depth, creating a stunning visual. Their sweet fragrance wafted through Astor Hall, mingling with the scent of old books and polished marble.

Our wedding theme effortlessly combined elegance with a cozy warmth. Thanks to our skilled wedding planner, we created an ambiance that seemed like something straight out of a fairy tale. Pastel blues and soft ivories dominated the color palette, symbolizing our love's tranquility and purity, while silver grey accents added a dash of luxury. It was like stepping into a dream, only better because it was real and it was ours.

Although I'd initially envisioned a simple wedding, just Richard and me in front of a judge, our circumstances required more. Given his status and my new role in my father's business, we couldn't escape a grand celebration. So, there I was, stepping out of the limousine, my heart fluttering like a butterfly.

The media, representing both Hollywood and Fleet Street, swarmed around us, their camera flashes.

In the midst of my emotional whirlwind, my father was my rock. He whispered, "I got you," steadying me with his arm. My mother, her eyes sparkling with held-back tears, dabbed at her eyes and then gave a glowing smile to everyone gathered. As I made my grand entrance, the whispers of silk and the rustle of tulle announced my arrival. My gown was a vision of lace and dreams, shimmering with every step I took, making me feel like a princess straight out of a fairy tale.

The wedding procession began, each movement a beautifully choreographed ballet. The flower girls led the way, their giggles muffled by the petals they scattered with youthful exuberance. They were enchanting little visions in their ivory dresses, each resembling a delicate blossom. Their dresses were adorned with tiny blue sashes that matched the bridesmaids' dresses, tying the motif together seamlessly. The skirts billowed out around them as they moved, creating an ethereal effect that was truly magical to behold.

Then came the bridesmaids, my college friends Jane and Lizzie, followed by Brittany Ginger — Richard's leading lady in the TV series *Back In Time*. Their gowns a sea of pastel blues that mirrored the early morning sky. My Maid of Honor Jenna was stunning! They walked with grace, their smiles radiant and warm. The dresses, made of flowing chiffon, were designed with a flattering A-line silhouette, creating an elegant and timeless look. Each dress was cinched at the waist with a silver-grey belt, mirroring the accents of the overall decor.

As the music swelled, signaling my arrival, my heart pounded in my chest as I walked down the aisle, the soft rustle of my dress the only sound in the room. My gaze was drawn to the Sungs seated together with Mavi, Tess, and Zaldy, chatting softly, their faces alight with anticipation. Hillary was seated next to my editorial team, her eyes brimming with happiness.

On the other side of the aisle, I spotted Yumi, Frank, Raymund, and the rest of the executives. Their presence was a stark reminder that the company supported me this day and moving forward.

"Breathe, Hope," I whispered to myself, clutching the bouquet tighter. I could feel the weight of their gazes, but I forced myself to focus on the end of the aisle. On the man waiting for me there.

I caught sight of Richard. Seeing him standing there, tall and handsome in his perfectly tailored tuxedo, my heart swelled with love. The groomsmen stood to the right of the groom — Tom, Jack, and Robin. Henry stood next to him as his best man. Both men were undeniably handsome, but my eyes were only for Richard. His eyes locked onto mine, a blue so deep it rivaled the ocean, and the speck of grey added a mystery. In them, I saw love, awe, and a promise of forever.

With each step I took down the aisle, a wave of emotions washed over me — excitement, nervousness, joy. The world seemed to shrink, leaving only Richard and the steady rhythm of my heartbeat. As I reached him, he extended a hand to my father and gently kissed my mother's cheek. Then he took my hand, his touch grounding me. Our eyes met again, and at that moment, I knew. This wasn't just a beautiful wedding day. This was the start of our life together.

The library, usually a place of hushed whispers, echoed with the solemnity of his words, "Darling, you're beautiful."

Our friends and family watched on, their eyes shining with shared joy. The cameras clicked away, desperate to capture every fleeting moment of our fairytale wedding.

Richard squeezed my hand, drawing my attention back to him. His gaze was soft, his smile tender. I could see his nerves dancing in his eyes, a mirror of my own anxiety. But beneath it, all was a certainty that grounded me. This was Richard, the love of my life.

His thumb traced circles over my knuckles, a comforting rhythm amid the symphony of emotions playing within me. The world seemed to shrink until it was just Richard, me, and the minister's soothing voice weaving our lives together with his words.

* * *

"Dearly beloved, we gather in this hallowed place today, under the watchful gaze of God and amidst these esteemed witnesses, to unite Richard and Esperanza in the sacred bonds of matrimony. This is a union that must not be entered into lightly but with reverence and sobriety. Marriage, as we comprehend it, is a sanctified and voluntary merging of two hearts and minds, exclusively dedicated to each other. It's a commitment to share life's joys and sorrows, victories and defeats, with patience and understanding."

The minister cast his gaze over us, his voice resonating with gravity as he continued, "With this in mind, let us proceed with this sacred ceremony. Richard, do you take Esperanza to be your lawfully wedded wife, to live together in the holy estate of matrimony? Do you pledge to love her, comfort her, honor and protect her, in sickness and health, and forsake all others, devote yourself solely to her for as long as you both shall live?"

Richard's deep-set eyes penetrated my gaze through the delicate lace veil. A warm smile graced his lips as he confidently declared, "I do."

With Richard's affirmative response, the minister turned his attention towards me, "Esperanza, do you accept Richard to be your lawfully wedded husband, to live together in the holy estate of matrimony? Do you promise to love, comfort, honor, and keep him in sickness and health, and forsake all others, devote yourself solely to him for as long as you both shall live?"

Tears welled up in my eyes as I echoed the sentiment, "I do."

"And now," the minister's voice resounded clear and steady throughout the grand library, "we come to the vows."

My heart echoed in my chest like a drum beat, reverberating the profound significance of this moment. As I turned to face Richard, his hand was a warm reassurance in mine, his gaze unwavering. Looking into his eyes, I saw a montage of our past, our present, and a glimpse of our future together. Laughter, tears, triumphs, trials, days bathed in sunlight, and nights blanketed by stars.

* * *

Drawing a deep breath, I steadied myself to voice the promises etched in my heart. Promises not just meant for today or tomorrow, but for all the days of our lives. Richard mirrored my actions, our chests rising and falling in synchrony. We were two halves of a whole, on the verge of becoming one.

The room was buzzing with anticipation as if it were a living being holding its breath while we prepared to say our vows. As someone who writes for a living, crafting my wedding vows took weeks. This wasn't a typical love script. This was real. This was about us. Our lives would become inseparably entwined in the moments that were about to unfold.

As the minister cued us, I drew a deep breath, my heart pounding like a captive bird against my ribcage. Richard's eyes, mirrors of the clear sky, offered silent encouragement. My voice rang out, steady despite the storm of emotions brewing within me.

"Richard, my love," I began, my voice bouncing gently off the marble walls of the library. "Today, I choose you. Not just as my partner but as my soul's confidante, my heart's keeper. I promise to walk with you, side by side, through every journey life takes us on. I pledge to love you, to support you, and to cheer you on in all of your pursuits. I vow to make time for our conversations, to hear you truly, and to nurture you. As we navigate the unpredictable seas of life, I will be your constant. Your strength when you need it, your solace in times of sorrow, and your partner in moments of joy. I will never leave your side. I will always be there for you, in sickness and health, till death do us part. My love for you will never falter. Today and always."

Each word I spoke resonated with sacred significance, each promise binding me closer to him. Richard's eyes glistened as he absorbed my words, his hand offering a comforting squeeze in silent acknowledgment.

Then it was his turn. Richard cleared his throat, a rare hint of nervousness coloring his otherwise steady gaze. He looked at me, his eyes deep oceans of sincerity and love.

"My darling, Hope," he began, his voice a steady lullaby, "Today, I bind my life with yours. Not only as your husband but as your friend, lover, and confidant. I pledge to cherish you, to stand by you and with you, to laugh with you in joy, to grieve with you in sorrow, and to grow with you in love, for as long as we both shall live."

His words washed over me, seeping into my very soul. A tear slipped down my cheek, and the overwhelming love consumed me. As he concluded, he reached up to gently wipe the tear away, his touch tender as ever.

The minister's voice cut through the stillness of the grand library, its timbre echoing off the marbled walls. "May I have the rings, please?" At his request, Henry stepped forth. His hands, usually steady from training in the medical field, trembled ever so slightly as he held out the delicate bands. The rings glinted under the soft glow of the chandeliers, each diamond a testament to the eternal love they symbolized.

"These rings," the minister began, his gaze softening as he looked at the precious symbols nestled in Henry's palm, "are symbolic of an unbroken circle of love. Love that is freely given has no beginning and no end. It knows no giver or receiver, for each person is both — offering their love and accepting it in return. May these rings serve as a constant reminder of the vows you've exchanged today." His voice resounded with solemnity as he blessed the rings, the weight of his words sinking into the hearts of everyone present.

With a nod from the minister, Richard took my hand, his touch warm and reassuring. He slipped the ring onto my finger, his eyes mirroring the promise etched onto the band. I reciprocated the act, the cool metal sliding onto his finger as smoothly as our lives had entwined.

"By the power vested in me," the minister announced, his voice ringing out clear and strong, "I now pronounce you husband and wife. Richard, you may kiss your bride." A ripple of anticipation washed over the room, the air thick with emotion. "Ladies and gentlemen, allow me to present Mr. and Mrs. Richard and Esperanza Collins."

The room burst into a symphony of applause. The sound washed over me like a tidal wave, but all I could hear was the booming echo of my own heartbeat. Richard gently lifted my veil, the intricate lace caressing my cheeks as it fell away. Solid yet tender hands cupped my face as he leaned in. The world around us receded into a distant hum as his lips met mine in a passionate kiss. It was a kiss that sealed our promises, the vows that were more than mere words. They were the foundation of our shared future, the tangible embodiment of the love that had navigated us to this poignant moment.

9

As Richard and I crossed the threshold into the Celeste Bartos Forum, it was as if we had slipped away from reality and stepped into an ethereal dream. The stately grandeur of the dome-shaped venue spread out before us, every inch adorned with intricate gold leaf detailing that glowed under the soft, romantic lighting. Spotlights strategically placed around the room cast an enchanting play of light and shadow, accentuating the architectural beauty of the space.

Suspended from the center of the dome, a chandelier of twinkling fairy lights hung like a celestial constellation, casting a magical glow over the entire room. Below it, tables swathed in champagne-colored linen were arranged with meticulous precision. Each table was adorned with towering arrangements of blush roses and trailing ivy, creating miniature gardens amidst the opulence. Crystal glasses shimmered under the ambient lighting, their reflections dancing on the polished silver cutlery laid out with military precision at each setting. It was a scene from our shared dreams, a perfect setting for our wedding reception.

The air buzzed with anticipation, filled with our guests' excited whispers and laughter. They were a colorful blend of elegance and joy, their outfits as diverse and beautiful as they were. From afar, I recognized faces from Hollywood, friends Richard had made over the years through his film career. Among them were George Clooney, with his captivating smile; Ryan Reynolds and Blake Lively, their love evident in their exchanged glances; Benedict Cumberbatch, radiating British charm; and Emma Watson, standing out with her grace and intelligence even in this crowd of stars. Their laughter and conversation added warmth and sparkle to the atmosphere.

There were also directors and producers Richard had worked with on past films, blending seamlessly with my business associates and colleagues from the publishing industry.

Suddenly, a wave of applause erupted from the entrance, growing louder and more enthusiastic as our guests parted to make way for us. The sound of their cheers and clapping filled the hall, the energy pulsating through the room and causing my heart to swell with joy.

Hand in hand, Richard and I made our way to our sweetheart's table, a little haven carved out just for us amidst the sea of celebration. Dressed in the same ivory silk as my gown, the table was adorned with a lush garland of ivory tulips, roses, and peonies. Interspersed between the blooms were flickering candles, their soft light casting a warm, intimate glow around us, creating a bubble of peace and love where we could bask in the joy of our special day.

Richard leaned into me, his voice a soft murmur over the hum of conversation that filled the room. "You look absolutely radiant, Mrs. Collins," he whispered, his eyes twinkling with adoration. My heart fluttered at the sound of my new title, a sweet reminder of our newly solidified bond.

"Thank you, Mr. Collins," I replied, my voice full of warmth. "And thank you for this enchanting wedding. It's exactly as I envisioned it when I was a little girl, dreaming about my fairy-tale day."

As we settled into our seats, a hush fell over the room as if the air itself was holding its breath. The spotlight shifted towards the stage area, where the heavy velvet curtains slowly pulled back, revealing the evening's surprise guest performer. A collective gasp echoed through the hall as the opening notes of 'Make You Feel My Love' filled the room. It was Adele! Her powerful voice, raw and heartfelt, brought a fresh, contemporary vibe to our classic reception, adding a unique touch that was quintessentially us.

Richard squeezed my hand under the table, his eyes shining with surprise and delight. We were both ardent fans of Adele, her soulful music often serving as the soundtrack to our relationship. Having her perform at our wedding was like a dream spun into reality. We sat there, completely captivated, as she poured her heart into the lyrics about an unwavering love. This sentiment resonated deeply with us on this momentous day of our lives.

The room was silent except for Adele's voice as she transitioned into 'Someone Like You,' another favorite of ours. Each song served as a powerful testament to love, commitment, and the promise of forever, echoing the sentiments that brought us together on this special day.

Applause erupted after each song, the guests' excitement palpable. The energy in the room was electric; everyone sang along, their voices blending beautifully with the music, creating a symphony of celebration and joy.

As the final notes of 'Hello,' yet another of her masterpieces, faded away, Adele bowed, a broad, genuine smile gracing her face. Then she looked into our table, "To this lovely couple, may your union mark the beginning of a journey filled with love and joy. As you embark on this beautiful journey of togetherness, may every day hold wonderful shared experiences! May your love story be a grand adventure filled with laughter, tenderness, and devotion. To Richard and Hope, here's to a lifetime of love, happiness, and an ever-lasting friendship. Wishing you both a wonderful and love-filled married life!" The room filled with thunderous applause and a standing ovation, a testament to the magic she had woven with her music.

We turned to each other, our eyes sparkling with unshed tears of happiness, and leaned in for a tender kiss. This moment, this day, was indeed the best day of our lives, brimming with love, joy, and the magic of music.

The grandeur of the New York ballroom was breathtaking, its magnificence amplified by an ongoing classical performance that echoed from the center stage. The symphony reverberated through the room, each note pulling at the heartstrings of the well-dressed audience members. As the music swelled, a different kind of ballet unfolded on the floor below, just as captivating and harmonious.

* * *

Waitstaff in crisp white shirts and pressed black trousers, moved like seasoned dancers among the sea of tables. Their hands held aloft silver trays, glistening under the soft light, each carrying meticulously arranged gourmet delicacies. The precision and grace in their movements were reminiscent of a well-rehearsed ballet, their rhythm matching the cadence of the orchestra's melody.

At the piece's crescendo, a waiter approached a table, his tray balanced with the expertise of a veteran performer. With gentle deftness, he placed a plate before each guest, his actions mirroring the elegance of the overhead music. The guests' faces brightened at the sight of the culinary artistry, a sensory delight for both the eyes and the taste buds.

Simultaneously, other waitstaff flitted around the room, refilling wine glasses and catering to every nuanced request. Their service was discreet yet attentive, a seamless blend of professionalism and courtesy, enhancing the overall ambiance of sophistication and refinement.

As the symphony peaked, so did the flurry of activity on the floor. Yet, amidst the hustle and bustle, there was no trace of hurriedness or disarray. Instead, the staff continued to move with a serene pace, their actions perfectly synchronized with the rhythmic pulse of the symphony.

The food distribution was a performance in itself, a dance choreographed to the beat of the classical masterpiece. Each movement was executed with precision, and each step was in harmony with the next, creating a mesmerizing spectacle that added another layer of charm to the evening. The scene was a testament to the beauty of perfect synchronization, a ballet of service unfolding under the enchanting notes of the orchestra, making the evening a truly unforgettable experience.

Henry, who was Richard's best man, was the first to raise his glass. His voice resonated through the hall, filling the room with a warmth that was both touching and amusing. His toast was a cocktail of heartfelt sentiments and humor, peppered with anecdotes that vividly depicted Richard's character.

* * *

"I believe not everyone's privy to the fact that I encountered Hope before she even met my old man," he began, a cheeky twinkle in his eyes. "We hit it off so splendidly that we nattered away for hours like long-lost mates. We got so carried away that we completely forgot to swap phone numbers!" This revelation prompted a wave of laughter among the crowd. Henry continued, "Our family is infamously anti-social media, so it didn't occur to me to seek her out... until it was a tad too late." The guests erupted into more laughter at this unexpected turn of events.

"When I bumped into Hope again, she was dating my father. Now, I've ended up being the stepson of my erstwhile potential girlfriend, who's now my delightfully wicked stepmother! So, chaps, when you reckon you've found the right girl, don't dither!" His jovial tone elicited a ripple of chuckles from the audience. "But on a serious note, to my dad, I'm absolutely chuffed that you finally found the love you were searching for. You've earned this happiness. To Hope, cheers for entering our lives and for remaining a top-notch friend to me. So, let's lift a glass to my father, who bagged the best girl in town. Here's to the start of your happily ever after."

The guests raised their glasses high, cheers echoing through the hall in a chorus of well wishes.

At the other end of the table, Jenna gently gathered the hem of her gown and rose from her chair. "One of the things that make this wedding truly extraordinary is that the bride chose a 56-year-old maid of honor!" Her statement elicited peals of laughter from the crowd.

"Kidding aside," she continued as the laughter subsided, "Richard is incredibly fortunate to have found this girl," Jenna looked at me lovingly and paused. "She's the sweetest, smartest, and kindest girl I've ever known. Despite everything that comes her way, she remains steadfast and grounded. When she fell in love with Richard, I initially opposed it. I believed Esperanza, as I fondly call her, deserved someone more private, away from the prying eyes of the media. But life isn't like one of my novels, where I can change the characters' circumstances. My wish for her is to live out her love story privately, away from the glitz and glamour." Jenna's voice wavered, and tears welled up in her eyes. "So, here's to Richard and Esperanza. May you grow old together in a quiet corner of the world, far away from the limelight."

With that, she raised her glass, prompting the guests to follow suit — the room filled with the tinkling sound of clinking glasses and heartfelt cheers.

A wave of emotion swept through the room as our parents rose to express their love and well wishes. My mother, her eyes glistening with unshed tears, was the first to speak. She unfolded a piece of paper on which she had written her prepared speech, took a deep breath, and carefully refolded it, tucking it under her wine glass.

She cleared her throat, met my gaze, and spoke from the depths of her heart. "Today, I watch you step into a new chapter of your life with immense pride and joy. As you walk down the aisle, my heart overflows with love and happiness for you. From the moment you were born, I knew you were destined for great things. You've matured into a strong, independent, and compassionate woman, and seeing you so deeply in love fills me with an indescribable joy."

She paused momentarily, collecting herself before continuing. "As you embark on this beautiful journey of marriage, remember that love is not just about finding the right person but also about being the right person. It's about patience, understanding, and forgiveness. It's about supporting each other, even when times get tough. Always cherish the love you share, nurture it, let it grow. Marriage is a garden that needs constant tending, and with care and respect, it will bloom beautifully."

Her voice faltered, and tears streamed down her cheeks, mirroring my own. My father handed her a white handkerchief, which she used to dab away her tears before resuming her speech. "I am here for you, always, in all ways, as you navigate through this new phase of your life. Remember, no matter how far you go, you will always be my little girl. Congratulations, my darling. May your married life be filled with love, joy, and endless blessings."

Unable to hold back my tears, I let them fall freely. Her words painted a touching picture of my transformation from a wide-eyed little girl into the woman I had become, standing on the precipice of a thrilling new journey. Richard enveloped me in his arms, and I noticed my father doing the same for my mother.

Richard's father, George, rose from his seat, his eyes brimming with warmth and kindness. He reached out to me, a gesture both grand and personal. Hand in hand, we made our way to the dance floor as the music enveloped us like a gentle wave. Despite his years, George moved with surprising agility, leading me across the dance floor with an unexpected grace.

"Hope," he began, his voice resonating with sincerity, "thank you for bringing such joy to my son's life. I haven't seen him this happy in a long time." His words warmed my heart, prompting a smile that lit up my eyes.

"George," I replied, echoing his sincerity, "I love Richard more than anything in this world." The truth of my words lingered between us.

"You can start calling me 'dad' now," he suggested, a playful twinkle in his eyes. We both broke into soft laughter, the sound rippling gently across the dance floor.

Then, it was my father's turn. He tapped George's shoulder. My father-in-law planted a kiss on my cheek before passing my hand to my father. As Dad enveloped me in his arms, a misty look in his eyes revealed his deep emotions. We swayed slowly on the dance floor, each step an attempt to recapture the missed moments from my childhood. His grip tightened slightly as he whispered, "I am so proud of you, Hope."

"Dad," I responded, my voice heavy with emotion, "you entered my life at just the right moment. I couldn't have asked for more." Overwhelmed, I held him close, imprinting this moment deep into my memory. This was more than a dance; it was a heartfelt exchange between a father and daughter, a cherished memory to be treasured forever.

An unexpected hush fell over the room as the opening strains of "Home" filled the air. The atmosphere, already heavy with emotion, took on a deeper resonance. Michael Buble and Blake Sheldon appeared on stage as the music swelled, their rich voices lending a surreal touch to the proceedings. They were singing our song, a moment that left everyone in the room, including us, utterly spellbound.

Finally, Richard stepped up to join me on the dance floor. Dad held me close before passing my hand to Richard. When his hands met mine, our fingers intertwined effortlessly, like puzzle pieces finally finding their match. We swayed to the rhythm of the music, and as I looked into his eyes, I saw not just the man I loved but also a future brimming with love, laughter, and infinite possibilities.

As the final note of our song dissolved into silence, we held each other close. Richard whispered, "I love you, my darling... more than you'll ever know."

"And I, you, my love," I responded, looking up into his eyes.

The applause that ensued was thunderous, a reflection of the love and warmth emanating from everyone present. Our day, our moment, was unfolding even more beautifully than we could have ever imagined.

Our wedding cake was wheeled to the center of the floor where Richard and I were dancing. A gasp escaped my lips as I turned my gaze towards the wedding cake. Erin had truly outdone herself, again. The cake stood tall and majestic, a stunning masterpiece of culinary art. It was adorned with delicate white tulips, each petal carefully crafted from icing, their purity and grace reflected in the soft glow of the room's lighting.

The sight of the tulips brought a smile to my lips. Richard had given me a bouquet of white tulips on our first date, and he knew they were my favorite. From then on, they became an emblem of our love story.

The way Erin had intricately designed each tulip on the cake was simply breathtaking. It was as if she had breathed life into the icing, transforming it into a field of blooming tulips. Each cake tier was wrapped in a garland of these sugar-crafted flowers, cascading down in an elegant fall.

* * *

Richard and I moved towards the grand wedding cake, our hands coming together over the hilt of a gleaming silver knife. A hush fell over the room as the blade sliced through the creamy frosting easily. Laughter erupted as we playfully fed each other, smearing icing on each other's noses in a moment of shared joy.

Richard, with the help of our wedding planner, made sure our wedding was a dream come true for every bride. They ensured it incorporated all the traditions of an American wedding, including the garter toss. Richard knelt before me, his eyes sparkling with playful mischief as he reached for the garter. His hand gently rested on my thigh, and he looked up at me, biting his lower lip in a way that was irresistibly sexy. He whispered, "I really wish I could keep this garter, darling." His words, barely heard amidst the lively chatter of our guests, sent a thrill through the crowd. With a teasing wink, he threw the garter towards a group of eager bachelors. Henry, always athletic, jumped and caught it, his face glowing with surprise and pleasure. The room burst into applause as he proudly held up the garter, his smile wide and victorious.

Then, it was my turn for the bouquet toss. My back was to a crowd of hopeful single ladies, their eyes fixed on the bouquet in my hands. With a silent prayer, I released the flowers into the air. The gasp from the crowd was quickly replaced by a cheer as Tess emerged victorious, a stunned look of joy on her face, and screamed, "I'm next... 'gotta find me a groom!"

As the night wore on, Richard and I shared our last dance, losing ourselves in each other's eyes as we swayed to the soulful notes of our song. It was a moment suspended in time, a moment we had dreamed of.

Finally, it was time to say goodbye. Hand in hand, we walked down the aisle one last time, our friends and family showering us with rose petals and well wishes.

Richard leaned in close, his voice soft. "Are you ready?" His question hung in the air, filled with promise and anticipation. Looking up at him, I replied, my voice thick with emotion, "I've never been more ready."

With a final wave, we stepped into the waiting car, ready to embark on our next adventure. As we drove off, I nestled closer to Richard, my heart full and my spirit soaring. We were leaving behind a cherished chapter in our lives, but ahead of us lay a thrilling journey filled with unknowns and infinite possibilities. As long as we were together, I knew we could face anything. And with that thought, we headed off into the night, ready to start our honeymoon and begin the rest of our lives together.

10

The amber glow from the cabin lights danced off the rim of the wine glass I held, its contents a dark, rich red that mirrored my anticipation for this honeymoon. With a graceful maneuver, I extended the glass to Richard, our fingers grazing in a fleeting yet electrifying touch that sent a ripple of excitement up my arm. The clink of crystal against crystal reverberated within the confines of the lavish cabin, a stark contrast to the soft whispers of our conversation. I really needed to get used to this no-ordinary setting — like my father's private jet, a symbol of wealth and power, was as intimidating as it was impressive.

Richard's gaze, a mesmerizing blend of curiosity and amusement, was locked onto me, his attention undeterred by the luxurious surroundings; he was used to it. With deliberate slowness, I moved to straddle his lap, the hem of my cotton powder-blue dress riding up my thighs. A sense of daring, unfamiliar yet thrilling, coursed through me. His hand found its way to the back of my left thigh, lingering just above my knee, a silent promise of the intimacy we were about to share.

The comforting hum of the jet engines provided a rhythmic backdrop to the unmistakable tension between us, their steady drone a soothing lullaby to my quickening breaths.

"Darling," he began, his voice a gentle caress against my heightened senses. But the words died on his lips as I pressed a finger against them, silencing him with a playful warning. My other hand lifted the wine glass to my lips, and I took a slow sip, allowing the rich flavor to linger on my tongue. The taste of the exquisite vintage was a compelling accompaniment to the thrill coursing through me. His hands, solid and warm, shifted to my hips, anchoring me in place and reinforcing our shared connection.

"Surprised?" I asked, a cheeky smile playing on my lips as I reveled in this newfound control. His response was a chuckle, a low, rumbling sound that vibrated against my chest, sending a delightful shiver down my spine.

"I can't say I had expected you commandeering our honeymoon plans," he confessed, his voice a harmonious blend of warmth, surprise, and unabashed admiration. "But I must confess, this air of mystery you've donned is quite... enticing. And, I love this flirty and sexy side of you." His eyes sparkled with intrigue, hinting at the thrilling journey ahead.

His words sent a ripple of satisfaction coursing through me, a warm affirmation of the intricate dance we shared. It was a game of emotional chess between us, a delicate balance of personalities where he was the calming balm to my fierce spirit, the steadying anchor to my whirlwind spontaneity. We were two halves of a harmonious whole, and I reveled in the intoxicating rhythm of our synchronicity.

With each beat of my heart pounding a wild, frantic tempo within my chest, I leaned in closer, the electric charge between us pulling me like a magnet. My eyes, drawn by an irresistible force, flickered to his lips before darting back to meet his gaze. "Good," I whispered, my voice barely audible over the hum of the jet engines, "because the surprises have just begun."

In a move as natural as breathing, I closed the remaining distance between us, pressing my lips onto his in a passionate kiss. It wasn't just a mere meeting of lips; it was a promise, a silent vow of the thrilling adventures that awaited us in the snow-cloaked landscapes of Finland and beyond. As I pulled back, a spark ignited in his eyes, mirroring my own bubbling excitement and anticipation.

Richard reciprocated the kiss with a fervor that left me breathless, his hands moving up to cradle my face as his fingers threaded through my hair, deepening our connection. It was more than desire; it was a hunger, a yearning echoing my own sentiments, a silent conversation between two hearts beating in unison.

Our world had contracted to this moment, to the lingering taste of red wine on our lips and the heat radiating from our entwined bodies. Just when I was about to surrender entirely to him, a polite cough drew us back into reality.

Turning my head, I saw the stewardess standing at a respectful distance, a tray laden with delectable dishes held securely in her hands. A blush crept up my cheeks, but I managed to flash a small, sheepish smile.

"Your lunch, Mr. and Mrs. Collins," she said, her voice laced with a twinge of embarrassment at having caught us in our intimate moment.

"Thank you," I replied, my voice barely louder than a whisper. As Richard gently helped me off his lap, the stewardess proceeded to set the tray on the small table nestled between us.

"Enjoy your meal," she added, her professional smile firmly back in place before she retreated to the front of the jet.

A soft chuckle bubbled up from within me as I settled onto the plush couch opposite Richard. Picking up my fork, I glanced over at Richard, who was watching me with an amused grin dancing on his face. "Guess we got a bit carried away," I admitted, a peculiar blend of embarrassment and exhilaration washing over me.

Reaching across the table, Richard captured my hand in his, his touch a comforting presence. "I wouldn't have it any other way, darling," he confessed, his eyes shimmering with the promise of more stolen moments, more passionate kisses, more shared laughter. With that, we savored our lavish meal, high above the ground, nestled in our own little world.

———

The crisp, clean Finnish air filled our lungs when we stepped off the private jet. It was a purity unlike anything I'd ever breathed in before, a coldness that was both biting and exhilarating, filling our lungs with a freshness only found in the heart of winter.

Richard glanced at me, his ice-blue eyes — their hue deepened now, a shade bluer than usual, speckled with grey — mirroring the snow-kissed expanse around us. His gaze held a curious mix of anticipation and wonder, like a child on Christmas morning.

"Welcome to our winter wonderland," I murmured softly, my breath crystallizing into a cloud of warmth against the freezing backdrop, starkly contrasting the frosty atmosphere.

His laughter echoed through the silent landscape, a rich, warm sound that seemed out of place in the frozen wilderness. "Darling, I'm positively bursting with anticipation here. You know I'm not accustomed to my wife keeping secrets from me," he quipped, his lips brushing the top of my nose in a playful kiss. "Can you let me in on this grand surprise now?"

With a teasing smile, I replied, "Patience, my love," standing on tiptoe to plant a quick, playful kiss on his lips.

A sleek black car, an elegant beast against the pristine white, awaited us, its engine purring softly in the still night. As we journeyed through the forest, the snow-draped trees stood tall like silent sentinels, guarding the secrets of their icy realm—our destination: a glass igloo hotel nestled in the heart of this frozen paradise.

As we arrived, a sight straight from the pages of a whimsical fairy tale greeted us. The entrance sign glimmered under the soft luminescence of the moon – Kakslauttanen Arctic Resort. Nestled amidst the snow-cloaked pines, the glass igloos shimmered under the starlit sky, their domes reflecting the celestial tapestry above. The Northern Lights, those ethereal dancers of the night sky, began their mesmerizing performance, casting an otherworldly glow over the entire scene.

Richard's grip on my hand tightened, his excitement pulsating through his touch. "Surprise is an understatement, darling," he whispered, radiating a warmth that seemed to melt the very ice beneath our feet. We were about to embark on our first adventure as a married couple in this bewitching, frost-kissed wonderland.

The instant we alighted from the car, we were warmly welcomed by a hotel staff member. Her rosy cheeks, flushed from the cold, and radiant smile contrasted sharply against her pristine, snow-white uniform. "Welcome to Kakslauttanen. I am Eeva," she introduced herself, her Finnish accent lending a delightful cadence to her words.

Eeva guided us along a lantern-illuminated path that meandered through a forest of frosted pines. The rhythmic crunch of our snow boots punctuated the tranquil silence of the wintry night. The air was alive with the crisp scent of pine needles, carrying the whispers of new beginnings on its icy breath.

Our igloo, a glass gem, was nestled in a secluded nook of the resort, offering an intimate haven with an unhindered view of the celestial tapestry above. As Eeva swung open the door, it revealed a cozy and majestic space. Our igloo was a sanctuary of warmth and luxury amidst the frigid wilderness. Dominating the room was a king-sized bed swathed in plush fur blankets strategically positioned under the transparent ceiling for optimal stargazing. A bottle of champagne sat chilling beside a bouquet of vibrant wildflowers and a vintage 1994 Bordereaux on a quaint table — another gift from my father — while soft, ambient music wafted through the air, further enhancing the romantic ambiance.

Richard drew me close, his breath warm against my ear as he whispered, "Damn, I want to make love with you now, under this star-studded sky." His husky words sent shivers coursing down my spine, not from the biting cold but from the thrilling anticipation of the intimate moments soon to unfold.

With a twinkling farewell, Eeva wished us a good night. Her eyes held a gleam of shared joy, a sentiment only known to those privileged to create such magical experiences for others. As she departed, I turned to absorb the enchanting panorama of our honeymoon suite fully. The Northern Lights had amplified their dance, their colors more vivid and stunning than before. The entire room was bathed in a soft, otherworldly glow, making everything feel beautifully surreal, like a dream spun from ice and starlight.

* * *

"Welcome to our private cosmos," I murmured, my fingertips tracing his tousled hair as I rose on my tiptoes to meet his lips. Our surroundings, an ethereal cocoon of glass and stars, were the perfect backdrop for the blossoming of our shared journey.

"Are you ready, darling?" His question was laced with a playful undertone, his eyes twinkling in harmony with the constellation above us. I responded with a nod, my heart pulsating like a wild drum, echoing the rhythm of my anticipation.

Gently unwinding my arms from his sturdy frame, I offered a soft plea, "Give me a few moments to freshen up."

His response was a whisper, laden with promise and longing. "Don't keep me waiting too long, Mrs. Collins," followed by a lingering kiss that tasted of sweet wine and unspoken desires. As he released me, his right arm casually draped around my waist, his fingers lightly brushing against the small of my back.

While he patiently awaited my return, I indulged in a refreshing bath, preparing myself for the intimate rendezvous ahead. Emerging from the bath, my skin felt smooth, primed for the caress of his touch. I wore nothing under my white silk kimono, which cascaded down to my ankles. The fabric felt cool and sensual against my bare skin.

After one final appraisal in the mirror, a surge of confidence washed over me. Tonight felt like a new beginning with Richard, an exciting chapter in our shared narrative. I stepped out of the bathroom with a deep breath to quell any lingering nerves.

The room's ambiance was subtly romantic; the dim lighting from the flickering candles cast long, dancing shadows on the glass dome ceiling. The air was fragrant, with the comforting scent of vanilla mingled with a hint of exotic spices. Despite the initial wave of nervousness that threatened to overwhelm me, Richard's calming presence was an anchor amidst the storm of my emotions.

He lay there, relaxed and inviting, on our bed. His clothes were carelessly strewn across the room. He held a glass of wine in one hand, the ruby liquid reflecting the mesmerizing dance of the Northern Lights overhead. The sight was breathtakingly beautiful — a man, lost in thought, under the celestial ballet of the aurora borealis.

With a bold move, I let the kimono slip from my shoulders, pooling at my feet. Richard's gaze darkened, his usually blue eyes now a smoky grey — a telltale sign of his mounting desire. I slid under the plush duvet, the crisp white sheets cool against my bare skin. Nestling against him, I teased my leg along his, our bodies moving in a slow, rhythmic dance. He placed his wine glass on the bedside table, his eyes never leaving mine.

Our night of passion was about to begin, and the anticipation was as electrifying as the Northern Lights dancing above us.

He grabbed my head, and suddenly, his mouth was on mine. His tongue was probing, searching, and dueling with mine. The relentless pressure of his mouth on mine was intoxicating. I wanted Richard more than anything at that moment. He held me tight to his body, wrapping his arms around my back. His boxers were still on, but I could feel his hardness against my stomach.

I needed to get closer; I sat astride his hips and leaned down. I took the bottle of wine from his side and drank straight from it. Richard gave me his devilish smile that showed how fascinated he was with this wild side of me. I took over, kissing the life out of him. I couldn't resist caressing his hardness. Stroking him through the material while kissing his lips turned me on more. I had control, even if it was only for a few minutes. I enjoyed setting the pace of the passionate kissing. My tongue ran in and out of his mouth and caught his lips in my teeth. If I kept up this wild pace, I would have reached my peak even before I'd stripped him naked.

Richard took the bottle from my hand and took a swig before he ran his tongue over my sensitive nipples and seized them, one after the other, in his mouth. This only resulted in my desire rising. I was more desperate to have him inside me. He knew my body well — his actions drove me crazy.

I couldn't wait any longer. I scooted down the bed, pulled off his remaining piece of clothing, and enjoyed the view. I heard him groan quietly when my soft hands held his hardness. It was thrilling to have him at my mercy — stroking him firmly before my mouth followed through. I glanced at Richard; his eyes were closed, and his breathing was fast as he held my head firmly; his hips matched my mouth's tempo.

Suddenly, he moved me up to his taut, muscled body and positioned me in the exact place he wanted me to be. I held my breath and dropped down on him, wasting no time. I needed to feel his friction inside me and support myself, placing my hands on his chest and sliding myself up and down his length. It felt amazing, and we were just getting started. I needed his passionate kisses. Leaning forward, I sucked on his lower lip until he caught the nape of my neck with his hand and pulled me in for a deeper kiss.

I was desperate for my own release. My movement became erratic, and I held onto the headboard for support. I also felt Richard's tension; his movement matched mine, and he grabbed my breasts and sucked on my nipples as I came down from my high. We were both soaked with sweat as our fingers interlocked. I needed to kiss him again and stretch my neck back. He helped by pulling on my chin and licking my mouth, not bothering with kissing my lips, just dueling tongues.

His attention was finely tuned to my every desire as he clasped my hips. The low groans spilling from his lips signaled his nearing peak, yet he held back, waiting for me to join him. It wasn't long before a cry of his name escaped my lips — swiftly followed by my name resonating from his. The world beyond our private sanctuary ceased to exist; it was solely Richard and I, adrift in our intimate universe. Above us, the Northern Lights whirled in a dizzying dance, their hues morphing and shifting, crafting an ethereal masterpiece only nature could imagine. Our connection transcended the physical — it was profound, emotional, and spiritual.

As we reclined on the plush bed, our bodies intertwining like entangled vines, time seemed to decelerate to a languid pace. Richard tenderly swept a stray lock of hair from my face, his touch sparking electric currents across my skin. "I love you, Hope," he murmured, his breath washing over my cheek like a warm summer breeze.

* * *

"And I love you, Richard," I echoed, my voice barely audible amidst the symphony of our beating hearts.

Our igloo was an oasis of warmth amidst the frigid wilderness. It was a haven of luxury and comfort, topped with a transparent ceiling offering an uninterrupted night sky panorama. Richard drew me closer, wrapping his arm protectively around my shoulders — our bodies covered with the white blanket.

"It's enchanting, isn't it?" His voice was calm, filled with awe and reverence for the celestial spectacle above us.

"Yes, it truly is," my voice scarcely a whisper. I was captivated by the mesmerizing display unfolding overhead. It felt like the universe was staging a performance exclusively for our eyes. My heart swelled, overflowing with love for the man beside me and the extraordinary journey we were embarking on together.

Through the canvas of the night, under the ballet of the Northern Lights, Richard shifted and towered over me. "Oh god, you're beautiful, darling. I can't get enough of you," he said, trembling. Throwing the covers away, his right hand brushed my inner thighs lightly, teasing me. I looked into his eyes and saw the same desire he had a while ago. Oh, I wanted him again, but he had another plan. He wants to take his time relishing how my body responded to him. He knew I enjoyed some good pleasure delay. I watched him worshiping me, and I saw his intent, his message: he didn't want it to be over this time... and neither did I.

He opened my legs wider; his fingers danced between them. "Oh, Richard!" I cried. I closed my eyes as I lifted my hips to meet his fingers.

"Don't close your eyes on me, Mrs. Collins," his devilish smile almost drove me wilder. When he claimed my mouth, his kisses made me lose my mind, and when his tongue danced across my already-hardened nipples, I begged, "Richard, please," I gasped, and with that, he knew I was ready.

* * *

"No, darling. Not yet," he said as he looked into my eyes. "I want you to prolong your pleasure."

"I don't want to wait. I want it now. Please, Richard," I continued to beg. He continued his magic on my body. He was always a good lover, but at this moment, I think it's even better than before, if that's possible. He's got a look in his eye I never saw back then — he's enjoying my own desire. I felt more pressure from his fingers inside me as he bit my nipples harder.

Richard was showing me he didn't just enjoy my pleasure. He required it. I added my hand on top of his, encouraging him to go deeper. I felt his erection throb against my thigh.

Then he dug his fingers further inside me, opened me up as he hit the spot, and sent me spinning out of control. His masculinity teased at my feminine tenderness until I could no longer bear it and needed to respond to all the ways in which he could touch me like this, intimately, manipulating all of me.

This is it. I needed more as much as I enjoyed his tongue, hand, and mouth. I pushed his hand deeper, aiding him as I arched and cried out. When tears started falling down my cheeks, Richard kissed me passionately; his tongue danced on mine, and without warning, he removed his hand between my legs, entered me, and started moving slowly, increasing his tempo.

"Open your eyes. Look at the sky above," he commanded. Snow fell from the sky, touching the clear globe ceiling above us. I wrapped my legs around his buttocks the way he liked it. My fingers dug into his back without mercy — all the tension in the center of me was about to be released. I was floating on a cloud, pulsing. When I moved my hand between his legs while it connected to me, I made him scream my name repeatedly.

The hours have melted away in a blissful fog, each moment etching itself indelibly into the tapestry of my heart. We made love again. And again. As dawn's first light pierced the horizon, I found myself surrounded in Richard's arms, our bodies still tangled in a loving embrace. This was precisely where I longed to be — in this magical enclave, with Richard at my side, under a sky ablaze with the echoes of our shared passion.

———

The honeymoon was a whirlwind, a fleeting yet precious moment in time where it was just Richard and I, far removed from the bustling world of work commitments and corporate negotiations. Both of us were captives to our respective careers — he to the glitz and glamour of Hollywood for a pre-production and casting meeting for his upcoming movie The Getaway. And I to the cold, calculated boardroom to start negotiations with the tech firm for our expansion before anyone changed their minds.

But here in this snowy wonderland, our marriage blossomed amidst the frost-kissed wilderness on snowmobiles that roared through the silent forest. We were hunters on a quest, not for prey, but for nature's elusive light show - the Aurora Borealis. The thrill of the chase was intoxicating. My heart pounded in my chest each time the snowmobile lurched over a snowdrift, the biting wind whipping against my face. Richard's laughter echoed in my ears, a balm to the icy chill.

"Are you scared?" He teased, his eyes twinkling with mischief beneath the woolen hat that covered his dark curls.

"Terrified," I admitted, gripping the handles tighter. But it was more than just the physical thrill. It was the fear of this ephemeral bliss ending, of returning to reality where Richard and I were oceans apart.

We sought refuge in winter sports the next day, strapping on our skis and carving up the slopes. The adrenaline rush, the pure joy of freedom, was a welcome distraction. Richard was a natural, his athletic body moving with grace and ease. I struggled to keep up, often landing face-first in the snow. His laughter would ring out, followed by a helping hand and a gentle kiss that tasted of cold air and warm promises.

Fishing on the Sotajoki River was another adventure I will never forget. Guided by an old local, we waited patiently for our catch, huddled together for warmth. Lunch was always fresh fish grilled over an open fire, the smoky flavor a delicious contrast to the biting cold. Sitting side by side, hands entwined as the fire crackled before us, were the most peaceful moments. We spoke of dreams and fears, our voices barely above whispers, as if scared to disturb the serenity around us.

We retreated to our igloo at night, seeking solace in each other's arms. We made love until dawn, fueled by the urgency of our impending separation. His touch was familiar and new, thrillingly exploring uncharted territories. Each kiss and caress was a promise, a vow to return to each other, no matter how far apart we were.

And then, just like that, it was over. Time, the ever-fleeting thief, had robbed us of our brief respite. We found ourselves boarding the jet at the airport — me to New York, him to Los Angeles. As the plane took off, I looked out the window, the snowy landscape below fading into a blur, then to the beautiful man beside me. I clung to the memories, etching them into my heart. Our love story wasn't over; it was just beginning.

11

When Richard walked through the front door, I knew something was off. His face was a troubling blend of sadness and distress, making my heart race in anticipation of whatever harrowing news he was about to disclose. It felt like the air in the room had thickened, making breathing difficult.

Only a couple of days prior, I had received an abrupt call from him in Sydney. He was urgently leaving his film set for a few days and needed to return to London. The details he shared were scant; he briefly mentioned that someone he was acquainted with had tragically passed away, and his presence was required. I refrained from prying any further, choosing instead to put my faith in Richard, as I always did.

Today, however, our usual routine was broken. Instead of enveloping me in his comforting embrace upon his return, Richard merely planted a fleeting kiss on my forehead before striding purposefully toward the dining room. This change in his behavior was a clear indicator that we were about to get into a grave conversation. With each echoing footstep that followed him, my heart pounded furiously against my ribcage. I found myself standing hesitantly behind one of the dining chairs.

Richard reached for two glasses and uncorked a bottle of wine, filling both glasses nearly to the brim. Handing me one, I noticed a tremor in his grip that wasn't usually there. He downed his drink in one swift motion, replaced the empty glass on the table, and took both my hands into his own. As his gaze met mine, the profound sadness reflected in his eyes was unmistakable — I braced myself for the impending storm of bad news.

"Hope, there's something I must tell you, and I'm dreadfully terrified... that it might turn our world upside down," Richard began, his voice trembling with an undercurrent of fear.

"What is it, Richard? You can tell me anything, no matter the gravity of the situation," I responded, attempting to exude an air of calm despite the mounting dread within me.

He paused, seemingly collecting his thoughts, before drawing a deep breath. "During my trip to London, I learned that someone from my past had departed this life. We were... intimate briefly, a considerable time ago, before you entered my life."

His words hit me like a freight train, leaving me dizzy and disoriented. My mind was a whirlwind of questions, emotions, and fears. A sense of betrayal washed over me, even though I knew it was irrational. It was a relationship that predated our own, yet the thought of Richard being intimate with someone else was a bitter pill to swallow. His expression, however, suggested that there was more to the story.

"And?" I urged him, bracing myself for whatever came next.

Richard swallowed audibly. "She had a little girl, Hope. The child is 11 years old now, and... she's my flesh and blood. I had a paternity test done to confirm it."

The room spun around me, and I felt my knees give way. I pulled my hands from his and clutched the arm of the chair to keep myself steady. My mind raced with questions, emotions, and fears. This revelation would undoubtedly alter everything, and I couldn't help but feel a sense of betrayal.

"How could you not know about this, Richard?" I asked, my voice barely above a whisper.

"I honestly had no clue, Hope. She never let on. Had I known, you would've been the first to know," he replied, his eyes pleading with me to understand.

I remained silent, lost in the depths of my thoughts.

Richard reached out to clasp my hands again, his grip firm yet gentle. "I'm terribly sorry, Hope. I never intended to inflict any pain or disappointment upon you. You mean the world to me, and the mere thought of losing you over this... it's simply unthinkable."

I drew a deep breath, attempting to quell the flurry of thoughts swarming within my mind. "Richard, I need to understand the whole picture. Who was she? Why didn't she tell you about this child?" I asked, trying to navigate through the fog of confusion.

"She was an old flame, someone I knew long before our paths crossed. Perhaps she didn't want to impose the responsibility upon me or feared how I might react. I can't be certain, Hope," Richard explained, his voice laden with regret.

Tears filled my eyes, a bitter cocktail of sadness, anger, and fear. As they spilled down my cheeks, I realized I was grieving for the life we had built together and our envisioned future. Our reality had been irrevocably altered instantly, and I knew that things would never revert to how they once were. I wanted to stand by Richard, but my heart and mind were in turmoil. "Don't you realize you're asking too much of me?" I sobbed.

Richard gently cupped my face, wiping away the tears with his thumb. "I deeply regret all of this, Hope. I love you... you are my everything."

A piercing pain coursed through my chest as if an unseen hand had reached in and cruelly squeezed my heart. The sheer shock of the revelation left me disoriented, grappling with the enormity of our situation. Despite Richard's recent discovery of his daughter, I couldn't shake off the feeling of betrayal. The thought of him entwined with another before we met was akin to a poisonous arrow piercing my heart. I had always romanticized our love story as one unblemished by past entanglements, and this disclosure ruthlessly shattered that ideal.

* * *

My mind raced with questions: How could he not have known? Why didn't she tell him? Would he have chosen her over me if he had known? The uncertainty gnawed at me, threatening to consume me, sowing seeds of insecurity and doubt.

I desperately tried to reassure myself that Richard hadn't willfully concealed this from me, yet it did little to assuage the hurt. It felt as though the very bedrock of our relationship had been jolted, leaving me to ponder what other secrets might be lurking in the shadows. It was as if a gaping chasm had opened up between us, and I was left wondering how—or even if—we could ever bridge it.

Despite the anguish troubling me, I knew I loved Richard and couldn't imagine my life without him. So, wiping away my tears and drawing a deep, steadying breath, I found the strength to ask, "So, what do we do now, Richard?"

His gaze met mine, his eyes seemingly on a quest for answers. "I honestly don't know. I yearn to be a part of her life, my daughter's life. Yet the thought of losing you, Hope, is utterly unbearable."

I nodded, recognizing that our relationship would be tested in ways we never imagined. "We'll need to discuss custody arrangements, child support, and how we will integrate her into our lives. This won't be a walk in the park, Richard."

"Samantha—that's her name. My daughter. She's all alone now, what with her mother's passing. I want to bring her home." Richard wasn't asking for my permission; he was informing me of his plans. The moment he uttered 'my daughter,' I knew I had lost a piece of him. He was no longer just my Richard.

Richard cupped my face, his thumb tracing the line of my jaw as if preparing to kiss my pain away. But for the first time, his touch failed to bring me the slightest comfort. "I love you, Hope. I'm truly sorry for all this mess. But please, don't make me choose."

"I won't, Richard," I responded, sorrow tinging my voice. I held his hand and looked at the man who had once made me the center of his universe, "Because I already know you'd choose her." Then, I gently removed his hands from my face, bestowed a tender kiss on his cheek, and walked away.

———

Unlocking the door to my former apartment on 89th Street, I was enveloped by a surge of nostalgia. This refuge had been my sanctuary before Richard entered my life, and it felt fitting that I would return to its familiar embrace for solace amidst the storm that had upended my existence.

When I left Richard wrestling with his own struggle in our dining room, I found myself aimlessly riding the elevator. Our doorman, Fred, an old acquaintance from before Richard purchased the penthouse, intuitively gauged my plight. With a subtle signal, he dispatched the valet to alert Chen and Arthur. Moments later, Arthur appeared in the lobby, while Chen waited in the car.

"Take me to my apartment," I requested. Arthur swiftly escorted me to the vehicle, simultaneously instructing Leticia over the phone to retrieve my handbag. The ride to my old place was cloaked in silence. Both men were well-versed in the art of discretion.

Stepping inside, I was welcomed by the familiar scent of the apartment, triggering a cascade of memories from my former life. Life had been less complicated then, devoid of the intricate web of heartache that now ensnared me. I strolled through the modest living room, my fingers tracing the spines of the books that still adorned the shelves—echoes of a time when my own company had been enough to satiate my need for contentment.

I turned on the heater and the lights and walked to the reading couch behind my tiny balcony. As twilight descended, a gentle snowfall began to grace the little balcony of my apartment. The sky was painted with soft lavender and warm orange hues, merging together to create a breathtaking canvas. The city's skyline cast a shadowy silhouette against the backdrop of this enchanting scene.

Delicate snowflakes, each unique in their intricate design, drifted lazily through the air, catching the last glimmers of sunlight as they spiraled toward the ground. They landed gracefully on the cold metal railing and the wooden floorboards, forming a thin blanket of pristine white.

The once-bustling city seems to slow its pace as if to pause and appreciate the serene beauty of the moment. The distant hum of traffic and the chatter of pedestrians below faded into a gentle whisper, allowing the hushed sound of snowflakes kissing the ground to take center stage.

My breath fogged the glass door leading to the balcony, creating a frosty filter through which I watched the snowfall. The icy air nipped at my cheeks and nose, filling my lungs with a crisp freshness invigorating the senses. Somehow, I couldn't help but feel a sense of peace wash over me.

How long did I stay here? I couldn't say. All I wanted was for the world to pause, just for a moment. Snowflakes continued their gentle descent, gradually transforming the urban landscape into a breathtaking winter wonderland. As street lights flickered to life, they cast a warm glow that danced across the pristine snow, creating a mesmerizing contrast against the cool shades of twilight. The magic of this moment enveloped me, filling me with gratitude for the simple beauty of life.

The sadness I carried weighed heavily on my chest, making breathing difficult. I slumped onto the well-worn reading chair, tears streaming down my cheeks as I imagined what our lives would become now that Richard's daughter, Samantha, was in the picture. Would there still be room for me in his heart? Or would I be pushed aside, overshadowed by this new and unexpected addition to our family?

I knew I needed to prepare myself for the impending shifts in our dynamics, but the prospect of sharing Richard—and our home—with Samantha seemed almost impossible. It might be construed as selfish, but over time, I had grown comfortable being the sole woman in Richard's life. Now, I was confronted with the reality of sharing him with someone born from an intimate liaison he'd had in his past. As I sat there, trapped in my musings, I resolved that confronting my fears directly was the only viable path forward.

* * *

A knock on my door interrupted my thoughts; it must be Charlie Sung from the flower shop downstairs. He saw me hurry to the second floor a while ago. I hadn't visited this place for a long time, and maybe he was wondering about this surprise visit. I rose from my seat, opened the door, and sure enough it was Charlie, greeting me with his warm smile and a bowl of noodle soup. "I knew you were here and must be hungry," he said.

I stepped aside as Charlie entered the room and headed straight for my small kitchen. He placed the bowl of soup on the table and looked at me. "Eat first, then sleep. You'll start feeling better," he advised.

I wrapped my arms around him. "I missed you. Thank you, Charlie." One of the things I appreciate about Charlie is that he doesn't hover. He patted my back, his way of offering comfort. "Eat before it gets cold. I'll invite your bodyguards to join me in my kitchen and eat as well. It's chilly outside." In my haste, I had forgotten about Arthur and Chen.

"Thank you again, Charlie." With that, he left the room and closed the door behind him.

The delicious aroma immediately awakened my senses as I lifted a spoonful of Vietnamese noodles to my lips. The steam swirling above the bowl carried with it the comforting notes of ginger, garlic, and lemongrass — creating a symphony of scents. As I continued to eat, the warmth of the Vietnamese noodles seemed to seep into my very soul, lifting my spirits and alleviating some of the heaviness in my heart.

My phone persisted in its clamor, ringing incessantly. Even without checking, I knew it was Richard and likely my parents trying to reach me. When I had walked away from Richard, I never looked back — I grabbed my coat and left. Ignoring the noise, I retreated to my old room. The inviting bed was neatly made, and I reminded myself to thank Leticia for keeping it clean despite my absence. I removed my boots and pants, then opened my closet. My old clothes were carefully folded and hung; I selected an oversized white T-shirt with a sunflower print at the hem and picked out yellow cotton panties from my drawer.

* * *

After a warm shower, I padded barefoot into the living room, settled onto the reading couch, and closed my eyes. Tonight, I didn't want to think about being Hope Ortega-Collins. I yearned to be Hope Williams, the ordinary girl who juggled writing gigs to cover the rent, not the privileged daughter of a billionaire and spouse of a Hollywood star.

The commotion in the hallway jarred me from my peaceful nap. Heated exchanges reverberated just outside my door. I swung it open on instinct to find Richard locked in a dispute with Chen and Arthur, who were steadfastly barring his entry. Jeffrey loomed behind Richard.

"Remove your bloody hands from the door this instant!" Richard's British accent was more pronounced in his ire. "I demand to see my wife!"

"I shall be forced to dial 911 if you persist," Chen responded with unruffled calm.

"Do whatever the bloody hell you fancy, but I'm getting in!" Richard became aware of my presence; worry etched lines into his tense face. "Hope, I beg of you..." His eyes implored me.

Glancing at my steadfast bodyguards, I murmured, "It's okay." I then eased the door wider to admit Richard.

When he closed the door behind him, he cradled my face in both hands and kissed me. His lips demanded that I match his fervor. My mind urged me to break away, but my heart needed this connection. I needed Richard, even if just for tonight. I closed my eyes and allowed his tongue to part my lips further, deepening the kiss. He recognized my surrender. His hands left my face. His right hand went to the back of my head, grabbing my hair, while the other one moved inside my T-shirt to cup my bare breasts. I cried in his mouth. He knew in that instant, I was his. He left my mouth and trailed kisses down my throat. He pinched and pulled my nipple under my shirt, then bit and sucked it over the cotton material. That was erotic — Richard knew how my body responded to him. His right hand moved lower, between my legs, and ran a finger above my underwear — my body convulsed. He left my nipple, leaving a wet spot over my shirt. He looked at me and boldly said, "Damn, I want you, my darling." Then he swiped my underwear and roughly put his finger inside me. I lost it. I cried in ecstasy.

Richard moved onto the couch without breaking the contacts on my body. I unbuckled his jeans and touched the place I knew would drive him crazy. His breathing was rough and short. I pulled his pants and underwear down his ankle and pushed him on the couch. I landed on his lap, and I was towering above his head.

"Ride me now, darling!" His voice was bold and commanding. He didn't bother to remove my panties and my T-shirt. He just moved them aside and entered me without warning. That's all it took for me to forget everything, but just the pleasure of what our body was creating.

———

Richard and I lay entwined on the living room floor as our passionate lovemaking finally subsided. My yellow carpet served as the canvas of our naked forms draped in grey-and-white-striped reading blankets. Our bodies were still warm and tingling from the love we had just made. Richard traced his fingers gently along my spine, sending shivers throughout my body. My head nestled comfortably between his shoulder and chest, allowing me to listen closely to his steady heartbeat. I listened to the rhythmic sound, and a sense of contentment washed over me. Despite all the doubts and fears that had plagued me earlier, at this moment, it felt as if everything was going to be okay.

Richard's breathing slowed as he began to relax in my arms. His robust and protective presence was a comfort I hadn't realized I'd been craving. I found myself tracing the contours of his face with my fingertips, memorizing every detail as if it were the first time I had ever touched him. The intimacy of this simple act brought tears to my eyes, and I couldn't help but feel grateful for the connection we shared.

As I held him close, I pondered the future that awaited us. There would undoubtedly be challenges as we navigated the complexities of our new family dynamic, but I now felt confident that Richard and I could face anything together. The love we shared was powerful, and I knew it would guide us through even the most difficult times.

* * *

With a deep, contented sigh, Richard shifted in my arms and looked into my eyes. A tender smile played on his lips as he whispered, "I love you, Hope." My heart swelled with emotion, and I smiled back at him, feeling an overwhelming sense of love and belonging.

"I love you too, Richard," I whispered in return, and as we lay there, wrapped in each other's arms, I knew that we would find a way to make our new life together work.

His voice vibrated in my ear as he spoke, "You once said that I wouldn't choose you, but my darling, there are no choices when it comes to you. You are my only option; everything else is up for discussion." He continued, his words filled with conviction, "With you, no one even comes close. I would choose you over my own life."

I tightened my hold on Richard, burying my head deeper into the crook of his neck, and sobbed softly. He tenderly brushed my hair with his long fingers, comforting me. "I almost lost you once, and I won't ever go through that again," he whispered.

Taking a deep breath, I resolved to make an effort to understand his plans for Samantha and to really see who she was and what she needed. If Richard cared for her, then I owed it to him—and to myself—to at least try to care for her as well. "How is she? And what are we going to do?" I emphasized the word 'we'.

"Her mother's younger sister is willing to care for her," Richard explained. "She's proposing joint custody and regular financial support for both of them. Jenny, Samantha's mother, was specific in her last will, though — she wanted me to be Samantha's sole guardian."

I looked up at the man I had fallen in love with and gently ran my finger across his lips. Richard was my world, but I also knew that I couldn't lose myself in the process. I need to find a balance between embracing this new chapter in our lives and holding onto the person I was before Samantha entered the picture. It wouldn't be easy, but I was determined to make it work. "Let's go get her, Richard."

He held me tightly as if he would never let me go. "We don't have to decide now. Tonight is about you and me." Then he rolled me onto my back and kissed me passionately. I knew I would never tire of making love to Richard.

12

As I sat shielded in the plush chair of my high-rise office, I found myself drifting into a reflective trance, my gaze transfixed on the sprawling panorama of Manhattan spread out below me. The city was a vibrant tableau of life, painted with kaleidoscopic hues, its skin lightly dusted with the remnants of last winter's snowfall. The once pristine white blanket that had gracefully draped over the towering skyscrapers and labyrinthine streets had begun to thaw, heralding the imminent arrival of spring.

The bustling district was alive and humming as it busied itself with preparations for Valentine's Day. From my vantage point, I could see the tiny ant-like figures of people scurrying about below, their lives as intricate and complex as the cityscape itself. Flower vendors peddled their lushest roses, their petals a passionate crimson, while confectioneries showcased their most tantalizing treats, adding to the city's symphony of love and anticipation. This pulsating vibrancy starkly contrasted with the peaceful solitude of my office that towered above, a quiet oasis amidst the whirlwind of urban life.

On this day, traditionally reserved for lovers, my husband was miles away in Sydney, swept up in the whirl of his latest movie shoot. Adding to the geographical chasm between us was our ongoing process of adopting his daughter Samantha, a process unfolding across the Atlantic in London. The strain of distance was noticeable, but our bond remained unbroken, our love steadfast and unwavering. Sometimes, I wished for the simpler times when I was just a writer, able to accompany Richard around the globe. But now, with my evolving role in my father's business empire, life has become more complex.

Richard's absence today felt like a missing piece in an otherwise complete puzzle, leaving our picture of domestic bliss incomplete. Yet, I understood his commitment and admired his unwavering dedication to his craft. Richard was not just a husband; he was also a dedicated father and a passionate actor, a man who wore many hats with grace. We were both entangled in the roles we had chosen, bound by the promises we had made – to ourselves, each other, and the world that watched us.

I found my gaze drifting towards the photograph perched on my desk. It was a candid shot of Richard and me, our smiles frozen in time by the unassuming lens of a smartphone camera. A sigh escaped my lips as I turned my gaze back to the cityscape. The snow was now surrendering to the sun's warmth, each falling droplet a poignant reminder of time's relentless march. Spring was inching closer, bringing with it the promise of fresh beginnings and rekindled hopes. And with its arrival, I yearned for the day when Richard and I would finally bridge the chasm of distance between us.

Caught in this whirlpool of thoughts, I was jolted back to reality as the door to my office swung open with a thud. Hillary, my personal secretary, strode in, her face etched with a sense of urgency that was uncharacteristic of her usual composed demeanor. "Ms. Hope," she gasped, trying to catch her breath, "there's an out-of-city meeting lined up for you. The jet's all prepped."

"A meeting?" I echoed, surprise creeping into my voice. "What meeting?"

"I'm afraid I don't have the specifics," Hillary responded, her tone apologetic, "The briefing pack is already on the jet."

My heart pounded against my ribcage at this unexpected development. This must be some urgent company matter that necessitated my stepping into my father's shoes. With a brisk nod to Hillary, I gathered my belongings and straightened my business suit, mentally bracing myself for whatever awaited me. Though a part of me dreaded the unknown, another part welcomed this sudden distraction from the loneliness that Valentine's Day had draped over me.

As I navigated my way toward the private airstrip, I was flanked by Arthur and Chen — my most trusted aides. The familiar Manhattan cityscape gradually receded, replaced by the expansive tarmac where our family's sleek jet stood poised for takeoff.

Upon boarding, my eyes were immediately drawn to a pair of elegantly wrapped boxes nestled on the supple leather seating. One was a large Dior box, its glossy exterior reflecting the soft cabin lighting. The other, smaller yet equally as enticing, bore the unmistakable insignia of Cartier.

A flutter of excitement stirred in my chest as I delicately opened the Cartier box. Inside, nestled amidst soft velvet lining, was a handwritten note from Richard. "See you soon, darling," it read. A wave of exhilaration washed over me, replacing my earlier apprehension with giddy anticipation. This wasn't some urgent business meeting; it was a surprise orchestrated by Richard!

"Welcome aboard, Mrs. Collins," a voice interrupted my thoughts. I turned to find a stunning blond stewardess extending a glass of champagne towards me. "I'm Christine, your flight attendant for this journey."

"Thank you, Christine," I responded, accepting the glass and taking a small sip. The bubbles danced on my tongue, mirroring my buoyant mood.

"I can carry the gown to the dressing room," Christine offered, gesturing towards the Dior box. "And if you need any assistance with your makeup, don't hesitate to ask."

Her offer was met with a grateful nod from me. "That would be wonderful, Christine. Thank you," I replied, trailing after her into the jet's private dressing room. As the door clicked shut behind us, I couldn't help but marvel at the day's unexpected turn of events.

* * *

Gently lifting the lid of the Dior box, I found a stunning evening gown crafted from lilac silk. "Oh, Richard," I whispered to myself, "you do know how to make a woman feel beautiful."

Christine proved to be a maestro with makeup and hair styling. As she worked her magic, I felt like I was being transformed into a princess from a storybook. The gown was breathtaking– luxurious silk in a soft lilac shade that added a hint of romantic allure. Its structured bodice hugged my curves before gently cascading into a full, sweeping skirt. The neckline was a bold yet tasteful plunge, adding an element of drama to the elegant ensemble. The gown was adorned with intricate hand embroidery and delicate lace detailing, amplifying its charm. The back featured a low scoop, ensuring the dress was as captivating from the rear as it was from the front. The lilac hue shimmered subtly under the cabin lights. A simple diamond necklace and matching earrings from Cartier were the perfect finishing touches.

"Mrs. Collins, you look absolutely stunning tonight," Christine complimented, applying the final stroke of lipstick to my lips.

"I can't thank you enough, Christine," I said, admiring my reflection, "you've truly outdone yourself." The old me would have enveloped her in a warm hug, perhaps even planted a kiss on her cheek. But my father's teachings echoed in my mind — maintain a professional distance from those in our employ. So, instead, I flashed Christine the most genuine smile I could muster.

———

Several heartbeats later, I found myself stepping into the grand entrance of L'Oiseau Blanc. Nestled on the sixth floor of The Peninsula Paris, this rooftop restaurant boasted one of the best views of the Eiffel Tower. The gentle flicker of candlelight from the tables cast an enchanting glow around the room while the soft hum of hushed conversations and the tantalizing aroma of gourmet cuisine filled the air.

And there he was, standing tall in a meticulously tailored tuxedo accentuating his lean physique. Richard looked every bit the movie star he was, with that trademark charm that had always left me breathless.

Despite the miles we had traversed, the surprise, and the anticipation, we were finally together on Valentine's Day. His warm smile made my heart flutter, and as he drew me into his arms, all the day's stress and worry ebbed away. "Darling, you're so beautiful," he murmured, his voice barely above a whisper.

I looped my arms around his neck, pressing my body close to his, "I've missed you, Richard," I confessed softly. This was us, snatching precious moments from our hectic lives, clinging to each other as if the world outside didn't exist.

His voice dropped lower as he leaned in, his words laced with passion, "With you here in my arms, we have two options. One, we leave this place and surrender to our desires. I would love nothing more than to peel off this beautiful dress. Or two, we enjoy a romantic dinner and save our passions for later."

His words sent a thrill through me, but I knew which option appealed to me most at that moment. "As tempting as the first option is, I think we should go with the second. I want to savor every moment of this romantic surprise," I replied, my eyes meeting his.

Seated beneath the soft, romantic illumination of the restaurant's lights, with the city's sparkling skyline as our backdrop, Richard and the magic of Paris enveloped me. But the crowning glory was the enchanting view of the Eiffel Tower, standing tall and proud against the night sky.

Richard followed my gaze to the iconic structure, then gently took my hand, pressing tender kisses to each finger. "Did you know that this place is designed to evoke the feel of a vintage airplane cabin?" he asked, his eyes twinkling with curiosity. At the shake of my head, indicating my interest, he elaborated. "It's a tribute to the L'Oiseau Blanc aircraft, after which the restaurant is named."

"Hmm. Moments like these always remind me how lucky I am," I said, my eyes filled with adoration. "Not only am I married to the most handsome man on earth, but also the most knowledgeable."

* * *

Our waiter for the evening was a compact man in a crisp white shirt and black vest, his demeanor professional yet warm. He presented us with a bottle of rich Burgundy, expertly uncorking it and filling our glasses. "Tonight's menu has been specially curated by Chef David Bizet — a gastronomic journey in itself." He described the starters, his words painting a tantalizing picture of blue lobster paired with Swiss chard, roasted pistachios, and charred mackerel served with a tangy citrus accompaniment.

The ambiance was magical; each table had its dedicated wait staff and sommelier, ensuring every dish was served precisely and at the perfect temperature. Each plate was a visual feast, a riot of colors and textures.

Richard chose the 6-course tasting menu for the main course, promising a culinary adventure. The highlight was a succulent duck breast, cooked to perfection, accompanied by a medley of seasonal vegetables.

"The last time we dined out in Paris, I ended up sleeping in the tub!" I chuckled, reminiscing about our past adventures in this city of love.

"This city suits you," Richard observed, his blue-grey eyes meeting mine with an intensity that took my breath away. "The food, the sightseeing, the books... Let's buy a house here, darling."

"I would love that," I sighed, "but our lives are in New York. However, having a reading parlor here, where we could spend spring or summer... that sounds perfect."

When the dessert was served, it was a total showstopper — a beautifully crafted sorbet that was as delightful to look at as it was to eat. As we savored each spoonful, the sweet and tangy flavors of the sorbet provided the perfect end to our meal.

But what truly made our dinner special was the wine. The Head Sommelier had carefully selected wines to pair with each course. From crisp whites to robust reds, each glass of wine enhanced the flavors of the dishes, creating a symphony of tastes that elevated our dining experience.

* * *

Casually, I broached a topic close to our hearts, "How's the adoption process coming along?"

Richard's face softened as he replied, "It's progressing well. We're looking at about three more weeks; then we can bring her home." He tenderly caressed my jaw, his fingers lightly tracing my lips. "Let's put that aside for now. Tonight is just about you and me," he gently insisted, leaning in to kiss my lips softly.

As we savored our wine, we found ourselves immersed in our own world, lost in deep conversation. The gentle hum of the restaurant, the clinking of glasses, and the sporadic bursts of laughter from neighboring tables orchestrated a soothing background symphony.

As the night wore on and our dinner neared its end, Richard and I found ourselves lingering, reluctant to break the spell. We knew our brief escapade would soon draw to a close, and we would once again be continents apart.

Suddenly, Richard rose from his seat, wiping his mouth with a napkin. He extended his hand to help me up, a glint of impatience in his eyes. "I can't wait any longer, darling," he confessed, signaling our waiter to ensure everything was charged to his room. With that, we decided to retreat to the privacy of our suite at The Peninsula Paris, eager to savor the rest of our night together.

———

Our suite was a haven of luxury, its lavish decor and breathtaking views of the Parisian skyline creating an ethereal setting. As Richard uncorked a bottle of champagne, I found myself drawn to the balcony, captivated by the sight of the Eiffel Tower twinkling against the night sky. The soft strains of a piano serenade drifted up from the streets below, a sweet reminder that the city of love never ceased its romantic lullaby, especially on Valentine's Day.

I felt Richard's arms encircle me from behind, his warmth seeping into my back. I glanced up, catching his gaze in the reflection of the glass. An unspoken promise passed between us as he gently spun me around to face him. His arms cradled me, our bodies swaying in sync with the music, our eyes locked in a silent conversation.

The champagne was forgotten as Richard dipped his head to claim my lips. Our kiss was unhurried and tender, brimming with suppressed emotions and longing. I reciprocated fervently, my fingers threading through his hair as I deepened our embrace.

We moved towards the bedroom, our bodies joined together like two pieces of a jigsaw puzzle that fit perfectly together. Our hearts drummed a harmonious rhythm as we surrendered to our shared desire. Our lovemaking was passionate yet gentle, a beautiful ballet of love that only we could orchestrate.

As the first light of dawn painted the sky, we held each other close, the memory of our shared passion forever etched in our hearts. The city of love had cast its spell, making this day unforgettable. Looking into Richard's eyes, I understood love wasn't just about grand gestures or candlelit dinners. It was about these stolen moments, these heart-fluttering surprises, and the sheer determination to navigate obstacles.

I closed my eyes momentarily, keenly aware that this enchanting interlude would end in a few hours. Though we were bound for different continents, the memory of this night would stay with me, a poignant testament to our enduring love.

13

Over the past few weeks, Richard had been attending meetings with barristers — yes, lawyers — and the London legal team orchestrating Samantha's paperwork. Living with Richard, and with Henry's occasional visits, I gradually acclimated to their distinct mode of speech. Richard, too, was picking up on a few American idioms.

Today, Richard was providing me with an update regarding the progress of the child arrangements order. I set aside the manuscript I had been engrossed in and shifted my attention to Richard's image on the screen before me.

"Bring me up to speed, Richard," I urged.

"Well, Jenny's family has been contesting for custody, questioning my capability to raise a child given my frequent travels for film schedules. Nevertheless, Raphael and his London contingent remain optimistic that we could secure full custody. After all, she left a will giving exclusive custody to me, corroborated by the paternity test result," he elaborated.

"It seems like the plan is coming together... although I sense a few snags," I observed.

Richard explained that to establish Samantha's legal status as Richard's daughter and sole guardian, the solicitor specializing in family law had suggested an alternative to the court-issued child arrangements order. "Since you're married to me, we could both legally adopt her and become her lawful parents. Your presence would lend a more stable environment for her."

"Hold on," I interjected. "I thought in the UK, adoption is typically reserved for scenarios where a child is permanently placed with new parents who aren't biologically related?"

"Indeed, adoption is generally not the appropriate course for a biological father to establish paternity and acquire legal rights over their child. However, it remains an option worth considering," he conceded, but quickly added, "Darling, you're under no obligation to do this," Richard reassured gently.

"I want to, Richard. But let's keep this under wraps until she's ready. She's got a lot to process. We'll navigate this one step at a time." Richard traced his fingers on the screen as if attempting to caress my face in his familiar fashion.

I must admit, I was unprepared for this new dynamic, but my love for Richard was solid. What's more, Samantha found herself in a difficult situation with her mother's untimely departure, and Richard's initial plan to send her off to a boarding school seemed excessively severe. Having navigated the challenges of growing up with a single parent, I couldn't grasp how much harder it would be for her to be without both.

Richard and I delved deeper into the logistics of relocating Samantha to New York. "Henry is aware of her existence, but Samantha isn't aware that she has a half-brother yet. Perhaps we should arrange their first meeting there," he proposed.

"Alright, you inform Henry. Meanwhile, I'll engage a designer specializing in children's interiors to repurpose one of our rooms for her," I offered. "Do you happen to know her dress size? Never mind, I'll handle it."

Richard chuckled, "I'm certain she'll take a shine to you. With a sixteen-year age gap, you two could easily pass as sisters."

"I was hoping for that, too," I said. An immediate thought seized me,

"Richard, if we adopt Samantha, she'll bear the Ortega-Collins name."

"Darling, you don't need to go to such lengths. I understand that name carries significant weight and is reserved for our biological children..." Richard began, but I cut him off.

"If we're embarking on this journey, we must commit wholeheartedly. She will be ours, and she must be safeguarded in all legal matters she might encounter," I asserted.

"What did I ever do to deserve such a beautiful and kind wife?" He asked affectionately.

"Nothing at all. You're simply one lucky guy," I retorted, eliciting laughter from both of us.

Thus, we resolved to open our home to Samantha and raise her as our own. It wasn't a decision taken lightly, but we knew it was the right thing to do.

14

While Richard was in London attending court appearances, I sent my own lawyer to represent me in the adoption process. In the meantime, I took a leave of absence from work and spent the next few days preparing for Samantha's arrival. I created space for her in our apartment, decorated her room, and purchased clothing and other essentials.

Once the interior designer had worked his magic, Samantha's room was transformed into a sanctuary that perfectly catered to her pre-teenage sensibilities while providing a comforting and nurturing environment.

The room was awash with a soft palette of pastel colors, creating a relaxing atmosphere. The walls were painted in a soothing shade of lavender, accented by whimsical murals of abstract blossoms and birds in flight, adding a touch of youthful charm without being overly juvenile.

A plush, queen-sized bed held court in the center of the room, dressed in crisp yet comforting white linens and an array of cushions in varying shades of purple, soft pink, and mint green. A tufted, velvet headboard in a deeper shade of purple added a luxurious touch and a sense of maturity, bridging the gap between childlike whimsy and adolescent sophistication.

Opposite the bed, a modern, white desk was set against the window, allowing natural light to illuminate the workspace. It was equipped with all the necessary stationery supplies and the latest iMac for schoolwork. Plus, a new iPhone and iPod lay on top of the study table, waiting for their new owner. Beside the desk, a towering bookshelf was filled with an array of books ranging from classic literature to contemporary YA novels, hoping for Samantha's love for reading.

One corner of the room was dedicated to a comfortable lounge with a plush, oversized bean bag chair and a low coffee table, perfect for casual reading, listening to music, or simply daydreaming. Adjacent to this, a cork-board wall allowed space for Samantha to pin up photos, notes, and personal mementos, making the room truly her own.

The room was thoughtfully lit with a combination of a chandelier casting a warm, diffused light and strategically placed lamps for task lighting. A large, vintage-style mirror hung on one wall, while the opposite wall featured a flat-screen television.

The final touch was a walk-in closet, thoughtfully designed with abundant storage for clothes, shoes, and accessories. It was complemented with full-length mirrors and adaptable, efficient lighting. Yumi and I had taken great delight in shopping for clothing and shoes, and it was fair to say we had lavished this area with an excess of attention.

The revamped room was a symphony of comfort, functionality, and style. It offered Samantha a secure and welcoming space to flourish, learn, and dream.

As Leticia and I retreated to survey our handiwork, she turned to me and remarked, "Madam Hope, she's very lucky to have you as her mother."

I returned her sentiment with a smile, "I can only hope she'll take to me, Leticia."

"If she doesn't, she must be *loca*," Leticia quipped.

Casting a final, approving glance at the room, I closed the door, my heart fluttering with anticipation at the thought of finally meeting Samantha. It was then that I remembered to ask whether Henry's room was prepared for his impending arrival.

"It's been ready since yesterday," Leticia confirmed.

Henry and I had always enjoyed a smooth relationship, having hit it off from the start and quickly becoming good friends. I was optimistic that my relationship with Samantha would be just as effortless, given our shared gender and my long standing desire for a younger sister.

"Thank you, Leticia. He'll be arriving shortly," I informed her.

As if on cue, the doorbell chimed, and there was Henry! He greeted me with a broad grin and a warm hug.

"How're you holding up?" he enquired, his British accent adding a touch of charm to his words.

"Here I am, adjusting to a new role," I responded.

"You're a natural, Hope. Everyone's taken to you," he reassured me.

"By everyone, you mean just you," I retorted playfully, draping my arms around his waist. I guided him towards the dining room as Leticia whisked away his suitcase to unpack in his room. Today marked Henry's first encounter with his half-sister, and he had chosen to take a separate flight from them.

He turned to me, a hint of gloom in his eyes, "You truly love him. You're too young to shoulder the responsibility of two stepchildren."

"You've never been a burden to me. As an only child, I've always longed for a large family. If you were still underage like Samantha, I wouldn't hesitate to adopt you, too," I assured him.

In response, Henry tenderly kissed my forehead.

"Alright, take some time to rest or freshen up; they'll be here soon. I'll be in the kitchen with Leticia." With that, I reciprocated his affectionate gesture.

* * *

———

As Samantha's arrival drew near, the mood in the house thrummed with anticipation. Henry and I had gone to great lengths to create a welcoming ambiance, hoping to make her feel right at home from the moment she crossed the doorstep. I had even baked sugar cookies, which I was now carefully arranging in a large, clear jar.

"Henry, do British girls prefer orange juice or lemonade? Or perhaps soda... no, scratch that," I mumbled, my voice laced with uncertainty.

"They're not all that different from American girls, not particularly partial to orange juice or lemonade. However, you can seldom go wrong with a warm cup of tea to accompany those sugar cookies," he responded in his charming voice. "Hope, you need to relax. You're not the one who needs to impress her; it's quite the contrary."

Just then, the doorbell chimed. As approaching footsteps echoed through the house, Henry and Leticia moved towards the living room. I hung back for a moment, my heart pounding, a cocktail of excitement and anxiety coursing through my veins. Gathering my courage, I followed suit.

The door swung open, revealing an 11-year-old girl whose striking features were a mirror image of her father's. Her wavy, chestnut hair cascaded just below her shoulders, framing a face adorned with piercing blue eyes and a dusting of freckles across her nose. She possessed an air of vulnerability entwined with resilience, suggesting a childhood that had already encountered its fair share of trials.

Samantha clung to Richard like a lifeline, her tiny hands gripping his arm tightly. Richard responded by patting her back gently, providing reassurance and comfort. He then turned towards me, his eyes brimming with love and longing. It had been weeks since we last saw each other. Richard approached me, wrapped an arm around my waist, and planted a tender kiss on my lips.

When he pulled away, he turned back to Samantha, who was again holding onto his hands, seemingly reluctant to let go. "Sam," he began softly, "this is Hope." His gaze shifted back to me, "Darling, meet

Samantha." We had decided not to disclose to Samantha that I was, in fact, her legal mother through adoption.

After a moment's hesitation, Samantha released her hold on Richard. She extended her hand, offering a formal handshake and a small, tentative smile that instantly warmed my heart.

"Hello, Sam. Welcome home," I greeted her. I took her small hand into mine, attempting to convey my love and acceptance. "We've prepared a room especially for you. Would you like to see it?" She nodded in affirmation, still clinging to her father.

At that moment, Richard's gaze fell upon Henry. Father and son embraced as Richard introduced him, "And this, Sam, is your big brother, Henry."

"Hello there, kiddo," Henry greeted her, his smile warm and welcoming. In response, Samantha beamed at him before darting into his open arms. With effortless ease, Henry scooped her up and swung her around, eliciting peals of laughter from Samantha.

"Put me down. I'm not a baby anymore," she protested, her voice echoing with mirth.

I found myself leaning into Richard, his arms wrapping around me in a comforting embrace, as we watched the heartwarming scene of two siblings meeting affectionately for the very first time.

Then, turning his attention back to Samantha, Henry suggested, "Shall we peek at your room?" She nodded once more, this time attaching herself to Henry.

As we walked towards her new room, she spotted Salem and promptly informed us about her cat allergy. "Daddy, I'm not overly fond of cats."

"Don't worry. Salem usually stays in my room or office. Leticia and I will ensure he stays well clear of you," I reassured her. Salem, who could sense when he wasn't wanted, hissed at her and walked away.

When Samantha twisted the doorknob to her bedroom, and the door creaked open, her eyes widened in amazement. Her new room was bathed in soft sunlight filtering through a large window, casting a warm, inviting glow on everything it touched. A gasp of wonder slipped past her lips as she stepped into the room, her small feet sinking into the plush carpet. She ran her fingers over the comforter, then over the walk-in closet door. Her eyes sparkled with uncontained delight as she explored every corner of her private sanctuary. Avoiding my gaze, she turned to Richard and asked, "All these are mine, Daddy?"

"Yes, Sam. Hope arranged everything for you," he confirmed, his gaze adoringly meeting mine. "Thank you, darling," he murmured, leaning in to plant another tender kiss on my lips.

"Do you like it?" I asked her, my heart pounding in anticipation.

She nodded and whispered, "Thank you," before turning to her father and wrapping her arms around his waist.

"Hey, Sam! Fancy seeing what else Hope has prepared for you?" Henry chimed in. "Come along. She's baked some lovely sugar cookies just for you."

Richard looked at me, amusement dancing in his eyes; he knew of my somewhat disastrous track record in the kitchen. "Really? Another round of Erin's Baking 101?"

"Actually, she volunteered to have fresh cookies and cakes delivered here every day, but I fancied trying my hand at some traditional English biscuits," I countered, my voice thick with pride and confidence.

We made our way back downstairs to the dining room, where Leticia was pouring warm tea for everyone and arranging cookies on saucers. Richard picked one up and declared, "These are rather good, darling!"

I playfully brushed the crumbs from his lips and planted a kiss on the corner of his mouth. I asked Samantha, who was pulling out a chair, "Would you like some milk in your tea?" She nodded in response.

* * *

And so, our first meeting proceeded. Samantha was still distant from me, but I understood. She needed time to familiarize herself with me and adjust to life in New York instead of what she was used to in London. Dinner was informal, consisting of pepperoni and classic New York pizza from our favorite local spot. Considering how exhausted Samantha must be from the flight, Richard tucked her into bed early that night.

———

The first few days of Samantha's transition into our lives were far from easy. She was accustomed to a different lifestyle from her mother, so we had to adapt to her needs. She was claustrophobic, so I was grateful that the interior designer had made her room spacious and airy. The most challenging aspect was coming to terms with our sudden roles as parents. Although Richard and I were used to living together as a couple, we were novices when it came to child-rearing together. Nonetheless, observing Richard's daily interactions with Samantha was nothing short of heartening. His ease in parental roles was apparent; look at how he raised Henry and their strong bond.

Richard had an innate knack for connecting with children, so Samantha took to him like a moth to a flame. "Daddy, might you be able to stay a wee bit longer before you return to filming?" Samantha one day inquired, her eyes brimming with hope. My heart welled up with emotion as I watched their tender exchange.

"Absolutely, kiddo," Richard responded, his hand affectionately tousling her hair.

I decided not to interrupt their precious moments together. Instead, I changed into my running gear and quietly slipped out of the house. Richard and Sam were cozily cuddled together in the living room, engrossed in a Disney movie, as I left them to enjoy their time together.

As I stepped out of our apartment building, I took a deep breath, inhaled the fresh air, and began my jog to clear my head. Chen and Arthur, who would tail me wherever I went, received my phone as I handed it to them. The city was coming back to life after a long, cold winter, and the signs of spring were everywhere.

The sidewalks were bustling with people enjoying the warmer weather, and I couldn't help but smile as I weaved through the crowd. As I approached the Metropolitan Museum, I marveled at its grand facade, proof of the rich history and culture housed within its walls. I made a mental note to pay a visit soon — it had been too long since my last visit.

Crossing the street, I entered Central Park, leaving the concrete jungle behind and immersing myself in the beauty of nature. The park was alive with colors, from the vibrant green grass to the budding flowers that adorned the trees and gardens. The sweet scent of cherry blossoms filled the air, and I paused momentarily to take it all in.

As I continued my jog, I noticed families having picnics on the lush lawns, children enjoying the playgrounds, and couples strolling hand in hand along the winding paths. The laughter and chatter of park-goers filled the air, creating a symphony of joy that seemed to echo through the trees.

I picked up my pace, feeling the gentle breeze against my face as I passed by the serene lake. The water shimmered under the golden sunlight, and I could see ducks and swans gliding gracefully across its surface. I missed Henry, who had taken a short trip to DC today with his friend. Feeding the ducks was our thing. I saw a group of rowboats drifting lazily nearby, their passengers enjoying a peaceful afternoon on the water.

The further I jogged into the park, the more I was captivated by the sheer beauty of spring in full bloom. The world around me seemed to be awakening from its slumber, bursting with new life and endless possibilities.

As I made my way back toward our apartment, my thoughts turned to Samantha and the challenges we faced as a new family. How could I break down the barriers between us and help her feel at home?

With every step, I reminded myself that just like the flowers blooming around me, our relationship could grow and flourish — all it needed was time, patience, and the nurturing warmth of love.

But the moment I stepped into the living room from my usual Saturday run, I immediately sensed the tension between Samantha and Salem. She shot an icy glare at my cat, who nonchalantly sashayed past her, his tail swishing in the air with defiance. I released a resigned sigh, aware that her disdain for him stemmed solely from his being mine. Their ongoing feud had been a constant source of discomfort in our otherwise peaceful home.

"Sam, why not give petting Salem a try? He's genuinely friendly, I assure you," I suggested, attempting to bridge the gap between them. I hoped that maybe, just maybe, they could find some common ground and learn to coexist peacefully.

"I'm not fond of cats, and on top of that, I'm allergic. Do you fancy watching me suffer, or worse, get killed?" she retorted, her voice frosty and her gaze averted. It was evident from her tone that her frustration was aimed not only at Salem but also at our current situation. Richard was about to say something, but I gave him a look that said, *'let me handle this.'* She blurted out, unable to mask her true feelings, "I yearn to return to London. I absolutely loathe New York."

Her words stung, but I did my best to maintain composure. It wasn't easy to hear that she was so unhappy, but I knew it would take time for us to adjust to our new life together. "I'm sorry. I understand it's a significant change, Sam, but give it some time. You might eventually warm up to our life here."

She crossed her arms over her chest and turned to her father, Richard, who was busy reading a script and quietly observing our exchange. "Daddy, can't we just go back home? I miss London and my friends."

Richard sighed, put down the script, and knelt beside her, putting a comforting arm around her shoulders. "Sweetheart, we've talked about this. We're here because of my work, and we need to give it a chance. Besides, I think you and Hope could become great friends if you just give her a chance, too."

Samantha looked at her father with pleading eyes, but he didn't waver.

She finally turned to me, her expression softening just a little. "Fine. I'll try. But I still don't like cats."

I smiled, grateful for the small victory. "That's all I'm asking, Sam. Let's try to make the best of this together, okay?"

She nodded at her father without looking at me. Richard squeezed her shoulder before standing up. "Why don't we all go out for ice cream? It's a beautiful day, and we could use a treat."

Samantha's eyes lit up at the mention of ice cream, and I could see a glimmer of hope that she somehow forgot about her desire to return to London. "Okay, Daddy. Can we go to that place with the giant sundaes?"

Richard chuckled and nodded. "Of course, sweetheart. Let's get going."

As we headed for the door, Samantha hurried to her father's side, clinging to his arm. I could see that she was still hesitant to include me in their little world. Richard looked at me apologetically, and I tried to mask my disappointment with a reassuring smile. I couldn't help but glance back at Salem, who was perched on the windowsill, watching us with his curious yellow eyes. I hoped that one day Samantha would learn to love him too, but I knew I had to be patient and give her time to adjust to her new life here.

"Hey, Samantha," Richard suggested, "why don't you and Hope walk together? I bet she knows a lot about New York and can tell you some interesting stories."

Samantha's grip on her father's arm tightened, and she shook her head vigorously. "No, Daddy, I want to walk with you."

Richard glanced at me again, his eyes filled with concern. I didn't want him to feel like he had to choose between his daughter and me, so I gave them some space.

"That's fine, Richard," I said, forcing a smile. "You two go ahead. I'll catch up with you later."

* * *

He hesitated for a moment before nodding reluctantly. "Alright, but we'll save you a seat at the ice cream parlor, okay?"

I nodded, watching as they walked away, hand in hand. Samantha glanced back at me over her shoulder, her expression unreadable. I couldn't help but feel a pang of jealousy, wishing she would give me a chance to be part of her life, too.

As I stood there alone on the sidewalk, I thought about what I could do to win Samantha's heart. It wouldn't be easy, especially since she seemed determined to keep me at a distance. But I loved Richard and knew that if I wanted our new family to work, I needed to find a way to connect with his daughter.

With a deep breath, I started walking towards the ice cream parlor, determined to make an effort to bond with Samantha, no matter how long it took. Little by little, I hoped she would eventually open up to me and allow me to be part of her world.

15

I could feel the tension hanging in the air like a thick fog when I stepped into our home. Leticia stood in the living room, hands on her hips, glaring at Samantha. Samantha's arms were crossed defiantly over her chest, and I could tell she was fighting back tears.

"What's going on here?" I asked, my voice slicing through the silence.

"Samantha and her new friends thought it would be amusing to spray-paint Salem!" Leticia exclaimed, her eyes ablaze with fury. Samantha had recently befriended a pair of twins who were close to her age. I was relieved to see her making friends within the neighborhood, as it seemed she was gradually adapting to her new life with us.

I glanced down at my poor black cat, now marred by neon pink and green paint splotches. Salem gazed up at me, wide-eyed and pleading as if begging for rescue from his nightmare. I knew his eyes were pained; he wasn't the type of cat to appear frightened without reason.

"It was just a game," Samantha mumbled, her voice barely audible. "No big deal."

My heart ached for Salem, and I couldn't let this pass. "Samantha, you know better than to do something like this," I said firmly, attempting to keep the disappointment from my voice. "Salem is a living being, not a toy or canvas for your amusement." Turning to our housekeeper, who continued to seethe, I asked, "Leticia, could you please help me clean Salem? We must be gentle to avoid hurting his eyes or damaging his fur."

"Yes, Madam Hope," she replied, her voice softening.

As I attempted to comfort Salem, Samantha's expression shifted. Instead of appearing remorseful or upset, she glared at Salem with resentment.

"It's all Salem's fault anyway," she huffed, folding her arms across her chest. "If you didn't have a stupid cat, I wouldn't have done this."

My heart sank as I realized that Samantha wasn't taking responsibility for her actions. Instead, she shifted the blame onto Salem, who remained visibly distressed.

"Samantha," I said firmly, trying to keep my voice steady, "you must understand that it's not Salem's fault. You chose to spray-paint him, and you must take responsibility for your actions."

She rolled her eyes, clearly not interested in hearing what I had to say. "Whatever. It's just a cat," she muttered, turning her back on us.

The front door swung open, and Richard and Henry stepped into the tense atmosphere. Sensing imminent trouble, Samantha's eyes filled with tears. "It wasn't me, Daddy. My friends spray-painted the cat!" She sprinted to Richard and clung to him, seeking refuge.

"Let me check on him, Hope," said Henry, concern evident in his voice.

"What's going on here?" Richard asked, his eyes searching for answers. I exchanged a worried glance with Henry, who was gently wiping paint from around Salem's eyes with a damp cloth. I knew that merely scolding Samantha wouldn't be enough to instill empathy and responsibility within her. Distraught and frustrated, I fought to hold back my tears. Sensing my distress, Richard walked over to me and wrapped his arms around me, offering comfort as I continued to stroke Salem, trying to calm him down.

At that moment, Samantha decided to escalate the situation with a tantrum. "I hate it here! You care more about that stupid cat than me!"

* * *

"Enough, Samantha!" Richard's authoritative voice echoed throughout the room. He ran a hand through his hair, attempting to relieve the sudden stress that weighed on him.

Henry, still tending to Salem, offered reassurance. "He's going to be fine. Let's just take him to the vet to ensure there's no paint in his eyes or any irritation to his skin." Salem began to lick Henry's hands, seemingly grateful for the gentle care. He then cast a sidelong glance at Samantha, as if mentally concocting a plan for retribution. My cat had returned to his mischievous state, and I knew he would recover.

"Thanks, Henry," I said, grateful for his help and expertise. I carefully scooped up Salem in my arms and ran the stairs to our room, leaving Richard and Samantha behind to address the underlying issues and clean up the colorful mess left in the wake of her actions.

I gently placed Salem on our bed, ensuring he was comfortable as I gathered a few necessary items in my bag. Hearing Richard's footsteps approaching, I felt his arms encircle me. "I'm so sorry, darling," he murmured.

Taking a deep breath, I turned to face him. "I'll take Salem to the vet and then to Charlie's place. He'll stay there for a few days while we sort things out here."

"Would you like me to go with you?" he asked, concern etched in his features.

"No need, Richard. Just handle this situation with your daughter," I emphasized the words 'your daughter,' making it clear that he needed to address Samantha's behavior. With that, I picked up Salem, cradled him in my arms, and left Richard alone in the room, contemplating how to mend the rift within our family.

—

The following day, hiding away at my desk, I was meticulously sifting through the pile of morning paperwork when an unexpected figure drew my attention. Richard filled my office doorway, radiating a tangible mix of guilt and worry. It was apparent he had come to discuss the recent unsettling incident involving Samantha and Salem.

I found myself studying him involuntarily– the man I now proudly called my husband. His towering stature, broad shoulders, and sculpted jawline embodied masculine allure. His arresting blue-grey eyes seemed to delve into the depths of my soul, while his impeccably styled dark hair framed his face beautifully, eliciting sighs from the female contingent at the office. However, my lingering annoyance from the previous episode with Samantha and Salem had inadvertently spilled over onto Richard. It might seem petty, but yes, I held him accountable.

"Hello," he began, his voice low and velvety, sending a shiver of anticipation down my spine. Even after all this time, I was far from immune to his magnetic pull. "Might I pop in?"

"By all means," I responded, striving to mask my mixed feelings of surprise, curiosity, and irritation.

As Richard approached my desk, I noticed my female colleagues swiveling their heads through the clear glass, trying to catch a glimpse of him. Even the most stoic among them couldn't resist staring as he passed by. It wasn't just his looks that captivated them; the aura of confidence and mystery that enveloped him was irresistible.

Richard pulled out a chair and sat across from me, folding his hands on my cluttered desk. He took a deep breath, and I could see the weight of the situation bearing down on him.

"I'm here about Samantha," he began, his eyes filled with sincerity. "I know what she did to Salem was... unforgivable. And I want to make it right."

I nodded, uncertain of where this conversation was heading.

"I need to get back to filming," he continued, "and you're the only person I trust to look after her while I'm away because you're now her mother. Can we tell her, darling?"

* * *

I gazed at Richard, almost pleading, "We can't, Richard. There's so much adjustment on her side. We forced her to start school before spring break. She will be in a new environment without friends, and that's too much for an 11-year-old child. I couldn't add more confusion and change. She's going to hate me even more."

Before I could elaborate, Hillary opened the door and reminded me of my meeting, "Mr. and Mrs. Collins, I'm sorry to interrupt, but your meeting is about to start in Conference Room 2," she said.

I glanced at my watch and saw Richard preparing to leave. "Hillary, can you ask someone from my team to attend the meeting? Tell them I have a pressing matter that I need to attend to now."

"No, darling. We can talk about this tonight when you get home."

"Our family comes first. That's our deal from the beginning," I reminded him. Hillary closed the door, leaving us alone again.

"So, what are we going to do with our daughter?" I asked. Richard smiled at my use of *our daughter.* "If she's going to pull that stunt again, I swear on all that's holy, Richard, I'll strangle her!"

Richard chuckled, rose from his seat, and walked over to me. He gently pulled me up, cradling me in his strong arms. He tilted my chin upwards and kissed my lips tenderly, "You and Sam are more alike than you realize. You're both fiercely independent and stubbornly persistent."

"Now that you're leaving again, I'm left with no choice but to play nanny to that little terror," I retorted, my words softened by the smile on my face.

Richard flinched slightly at my choice of words. "Not a nanny, per se. More like... mentoring her, guiding her. I believe she needs a figure like you in her life. Someone who can empathize with her. She's on the cusp of womanhood, and you're the only one who can steer her through this journey."

* * *

I mulled over his proposition for a moment. It was an unconventional request, but perhaps it was worth considering.

"Fine," I conceded reluctantly. "I'll do my best to guide her, but I'm unsure how to proceed. My growing up years were rather complicated, too."

Richard's face brightened into a grin, and he enveloped me in another warm embrace. "Thank you, darling," he expressed sincerely. "I truly appreciate it."

As I pressed my face against his chest, I couldn't help but wonder what I had just signed up for. But one thing was certain – with Sam's presence now part of our life, things were about to get complex.

——

The day designated for Richard's departure has finally arrived. The cool, refreshing spring morning air filled my lungs as I stood alongside him and Samantha outside the imposing school gates. Cherry blossoms danced gracefully in the breeze, their radiant hues creating an idyllic backdrop for what was to be Samantha's first day at her new school. In a joint decision, Richard and I had resolved to accompany her today before he was due to depart from La Guardia for his flight to Dublin. Samantha fidgeted nervously, clutching her backpack tightly as she eyed the bustling school grounds. Richard placed a comforting hand on her shoulder, offering an encouraging smile.

"Don't worry, Samantha," he said softly. "You'll do great here. Remember, everyone feels nervous on their first day, even if it's not technically their first day."

Samantha nodded, attempting a brave smile. "But Daddy, this isn't their first day. It's just... I've never had to start in the middle of the school year before."

Richard looked at me, his eyes seeking reassurance. I smiled and said, "Samantha, I promise you'll be fine. Jeffrey will be here, and he'll always keep an eye on you."

Her eyes flickered, and she looked directly at her father. "Daddy, please don't leave me," she pleaded.

"I'll be back on Saturday," Richard reassured her. "Be good, don't give Hope and Leticia any trouble, and no more incidents with Salem. Promise me."

Just then, the school bell rang, signaling the start of the day. Students hurried towards their classrooms, leaving us standing by the entrance.

"Alright," Richard said, his voice filled with pride and a hint of sadness. "It's time for you to go in. I have to catch my flight. Hope will accompany you inside and introduce you to your teacher." He kissed the top of her head and whispered, "I know you'll do wonderfully."

He pulled Samantha into a tight hug, and she hugged him back fiercely. Richard looked at me as they separated and whispered, "Please take care of her."

"I will," I promised and kissed him passionately.

With one last deep breath, Samantha stepped away from her father and walked towards the school building. We both looked back at Richard and waved goodbye. As we entered the hallway, I could sense her anxiety growing.

"Hey," I said gently, trying to lighten the mood. "What do you say we find your first class together? I bet you'll make friends in no time."

Samantha looked at me with a small, hopeful smile. "Okay," she agreed, her voice barely audible.

As we navigated the bustling halls together, I couldn't help but feel a sense of responsibility for Samantha's well-being. Though she seemed vulnerable now, I knew that with time and support, she would thrive in her new environment. And just like that, I became the sole parent to an adolescent while Richard was away. I felt as if I had aged all of a sudden.

* * *

In the following days, my life transformed into a whirlwind of activity. Juggling work and caring for Samantha left me feeling stretched thin, my energy reserves dwindling with each passing day. Yet, despite the challenges, I sensed a subtle improvement in our connection. Whenever I inquired about her day or how school was going, she managed to respond with more than just a single word.

I made it a point to be there for her before she left for school each morning, acutely aware of how much she missed her dad and Henry, who had returned to London a few days prior.

Every morning, I rose early to prepare her breakfast and pack her lunch before heading to work. As I meticulously arranged sandwiches and apple slices in her lunch container one day, I casually asked if she would like to have dinner outside the house for a change.

"I'm fine," she replied, a hint of annoyance in her voice. "You don't have to be so nice to me. When's daddy coming home?"

"He'll be back on the weekend," I reassured her, trying to sound upbeat. "I'm booking his flight for Friday. How about we order pizza tonight and watch movies after you finish your homework?"

"Okay," she agreed, her tone softening ever so slightly. She picked up her lunch bag and headed toward the door without saying goodbye. Despite the lingering tension, I couldn't help but feel a sense of relief. This was a better day – at least we weren't quarreling.

As she disappeared from view, I dialed Jeffrey's number to let him know that Sam was on her way to the lobby.

———

The moment I settled into my desk chair, Hillary appeared by my side, placing my schedule in front of me. It revealed a last-minute meeting that hadn't been there before. "Hillary, is there any chance you could reschedule that final meeting to an earlier slot? I need to be home in time for dinner with Sam," I implored.

* * *

Her brows knitted together as she considered the request. "I'm afraid you have another meeting penciled in just before that one. Would you like me to handle any necessary preparations at home on your behalf?" she offered.

A wave of relief washed over me, and I couldn't suppress my gratitude. "You're a lifesaver, Hillary. Instead of resorting to pizza, could you ring my housekeeper and inquire about Samantha's dinner preference? That way, we can all enjoy something together."

Her face lit up with a smile, and she reassured me, "Rest easy, I'll see to it."

As she turned to leave, I was struck by a sudden realization. "You know what?" I said, my smile mirroring hers. "You're pretty awesome, Hillary."

Her smile grew wider, lighting up the room. "Thank you," she replied before closing the door softly behind her.

At the stroke of noon, my phone buzzed with an incoming call. Glancing at the screen, I saw Richard's name light up.

"Hey there, how's my beautiful wife doing?" he asked, his voice warm and comforting.

"Trying to balance work and taking care of your daughter. She's really missing you. You know — she's been pretty lonely. I tried cheering her up, but she just stayed in her room," I replied, a hint of concern in my tone.

"She'll need to adjust. You remember how it was when I wasn't around much while Henry was growing up," Richard sighed softly. "Thank you, darling, for being there for her."

"It's not just Sam who misses you," I said longingly.

"I know, darling. I miss you too." I could hear the heaviness in Richard's breathing, and I knew he longed to be back home. "So, how are you two getting along?" he asked, trying to lighten the mood.

* * *

"Well, there's been some progress. At least we're not pulling each other's hair out," I joked. Richard joined in with a chuckle, likely picturing his wife and daughter engaged in a brawl.

Just then, Hillary entered the room, gesturing that everyone was already gathered in the conference room, waiting for me to start the meeting. I raised a hand, signaling her to give me a few more minutes. I didn't want to end my conversation with Richard just yet.

We talked for a bit longer before he finally said, "I love you, and I miss you."

"Me too. Please take care of yourself for me, okay? I love you," I responded, my voice filled with affection. With a reluctant sigh, we ended the call, and I turned my attention to the meeting that awaited me.

16

The moment I stepped through the front door of our home, an eerie silence enveloped me. It was out of character for Samantha to be absent from the living room at this hour. My instincts guided me first to her bedroom, then to ours. A wave of unease washed over me, leaving a persistent feeling that something was amiss.

I wandered from room to room, searching for any signs of her presence. In the laundry room, Leticia was sorting clothes with a focused expression. "Leticia, have you seen Samantha?" I asked, my voice tinged with concern.

"She was heading towards Señor Richard's office earlier," she replied.

Puzzled, I made my way to the last place I'd expected to find her — her father's study. There she was, hunched over the desk, papers scattered around her like autumn leaves strewn across a sidewalk. My heart skipped a beat as I recognized the documents — these weren't the scripts Richard usually kept in his office. They were the adoption papers we had hidden away months ago, never intending to reveal the truth until Samantha was ready and adjusted.

The room was heavy with unspoken tension, an unmistakable aura of hurt radiating from her. I lingered in the doorway, uncertain how to approach the subject, but finally summoned the courage to speak.

"Samantha," I started cautiously, "I see you've discovered the adoption papers."

* * *

She glanced up, her eyes glistening with unshed tears, and I could feel the weight of her pain. "So it's true then? You and Daddy adopted me?" she asked, her voice barely more than a whisper.

After a confirming nod, I took a moment to compose my thoughts before elaborating. "Yes, sweetheart. But you need to understand that you're your father's biological child. The legal procedure was necessary to ensure we could bring you home with us," I explained. "We've always meant to tell you but thought it best to wait until you were ready and had adjusted to this new surroundings."

Samantha's gaze fell back on the papers, her hands trembling. "Why didn't you tell me? My teachers insist I'm Samantha Ortega-Collins, not Samantha Willis," her tears fell down her cheeks unceasingly. "I kept telling them they were mistaken!"

"I'm sorry, Sam... this is not how we planned it. We never meant to cause you pain, Sam. We were merely trying to protect you," my voice nearly pleading.

"Stop pretending you are my mother! You're not my mum, Hope! You never will be!" Her words were a guttural cry, piercing my heart like a dagger. She hated me now, more than ever, and my tears welled up.

Taking a deep breath, I struggled to find comforting words. "You are our daughter in every way that counts. Being adopted doesn't alter how much we love you or how much you mean to us."

Tears traced down her cheeks as she looked up at me, her eyes a storm of anger and confusion. "I hate you! Both you and Daddy! And Henry, too! You all lied to me!"

"That's not true, sweetheart. Your dad wanted to tell you, but I asked him to wait until you were settled." As I moved closer, hoping to console her, she pushed me away and ran to her room, slamming the door shut behind her.

As I stood there, the sound of Samantha's door slamming still ringing in my ears, a mixture of heartache and worry overwhelmed me. Her anger and pain seemed to rest heavily upon my shoulders, and I couldn't shake the feeling that I had failed her.

With Richard in the middle of filming, I knew I couldn't burden him with this news right away. I needed to give myself time to process the situation and figure out how to mend the rift that had formed between Samantha and me. The thought of facing this challenge alone only intensified my anxiety.

Feeling defeated, I retreated to the sanctuary of our bedroom, hoping to find some solace in the familiar surroundings. As I closed the door behind me, the room appeared to echo my own emotional turmoil. The once warm and inviting space now felt cold and distant, mirroring the chasm that had opened up within our family.

I sank onto the bed, my body trembling as the gravity of the situation finally hit me. Tears streamed down my face, each proof of the fear and worry that filled my heart. How could I bridge the gap splintered between Samantha and me? Or piece together the rapport she once shared with her father and Henry? How could I make her understand that our love for her was unconditional, regardless of the circumstances of her adoption?

As I sat there, consumed by my thoughts, the walls of the room seemed to close in around me, amplifying my sense of isolation. The world outside continued to turn, oblivious to the storm raging within our home, leaving me feeling more alone than ever.

Despite the anguish that gripped me, I knew I couldn't let these emotions consume me. I needed to be strong — not just for myself and Richard, but for Samantha as well. With a deep, steadying breath, I wiped away my tears and resolved to face the challenges head-on. No matter how long or complicated it took, I would do everything to prove to Samantha that she was, and would always be, family. And with time, I hoped that she would come to see that my love for her was as genuine and enduring as if she were my own flesh and blood.

———

As I slowly awakened from a restless sleep, the first rays of sunlight peeked through the curtains, casting a warm glow across our bedroom. The events of last night rushed back to me, and my heart constricted at the memory of Samantha's pain and anger.

With a heavy heart, I pulled on my robe and hurried to the dining room, hoping to catch Samantha before she left for school. Perhaps we could have a brief conversation. But as I entered the dining room, Leticia greeted me with a sympathetic smile, her eyes reflecting an understanding of our family's situation. "Samantha already left for school early this morning," she informed kindly.

A pang of disappointment washed over me, but I nodded in acknowledgment. "Thank you, Leticia."

Realizing that I needed to carry on with my day despite my emotional state, I returned to my room and readied myself for work. As I dressed, I speed-dialed Richard. His phone was unreachable — he must have been in the middle of filming.

Once prepared, I grabbed my bag and headed to my office, steeling myself for the hectic day ahead. The familiar routine of work offered a reprieve from my personal troubles, but my thoughts of Samantha continued in the corners of my mind.

Throughout the day, I found myself repeatedly glancing at the clock, counting down the hours until I could go home and attempt to reconnect with Samantha. She needed me now more than ever. In the midst of a read-through meeting for a new book launch, Hillary interrupted us, my phone in her hand.

"I'm sorry, but you need to take this," she said, handing me the phone.

It was Jeffrey. "I couldn't find her. Most of the kids have already left the classrooms. Her mobile phone is off. I couldn't track it anymore" he explained, his usual calming voice tinged with anxiety.

"What? You can't miss her, Jeffrey!" My voice trembled with panic. "Find her! I'm on my way!" I hastily ended the call and dialed Chen and Arthur. "Pick me up in the lobby now," I instructed. Without a word of farewell, I hurriedly left the room.

* * *

As I rushed out of the meeting room, my heart raced with fear and anxiety. The thought of Samantha being alone, feeling lost and betrayed, was too much to bear. I couldn't help but blame myself for not being there when she needed me the most.

I reached the lobby in record time, my breaths coming in short gasps. Chen and Arthur were already waiting for me, their faces etched with concern. They could sense the urgency in my voice when I called them. We jumped into the car and sped off toward Samantha's school without delay. I tried to reach Richard's mobile again, but it remained unreachable.

The ride felt like an eternity, each passing minute amplifying my worry. As we approached the school, I tried to calm myself, knowing that panicking would only make matters worse. My thoughts raced as I considered all the possible scenarios — where could Samantha be? What if she had run away or found herself in danger?

We finally pulled up to the school, and I leaped out of the car before it even came to a complete stop. Scanning the area, I desperately searched for any sign of Samantha. Jeffrey greeted me at the entrance, his countenance mirroring the worry gnawing at my insides.

"I'm sorry, but there's still no sign of her," he admitted, his voice heavy with a sense of failure and concern.

As I approached the principal's office, I spotted a huddle of Samantha's classmates. I approached them with a glimmer of hope that someone might have seen her or knew her whereabouts. As I began questioning them, one hesitant and visibly nervous girl decided to speak up.

"I saw her leaving the school grounds right after classes ended. She was with Liam's friends. She seemed really upset," the girl said, her eyes downcast.

"Who's Liam? Did you see which way they went?" I asked, trying to keep my voice steady.

"Liam is in ninth grade. I don't know why she was hanging out with the big guys," the girl said. I thanked the girl and immediately headed to the principal's office, Chen, Arthur, and Jeffrey following close behind.

———

The tension in the air was intense as I entered the principal's office, like a storm cloud on the verge of releasing its torrential downpour. My gaze darted around the room, settling on Samantha's teacher, Mrs. Thompson. She sat, wringing her hands nervously, her face etched with concern.

My heart raced as I struggled to suppress the panic welling within me. Where could she be? Taking a deep breath, I forced myself to focus. "Mrs. Thompson," I began, my voice barely audible. "I spoke with one of Samantha's classmates earlier. She mentioned seeing her with Liam's group – that older kid from school."

The principal, Mr. Johnson, immediately straightened in his chair, his eyes narrowing. "Liam? I see. Thank you for informing us, Mrs. Collins. We'll handle this."

As he reached for the phone, I paced back and forth, my mind conjuring up various scenarios that could have transpired. I retrieved my phone from my bag and attempted to call Richard — still unreachable. "Where are you, Richard?" I murmured. What if Samantha had been coerced into something dangerous? What if she was injured or lost? I knew I needed to remain strong, but fear threatened to overwhelm me.

Mr. Johnson's voice pulled me back to reality as he spoke into the phone. "Yes, hello. I'm calling on behalf of Hillside Middle School. We have a situation involving your child, Liam, and another student named Samantha Collins..."

I listened intently as he proceeded to call the parents of Liam's friends, updating them on the situation and urging them to contact their children. With each conversation, a flicker of hope ignited within me — perhaps one of these parents would provide the answers I desperately sought.

* * *

At last, the final call was made. Mr. Johnson hung up and turned to me, his expression grave. "Mrs. Collins, we've alerted all of the parents. They'll contact their children and update us as soon as possible. We also need to involve the NYPD."

I nodded, fighting back tears. "Thank you, Mr. Johnson. I just... I need to find her." As Mr. Johnson spoke with the police, I dialed my father's private number. He answered on the first ring. "Dad, we're in trouble. We can't find Samantha, and Richard isn't answering." I said.

"Calm down, Hope. Tell me everything. Start from the beginning," he said soothingly. I recounted the events, starting with Jeffrey's inability to locate her after school and ending with my arrival at the principal's office.

"Dad, I need to find her. She must be terrified right now," I choked out.

"Hand the phone to Arthur, sweetheart. I will contact Richard myself and send the jet to fetch him," he instructed. I passed my phone to Arthur. Then Jeffrey's phone rang, and he gestured that it was Richard. I snatched the device and exclaimed, "Richard! I've been trying to reach you. I'm at Samantha's school, and we can't find her. She must be frightened. We need to locate her!"

Richard's voice trembled with worry, but he attempted to remain composed for my sake. "Darling, I'm getting the next flight. We'll find her. Give the phone to Jeffrey; let him coordinate while I travel."

"Dad's speaking with Chen and Arthur now. He'll call after, he's sending the jet for you. I didn't know what else to do, so I called him."

"You did the right thing, darling. We'll find her." I handed the phone to Jeffrey.

Mr. Johnson placed a reassuring hand on my shoulder. "The police are en route. We'll do everything in our power to assist you, Mrs. Collins. We'll find your daughter."

Taking a deep breath, I braced myself for the search that lay ahead.

Jeffrey returned his phone to me. Richard's voice was now calmer, "Darling, I have to go. Jeffrey, Chen, and Arthur will work with the police. Try to relax. I know it isn't easy, but our daughter needs us, and we won't rest until she's safe in our arms again. I love you."

"I love you too. Be safe," I replied before ending the call.

The moment the police sirens echoed through the school halls, I could feel the tension rise in the atmosphere. Officers rushed inside, their heavy boots pounding against the marbled floor. I was approached by a tall, stern-looking man who introduced himself as Detective Morris.

"Can you give us any information about Samantha?" he asked, his eyes scrutinizing my face for any signs of deception.

I nodded, swallowing hard, "Yes, she's my daughter. She was safely dropped off here in school this morning. Her security detail was guarding her at the gate as he always does daily. He called me when she failed to show up at the gate after school."

"Do you have a recent photograph of her?" Detective Morris inquired.

I pulled out my phone and showed him a picture of Samantha laughing with Henry, both of them looking carefree and happy. He took a snapshot of the screen with his phone and thanked me.

Just then, the parents from Liam's group arrived, their faces etched with worry and confusion. They were frantically searching for their children, who were also nowhere to be found. The chaos escalated as we started blaming one another, our voices rising like a cacophony of fear and anger.

"You should have kept an eye on them!" one mother shouted at another.

"Well, maybe if your son weren't such a bad influence, they wouldn't be in this mess!" retorted the other.

In the midst of the commotion, a timid-looking boy appeared in the corner. He seemed frightened, his eyes darting around the room as if searching for an escape route. "What's your name?" I asked as I stared deep into his eyes.

"Jake. I've nothing to do with her," he said quickly.

"Jake, you have to tell us where Samantha is," I pleaded, my voice trembling with desperation.

He hesitated, his gaze shifting from me to the agitated parents and then back to me.

"If you don't," I threatened, my voice low and menacing, "I'll tell everyone you were involved in their disappearance."

Jake's face paled, and he finally relented. "Okay, okay," he stammered. "Liam hid Samantha with his jacket so her bodyguard wouldn't see her. He said he'd show her our hideout at the abandoned warehouse by the river. Samantha wanted to return to London, so we said we'd help her and discuss the plan at our hideout." Jake's voice trembled as he continued. "Once we arrived, Samantha got scared and cried. She said she wanted to go home. Liam locked her inside and threatened to leave her there. They wanted to get rough on her. That's why I got scared and left."

"Oh, my God! She's terrified of enclosed spaces!" I panicked. I glared at Liam's parents and shouted, "If anything happens to my daughter, I'll make sure your son spends the rest of his life in jail!" I had never felt so angry in my life, and at that moment, knowing Sam was locked in a room without light or windows, she must be fearing for her life.

With this critical piece of information, Detective Morris quickly relayed the news to his team, and they prepared to head out immediately. I grabbed my bag and gestured to my three bodyguards to follow the police. Detective Morris stopped me, "Mrs. Collins, let us do our job. Your presence will only put us at a disadvantage. Please stay here."

I stared back at him, my eyes steely. "You can't make me stay here. I'm going with you to find my daughter!" With that, I left the room, followed by Jeffrey, Chen, and Arthur.

* * *

———

As we made our way through the desolate warehouse, my heart ached with the overwhelming need to find Samantha safe and sound. I longed to hold her close, reassuring her that she was loved and cherished, no matter what. As the police officers swept the area, the boys inside panicked and started to run. Desperation filled my voice as I called out, "Samantha!"

Silence. My panic escalated. Detective Morris instructed everyone to call her name. At the top of my lungs, I called out again, "Sam! Where are you, sweetheart?"

From a distance, I heard a faint voice, "Mummy!" My heart soared. She was calling for me – she called me Mummy. Tears streamed down my cheeks as relief washed over me — she was alive!

"Tell me where you are! Keep talking, sweetheart!" I yelled back, desperate to pinpoint her location. Arthur and Chen scrambled around the warehouse to determine where her voice came from.

"I can't see. It's too dark. I can't move!" she cried. Memories of my own ordeal in London resurfaced, but I pushed my fears aside to stay strong for Samantha. That's when Chen spotted an abandoned, empty water tank near the back. It was padlocked, but he forced it open. There she was — tied to a post, her tear-streaked face reflecting the terror she had endured.

I rushed to her side; my voice choked with emotion as I whispered, "Samantha." Arthur and Jeffrey untied her, and she flung her arms around me, sobbing, "Mummy, I knew you'd find me."

"Of course, sweetheart. Let's get you out of here," I replied, embracing her tightly.

Two female officers and paramedics approached us, and Samantha clung to me even more. I looked into her eyes and reassured her, "Sweetheart, they need to check on you. Just let them do their job. I won't leave you. I'll be right beside you." Remembering how scared I was when Richard had found me after his ex-wife kidnapped me in

London, I couldn't bear to leave Samantha's side.

As they asked her sensitive questions about whether the boys had touched her, she bravely replied, "No, I didn't let them, but they tried. They punched me instead and tied me up." I held her in my arms and kissed her hair, proud of her courage.

Detective Morris approached me, requesting that I give a statement at the precinct. "My daughter needs me. Our lawyers will be there. I want those kids locked up," I said, anger seething through my words. I signaled Chen to call Raphael, our lawyer, and brief him on his way to the police station.

"Mrs. Collins, we have another situation. We tried to block some paparazzi, but they swarmed the area. Someone must have leaked the information to them," Detective Morris explained. I couldn't bear the thought of Samantha's photos appearing on the front page or online. Being Richard's daughter would only amplify the attention. I dialed Yumi's private number.

"Yes, Hope. How's Samantha?" She asked.

"She's fine. I need your help. Those paparazzi are all over the place. I don't want to see photos or news about this incident. Please, Yumi, make it go away. Not a single photo," I pleaded.

"Consider it done, Hope – I'll take care of it. By the way, the jet already picked up Richard. They'll be airborne in a few minutes." She ended the call without waiting for me to express my gratitude. If there was one thing I admired about Yumi, she could get things done.

17

As we stepped into our home, I felt the weight of the world lift from my shoulders. Jeffrey ushered Samantha and me inside while Arthur and Chen remained with the police to handle the paperwork alongside our lawyer. Our home's atmosphere blended relief with a lingering sense of anxiety.

Our family physician, Dr. Peters, was already there, prepared to examine Samantha. Gently unwrapping the blanket around her, I knelt down and met her gaze. "Sweetheart, I'm going to help you take a shower. We need to remove these clothes so Dr. Peters can check on you properly. Is that okay with you?" I asked.

"Okay, but will you stay with me?" Her voice wavered, her lips trembling.

"Of course, I'll be right there in the bathroom," I reassured her, planting a tender kiss on her forehead.

After assisting her with the shower and helping her change into cozy pajamas, I tucked Samantha into bed. "Sweetheart, I'm going to let Dr. Peters take a look at you now, but I'll be right here. I just want to make sure you're okay," I told her. She nodded, grasping my hand tightly, unwilling to let go.

At that moment, Leticia entered the room, carrying a tray of comfort food — mac and cheese and a glass of milk. "Try to eat, even if you don't feel like it. And guess what? Daddy's already on his way; he'll be here when you wake up," I said, gently stroking her cheek.

After managing to eat half of the food on her tray, Samantha handed it back to Leticia. Dr. Peters meticulously checked her vitals and examined her for any bruises or fractures. She applied a soothing balm to Samantha's bruised wrists. "I'll give something to help her sleep and recover from this ordeal. I'll return tomorrow morning to check on her again," she informed me.

"Thank you," I expressed my gratitude. "Please send the bill to my office; Hillary will handle it."

———

I remained by Samantha's bedside, watching her cuddle her pillow as she gradually drifted off to sleep. Once the medicine took effect and her slumber deepened, I carefully retreated from the room, leaving the door and night lamp open before heading to my own room for a much-needed shower and change.

As the warm water cascaded over me, I couldn't help but reflect on the emotional turmoil we had all endured. The fear and worry that once consumed me were now gradually replaced by relief and gratitude for finding Samantha safe. After changing into cozy lilac silk pajamas and grabbing a manuscript to review, I settled onto the couch in Samantha's room, thankful that she slept peacefully.

Halfway through the manuscript, I, too, succumbed to sleep. I was exhausted from today's event. I was later awakened by sounds from the living room—Richard had finally arrived. He rushed to check on Samantha, and I could see the relief flood his face as he found her resting peacefully. I wrapped my arms around him, and he held me tightly, pressing his lips against mine. The taste of alcohol lingered on his breath; he had likely been drinking on the plane to ease his worries.

Pulling away from our kiss, Richard asked with worry, "How is she?"

"She's doing okay," I reassured him. "The doctor gave her something to help her sleep. She'll need some time to recover, but I think she'll be fine."

* * *

Richard nodded, and together, we stood at the foot of Samantha's bed, our arms entwined, watching her sleep.

I led him out of the room so we could talk quietly without disturbing Samantha's rest. Once inside our own bedroom, I recounted the harrowing events, from Samantha discovering the adoption papers to rescuing her from the warehouse.

"I'm sorry I wasn't here for you and Sam," Richard's voice was laden with regret and pain. Tenderly, I touched his face, traced his jaw with my fingers, and kissed him passionately. At that moment, I wanted both of us to forget the day's ordeal and let go of our lingering fears. As our kiss grew more urgent, my soft lips brushed gently against his, my tongue seeking solace in our connection. Then I felt his arms wrap around my body. His fingers touched the bare flesh between my pajama top and bottoms. I could feel goosebumps trickling between my breasts, warming me up.

Finally, we parted our lips. Richard looked into my eyes. His blue-grey eyes were now more grey than blue, and he whispered, "I need you, Hope." There was hunger in his voice.

"Make love to me, Richard," I said, tracing his lips with my finger. He caught it between his lips and sucked it gently. Then, he gently kissed my neck as I arched my head back, exposing my neck even more. He licked at my neck — a small moan of pleasure escaped from my lips, and I felt his gentle and warm kisses trail down from my ear to my collarbone. I reached out and ran my fingers through his soft hair, rubbing the back of his neck.

His hands found my breasts and squeezed them. His kisses trailed down the hollow of my breasts. I felt his tongue flick across my left nipple before taking it into his mouth and sucking it as he gently played with my right nipple. I can feel the pleasure arising from his touch. I gasped out loud as he rubbed my nipples, getting them to turn to rock-hard flesh.

His tongue felt so good, so soft and wet. My moans were louder now. I was pleading for him to continue. The pleasure was so intense that I started to breathe heavily, feeling the pleasure consume my body. He sent my body into an uncontrollable spasm, pushing me to the edge. When Richard finally raised his head to see my fully pleasured state, he pushed me gently to the bed and unbuttoned his jeans and shirt. He pulled my pajama bottoms and gently rubbed his fingers between my legs as his face approached mine.

Once again, our lips and tongues played together, tasting and feeling each other's warmth and softness. As we kissed, I felt him pressed inside me, and I was lost in pleasure. Richard looked down at my face and stared deeply into my eyes as he moved inside me. "Don't close your eyes, darling," he whispered.

I felt his hips slowly move to join my rhythm, and we both sighed and moaned in the intense pleasure that neither of us had ever felt before. I almost screamed out in pleasure. Passion swelled intensely in my body as we kissed deeply. At that moment, there was no one else in our world, just Richard and me.

Exhausted, he collapsed onto me before tenderly pressing his lips to mine again. Rolling onto his back, he cradled me in his arms, holding me close. I lifted my head, gazing at my husband's handsome face. "Just sleep, my love," I whispered, brushing my lips against his. "Everything is fine now," I assured him as I nestled back into his embrace and closed my eyes.

———

In the middle of the night, I was jolted awake by Samantha's screams. "Mummy!" she cried out, her voice laced with fear.

I sprang from my bed, hastily threw on my clothes, and dashed to her room, my heart pounding. As I entered, I saw her sitting upright in bed, tears streaming down her face.

"Mummy, I had a bad dream," she sobbed, extending her arms toward me.

I swiftly crossed the room, enfolded her in my arms, and held her close. "It's okay, sweetheart," I whispered, soothing her. "You're safe now. I'm here."

* * *

As I held Samantha, she buried her face in my chest and closed her eyes tightly to take out the nightmare. I couldn't help but feel grateful that we had found her and brought her home. The worry and fear that had gripped us were beginning to fade, replaced by relief and a resolve to help her heal from this experience. Sensing Richard's presence on the bed behind me, I encouraged her softly, "Open your eyes, sweetheart, and look who's here?"

"Daddy!" she exclaimed, her face lighting up with joy. "You're here! I missed you so much!"

Richard embraced her tightly, lifting her from the bed and out of my arms. "I missed you too, sweetheart," he said, his voice thick with emotion. "I'm sorry I wasn't here."

"It's okay, Daddy. Mummy found me," she said as she nestled her head against Richard's shoulder.

"I knew Mummy would find you, sweetheart," Richard replied, kissing her hair tenderly. He looked at me lovingly as he heard Samantha call me mommy.

As I rose from the bed, he turned to me, his eyes brimming with gratitude. "Thank you," he whispered, drawing me into a passionate embrace. "For everything."

As the three of us stood there, our arms entwined, I knew our family had been changed forever – and for the better.

"Why don't you sleep in our room tonight? Would you like that?" I asked her. She nodded enthusiastically.

"Come on, girls. Let's go." Richard gathered Samantha into his arms as I encircled my arms around his waist; together, we walked to our bedroom. Though the road ahead was bound to be filled with challenges and complications, I clung to the hope that we could face anything life threw our way.

* * *

I gradually opened my eyes, basking in the sun's warmth on my face. Glancing around, I noticed Samantha sleeping soundly between Richard and me. Her chest gently rose and fell, her soft breaths a soothing lullaby that had lulled me to sleep the previous night. I couldn't help but smile as I observed her, the morning light highlighting her angelic features.

Richard, too, was fast asleep, his arm protectively draped over Samantha. The sight of them both filled my heart with an indescribable warmth. Moments like these made me realize just how deeply I cared for them. The room's glass wall allowed the morning sun to filter in, casting golden beams throughout the space, making it feel like our personal sanctuary.

I kissed each of them tenderly, careful not to disturb their sleep. Silently, I slid out of bed and tiptoed toward the kitchen. The aroma of fresh coffee greeted me as I entered. Leticia was already bustling about, preparing breakfast. She turned to me with a warm smile.

"Good morning, Madam Hope," she said, her voice gentle and welcoming.

"Morning, Leticia," I replied, mirroring her smile. "It smells delightful in here."

"Thank you," she responded, her eyes sparkling with pride. "I thought I'd make pancakes today. I know how much Samantha loves them."

My heart swelled, grateful for Leticia's thoughtfulness. "That's incredibly kind of you. She'll be ecstatic."

As she poured me a cup of coffee, an unsettling feeling crept in that there was something urgent I needed to address. Then it struck me — I had scheduled a meeting with my father at lunchtime. He was due to arrive this morning from Barcelona. And there's the need to send the reviewed manuscripts to our agents to offer contracts and assign editors to the projects. I resolved to work from home today, allowing me more time to care for Samantha.

It was now past nine in the morning, and Hillary would already be at her desk. I quickly dialed her number and spoke to her. "Hey, can you do me a favor? Check if Oliver Ortega has arrived and cancel my meeting with him through his secretary. I'll call him myself. I'll be working from home today."

"Of course," my assistant replied. "I'll take care of it right away."

"Thank you. Also, I'll be sending some manuscripts with my notes to you. Give them to Timmy, tell him to assign it to one of our literary agents... whoever is available," I said before hanging up.

Sitting at the kitchen counter, sipping my coffee, I couldn't help but feel grateful for the tranquil morning. It was a rare moment of respite amidst life's chaos, and I knew I had to cherish it. Last night was traumatic for all of us, but I chose to be grateful that we found her. Taking a deep breath, I allowed myself to absorb the sun's warmth fully. Today was going to be a good day.

Richard emerged from the bedroom, rubbing his eyes and yawning. His tousled hair and sleepy expression brought a smile to my face. He walked over to me, planted a gentle kiss on my cheek, and settled into the chair beside me.

"Mornin'," he mumbled, his voice still thick with sleep.

"Morning. Sleep well?" I asked, passing him a cup of freshly brewed coffee.

"Blimey, Samantha is a proper bed hog, just like you. I wouldn't survive another night with you two in bed," he joked, taking a gulp of his coffee. "Thanks for this, darling. It's just what I need to start the day."

I let out a hearty chuckle. "How's Samantha? Is she still asleep?"

Richard gave a reassuring nod. "Yeah, she's out like a light. I reckon yesterday's events have finally taken their toll on her."

A comfortable silence enveloped us as we enjoyed our coffee. The atmosphere was warm and inviting, the sun's rays streaming through the windows, casting a golden glow over everything. "I'll work from home today until Samantha is back to her usual self," I said as Leticia set down two plates with pancakes and bacon strips. "I'll send some manuscripts to the office and call Dad to let him know I can't meet him for lunch today."

"Oliver's here? Thought he was off in Barcelona?" Richard asked, a hint of surprise in his voice.

"He was — but he's due to land in New York this morning," I responded.

"But he let me borrow his jet last night," Richard said, a furrow forming in his brow.

"No need to worry about that. The pilot likely got back in time to fly him here, or he used a different one," I explained, drizzling syrup over his pancakes.

"Thank you, darling," he said, spreading the syrup evenly over his pancakes and cutting them into neat diagonal pieces. "So, he's got more than one jet, has he?"

"I honestly don't know. When I've flown with him, I didn't pay attention to whether it was always the same jet," I admitted, taking small bites of my bacon while Richard enthusiastically tucked into his pancakes.

Richard set down his cutlery and reached across the table, capturing my hands in his. Gently, he lifted them to his lips. "You know, there's something I've been meaning to tell you," he said, his voice soft. His thumb traced the curve of my lower lip as he paused, "This unfortunate incident has, in a rather unexpected manner, led to something quite positive. I'm over the moon about your and Samantha's progress." He flashed a warm smile before continuing, "Last night, I heard her call you 'Mummy' for the first time. It completely took me by surprise, but in the best possible way."

His words filled my heart to the brim with joy. "When we were searching for her, she cried out 'Mummy'. It felt like she was truly expecting me to find her." Tears shimmered in my eyes as I recalled the moment. "I was taken aback, too. I didn't expect such a strong bond to form between us so quickly. She wouldn't let go of my hand."

"I reckon it's testament to how splendid you've been with her and how much she trusts you... relies on you. Despite the circumstances, I'm ever so grateful for the bond you two have established."

Tears streamed down my cheeks, and I tightened my grip on his hand. "I'm thankful too, Richard. I never imagined I could love another person's child as if they were my own, but Samantha has proven me wrong. She's brought such joy into our lives."

He tenderly wiped away a tear that had trickled down my cheek. "We're all so incredibly fortunate to have you in our lives — myself, Henry, and Samantha."

"It was hard for me to even mention our little bean... somehow, your children have filled the void left by his loss." My hand instinctively moved to my stomach, "I don't want to forget him, Richard, even if it's still painful." Seeing the emotion welling up within me at the memory of our unborn child, Richard rose from his chair, gently pulled me to my feet, and enveloped me in his arms as tears flowed freely.

"Oh, darling," Richard murmured, kissing my forehead gently and holding me close.

And so we stood there, bathed in the warmth of the sunlight, our thoughts lingering on our little bean.

18

As I sat on the couch near the window, the morning sun filtered through the living room's glass wall, casting a warm and inviting glow on everything in its path. I couldn't help but smile as I glanced up from the manuscript I was reviewing for publishing. Samantha and Henry were in the throes of playful banter in the middle of the room.

Henry had taken a brief hiatus from his hospital duties as a first-year intern to spend the weekend with us. The house was unusually lively. Even Salem, who had taken a break from his usual grumpy demeanor, sat beside me, demanding ear scratches. Henry sprawled out on the couch, teasing Samantha — who was seated on the plush carpet — about her newfound fondness for cookies.

"You know, Sam, if you keep scoffing down all those biscuits, you'll morph into one!" he quipped, his eyes dancing with mischief.

Samantha rolled her eyes, but her broad grin betrayed her amusement. "Oh, give over, Henry. At least I'm not the one spending my days jabbing people with needles!"

"There's more to medicine than just jabbing needles. We also advise children like you to cut down on sugar to avoid falling ill," he retorted, playfully chastising his sister.

"We only live once, big brother, so I say bring on the sugar!"

Their laughter echoed throughout the room, causing my heart to brim with joy. I stole a glance at Richard, who was engrossed in a script for his upcoming film. He lifted his gaze, meeting my eye, and shared a knowing smile, reflecting the warmth and satisfaction wrapping around me.

Weekends like these — brimming with laughter and the pure delight of family togetherness — hadn't always been our norm. There were periods when our lives were consumed by work, responsibilities, and the challenges that came with blending into a new family. But in moments like this, I was reassured that every hurdle had been worth overcoming.

Following Samantha's ordeal, we all decided to take a break from work, Henry included. We did not stop completely, but we always try to be home. Occasionally, when office meetings beckoned, I would bring Samantha along. She was captivated by the workings of my job and basked in the attention she received from my co-workers. Once, she was even invited to have lunch with my father, just the two of them. When I inquired about it, they both responded with a mischievous twinkle in their eyes, claiming it was their little secret.

"Henry, why don't you just stay here with us in New York? You could switch schools. It's much more fun when you're around," Samantha casually proposed, while nibbling on her cookies.

"It's not that simple. I'm still a Brit, just like Dad and you... though you're half-American now, thanks to Hope. Dad's here on a work visa, and he's married to an American. As for me, I can't just up sticks and live here," he responded, swiping a cookie from his sister's stash.

"So, why don't we all just move to London then?" she queried.

"Because your school is here, and you can't just drop out," I interjected, rummaging around for a colored pen to highlight some parts of the manuscript.

"Why do I need to go to school? We're loaded. Grandpa Oliver said we own shopping malls and skyscrapers in every major country, and Daddy is an actor raking in millions per film," she countered. Then she whispered to her brother, but loud enough for everyone in the room to hear, "But Mummy is wealthier than Daddy, I'm certain of that."

"I heard that," Richard said without lifting his gaze from the script.

I put down the manuscript and looked at Samantha, giggling beside her brother. "If you don't go to school, you'll end up scrubbing bathroom floors in malls and buildings for the rest of your life," I cautioned.

"What? You can't make me. I'm a trust fund baby," Samantha protested.

"Who told you that?" I asked, raising an eyebrow at her newfound knowledge.

"I overheard Raphael—Daddy's solicitor. And I'm an Ortega-Collins," she retorted confidently, her eyes sparkling with the satisfaction of having caught us off guard.

"Richard! Are you listening to this?" My attention shifted to Richard, who was engrossed in his script.

"You're in for it now, Sam! Let's see how you squirm your way out of this one," Henry goaded his sister, relishing the unfolding drama.

Richard set down his script and sauntered over to join us. "Sam, did you know Mummy has the final say on anything I do or say? She could make Raphael change everything."

Samantha looked startled but quickly regained her composure. "Oh, Daddy! Mummy wouldn't possibly make me scrub loos."

Henry laughed. "You reckon so?"

"If you would like to sit at my desk someday, you'd better see school through; otherwise, your future is in the lavatories," I warned her, but she simply rolled her eyes at me.

"So, you fancy being like Mummy now, do you? And here I thought you wanted to have a go at acting like Daddy?" Richard teased, pretending to be wounded.

* * *

"I don't fancy being an actress anymore, Daddy. I want to command the boardroom like Mummy," Samantha asserted.

Richard feigned shock and betrayal. "You turncoat!" he exclaimed, rising to his feet and tickling her tummy, instigating a wave of uproar and laughter that swept through the living room.

We all joined in the laughter, and I felt overwhelming gratitude for the love and joy permeating our home. The sun continued streaming through the window, bathing us in its warmth and light, and I knew this was what happiness should be.

As we continued to chat and jest together, I couldn't help but reflect on the long journey that had led us to this moment. The hurdles we'd surmounted, the love we'd nurtured, and the family we'd molded all culminated in this idyllic scene. And as I surveyed the beaming faces of my loved ones, I knew that I wouldn't exchange it for anything in the world.

19

Gently adjusting the soft cashmere blanket over Samantha, I marveled at her serene expression. She slept soundly on one of the plush couches in our private jet as we flew to Manila for the first time. With spring break upon us and Richard filming in Canada, we thought it was the perfect opportunity to bring her along.

Gazing out the window at the clouds, I reflected on this new chapter in my life. At just 28 years old, it wasn't long ago when I considered my life ordinary, even a failure at times. As the sole heir of Ortega Holdings, my responsibilities had grown exponentially. I was being groomed to manage the extensive global business network. In addition, I was married to a Hollywood star, and together, we had Samantha to care for during her critical adolescent years. The challenges were immense, but I welcomed them with open arms.

My eyes wandered over to my father, who sat at his makeshift workstation, surrounded by scattered papers. He looked up from his work and caught my gaze, his eyes brimming with warmth and pride.

"Is she asleep?" he inquired, nodding towards Samantha.

"Yes, she's out like a light," I responded with a smile. "I think all the excitement of the trip has worn her out."

My father chuckled softly and leaned back in his chair. "It's a big adventure for her, that's for sure. And for you, too. I know taking over the family business one day is no easy task, especially at such a young age." He removed his eyeglasses and looked at me intently, "Manila is where we started this business. This is one of our most crucial operations, and this is where I want you to learn."

I sighed, feeling the burden of responsibility on my shoulders. "Sometimes it feels like I'm juggling many roles – wife, mother, businesswoman. There is so much to take in. Occasionally, I just want to be just an ordinary young wife tagging along with Richard."

My father laughed, "You're saying that now because you have choices, but I know that isn't the life you would choose. You've always been independent and wanted to forge your own path, not just follow someone around."

"But I'm scared, Dad. This is a huge assignment. Sometimes, I doubt myself and wonder if I'm really up for the job," I confessed.

"You're more than capable. Look at the publishing firm; it's one of our fastest-growing businesses. You did it on your own without my interference," my father said, his voice filled with admiration. "That makes you the perfect person to carry on the Ortega legacy. You have the passion, drive, and heart this company needs."

I glanced back at Samantha, her chest rising and falling gently as she slept. "I want to make you proud, Dad. I want to show Samantha what it means to be strong, independent, and capable of achieving anything."

My father stood up and sat before me, reaching across the table to place his hand on mine. "You already have, Hope. You've proven time and time again that you can handle anything life throws at you. And remember, you're not alone in this journey. I'll always be here to support you, as will Richard and the rest of the family."

A warm feeling washed over me as I squeezed my father's hand. "Thank you, Dad. I couldn't do this without you."

———

As our private jet touched down at Ninoy Aquino International

Airport, the atmosphere starkly contrasted with the serenity of our flight. The moment we stepped off the plane, the bustling energy of the airport surrounded us. The cacophony of sounds — travelers chattering excitedly, luggage wheels rolling on the tiled floor, and announcements echoing throughout the terminal – enveloped us in a chaotic embrace.

"Welcome to Manila, my dear," my father said with a grin as he ruffled Samantha's hair, clearly amused by our wide-eyed reaction to the chaos. "You'll get used to it soon enough."

Thanks to my father's connections, we bypassed the long queues at immigration, quickly getting our passports stamped as someone was collecting our luggage. As we made our way toward the exit, I couldn't help but notice the stares and whispers from fellow travelers who recognized us, or perhaps more accurately, recognized my father.

Upon stepping out of the airport, we were greeted by an army of bodyguards, their faces stern and professional. They ushered us into a sleek black SUV waiting in a reserved pick-up area.

"Manila traffic is notorious, so buckle up and be prepared for a slow ride," my father warned as we exited the airport and merged onto the congested highway.

As we inched along the road, I gazed out the window at the cityscape, taking in the vibrant colors, the mix of modern skyscrapers and historical buildings, the slums and makeshift houses right along the roads, and the seemingly endless stream of cars, buses, and motorcycles weaving through traffic.

"Dad, how do people manage to get anywhere in this city?" I asked, feeling overwhelmed by the sheer volume of vehicles on the road.

He laughed heartily, "It's all about patience and embracing the chaos, Hope. You'll learn to navigate it just like everyone else. Besides, this horrible traffic is making some people rich."

"Grandpa, is this where Mummy was born?" Samantha inquired.

* * *

"No, Sam. Actually, this is your mommy's first time here, just like you," my dad replied, amused by how naturally Samantha referred to me as her mother.

"This is taking forever; it looks like the road is just one big parking space," she grumbled, rolling her eyes in a way that signaled she was either about to complain or bored. "Mummy, is Daddy joining us here?"

"He'll try, sweetheart. Right now, Daddy is busy filming in Toronto. So, it's up to us to have all the fun on the islands," I reassured her.

"I already miss him."

"I know, sweetheart, so do I," I said, pulling her close and tucking her head into my chest.

After what felt like an eternity, we finally entered a gated community filled with magnificent houses, manicured lawns, and towering gates.

"Wow! They look like mini castles!" Samantha exclaimed, her eyes wide with delight. "This is totally awesome!"

"Now you're starting to sound like an American!" I laughed.

As we approached my father's residence, its grandeur took my breath away. The impressive wrought-iron gates slowly opened, unveiling a beautifully manicured garden adorned with lush greenery and vibrant flowers along the driveway. Tall trees swayed gently in the breeze, casting dappled shadows on the cobblestone path. Security personnel, accompanied by large dogs, stood guard at the entrance. A line of uniformed servants greeted us as soon as we parked the vehicle.

"Mummy, it feels like we're on the set of Downton Abbey," Samantha giggled.

The mansion was a stunning example of classical architecture, featuring white marble columns and intricate stone carvings adorning its facade. As we stepped through the ornate double doors, I was struck by the luxury of the interior. Just then, my phone rang — it was

Richard.

"How's my lovely wife?" he greeted me warmly.

"We just landed, and your daughter is quite amazed by her new surroundings," I replied, stepping into the entrance hall that boasted a sweeping marble staircase with a glittering crystal chandelier hanging from the high ceiling. Fine art adorned the walls, each piece meticulously curated and beautifully displayed. The polished marble floors reflected the warm light, creating an inviting atmosphere.

To one side of the entrance hall, a spacious living room showcased plush seating arrangements and floor-to-ceiling windows that offered stunning views of the garden. On the other side, the elegant dining room was set for a formal dinner, complete with gleaming silverware and fine china.

"Stay tuned for the next episode of 'Mummy is Way Richer Than Daddy'," Richard quipped in his most dramatic, deflated voice. We both erupted into laughter.

"So, are you joining us soon?" I queried.

"I'm not certain yet, darling. I'll give it a go, I promise. I can't wait to see my beautiful wife in her scanty swimwear on the island," he ribbed.

"You'd better make it here, or you'll regret it," I threatened playfully.

"Is that a threat, Mrs. Collins?" he asked, amusement lacing his voice.

"I believe it is," I retorted. Richard let out a chuckle on the other end of the line.

"That means I'll have to nail our filming scene in one take."

"I miss you," my voice conveying longing.

"I know, darling. I miss you too, more than you can imagine," his voice echoed my sentiment. I knew he was in the midst of work as someone called his name in the background. "Alright, I must get back to work. I'll ring you and Sam before bedtime. Enjoy yourselves."

"I love you," I said gently.

"I love you, darling." And with that, our call concluded.

I held the phone close to my chest, reluctant to relinquish the feeling of Richard's presence, even if it was just through a phone call. Suddenly, my dad wrapped his arm around my shoulder. "Was that Richard?"

"Yes, and I already miss him," I admitted.

"Don't worry. As soon as he's done with his filming, I'll have the jet pick him up," he said, planting a kiss on my forehead.

"Was that Daddy?" Samantha bounced back to us excitedly and grasped my dad's hand. "That's why I don't want to have a boyfriend or get married, ever! Mummy is always sad when Daddy isn't around."

"Then don't get married, you can just help Grandpa run one of the businesses," Dad suggested, clearly enjoying her company.

"See, Mummy, I won't have to clean the loos when I grow up," she declared confidently.

"As long as you finish school — that's non-negotiable, young lady!" I asserted.

"Here we go again!" She rolled her eyes and ventured further into the house. Following her lead, we discovered a state-of-the-art kitchen, a cozy library brimming with leather-bound books, and a luxurious home theater. Each room was impeccably designed and furnished, showcasing my father's exquisite taste and attention to detail.

On the inaugural day of my acquaintance with the nerve center of Ortega Holdings, I opted for a sophisticated ensemble — navy blue pinstripe pants from Dior, coupled with a tailored coat, all layered over a luxurious creme silk blouse. The three-inch nude heels from Manolo

Blahnik added a hint of elegance to my stature, accentuating my height of five feet and seven inches.

"Mummy, could you assist me with the zipper on my dress?" Samantha's voice drew my attention toward her. She looked adorable in the beige and black horizontal striped dress we had recently picked up from Zara. Her tiny feet were snug in her nude ballet shoes. Our color palettes mirrored each other, creating an unplanned yet delightful mother-daughter duo.

"You're quite the fashionista, aren't you? How about we add a touch of elegance with mummy's pearl earrings?" I proposed. Upon seeing her enthusiastic nod and radiant smile, I proceeded to retrieve the delicate drop earrings from my drawer. As I gently fastened them onto Samantha, I couldn't help but admire her in the mirror. "There, perfection personified. You look exactly like your daddy," I commented, smiling at her reflection.

"But, Mummy, I want to look like you," Samantha replied, wrapping her arms around me. Her words tugged at my heartstrings, causing a rush of warmth to spread through me. I returned her affectionate hug.

"Well, my love, you might bear a striking resemblance to your father, but there's no denying that you've inherited my style and demeanor. Isn't that a deadly combination?" I quipped, eliciting peals of laughter from both of us. Regaining my composure, I added, "Let's get going now. It's time to meet the people who manage the Ortega Holdings, a legacy which you and your siblings are destined to inherit someday."

Hand in hand, we exited my room, heading towards the living room, where my father awaited our arrival.

The Philippine business center sprawled out before me, an intricate canvas of towering skyscrapers reaching toward the cerulean sky. The city pulsed with life, the symphony of bustling traffic and pedestrian chatter a testament to its vibrant heart. Our destination was the 35th floor of the Ayala Tower, a prestigious emblem of corporate superiority nestled in the heart of Makati.

* * *

Upon entering the conference room, we were met by a stark contrast to the colorful cityscape outside. The room was a harmonious blend of sleek lines and minimalist design aesthetics. Floor-to-ceiling windows offered a commanding view of the metropolis, and a long mahogany table gleamed under the soft, white glow of recessed lighting. Plush leather chairs, representatives of luxury and comfort, lined the table's length.

As we entered, the room was already beginning to brim with various executives, each exuding an aura of quiet confidence. Their sharp suits spoke volumes about their professional demeanor. The air buzzed with hushed conversations, punctuated by the occasional clink of coffee cups meeting the glass tabletop, as they exchanged pleasantries and discussed business strategies.

My father sat at the head of the table, his presence formidable and commanding. His dark eyes scanned the room, each gaze seemingly piercing through every individual present. He was a man of few words, but when he spoke, it was with an authority that commanded attention.

Rising from his chair, he instantly silenced the room. "Thank you all for being here," he began, his voice firm yet warm. "Today, I want to introduce a very important person to this organization." I was seated to his right, while Samantha was accommodated with a small table and chair behind me. Yumi, as always, was right by my side, dressed in her signature stylish business suit. "Ladies and gentlemen, please welcome the newest board member and executive committee member, our Executive Vice President Esperanza Ortega-Collins. She is currently spearheading the operations of our newly established publishing firm in New York, which has shown remarkable growth in a short period. I am confident that she will bring fresh ideas to the table." Hearing my legal name and my new executive title felt strange; I was more accustomed to being addressed as Hope Williams back in New York.

I rose from my seat, projecting confidence. "It's an honor to meet all of you. I look forward to learning from each of you and contributing to the growth of Ortega businesses." To my surprise, each executive stood up, approaching me one by one to shake my hand and introduce themselves.

* * *

One gentleman, likely in his late thirties or early forties, stood out. His well-maintained, athletic physique accentuated his Asian-American features. His well-sculpted body and broad shoulders were evident beneath his sharp charcoal gray suit. His face was marked by intelligent, well-defined features — a high forehead, strong jawline, and chiseled cheekbones framed by deep brown eyes. His short, dark brown hair was styled in a sleek, modern fashion, adding to his polished image.

"Finally, we meet in person. Your father has spoken highly of you. I'm Michael Yang, CEO of Ortega Corp in Singapore," he said, extending a firm handshake. He could easily pass for a movie star, too.

"The pleasure is all mine, Michael," I replied.

Suddenly, Samantha interjected, "I'm Samantha Ortega-Collins, Richard and Hope Collins' daughter," she extended her hand toward him. I couldn't help but smile at her protective stance.

"Delighted to meet the young heiress of Ortega's Holdings," Michael said warmly, shaking Samantha's hand. He glanced between us, adding, "You have a wonderful and smart daughter, Hope."

"Because my Dad is one of the most handsome and hottest celebrities in Hollywood and Britain. You know Richard Collins, I suppose?" Samantha quipped, her tone laced with a blend of pride and cheekiness that sent another wave of laughter around the table. Her innocent boast about her father was both endearing and hilarious.

"Of course, I've watched some of his movies," Michael responded, a smile playing on his lips as he directed his gaze toward me.

Yumi chimed in, "She may look like Richard, but she's starting to sound more like you, Hope."

"I've noticed that too," I laughed. "But her wit? That's all Richard."

"Will he be joining you on this trip?" Yumi asked.

* * *

"I hope so. He's filming in Toronto but will try to meet us here," I responded.

Before our conversation could continue, the remaining executives approached me, eager to introduce themselves. I made a mental note to remember their names and faces, marking the start of this new chapter in my career.

The room hummed with anticipation as the meeting commenced post-introductions. Ideas began to ricochet across the table like well-aimed arrows, each carrying the weight of potential success or failure. Strategies were unfurled, akin to intricate maps leading to uncharted territories, and critical decisions were made with a calm deliberation that spoke volumes about the experience of those present.

Despite the high stakes, the atmosphere was surprisingly pleasant, marked by an undercurrent of mutual respect. This was a testament to my father's influence and the professional culture he had nurtured over the years. The scale and complexity of the discussions were overwhelming, and I found myself scrambling to keep up, my pen dancing across my notepad in an attempt to capture the essence of the conversation.

Most of the topics discussed were alien to me, their nuances lost in the labyrinth of corporate jargon. Sensing my struggle, my father shot me a reassuring smile, his eyes reflecting a promise that gaps in my understanding would be bridged over time. I returned his smile gratefully, taking a moment to glance at Samantha.

Seated not far from the main conference table, she was engrossed in an iPad, her small fingers deftly navigating the screen. Likely, one of the executive assistants had provided it to keep her occupied while the adults delved into the business world. Despite her young age, she seemed to understand the importance of the occasion and was content to amuse herself quietly.

As the meeting drew to a close, we collectively exhaled, the tension in the room dissipating. We exited the conference room, leaving behind a tableau of coffee-stained cups and scribbled notepads. Our next destination was a luncheon hosted at the hotel adjacent to the Ayala

Tower.

Upon stepping into the dining area, a familiar figure caught my eye —
Michael Yang was already there, evidently awaiting our arrival. His
presence was unexpected, yet it hinted at the prospect of intriguing
discourse over lunch.

"What's he doing here? Can't he find someone else to hobnob with?"
Samantha blurted out, her young face scrunching up in visible
annoyance. I couldn't help but chuckle at her candid protest.

"He's one of Grandpa's top brass," my father explained, his eyes
gleaming with amusement. "He's simply trying to make a good
impression and curry favor with you and your mummy."

"I just don't fancy the way he ogles Mummy," Samantha confessed, her
tone grave.

Yumi burst into laughter next to me, her eyes sparkling with joy. "Now
it all makes sense why Richard insisted you bring her along
everywhere!"

I turned to Samantha, an eyebrow raised in mock suspicion.
"Sweetheart, did you make a pact with Daddy behind my back?"

"Absolutely not," she responded, a mischievous twinkle in her eyes.
"But he did instruct me to keep a watchful eye on you... and certain
individuals, you know, just as a precaution..."

Her statement was met with laughter as we all took our seats at the
table, the atmosphere lightened by Samantha's endearing
protectiveness.

———

I was hunched over my bed, the soft glow of the bedside lamp
illuminating the pile of papers strewn around me. The manuscript I
had been laboring over for weeks lay open, its pages filled with red
marks and scribbles. Beside it, a stack of papers awaited my approval,
silent evidence of the never-ending responsibilities that came with my

position.

My fingers traced the words on the page, my eyes heavy with sleep. The silk pajamas I wore did little to ward off the chill seeping in from the window, but I had no mind to deal with it.

The room in which I found myself was an ostentatious display of luxury. A king-size canopy bed draped in plush velvet took center stage, flanked by ornate Victorian furniture. A grand chandelier hung from the ceiling, its crystal droplets casting a kaleidoscope of shimmering patterns across the room. An enormous mahogany table stood on one side, crowned with an antique lamp. The extravagance was a stark contrast to the simplicity of my former New York apartment. Despite having spent many years alone, I often wondered why my father built such a grand house. Could he have foreseen that I would someday be part of his life?

Suddenly, the door creaked open, and in trotted Samantha. Her hair was a tousled mess, and she clutched a well-worn teddy bear we managed to bring with us in her small hands. Still dressed in her star-and-moon adorned pajamas, her wide eyes surveyed the room before settling on me.

"Mummy," she whispered, her voice barely audible as she hopped onto the bed, scattering papers in her path.

"What is it, sweetheart?" I asked her, setting my pen aside and brushing a stray hair from her face as she nestled into my lap.

"I can't sleep," she confessed, her small fingers toying with the buttons on my pajama top. "I miss Daddy."

I heaved a sigh, my gaze flickering between the manuscript, the impending deadlines, and the mounting pile of responsibilities. Yet, as I gazed down at Samantha, her eyes brimming with innocence and longing, I knew there was only one choice to make.

"I miss him too, sweetheart," I replied, pulling her closer.

Her fingers began to play with my Tiffany bracelets. "Mummy, you never take these off," she observed.

"Each charm is a chapter of your father's and my love story," I explained. "They represent the four seasons we experienced together — the leaf, snowflake, flower, and sun. In between those seasons are symbols of the places we traveled and created beautiful memories," I elaborated, showing her each charm.

"And the angel, Mummy?" She asked, touching the golden angel charm.

My voice faltered slightly. It was still a painful topic, but this innocent child beside me deserved to know. "This is Little Bean, your little brother. But he was taken away from us before he could join us in this world. Your daddy added him to our love story so he would never be forgotten," I said.

"Did you hate Henry because of what his mum did to you and Little Bean?" Samantha asked innocently, surprising me with her knowledge.

"Where'd you hear that, sweetheart?" I asked, curious about her source.

"I read it on the Internet. Remember the twins I befriended back home? They told me about how you were kidnapped and almost killed by Henry's mum. Then we looked it up online. I saw photos of Daddy looking really angry. Then I read about Henry's mum being in prison," she shared seriously. When she noticed the tears that fell on my cheeks, she tenderly wiped them away. "She's a bad person, Mummy."

"She is a horrible person. But Henry is one of the kindest people I've ever met. So, sweetheart, I don't hate Henry. You and he are my family, and I love you both unconditionally," I reassured her, planting a kiss on her forehead.

"I love you, too, Mummy. You're even nicer than my own mummy. She was always sick and often mad at me."

"Don't say that, sweetheart. She probably had a lot of troubles to deal with," I consoled her.

* * *

"I know. We were so poor. My clothes were mostly hand-me-downs, and they didn't fit me. My shoes were always either too big or too small, both uncomfortable. We also lived in a tiny house with a small Telly," she narrated innocently.

I hugged her tighter, "Oh, sweetheart! Your Daddy would have done everything to prevent that if he knew about you sooner."

"I know. He told me the same thing," she murmured sadly.

"Did you know that I was poor, too, before your daddy met me?" I asked her, adding, "That makes two of us!" Our giggles lightened the mood in the room.

"Mummy, will you still love me even when you and Daddy have your new babies?"

"Of course, sweetheart! You and Henry are part of this family. You are my daughter, legally. In the eyes of the law, I am your mummy, whether you like it or not. You will always have an equal standing with your future siblings." With that, we embraced each other, and I gently rocked her in my arms.

At that moment, amidst the luxury of the room and the weight of my work, I found a sliver of peace. Here was a love that was pure and unconditional, a responsibility that brought joy rather than stress. Samantha was not just my adopted daughter but my beacon of hope in a world that often felt too heavy. And as her eyelids slowly drooped, her breath evening out in the rhythm of sleep, I knew that whatever challenges lay ahead, I would face them head-on. For her.

As Samantha nestled in my arms, her soft breaths a lullaby against the silence of our room, my phone illuminated with the familiar Facetime ring. I glanced at the screen and saw Richard's name flashing. Gently cradling Samantha, I swiped the green button on my iPhone.

Richard's face filled the screen, still adorned in his film costume, props scattered haphazardly in the background.

* * *

"I see she's found comfort in your arms," Richard observed, a soft smile playing on his lips.

"Well, she misses you. We both do. We're trying to ease each other's loneliness," I admitted, the words heavy in the quiet room.

His eyes softened at my confession. "I miss you too. And I'd give anything to be in that bed with you."

"So, when are you joining us?" I asked, trying to keep my voice steady.

"Anytime soon, darling," he promised. A playful glint appeared in his eyes as he added, "So, how were your meetings today? I heard there's a new guy in town."

I rolled my eyes at his jest. "Oh, I see. Your little informer has been reporting back to you. Did you strike a deal with her? She's been overly protective, guarding me like a hawk!" I said, my laughter echoing in the room.

"No deal was struck, but I'm glad she's been keeping an eye out. Protecting her father's territory," he replied, his eyes twinkling with mirth despite his evident fatigue.

"There's nothing to protect in the first place, Mr. Collins. My heart belongs to you. Only you," I affirmed, my voice tinged with sincerity.

"I know, darling," he responded, his gaze intense. "But it's unsettling when someone looks at you like I do."

I pouted at his admission. "Now you know how I feel every time I watch you kissing another woman the way you kissed me on-screen."

"I've never kissed anyone, on-screen or off, the way I have kissed you, Mrs. Collins. Always remember that," he said, his voice warm with affection.

"I just miss you, Richard. I want you here with us. This separation is driving me insane!" I confessed, the tears welling up in my eyes and threatening to spill.

* * *

Before Richard could respond, a voice from off-screen interrupted our intimate conversation. "I'm sorry, darling," he apologized, his eyes mirroring my torment. "They need me on set. I promise I'll be back before you know it."

As he spoke, he reached out, his fingers tracing the contours of the screen as though he were caressing my face. It was a gesture so familiar, so intimate, that I could almost feel his touch for a moment.

With those final words hanging heavy between us, the call ended. The vibrant image of Richard dissolved into blackness, leaving me with only the echo of his voice and the weight of our shared longing.

20

The morning sun had barely risen when Samantha's excited squeals echoed through our home. Today was the day of our tour in one of Dad's grand malls in Manila. The sheer scale and grandeur of the place were a tangible manifestation of my father's vision. It was almost overwhelming. As Samantha and I walked hand-in-hand through the labyrinth of shops and bustling food courts, my heart brimmed with pride and deep admiration for my father's extraordinary accomplishment.

The mall was alive with a myriad of sights and sounds. Families with playful children, groups of boisterous teenagers, love-struck couples, and weary office workers seeking a respite from their demanding schedules. The air was thick with the hum of animated conversations, punctuated by peals of laughter and underscored by the gentle melodies drifting from the boutiques. The mall was a vibrant microcosm of life itself, pulsating with an irresistible energy and vitality.

Our entourage, an eclectic mix of vigilant bodyguards and dedicated executives from my father's company, shadowed us discreetly. Their eyes were perpetually scanning the crowd, their hands ever ready to lend assistance.

"Samantha," I began, stooping slightly to meet her enthusiastic gaze, "did you know this is the biggest mall in Southeast Asia?"

Her eyes ballooned in surprise. "Really, Mum? Even bigger than the one in Singapore?"

I nodded, a fond smile tugging at my lips as I recalled our last holiday. "Yes, sweetheart. And it's all thanks to your grandpa Oliver. This is his masterwork."

Samantha's innocent gaze swept across the mall, taking in the towering escalators, the ornate fountains gurgling cheerfully, and the sea of people flowing around us. "Wow," she breathed, visibly awestruck. "Grandpa did all this?"

"Yes, he did," I affirmed, a surge of pride welling up within me. "His dream was to create a place that would spread joy, a place where people could shop, eat, and create beautiful memories."

Upon hearing this, Samantha wriggled free from my hand and darted towards my father, who was observing us from a short distance away. "Grandpa!" she cried out, her voice ricocheting off the mall's high ceilings. Oliver spun around, his face splitting into a broad smile as he watched Samantha rushing towards him.

She took his hand and looked up at him, her eyes sparkling with unadulterated admiration. "Grandpa, this place is fantastic!"

Oliver's eyes twinkled as he glanced at Samantha, then at me. "Thank you, my dear," he responded, his voice laced with pride and affection. "Your words mean the world to me."

Samantha turned to me, her eyes gleaming with anticipation. "Mum, can we go shopping now?"

Before I could respond, Dad interjected, "Of course, you two can shop to your heart's content. Everything will be on Grandpa's tab." His eyes twinkled mischievously as he spoke.

"Grandpa, you're the best!" Samantha shrieked, her laughter echoing through the mall, adding to its symphony of sounds.

21

As the sun began to set, its warm, orange glow casting long shadows on the bustling streets of Singapore, Samantha and I found ourselves immersed in the vibrant cityscape. The stark contrast between the tropical heat and the biting cold of our home winters was not lost on us. This diverse city, pulsating with life and culture, had become our temporary playground.

Skyscrapers, towering high above us, seemed to reach out for the azure skies, their glassy facades shimmering in the golden sundown. The streets were a hive of activity, buzzing with individuals, each engrossed in their own worlds, contributing to the symphony of city life. The tantalizing aroma of exotic spices floated through the air, drawing us towards the bustling hawker stalls.

"Mum, d'you reckon we could give the food stalls a whirl tonight?" Samantha asked, her voice slicing through the noise of the city.

"Sweetheart, how about we save that for tomorrow? We're off to enjoy the night safari tonight," I responded.

"Yipee!" Samantha's pure and infectious laughter rang out, mirroring my joy.

The sun exited as soon as we freshened up and changed into more comfortable clothes. The moon paraded its beauty, accompanied by twinkling stars. It was a beautiful night.

* * *

Samantha's eyes widened in awe as we navigated the nocturnal jungle, her tiny hand gripping mine tightly as the mini wagon trundled through the various animal exhibits. Chen and Arthur were seated behind us, sharing our excitement. Samantha was captivated by the animal kingdom, particularly enamored by the regal lions and cheeky monkeys.

"Mum, check out the little cub. She's clinging onto her mama," she observed.

"And how do you know it's a girl cub?" I asked, amused by her certainty.

"Well, it's just like us, isn't it? Look, her daddy's nowhere to be seen," she responded innocently.

"Remember, your daddy will join us soon," I reassured her.

"He'd love this, wouldn't he? Can we come back when Daddy's not so swamped with work?"

"Absolutely, sweetheart," I said, kissing her head and gesturing towards another lioness and her cubs. Her laughter filled the night, blending harmoniously with the chorus of animal calls. It was a sound that tugged at my heartstrings.

After our exhilarating tour, we indulged in burgers that Samantha found far more appealing than the American variety. Although I usually monitored her sugar intake closely, tonight I decided to let loose, allowing her unlimited soda and ice cream.

Unsurprisingly, she fell asleep in my arms on the way back to the hotel. I didn't have the heart to wake her. Instead, I gently changed her into her cozy pajamas and tucked her into our shared bed, letting her dreams carry her through the night.

———

The luncheon meeting with the Singapore office concluded on a positive note, leaving Samantha and me feeling upbeat. We decided to seize the day and immerse ourselves in some retail therapy. Just the two of us, a mother-daughter duo, accompanied by our security detail, Chen and Arthur. I requested them to maintain a discreet distance; I wanted this to feel like an ordinary shopping day with Sam, as ordinary as it could be in our extraordinary lives.

Located in the heart of Singapore's iconic Marina Bay Sands complex, The Shoppes at Marina Bay Sands was more than just a shopping mall - it was a world-class destination for luxury and elegance. Covering over 800,000 square feet of high-end retail space, this flagship mall offered a unique blend of international luxury brands, emerging labels, and concept stores.

As you step inside The Shoppes, you will be transported into a realm of opulence and grandeur. The architecture was a stunning blend of modern and classic design, with high ceilings, wide-open spaces, and an abundance of natural light filtering through the glass roof. But what truly sets The Shoppes apart is its remarkable water feature.

Right in the heart of the mall was a stunning indoor water pool, proof of the mall's commitment to offering a unique shopping experience. This wasn't just any water feature; it was a marvel of engineering and design. The pool was beautifully illuminated, its shimmering waters reflecting the surrounding boutiques' lights, creating a mesmerizing spectacle that enchants visitors.

The sight of the water pool, combined with the soft sound of water gently lapping against the sides, added a serene and tranquil ambiance to the otherwise bustling mall. It was an oasis of calm amidst the shopping frenzy, providing shoppers with a moment of respite as they navigate their way through the vast selection of luxury fashion, watch, and jewelry brands.

"Mummy, look at that dress!" Samantha exclaimed, her finger pointing towards a Chanel store's display. Her eyes shone brightly, reflecting the twinkling lights that adorned the store's entrance. We made our way inside, the boutique's sleek modern aesthetics providing a stark contrast to the lively street outside.

The store was a veritable paradise for any fashion enthusiast, brimming with an endless selection of clothing, accessories, and footwear. Racks of meticulously arranged clothes in a rainbow of colors and textures beckoned invitingly, while glass shelves showcased a dazzling array of accessories.

"Let's give Daddy's credit card a workout!" I teased, eliciting giggles from Samantha.

Samantha was instantly drawn to a stunning dress, its vibrant teal color reminiscent of tropical seas. She held it against herself, twirling before the mirror. "What do you think?" she asked, her face glowing with anticipation.

"You look absolutely stunning, sweetheart," I responded, my heart swelling with pride. Watching her morph into a young lady was a bittersweet mix of joy and nostalgia. Deciding to purchase the dress, we moved on to other stores —each offering their unique blend of luxury and style.

Samantha was a whirlwind of energy, trying on outfits with an infectious glee. Her laughter echoed through every store, her enthusiasm adding a dash of extra sparkle to our day. I found myself drawn to a pair of sleek Louboutin heels and a Hermès bag from separate stores. At first, I hesitated at the price tags attached to these luxury brands. But their exquisite craftsmanship and timeless elegance were too alluring to resist.

As we moved from one store to another, my mind wandered. I found myself reflecting on how far I'd come. From being a young scriptwriter grappling with life's curveballs to an executive vice president, wife, and mother, each role shaped and transformed me.

When we passed Tiffany & Co., Samantha darted into the store, her eyes sparkling with curiosity. I followed her in and found her captivated by a delicate silver necklace adorned with an angel pendant, strikingly similar to the charm on my bracelet.

* * *

"Do you like it?" I asked her.

Her nod was enthusiastic, her grin radiant. Sensing her interest, the sales assistant encouraged her to try it on. "Mum, this is proper lovely," she whispered, her British lilt more pronounced in her excitement.

"And it suits you because you're beautiful, sweetheart," I responded, gesturing to the salesperson that we would take it.

Samantha wrapped her arms around me as the salesperson delicately packaged the necklace. "Thank you, Mummy," she said, her face glowing with happiness.

"You're welcome, sweetheart," I said, kissing her forehead. Looking at her joy-filled face, I realized these weren't just material possessions. They were physical reminders of a day filled with shared joy and deepened bonds. As we stepped back onto the bustling streets of Singapore, our hands were laden with shopping bags.

Before we headed back to our hotel, we found ourselves seated at a hawker's place, the aroma of local cuisine tantalizing our senses. Samantha's face lit up as she took her first bite of Hainanese chicken rice. Her lips curled into a satisfied smile, her taste buds reveling in the explosion of flavors.

Each spoonful was a journey, a dance of sweet, salty, spicy, and sour. Much like the city, the food was a melting pot of cultures, each dish telling a story of its own. It wasn't just about satiating our hunger but about experiencing a part of Singapore's soul. Every bite and moment was a testament to our adventure, an experience that would be etched in our hearts forever.

Witnessing Samantha's joy, her unfiltered excitement, was a heartwarming sight. These moments made the trip worthwhile, and we bonded over shared experiences, laughter, food, and stories of the city we explored together.

22

As the helicopter's blades began to whir, a surge of adrenaline pulsed through my veins. The cityscape, once sprawling and vibrant beneath us, slowly morphed into a seemingly infinite canvas of azure. Samantha clung tightly to my arm, her face pressed against the cool glass of the window in childlike wonder. This was her first time traveling aboard a chopper.

"Mummy, it feels like we've been swept up into a movie!" she squealed, her eyes dancing with the moment's thrill. A hearty laugh bubbled up from my chest as I tightened my hold around her.

"Indeed, sweetheart, it's our very own high-flying adventure," I shouted back, our words exchanged through the static hum of the headsets. My father's face, etched with amusement and joy, mirrored our elation. He reveled in seeing Samantha and me so engrossed in this weekend's escapade.

Our journey to Balesin Island was punctuated by panoramas that stole your breath away. This tropical island was located off the eastern coast of Luzon, one of the islands in the Philippines. It was situated in Lamon Bay and is approximately 60 nautical miles east of Manila. The vast cerulean ocean sprawled out beneath us, dotted intermittently by verdant islands. As our destination drew closer, the island's beauty unfurled like a flower at dawn. The coastline, a brilliant white ribbon, encased the lush green heart of the island. The sun's rays danced upon the turquoise waters, creating a shimmering spectacle. Quaint, rustic huts peppered the shoreline, adding to the charm.

* * *

Samantha's gasp of awe echoed my own sentiments. "It's even more dazzling than the pictures, Grandpa!"

Her enthusiasm was contagious, coaxing a grin out of my father. "Indeed, it is. And you're going to relish the food and water sports. Plus, it's an incredibly private getaway."

A whirlwind of emotions swept over me. Excitement, undoubtedly, at the prospect of a luxury island weekend, but there was also a pang of loneliness, a void echoing with Richard's absence. After our conversation the previous night, he had gone radio silent. His phone suddenly became unreachable. A part of me yearned to abandon my work, to follow Richard to the ends of the earth. But I had a responsibility toward Samantha. I couldn't simply abandon her.

As the helicopter descended and a cloud of dust swirled around us, I took a deep, steadying breath. I decided to make the most of this trip. Tonight, I'd attempt to reach Richard again. As if on cue, Michael emerged to welcome us as we disembarked from the chopper. His attire, a crisp white shirt paired with khaki shorts, accentuated his athletic physique.

"Welcome to the island!" he ushered us out, extending a hand to assist me.

"And here you are again," Samantha noted, her tone laced with annoyance despite the polite smile she offered.

"I'm going to be your personal tour guide. Isn't that exciting?" He laughed off Samantha's jibe.

Choosing to ignore him this time, Samantha entwined her fingers with mine. I shot Michael an apologetic smile, which he returned, signaling his understanding.

"Paradise," I whispered to myself, my eyes drinking in the beauty of the private island we had all to ourselves. The presence of Dad's security detail, including Arthur, Chen, and Jeffrey, was a subtle reminder that even in paradise, safety was paramount. Their primary responsibility was to ensure the protection of Samantha and me.

A Singaporean chef, along with his team, had been personally selected to cater to our every culinary whim. As we disembarked from the helicopter, a poised Asian waitress approached me, a chilled Mimosa cradled in her hands. Simultaneously, other staff members efficiently managed our luggage, their movements swift and precise.

Clad in a printed blouse and cut-off jeans, I could already feel the heat and was looking forward to changing into my swimwear and surrendering myself to the inviting water.

The accommodations on Balesin Island were nothing short of exquisite. Stepping into our assigned villa was like entering another world — an open design concept that was both luxurious and immersive. Large windows and doors filled the space with natural light, revealing breathtaking views of the surrounding landscape. The grand structure offered an unrivaled view of the sunset, painting the sky with hues of gold and crimson.

"Ma'am, this will be your suite," a staff member informed us, her voice soft yet professional. "Miss Samantha's room will be just across yours." She gestured towards the room tastefully furnished with a blend of traditional and modern aesthetics. A king bed, plush and inviting, sat in the center of the room, promising a night of restful sleep.

I took a quick peek into Samantha's room, a smaller version of mine but no less luxurious. It was equipped with modern amenities, including air conditioning and a large flat-screen TV, albeit without a minibar. The bathroom was equally extravagant, complete with premium toiletries, a large bathtub, and a separate shower area.

Additional staff arrived with our luggage, swiftly unpacking and organizing our belongings with practiced efficiency.

"Mummy, look! I have my own suite!" Samantha's voice echoed through the room. Her excitement was unmistakable as she bounced on the plush bed. "Did you know this island even has its own spa house?"

* * *

"Well, they do," I replied. "So you don't want to sleep in my bedroom?" I feigned shock, placing a hand over my heart.

"No, mummy. You'll be alright. I want to experience this luxury on my own!" She retorted, her eyes gleaming with mischief.

"You, traitor!" I teased, unable to suppress a smile at her audacity. "Don't forget your swimwear and sunscreen," I reminded her, shaking my finger playfully.

I retreated to my suite, slipping into a vibrant yellow two-piece bikini. When I bumped into Samantha in the hallway, I couldn't help but burst into giggles. She was clad in a yellow one-piece suit that made her look like a miniature version of me. Hand in hand, we strolled towards the beach, our laughter mingling with the rhythmic lullaby of the waves.

"Let's get some sunscreen on you," I said, applying the lotion on her delicate skin. Once I was satisfied she was adequately protected, I began to apply sunscreen on myself.

"Do you need help with your back?" The voice belonged to Michael, donned in a short blue board, surfboard tucked under his arm.

"No, thank you, Michael. Samantha would love to help," I declined politely, handing the tube to Samantha. Her small hands worked diligently, spreading the sunscreen luxuriously across my back.

"Mummy, may I go into the water now?" Samantha asked, her eyes sparkling with anticipation. Ever vigilant, Jeffrey was already by her side, ready to accompany her.

"Just stay where I can see you," I instructed, settling comfortably onto the recliner. I closed my eyes, surrendering to the warm embrace of the sun, the sounds of the ocean serving as the perfect soundtrack to this island getaway.

A soft lull had settled over me, perhaps a brief lapse into sleep when the distant hum of a helicopter snapped me back to reality. I lifted my sunglasses and squinted against the bright sunlight, scanning the horizon for the new arrival. It was likely another guest of my father's.

Engrossed in her sandcastle construction near the shore, Samantha seemed oblivious to the approaching aircraft.

As I was about to roll over onto my stomach, a familiar figure caught my eye—a tall, blond man in a light blue T-shirt. "Could that be Henry?" I found myself wondering. And sure enough, trailing behind him was a figure I knew all too well—Richard!

I sprang up from my recliner, calling out for Samantha. She immediately left her sandcastle masterpiece and sprinted towards me. Hand-in-hand, we made a beeline for the landing pad, where my father and Michael were already preparing to welcome our surprise visitors.

Upon reaching our destination and looking at Richard, I couldn't contain my excitement. I launched myself into his arms. He quickly caught me, his arms enveloping me possessively before pulling me into a passionate embrace.

"Hello, beautiful," he greeted, his voice breathless as we finally parted. Unable to resist, I leaned in to steal another kiss. Richard deepened the kiss this time, whispering, "Oh God, I missed you," between stolen breaths.

"Oh, how I've missed you," I murmured as I finally pulled away. His response was a warm, affectionate chuckle.

"I've missed you more, darling. The past few days were driving me crazy," he replied, his voice a soothing balm to my longing heart. He planted a lingering kiss on my forehead, making my heart flutter.

"Daddy!" Samantha's delighted squeal cut through the air, causing laughter to ripple through the small crowd.

"And how are you, my beautiful little one?" Richard asked, scooping Samantha into his arms. "I missed you too, sweetheart," he murmured as she buried her face into his shoulder.

Turning to Henry, I was met with a warm embrace and a kiss on the cheek. "Hello, Mommy dearest," he greeted.

"Oh, you're here. I've missed you!" I exclaimed.

"Hope, I'd like you to meet Agnes. She's a colleague from the hospital," Henry introduced, gesturing towards a beautiful blond girl with striking green eyes.

"Welcome to the island, Agnes. It's lovely to meet you," I said warmly, kissing her cheek. "And this is our daughter, Samantha," I introduced.

"Thank you for having me," Agnes replied shyly, her cheeks flushing a delicate pink.

Ever the lively child, Samantha jumped from Richard's hold and latched onto Henry, hugging his waist tightly.

Henry laughed and lifted her into his arms. "Well, hello there, princess! How's your vacation been?"

"It's been super!" Samantha chirped, her face lighting up with joy. "We made a huge sandcastle today!"

"Is that so?" Henry feigned surprise, his eyebrows shooting up. "I can't wait to see it."

While they continued their cheerful banter, I turned back to Richard. His comforting presence felt like home, making me forget about everything else.

"And what brings you guys here?" I asked, unable to keep the excitement from my voice.

Richard shot me a mischievous grin. "We thought we'd give you a little surprise."

"Let's all enjoy some refreshments and lunch," my father suggested, ushering everyone towards the villa with a welcoming smile.

The grains of sand beneath my feet felt like countless, tiny, warm kisses, each a delicate touch against the soles of my bare feet as I strolled along the coastline. The sun was bidding its daily farewell, its descent painting the evening sky with breathtaking hues of orange and pink. The salty sea breeze was a gentle caress on my face, carrying the scent of the vast ocean with it. My hand was entwined with Richard's, our fingers interlocking in a familiar grip, while Samantha, our little ray of sunshine, excitedly explored the beach.

We haven't been together for weeks. Richard was immersed in the filming of *The Getaway*. The absence had stretched us thin, the void tangible and hard to bear. But now, we were reunited. The joy and relief that filled my heart were overwhelming, washing over me like the waves lapping against the shore.

"Daddy, look!" Samantha's voice chimed in, her tone brimming with excitement as she sprinted toward us. Richard scooped her up, nestling her securely onto his shoulders. "Dolphins!" With wide-eyed awe, she pointed towards the horizon where the shapes of dolphins leaped playfully from the sea, their bodies shimmering under the setting sun. Her pure delight was contagious, prompting a warm smile across my face.

"Sam, isn't that a sight?" Richard responded, his voice echoing her wonder. He momentarily let go of my hand and hoisted Samantha up into his arms, both of them captivated by the spectacle unfolding before us.

Catching my gaze, Richard's eyes sparkled with unspoken joy. His voice was barely audible above the symphony of crashing waves. "I've missed all this," he murmured, a hint of longing seeping into his tone.

"And I, you," I confessed, resting my head against his shoulder. The familiar rhythmic thud of his heartbeat against my cheek provided a comforting melody, one that had always managed to quiet my worries and fears.

For a moment, we stood there, wrapped in each other's arms, with

Samantha squealing in delight at the sight of the dolphins, drinking in the tranquil scene. A calming peace washed over me, akin to being wrapped in a warm, cozy blanket on a cold winter's night. The anxieties and stress of the past few months seemed to dissolve, carried away by the receding tide beneath our feet.

"Dad, let's build a sandcastle!" Samantha's voice broke through our trance, her eyes sparkling with anticipation.

Richard's chuckle was deep and hearty — the sound of a pleasant rumble in his chest. He set Samantha down, and they dropped to their knees in the sand together. "Alright," he agreed, scooping up a handful of sand, "Let's see who can construct the most magnificent one."

As they commenced their friendly sandcastle challenge, I lowered myself onto the warm sand, my eyes taking in the heartwarming scene before me. Watching Richard and Samantha together, their laughter echoing across the beach and their playful teasing filling the air, a deep sense of contentment washed over me. It was a feeling that had been absent for far too long, one that was welcome in its return.

Amidst the grains of sand and the setting sun, a realization blossomed within me. These fleeting moments of togetherness, these precious snippets of time shared with my loved ones, were what indeed held value. They were the threads that wove our lives together, making a beautiful tapestry regardless of the physical miles that might separate us. Our love for each other was not merely a bridge spanning any distance but a powerful bond that transcended space and time.

The island was undoubtedly breathtaking, its beauty beyond words. However, it was the presence of Richard and Samantha that breathed life into it, their laughter and joy infusing the surroundings with a magic that was uniquely ours. As the sun made its final bow below the horizon, casting elongated shadows on the sand, I etched this moment deep within my heart, a memory to be cherished forever.

As the sun descended, casting a golden hue over everything, I turned to look at Richard. The fading sunlight danced in his blue-grey eyes, illuminating them with an ethereal glow. They shimmered like twin sapphires, holding an entire ocean of emotions within their depths —

love, joy, and a dash of that boyish mischief that had first ensnared my heart.

His physique, bronzed from days under the tropical sun, was only covered by a pair of blue board shorts. The shorts emphasized his well-toned legs, a testament to the countless hours he spent in the gym preparing for his movie roles. His broad shoulders and muscular arms were silhouetted against the setting sun, creating an image that was as mesmerizing as any masterpiece in a museum.

His laughter echoed around us, a sound that was so rich and full of life, it was music to my ears. Every time he laughed, his eyes would crinkle at the corners, and his perfect white teeth would flash in a smile that could light up even the darkest corners of my heart.

Watching him, I felt a wave of affection wash over me. His happiness was infectious, his presence comforting. His laughter, his smile, and his very being melted my heart in a way nothing else could. He was not just my husband but also my best friend, partner, and anchor. And at that moment, with the sunset painting the sky in shades of orange and pink, I knew there was no place I'd rather be.

My thoughts were abruptly interrupted by Samantha's high-pitched voice, ringing out with childish innocence. "Mummy is looking at you like a girl in love!" She giggled, the sound bubbling over like a clear brook as if she'd stumbled upon the world's most amusing secret.

Richard swiveled his gaze towards me, his blue-grey eyes twinkling with an intensity that set off a cascade of butterflies in my stomach. The corners of his lips twitched upwards in a knowing smile, a silent acknowledgment of our daughter's candid observation.

"Is that so?" He played along, his voice laced with joy. "And how does a girl in love look at someone?"

Samantha cocked her head to the side and scrunched up her face, deep in thought. After a moment, she giggled again, "She looks like... like mummy! All smiley and dreamy."

Richard chuckled at her response, his laughter warm and infectious.

"Well, I guess Mummy must really be in love then," he teased, returning his attention to me. His hand reached out, gently tucking a wayward strand of hair behind my ear. The tender touch sent an electric shiver down my spine, proof of the depth of our connection.

Richard turned to look at me, his blue-grey eyes sparkling with a warmth that made my heart flutter. Slowly, he leaned in, his gaze never leaving mine. His breath mingled with mine, a soft whisper against my lips before they met in a kiss. It was a beautiful kiss — slow and tender at first, like a sweet promise whispered in the quiet. His lips were warm, tasting faintly of sea salt and the fruity cocktail we had earlier.

The world around us seemed to fade away as he deepened the kiss, his hands finding their way to my waist, pulling me closer. It was passionate but not hurried, each movement filled with a love that spoke volumes. His lips moved against mine in a rhythm that was as familiar as it was exciting, a dance we had perfected.

I wound my arms around his neck, lost in the intoxicating sensation of the kiss. His fingers traced gentle circles on my back, sending waves of pleasure coursing through me. I could feel my heart pounding in my chest, matching his own rhythm.

When we finally pulled apart, my breath came in short gasps, my mind a whirlwind of emotions. His smile was soft, his eyes filled with a tenderness that melted my heart all over again.

"That's precisely why I don't want a boyfriend. I don't want to feel sad. Mummy always looks sad when you're away, Daddy." Samantha voiced her thoughts, her attention focused on the mound of sand before her.

Gently tucking a few stray hairs behind Samantha's ear, Richard asked, "Did you try to cheer up Mummy when she was feeling down?"

"Of course, I did! We went shopping together and swiped your card quite a bit!" She giggled, her eyes sparkling with mischief. "But at night, she would just stare at her phone, waiting for your FaceTime call, I think."

* * *

A hearty chuckle escaped Richard at his daughter's candid revelation. He turned towards me, his gaze filled with affection. His thumb gently traced my lips in a tender caress.

"Hey, Sammydoo! Quit playing gooseberry with Dad and Hope," Henry's voice echoed as he returned from his surfing session with Agnes.

"You know, Henriquedoo, you should keep your nose out," Samantha retorted, shooting her older brother a sideways glance. Their unique nicknames for each other never failed to make me smile. "Can you teach me how to surf?" she asked Henry.

"Anything for our little princess," he replied, his tone affectionate as he settled beside me. Agnes followed suit, joining Samantha in her sandcastle adventure.

"Our little bird has been chirping, and apparently, you've caught someone's eye," Henry teased, earning a smirk from Richard.

"So she's not just snitching to your father, but to you as well," I rolled my eyes and laughed. "But honestly, I'm so smitten by the two handsome men in my life that I hardly notice anyone else, even those with good biceps," I quipped.

"Well, you may be oblivious, but evidently, he's got a massive crush on you. But I put an end to that the moment we landed by marking my territory," Richard stated confidently.

"Is that why you kissed me passionately in front of everyone?" I questioned.

"No, I've been itching to do that for ages. But... I reckon it did the trick," he responded, extending a high-five to Henry.

"Agnes, just so you know, Collins men are possessive. In case you want to reconsider," I warned playfully, earning a giggle from Agnes.

"You truly are a wicked stepmother!" Henry feigned horror, triggering laughter among us all.

As I watched our family, our shared laughter and playful banter echoing around us, I felt an overwhelming sense of love. Richard, the ever-doting father, and Samantha, the apple of his eye; Henry and Agnes with their blossoming romance. This was my family, my sanctuary. Regardless of the time apart or distance, our bond had only grown stronger.

I reached for Richard, pulling him into another kiss. Beneath the canopy of a sky ablaze with the colors of the setting sun, I knew without a doubt that I was irrevocably, deeply in love with Richard.

23

The manuscript was all but alive in my hands. Words danced on the page, each sentence a tantalizing waltz of imagination and intrigue. I was lost within its rhythm, swept away by the magnetic pull of a story that promised to be more than just ink on paper. The author was unknown, yet his voice rang out clearly, echoing in the caverns of my mind with a resonance that was both haunting and beautiful.

Timmy's note lay beside me, his usually curt handwriting now brimming with enthusiasm. After the first season of *Back In Time*, I hired my writing team, including Timmy, who now acted as assistant editor. He, too, had been trapped by the story; his excitement showed even in blue ink. I could almost see his eyes twinkling as he wrote, "This is it, Hope. A masterpiece."

My office buzzed around me, a symphony of ringing phones, hurried footsteps, and hushed conversations. It was a chaotic ballet, each element a dancer in its own right. Yet, amidst this whirlwind, I found an island of calm in the manuscript before me. The morning sun streamed through the glass wall, casting long shadows across the room and painting the skyscrapers of New York City in shades of gold. It was as if the city itself was waking up, stretching its arms to embrace the day.

I paced back and forth, manuscript in one hand, a yellow marker in the other. I made notes, underlined sentences, and highlighted phrases that made my heart skip a beat. My heart was aflutter, not just with the thrill of a good story, but with the prospect of bringing it to life — not just in print, but on the silver screen.

But as I walked, a pang of longing tugged at me. I missed the sensation of a blank page beneath my fingers, the thrill of a story unfolding from my own mind. But that was my past, the old Hope Williams. My father's business empire occupied the top post for priorities. There was much to learn. The business was mine to inherit, a legacy that demanded my attention and respect. Still, I yearned for the freedom of the written word, the intimate dance between writer and reader. My excitement was so intense as I held a story that could change everything.

I tapped the speakerphone, "Hillary, could you please send Timmy to my office?"

"Of course," she responded, her voice crisp and professional. The line went dead.

I had barely finished digesting the words on the page when Timmy breezed into my office. "What's up, boss?" he greeted, his casual demeanor contrasting with the formality of the room.

"This," I said, gesturing towards the manuscript that lay sprawled across my desk. "What do you make of it?"

Timmy's face lit up. "It's phenomenal. The writing style is raw and unfiltered, and the story... It's unlike anything I've ever read. We're publishing this, right?"

"I was thinking of something more," I admitted, leaning back in my chair. "I want to produce it for a film adaptation."

A slow smile spread across Timmy's face. "I was actually going to suggest that. And not to overstep, but I think Richard would be perfect for the lead role."

"I'd considered that," I confessed. "But I want him to direct it."

"He can do both," Timmy pointed out. He was casually playing with a couple of highlighters from my desk. "Many seasoned actors are doing that nowadays."

"But I don't know how he'll react to me funding his film," I said, a hint of melancholy creeping into my voice.

Timmy laughed lightly. "Hope, Richard is a big boy. Plus, he's wealthy himself. Besides, he's one of the board's biggies who decide important matters here. I doubt he has any insecurities about this."

I sighed, "Alright, if Richard turns it down, we'll have to find the perfect cast."

Timmy nodded, "The story seems written for him. He'll see that when he reads the manuscript. Take it home. Let him look at it."

"Sounds like a plan, thanks, Timmy. After tomorrow, you can assign this to one of our editors while I talk to the agent who will handle it," I said.

"No, this is mine, Hope. I will be editing it myself," Timmy stood up, a determined look crossing his face, scooped a couple of candies from my table, and sprinted out of my room.

Now, I need to strike a balance between the world of corporate giants and the realm of narrative titans — I was ready for the ride.

———

As the evening sun descended, our living room was bathed in a warm, orange glow. Richard and I found our usual spots on the plush white leather couch, nestled between towering bookshelves that bore witness to our shared love for books. Most of the books were Richard's, but they felt as much a part of me as they were of him. Samantha was absorbed in her coloring book, sprawled across the floor with an intensity that only children possess.

In my hands were the contracts and memorandums that had been my nightly companions for weeks. They were more than just legal documents; they were the framework for our dreams. Richard, his reading glasses teetering on the edge of his nose, paced the length of the room, deeply engrossed in the manuscript. His dual roles as an actor and my husband made him my first and most discerning reader.

"Hope," he broke the silence, pausing mid-pace to catch my eye over the rim of his glasses. "This... this is nothing short of a masterpiece. The characters, the plot, it's all..." His voice trailed off, the enormity of his compliment hanging in the air.

A smile tugged at my lips. "That's precisely what Timmy thought," I replied.

Richard paused, his gaze thoughtful. "But Hope," he started again, "I want more than just a role in this. I want to direct it."

His words hung in the air, a silent plea. I put down the paperwork, my full attention now on him. "Timmy and I discussed it, Richard. We believe you can both star in and direct this piece."

Richard stopped pacing, his eyes wide. "We need to sit down and discuss this thoroughly, Hope. This... this could be an award-winning piece."

A sigh of relief escaped my lips, only to be quickly replaced by a sudden tension. Samantha's voice cut through the comfortable silence of our living room, clear, determined, and persistent. "Mum, Dad, I want to take a gap year from school."

Her words hung in the air, an uninvited presence. A knot of anxiety tightened in my stomach. "Samantha," I began, striving for calmness in my voice, "We've revisited this topic repeatedly. Education is important."

"But Mum," she interjected, her youthful exuberance undimmed, "I want to explore, to learn things beyond the confines of a classroom!"

I nodded, acknowledging her sentiment. "I understand and support your desire to discover," I replied, making air quotes as I added, "things beyond the classroom." I continued before she could reply, "But, your formal education — meaning the one in the classroom — is non-negotiable. You know that."

* * *

She straightened up, her young face taking on a serious expression that seemed far too mature for her 11 years. "Look, Mum," she began, her tone business-like, "I don't need formal education. I can always work at your company or Grandpa Oliver's." She paused, then added with a dash of audacity, "Or I could venture into filmmaking, like Dad."

Her words struck a chord, prompting a mix of amusement and concern. Here was our daughter, barely out of childhood, yet ready to leap into adulthood. It was a moment that highlighted the challenges and beauty of parenting — watching your child grow, make decisions, and shape their own future.

"Sam, how can you lead our companies with your siblings if you don't go to school? And for your information, young lady, your father finished school before he took to modeling and filming to ensure he performed his craft successfully."

Samantha rolled her eyes, a telltale sign that she felt cornered. "Mummy, you're overreacting. It's just a gap year!" she exclaimed, impatience seeping into her tone.

Feeling my patience thinning, I turned to Richard. "Richard, back me up here," I pleaded.

Richard, still engrossed in the manuscript, finally looked up. "Sam, listen to your mother," he said, his tone a blend of gentleness and firmness. The conflict in his eyes was evident — a father torn between supporting his child's dreams and understanding his wife's concerns.

"Okay, okay! Chill, parents," Samantha retorted as she stood up, rolling her eyes again. She shot a look at Richard that clearly said, '*She's your problem now.*' With a flick of her hand, she beckoned Salem, my cat, to follow her... who surprisingly had become her faithful companion despite their former rivalry.

Bewildered, I turned to Richard. "What's her issue with school?" I asked. Before he could respond, another question slipped out, "And when did she and Salem become best friends?"

* * *

Richard chuckled, a sound that eased the tension in the room. "Darling, she's 11. Remember how much you despised school at that age? And as for Salem, well, they bonded over their shared rebellious nature."

As our conversation continued, a whirlwind of emotions churned within me. Fear for Samantha's future if she chooses to stray from the traditional path. Frustration at her seeming inability to comprehend my concerns. Yet beneath it all, a glimmer of admiration shone. Our daughter stood her ground, much like I did when I convinced my father to let me pursue my passion for writing and build the company around it against all odds.

The room fell silent after Samantha's departure, the lingering tension from our discussion still apparent. Richard found his way back to the couch, the manuscript now resting on his lap. His face was a mix of emotions — a blend of admiration for the work I presented him and hesitation for the path that lay ahead.

"Hope," he began, his voice barely above a whisper, "I've been contemplating... perhaps it would be more prudent if I took this project under the wing of my own company. I could purchase the story rights, finance it, even produce it myself."

His words hit me like a gust of wind, leaving me momentarily speechless. His offer was generous but veered away from what I had envisioned. The story was not just a narrative; it was the lifeblood of our company.

I looked at him, stunned. His proposal wasn't what I had envisioned. This story is my company's brainchild. "Richard," I said, choosing my words carefully, "I appreciate your offer. But that manuscript belongs here, with us. I want it, too, not just the book publishing but its film adaptation as well. It's an integral part of this company, our company. It's as much yours as it is Henry's and Samantha's."

"I know, but the company isn't a family enterprise. You have a board to report to. I don't want to put you in a spotlight where they think you're extending a favor to me, your husband," he countered cautiously.

* * *

"Richard, you are no ordinary actor. You're a highly sought-after talent, with numerous film companies vying for your attention. And yes, I do have the advantage of steering things in our favor, but it's no less than what you deserve."

"But Hope," he persisted, "It's a gamble. If the film doesn't perform well, it could mean..."

"I know," I interjected, "I'm well aware of the risks. But with you leading the cast, I am confident that this will be the success we need."

He sighed deeply, his hand ruffling his hair in a gesture of unease. I knew he was trying to shield me from potential failure, but this was a risk I needed to take for both of us.

"Richard," I implored, reaching out to grasp his hand, "I need you to trust me. Trust in my vision. Trust in your remarkable talent. We can make this a reality together."

Our eyes locked, and at that moment, I saw a spark of understanding flicker in his gaze. This was more than just a film project; it was proof of our partnership, a leap of faith into uncharted territory. As I held his gaze, I felt an unwavering certainty that we would navigate this journey together no matter the outcome, just as we had done countless times before.

24

As I sat in the imposing conference room of Ortega Holdings' New York headquarters, I could feel the weight of the world on my shoulders. The room was filled with the CEOs from our different offices worldwide, including Michael Yang, who led our Singapore office. They all have flown in specifically for this meeting. My father sat at the head of the table, his aura exuding authority and power.

We were deliberating over our imminent expansion plans into Europe and Asia, a move that could redefine the landscape of our business operations. The air was thick with anticipation and a hint of nervous excitement. However, a storm of worry and apprehension raged beneath my composed exterior.

The hum of conversation buzzed in the background like a low-lying drone, punctuated by the occasional clinking of coffee cups and the rustling of refreshments. The huge flat-screen monitor flickered with images and charts, vividly depicting our expansion plans. However, amidst this symphony of corporate life, I felt an odd sense of detachment, as if I were a spectator in my own life.

My mind drifted towards Richard, my sanctuary in this ocean of chaos. He was wrapping up his filming schedule in Canada, and we eagerly looked forward to spending the fall together in New York City. We were also considering a trip to London, a city that held mixed emotions for me. It would be the first time I'd be visiting our home in Chelsea since my terrifying ordeal last year. Richard and I felt it was time to face my fears head-on, and I longed for Samantha to reconnect with her roots.

The sudden creaking of the conference room door jolted me from my daydream. My father's executive assistant walked in, trailed by Hillary, my secretary. Their faces bore an unnerving pallor, their eyes wide with a fear that sent an icy chill down my spine.

My father, the picture of stoic composure, looked up at them, his penetrating gaze demanding answers. "What is it?" he asked, his voice carrying an undercurrent of concern beneath its authoritative tone. My eyes darted to the phone clutched in Hillary's trembling hands, my heart pounding an urgent rhythm against my ribs.

Both women approached my father, whispering something in his ear. Despite straining, I couldn't catch their words, but the gravity in their expressions spoke volumes.

With a calmness that belied the tension in the room, my father rose from his chair and walked toward me. His hands enveloped mine, their warmth contrasting with the cold dread seeping into my bones. "Hope," he began, his voice sounding distant as if echoing from the depths of a well. "There's been an accident... Richard... he's been injured on the set in Canada."

His words hung in the air like a death knell, sucking the oxygen out of the room. The world seemed to tilt on its axis, throwing everything off balance. Richard. Accident. The mere thought was a cruel blow, a nightmare I had been thrust into without warning.

The room fell silent, the earlier hum of activity fading into a deafening quiet. My mind spun, the words echoing over and over again like a cruel mantra. My Richard. Hurt. It was unbearable, unthinkable. My breath hitched in my throat, my heart aching like it had been ripped out of my chest.

The faces around the table blurred, their expressions a mix of shock and sympathy. I was dimly aware of my father's hand on mine, his grip firm but gentle. But all I could see was Richard's face, his sparkling blue-grey eyes, his laughter. The man I loved more than anything in the world was in trouble, and I was miles away, surrounded by a sea of indifferent faces.

Pushing back my chair, I stood abruptly, the room spinning around me. "I have to go to him," I said, my voice a mere whisper. My voice was barely more than a whisper, the words catching in my throat.

My father, ever the rock in our storm, wrapped his arms around me, offering silent support. He gestured to Michael, indicating that he should take over the meeting. "I'll go with you," he said, his voice steady as he guided me out of the conference room and into his private office.

"No, Dad. I need you here with Sam. She adores you, and I can't bring her with me. I don't know how to break the news to her." The dam broke then, and tears began to fall freely. A wave of anguish washed over me. Richard was hurt, and I wasn't there. My father's comforting words seemed distant, muffled by the pounding of my heart.

"Let me take care of things here," he said. His office was now filling up with some senior executives, ready to take his instructions. Someone informed him that our private jet was on standby, and one of the twin goons had already packed a few of my essentials and was en route to the airport.

Suddenly, I remembered Henry! Frantically, I fumbled in my bag for my phone, my fingers shaking as I speed-dialed his number. He answered on the third ring, his casual greeting of "What's up? Everything okay?" starkly contrasting the turmoil I was in.

Struggling to keep my voice steady, I said, "Your dad's had an accident. I'm flying to Canada now. Can you meet me there?"

Henry didn't press for details or ask about the severity of the accident. He knew better than to add to my worries. Instead, he responded calmly, "I'll request an emergency leave and book the earliest flight."

"I'll send the jet for you as soon as they drop me off," I promised him.

Henry reassured me before we ended the call, "Everything will be alright, Hope. We'll get through this."

* * *

"Yes, as we always do," I managed to respond, ending the call. With that, I turned away, leaving behind the world of Ortega Holdings. Now, my world had shrunk to just Richard and me; everything else faded into insignificance.

———

Dashing through the sterile, white corridors of the hospital in Canada, my heart pounded in my chest like a drum, accompanied by the rhythm of my frantic footsteps. The distinct aroma of antiseptic filled the air, mingling with the hushed whispers of the medical staff that echoed ominously around me. My world had shrunk to the confines of this hospital, where Richard, my Richard, was fighting for his life.

Pushing open the door to his room, I was met with a sight that stole my breath away. Richard, my vibrant, energetic husband, lay motionless on the bed, a stark contrast to the man he was before his accident. His face, usually lit up with a warm smile, was pale and still, his chest rising and falling rhythmically with each breath he took.

A man in a blue scrub suit introduced himself as Dr. Simmons, the neurosurgeon who had operated on Richard, walked over to me. His face held a weary look, the lines etched deeper from the grueling eight-hour surgery. "Mrs. Collins," he began, his voice laced with both professionalism and sympathy. "Richard is stable now. However, due to the trauma to his spine, he may be temporarily paralyzed."

His words hung in the air, creating a chilling silence. "What does that mean?" I asked, my voice barely above a whisper.

"It means that Richard might have limited mobility," he confessed, his gaze never leaving mine.

The world around me seemed to shatter. Tears welled up in my eyes, blurring my vision. "Please," I begged, my voice hoarse with desperation. "Do everything you can. He's everything to me... to our family."

* * *

Dr. Simmons nodded solemnly. "We will do our best, Mrs. Collins. We won't give up on him."

"Will he ever walk again? I asked.

"There's a possibility. We're hopeful he could regain movement with intensive physiotherapy," Dr. Simmons reassured me.

With a nod, I turned back to Richard. I watched his sleeping form like a stab to my heart. His face was pale, so unlike the warm, sun-kissed complexion I had gotten used to. His typically animated face was peaceful in sleep, his chest rising and falling rhythmically. I reached out, gently brushing a lock of hair off his forehead. His skin felt unusually cool under my fingertips, a stark contrast to the warmth he usually radiated. His chest rose and fell steadily, the only sign that he was still with us.

The hospital room was filled with a deafening silence, broken only by the occasional beep of the monitors. The atmosphere was thick with anticipation, the sterile white walls seeming to close in on me.

A surge of willpower washed over me as I looked at Richard. I would not let this break me. I would fight for him, bring him back from the brink just as he had done for me countless times.

"Richard," I murmured, my fingers intertwining with his. "We've weathered storms before, and we'll weather this one too. I promise."

The doctors urged me to return to the hotel to rest, stating that Richard wouldn't regain consciousness for several hours due to his recovery from surgery. But I was stubborn about staying by his side. My parents each called to inquire about Richard's condition. Shortly after, George and Catherine rang me up, informing me that Henry had left London and was en route. After providing them an update, I ended the call and slumped in a chair beside Richard's bed.

———

The subdued hum of the hospital was interrupted by Henry's arrival. His imposing figure filled the doorway, worry etched deeply on his face. As he walked in, I felt a surge of relief. Amidst this crisis, having my family around offered me much-needed comfort.

"Henry," I managed to say, rushing into his arms. He embraced me tightly, his strong arms providing a sense of security I desperately needed.

"Hope," he responded, his voice wavering slightly. "How's Dad holding up?"

I pulled away, looking up at him. His eyes, so much like Richard's, were filled with concern. "He's stable, but the doctors say..." I paused, struggling to get the words out, "he might be temporarily paralyzed."

Henry nodded, his face pale but composed. He moved past me towards Richard's bed, his eyes scanning the medical chart at the foot of the bed. I watched him, noting the furrowed brow and tight jaw. Despite his calm exterior, I knew Henry was battling his own storm of emotions.

"Dad's a fighter, Hope," he said after a while, not taking his eyes off the chart. "He won't let this defeat him."

His words echoed my own thoughts. "I know, Henry," I replied, my voice choked with emotion. "We have to be strong for him now."

"Yes, we do," he agreed, finally looking at me. There was a determination in his eyes, a silent promise that we would get through this together.

As he settled into the chair beside me, gently clasping his father's hand, I was overcome by the courage he demonstrated. He was stepping up, preparing himself to face whatever lay ahead. "Stay with your Dad for a bit. I need to check on your sister," I instructed, my voice softer than usual. He nodded in response, and I quietly exited the room.

Glancing at my watch, I noted that it was already eight in the evening back in New York. I quickly dialed Samantha's FaceTime. The screen lit up, revealing Sam's anxious face. "Mummy, how's Daddy?" she asked, her voice wavering, her eyes glistening with unshed tears.

"Daddy's still sleeping, sweetheart, but he's out of surgery now," I replied, forcing a smile onto my face. "I'm sorry I didn't get a chance to see or call you before I rushed to be with Daddy."

"It's okay, Mummy. Both Grandpa and Grandma are with me," she reassured me. I was taken aback. Richard's parents were in New York? "Is that Grandma Debbie with you?" I asked, catching sight of my mother in the background.

"Yes, she and Grandpa are both here," Sam confirmed.

"Be good while I'm away, sweetheart. Don't give your grandparents any trouble, okay?"

"Yes, Mummy, but when are you and Daddy coming home?"

"Soon, sweetheart. We just need to take care of Daddy first. Can I speak to Grandma or Grandpa, please..."

Suddenly, my father's face filled the screen. "How's Richard?" he asked, concern etched across his features.

Tears welled up in my eyes, and I couldn't hold them back. "He hasn't woken up yet after the surgery. The doctor said there's severe damage to his spine... he might not be able to walk again."

"Hope, we live in an age of advanced medicine, and we have all the resources we need for Richard's treatment," he reminded me. "I'll come join you there. By the way, your mom is here to look after Samantha. I hope you don't mind."

"Thank you, Dad. I don't know how I'd manage without you and Mom," I sobbed.

"Wipe your tears, Hope. Richard's children need to see you strong. You must be their beacon of strength while Richard is recovering." His words lent me the strength I needed, and I wiped away my tears, ready to face whatever came next.

———

Exhaustion seemed to have stealthily claimed me as I kept a watchful eye on Richard's bedside. The rhythmic beeping of the monitors and the steady rise and fall of his chest had lulled me into a restless slumber. A gentle squeeze of my hand drew me back from the realm of sleep. My eyes fluttered open, greeted by Richard's familiar blue eyes. They were clouded with confusion, yet unmistakably awake, providing a much-needed glimmer of hope.

"Richard?" I whispered, a wave of disbelief washing over me. The morning sun peeked through the glass wall, casting a soft, golden glow on his face.

"Hey, beautiful," he murmured, his voice husky but filled with warmth. As our eyes locked, an overwhelming surge of relief and hope flooded me, bringing tears to my eyes.

"You gave us quite a scare," I managed to add, brushing a stray lock of hair from his forehead.

He offered a weak smile in response, his grip on my hand tightening slightly. It was a small gesture, but it felt like the most significant reassurance we could have asked for at that moment.

"Oh, Richard," I sobbed, clutching his hand tighter. Tears streamed down my cheeks as I leaned over, pressing my lips gently against his.

Richard gave me a small smile, using his thumb to wipe away my tears gently. "Don't cry, darling," he said softly. "We're in a hospital, not at a funeral."

His words, tinged with his signature humor despite our dire circumstances, broke the dam within me. I cried harder, my body shaking with relief, fear, and many other emotions. Richard was awake. He was here, with me, and that was all that mattered.

* * *

I called out, "Henry!"

He rushed into the room, relief washing over his face as he saw his father. "Looks like our patient is finally awake," he declared, leaning over to kiss his father's forehead.

"So, how much trouble am I in?" Richard asked Henry, his tone light but his gaze serious.

"You've just undergone an eight-hour surgery, Dad. That's how bad your fall was," Henry explained, attempting to put the situation in layman's terms. "Initially, you might not feel your legs, but with time and therapy, we're hopeful you'll regain control."

Richard glanced down at his legs stretched out across the bed. I could tell he was trying to wiggle his toes, but his evident frustration betrayed his lack of success. "Now, I know what you mean," he said, giving us a reassuring smile.

As I sat there, my tears falling onto our entwined hands, I felt a renewed sense of determination. "We have a long road ahead, Richard," I reminded him, "but we will face it all, one step at a time."

He nodded, his disappointment and fear hidden behind a brave smile. "Promise me," I choked out between sobs, "promise me you'll fight, Richard."

"I promise, darling," he replied, his gaze never leaving mine. His words weren't just a promise to fight; they were a vow to live, love, and overcome whatever life threw at us.

"I'm considering taking a leave of absence or applying for a transfer to New York," Henry said.

"Don't do that, Henry. I'm going to be fine, and we can afford doctors to look after me," he said.

"Dad, this isn't your decision to make. It's mine. Hope and Sam need us both. We will weather this storm just as we have all the others. Together."

* * *

I reached out and squeezed Henry's hand. At that moment, bathed in the warm sunlight streaming through the window, I realized that we had each other despite the fear and uncertainty. And as long as we stood together, we could face anything.

25

The cold, sterile hospital doors slid open with a disheartening hiss, the sound echoing in my ears like the end of a daunting symphony. I gripped the handles of Richard's wheelchair, the chill of the metal seeping through the thin fabric of my gloves. My heart fluttered with anxiety as I wheeled him out into the stark daylight, the world outside looking as gray and desolate as I felt inside. I adjusted the blanket draped across his legs, trying to ward off the chill.

"Thank you, darling," Richard said, gazing up at me. His voice was weak, but he was trying to put on a brave face, attempting to infuse some cheer into the bleak day. "I'm warm enough."

The past two weeks had been an emotional flurry for all of us. The sterile, white hospital walls had become an unwelcome sanctuary, a place we had reluctantly begun to call home. Richard's accident, which occurred on the set of what was supposed to be his triumphant return to action films, had left him bedridden. The doctors assured us it was temporary, but seeing his once vibrant eyes clouded with pain, a sight he tried so hard to hide from me, was heartbreaking.

"We're finally going home," I murmured, more to myself than to him. "Sam has missed you terribly." He took my hand that was resting behind him and gave it a gentle squeeze.

"Ah, Sam," he chuckled weakly. "She's been telling me non-stop about how bored she is and how your mother has constantly annoyed Salem." He glanced up at me, a hint of confusion in his eyes. "How come they're getting along fine now?"

I laughed, a welcome relief from the tension that had been building up. "They both found a common denominator — they don't like my mother."

Our laughter echoed along the hospital corridor as we made our way to bid farewell to the medical staff who had cared for Richard over the past two weeks. The stifling silence of the hospital was gradually replaced by the distant hum of city life outside. A few yards away, Henry was locked in a serious conversation with Dr. Simmons and Dr. Harper, the attending physician who had been overseeing Richard's treatment.

My fingers tightened around the handles of the wheelchair, the memory of endless nights spent in a hospital chair as he slept came flooding back. Praying for a miracle while Richard lay unconscious, wrestling with the fear and dread, waiting anxiously for him to awaken — the memories were still raw and painful.

"Hope," Richard's voice cut through my thoughts, drawing me back to the present. "I see that Henry is serious about his move to New York."

"Yes, he is," I replied, managing a small smile. "He's been in constant discussions with Raphael." Henry had been our pillar of strength during this ordeal, gracefully balancing his medical internship transfer with the emotional toll of his father's accident. His maturity had surpassed his years, and I couldn't have been prouder.

"I'm glad he's moving in with us, but I don't want my current situation to hinder his dreams and future," Richard murmured, his gaze lingering on Henry. "There's one thing I need you to promise me, Hope."

"What is it?" I asked. I stopped pushing his wheelchair and turned to face him.

"If ever you grow tired of hoping for my recovery, just tell me. You are young, and I want you to live your life fully. I don't want to burden you, especially when you're already taking care of a teenage daughter who isn't your responsibility," he said, a faint, bittersweet smile playing on his lips.

I crouched down in front of him. His words stung, but I knew they stemmed from his love and concern for me. "Richard, you are my life. We made a vow at our wedding — in sickness and health, till death do us part." My voice trembled as tears filled my eyes and spilled down my cheeks. "My heart will stop beating when yours does. But until then, I will never leave your side."

Richard looked at me with such love and tenderness that it took my breath away. He reached up, gently wiping away my tears with his thumb before pulling me in for a tender kiss. This was the Richard I knew and loved, always considering others even in his own time of hardship.

Straightening up, I gave him a determined look. "And as for Sam, she is as much my daughter as she is yours. Never forget that." With those words, I stood tall, pushing his wheelchair forward towards Henry.

As we neared them, their conversation wound down, and Henry gave Dr. Harper a firm nod before swiveling toward us. His eyes, mirroring the same spark as his father's, held a hint of optimism.

"Dad, Hope," he began, his voice conveying newfound confidence. "Are you ready to go home? Both Dr. Simmons and Dr. Harper believe... they are confident that you're prepared for the next recovery phase."

Richard extended his hand to both doctors, gratitude shining in his eyes. "I couldn't have been in better hands. Thank you."

Dr. Simmons grasped Richard's hand warmly, "Remember, this is just a temporary setback. It'll require hard work, but you have an ideal support system right beside you," he said, his gaze shifting between Henry and me.

"We've coordinated with your medical team in New York, and all your records have been forwarded. We'll visit you in a few weeks to meet with your team. Your wife was insistent that we continue to be part of your care team," he added with a smile.

Richard chuckled, "It's never easy to say no to her, is it?" The laughter that followed lifted the weight of the past weeks, if only for a moment.

"I just want the best for you, my love," I whispered, pressing a kiss to the top of his head.

Henry shared that Richard's care team, whom we had interviewed and selected, was already settled and prepared to assist us upon our arrival in New York. "They moved a couple of days ago," he informed me. We had purchased the apartment two floors below ours, converting it into both a rehabilitation center for Richard and a comfortable living space for his care team.

"Mrs. Collins, feel free to contact us anytime. With your husband's determination, he'll bounce back to his old self in no time," Dr. Harper assured me with a smile.

The relief washing over me was so potent that it nearly swept me off my feet. Richard squeezed my hand, his touch as comforting as ever. "I know. Thank you very much again," I replied.

Despite the trials we had faced, we were still here, together, ready to confront whatever lay ahead. I felt something other than fear for the first time in two weeks: hope.

———

As my eyes fluttered open, the first sight to greet me was the soft, golden glow of the dawn sun performing a delicate dance on the vast glass wall of our bedroom. Each morning, I would awaken, swathed in this divine light, with Richard's strong arm resting protectively over me. But today, as has been the case for countless mornings since the accident, the sunlight merely served to harshly illuminate the idyllic scene that now framed our drastically altered lives.

I turned over to Richard's side of the bed, his usual spot still indented from the weight of his once-constant presence. The sheets were cold, each thread woven with a chilling reminder of his absence. Once a sanctuary of love and shared dreams, our bed suddenly seemed too expansive, the room excessively large without his commanding presence.

"Richard," I whispered into the silence, my voice barely a murmur against the echoing emptiness. I reached out, fingers grazing the cool fabric where he should have been. A sigh escaped my lips, a silent testament to the longing that was now a constant companion. Once filled with shared laughter and whispered promises, our bedroom felt barren without him. His absence was a tangible presence, a void that even the most radiant dawn couldn't fill.

Richard no longer stayed in our room, instead confined to the spare bedroom two floors below us in our towering penthouse. Following the dreadful accident, the apartment had been hurriedly transformed into a makeshift rehabilitation center. The temporary paralysis had ruthlessly stripped him of his mobility and, in doing so, had stolen our intimacy.

I longed for the familiar brush of his fingers against my skin, the comforting heat of his body next to mine, and the soft whispers of affection we used to exchange under the cover of darkness. Instead, all that lingered were haunting echoes of our past, bouncing off the cold, empty walls of our present reality.

"Good morning, love," I whispered into the void, hoping that somehow, amidst the silence, he could hear me. But the only response was the constant purring of Salem, who was sleeping in our room.

Upon our return to the bustling metropolis of New York, we ventured to reignite the flame of intimacy that had once so fervently burned between us. I was acutely aware of Richard's struggle, and his attempts to ensure my satisfaction in the most intimate ways possible despite his limitations. Yet, the bitter truth was that our physical connection was a stark reminder of his current predicament.

One evening, Richard broached the subject as we sat in the dimly lit living room. "I think it might be best if I moved into the apartment below," he suggested, his voice steady but eyes hinting at an internal conflict. The room would allow for easier access to his rehabilitation equipment and, according to him, provide me with the privacy that his constant team of caregivers had inadvertently invaded.

But I knew the truth. Richard was shielding me from the harsh reality of his condition, not wanting me to witness the daily assistance he required, the humbling tasks like using the bathroom and being helped into bed.

Life, with its unyielding momentum, continued to push forward. Despite her persistent protests claiming the insignificance of education, Samantha dutifully attended school. My obligations as the head of the publishing firm were solid, although the expansion plans of Ortega Holdings into the United States and Europe were temporarily put on hold.

My father, sympathetic to the pressure of our circumstances, believed I needed more time to dedicate to our family, especially considering Richard's delicate health. He asked Michael to temporarily fill my shoes — a move I received with mixed feelings. It was not a critique of Michael's competence but rather a reflection on my own struggles in relinquishing control.

Michael was exceptional at his job. It came as no surprise that Dad entrusted him with primary, critical operations. A Harvard alumnus who graduated with top honors, Michael had returned home to Singapore to kickstart his career in business management before crossing paths with my father. He was undeniably handsome, occasionally reminding me of Daniel Henney.

What set Michael apart was his considerate nature. He intentionally kept me out of specific decision-making processes related to business expansion, and at times, he made sure my office and team were on track with the projects, allowing me to concentrate on the media and publishing business and, more importantly, on my family. If it weren't for my love for Richard, there might have been a chance for some form of attraction towards Michael. But I quickly dismissed such a thought...

Indeed, my life had found its new rhythm. It was a dance I was learning to perform solo, adapting to each beat as best as I could.

* * *

Brushing aside the remnants of my lingering thoughts, I slipped out of bed and silently made my way toward the dining room. The scene that unfolded before me was one I treasured deeply - Richard and Samantha, engrossed in their usual early morning ritual. Samantha was animatedly discussing her upcoming science project while Richard listened with undivided attention, his eyes gleaming with a mix of love and pride.

"Mum, come join the fun!" Samantha beckoned, punctuating her invitation with a flourish of her cereal-laden spoon.

I joined them at the table with a manufactured smile plastered onto my face. "Good morning, sweetheart," I greeted, playfully ruffling her hair. Then, I shifted my focus to Richard and asked, "Did you have a restful night?"

A fleeting shadow crossed his features, but he quickly masked it with a feeble smile. "As restful as one can hope for," he responded.

His words hung heavily in the air, a stark reminder of the battle we were navigating. I leaned over to plant a tender kiss on his lips, to which he responded by wrapping his arms around my waist.

"Dad, focus!" Samantha's voice broke through our moment, causing us both to chuckle.

I slid into the chair next to Samantha, allowing father and daughter to resume their bonding. "Are you not heading to the office today?" Richard queried.

"I've decided to work from home today. There are several manuscripts I need to review and decide on by next week," I explained, sipping the freshly brewed coffee Leticia had set before me.

"With Mum around, we better be on our best behavior," Richard teased Samantha, earning an exaggerated eye roll from her.

Shifting the conversation, I remarked, "I haven't seen Henry in a few days."

* * *

"I believe he's been buried in research on how to get his old man back in shape. He's attending interviews for internship programs, too," Richard filled in.

"And how's your training going?" I asked, keeping my tone casual despite the weightiness of the question.

"It's like a daily appointment with the torture chamber," he responded, his attempt at wit not entirely concealing the harsh reality. I reached across the table, intertwining my fingers with his. We were partners in this struggle, and no matter how daunting the obstacles, we would face them together. Glancing down at our joined hands, a flicker of hope sparked within me. Despite our current situation, we remained strong, still a family. And maybe, just maybe, that was enough.

26

The Upper East Side was a symphony of gold, the leaves pirouetting in the chilled autumn breeze as we strolled down the sidewalk. I felt the season's crisp coolness seep through my long woolen coat, creating a stark contrast to the sun's warmth that filtered through the towering buildings. Samantha, my little spark of joy, was swathed in a vibrant red scarf that mirrored her vivacious personality, her eyes alight with excitement.

"Mummy," she piped up, her small hand holding mine with an endearing tightness, "Do you reckon Daddy will be thrilled about the chocolate cake?"

A soft chuckle escaped me before I responded, "I have no doubt he'll absolutely adore it, sweetheart." As I spoke, I gave her hand a reassuring squeeze, a silent promise hanging between us.

As always, Chen and Arthur were just a few steps behind us. Their dark suits camouflaged them within the afternoon shadows, but their vigilant eyes never missed a beat, ceaselessly scanning our surroundings. Between them, they carried the carefully boxed birthday cake, handling it with an ease that only came from years of experience. Their laughter was contagious, echoing our joy and adding to the sense of normalcy we desperately sought.

"Chen," I called over my shoulder, "Ensure that cake reaches home in one piece. It has a very important mission tonight."

* * *

Their shared chuckle drifted forward on the breeze, and Arthur replied, "Fear not, ma'am. We've handled far more delicate operations than this."

The banter lightened my heart, painting our stroll through the city with a layer of ordinary joy.

The Upper East Side, just like the rest of New York City, pulsed with the enchanting spirit of autumn. The air was thick with the rich aroma of chestnuts roasting at nearby stalls, intertwining with the crisp scent of fallen leaves. Stylishly clad individuals bustled past us, their breaths fogging in the chilly air as they sought refuge in inviting cafes or boutique stores. Our boots crunched rhythmically on the leaf-strewn pavement, the cityscape providing a picturesque canvas for our walk.

Autumn has always held a special place in my heart, cradling countless cherished memories from my childhood to my first encounter with Richard, and even through my journey of self-discovery.

"You know, Samantha," I ventured, catching her eager gaze, "your father and I used to enjoy walks just like this when we were first courting."

Her eyes widened in surprise, "Really, Mum?"

I nodded, a nostalgic smile tugging at my lips, "Indeed, sweetheart. We both hold a deep affection for this season. He had this charming habit of trying to catch falling leaves. He believed that every leaf tells a story, just as every person does."

As the memory faded, Samantha wrapped her arms around my waist and clung to me, "Daddy will walk again, Mummy." Her tears tumbled freely down her cheeks. Despite her brave stance, she was still worried for her father. I returned her embrace before gently unwrapping her arms from around me. Kneeling before her, I wiped away her tears and kissed her forehead.

"He will, sweetheart," I reassured her, pulling her into a comforting hug. "Your father is doing everything he can to walk again."

* * *

On that tranquil afternoon, amidst the chill of autumn and the warmth of Samantha nestled against me, I closed my eyes and prayed silently. I prayed for brighter days ahead, strength for Richard's recovery, and hope for our family's future.

With a final wipe of our tears, we stood up and resumed our walk. A sense of peace washed over me, a soothing balm against the hardships Richard and I had faced. This simple act of procuring a cake for his birthday, of planning to celebrate it as a family, felt like a small yet significant victory against our adversities. I glanced at Samantha, her face radiant with anticipation for her father's birthday.

Today, we planned a private celebration of Richard's birthday — a quiet dinner with our close friends, Henry and Sam. My father had also promised to appear before he embarked on his journey back to Manila. The intrusive press had finally grown weary of hounding us for stories about Richard's accident. Thankfully, their attention had shifted to other celebrities, leaving us in relative peace. More prominent publications voluntarily withdrew their interest after Yumi threatened to pull advertising contracts from Ortega's Holdings. Business, it seemed, always took precedence in the media industry. At least their departure granted us a momentary relief.

The shrill excitement in Sam's voice pulled me out of my reverie. "Hello, Fred!" she called out as we approached our building.

Fred, our long-time doorman, responded with a warm smile. "Hello, Miss Sam," he greeted, then turned his gaze towards me. "Good afternoon, Hope." To Fred, I would always remain' Hope' regardless of the changes around us.

I returned his greeting with a soft nod, "Good afternoon, Fred." As I moved toward the elevator leading to our penthouse, I found myself enveloped in a sense of normalcy.

"Fred, how's your day been?" I asked, turning towards him. It was a small gesture, but one that often went overlooked in the hustle of the city.

* * *

He chuckled, a friendly twinkle in his eyes. "Oh, you know, Hope. Same old, same old. But thank you for asking." He said as the elevator doors closed behind us.

As we swung our door open, a tantalizing aroma wafted toward us. The dining room was buzzing with activity; four men garbed in crisp chef uniforms bustling around in a culinary ballet. "Wow, who are these people?" I asked Richard as he maneuvered his wheelchair toward me.

"Yumi sent them over," he replied, a grin spreading across his face. "She claims they're the best in town." His eyes sparkled with amusement, and I leaned over to press a kiss onto his lips.

"I bet this has made Leticia's day," I laughed, glancing at our housekeeper. She was observing the chefs with an intensity that suggested she was mentally cataloging their techniques.

"Daddy, we brought you a chocolate cake and some macarons from Laduree," Samantha said, her voice brimming with excitement.

"Really now?" Richard quirked an eyebrow, looking at Sam with playful suspicion. "Are those for me, or are they actually your favorite treats?"

Sam burst into giggles and promptly climbed onto Richard's lap. As he wheeled them both around the room, their laughter filled the air. It was a beautiful scene, reminding me that life had a knack for offering small joys for crafting moments that were nothing short of magical.

———

In the soft glow of our bedroom light, I stood before the mirror, slowly brushing my hair. The silky strands slipped through the bristles, falling gently against the backdrop of my nightgown. It was a delicate piece — pale blue silk that clung to my body, accentuating my curves. I caught Richard's gaze in the reflection, his eyes dark and filled with an emotion that made my heart flutter.

* * *

His stare, once filled with playful joy, was now softened by the anxieties we had faced. Still, his eyes held a deep love that warmed me from the inside out. I met his gaze in the mirror, a silent conversation passing between us.

The evening replayed in my mind, the joyous dinner we had shared with our family. Henry had broken into laughter over Samantha's antics — her youthful exuberance adding life to our gathering. And my father, his presence always a comforting constant, had shared stories of his travels, bringing the world to our dining table.

The meal was nothing short of spectacular, a symphony of flavors prepared by a renowned chef. Each dish was a work of art, from the mouth watering roast beef to the exquisite chocolate soufflé that had concluded our meal. The conversation around the table had been filled with laughter, shared memories, and heartfelt discussions.

"Remember when you first tried to cook, Hope?" Richard had teased, his eyes twinkling with mischief. Laughter erupted around the table as I recounted my disastrous attempt at making spaghetti.

As the memory faded, my thoughts returned to our bedroom with Richard propped up in our bed. His back leaned on the headboard. His wheelchair, a constant reminder of our reality, was parked nearby. I chose to ignore that. Tonight felt like a glimpse into our past, a tender moment shared in the privacy of our room.

I gently set the brush aside, the bristles still warm from running through my hair. The soft rustling of my silk nightgown against my skin filled the silence as I moved towards him. Bending down, I initiated a kiss that was more than just a meeting of lips. It was an exchange of love, hope, and strength. His hand came up to gently cradle my cheek, returning the intensity of the kiss with equal ardor.

"Hope," he whispered into the quiet space between us. "I don't want to let you down again, like last time." As I pulled back from our shared breath, I sought out his eyes. They held a certain sadness, perhaps tinged with worry. Richard, ever the protector, had a unique way of making me feel cherished in our relationship — everybody else gets frustrated, except me. This, in its own way, made me feel special.

* * *

I may not fit the mold of a temptress or a femme fatale, but I can play the part when needed. Richard taught me well. In the bedroom, Richard was always the skilled navigator, the pro, skillfully charting our course. But tonight, I felt a pressing need to take the helm, to be the aggressor. This wasn't merely about want, it was about need. My man needed me to step into this new role. I wanted Richard to see a different side of me, one bolder and more assertive than I usually allowed myself to be. Tonight, I wanted him to experience this new version of me.

"Richard," I began, my voice steady and soothing, "Don't dwell on it now... or ever, again. You have been everything I ever wanted, and more. Nothing will ever change that. Please, let me do this for you... for us," I implored. It was crucial for him to understand that he hadn't disappointed me on those nights. If anything, my concern was for him. I knew those nights could be frustrating for Richard, perhaps even painful, under the misguided belief that he had left me unsatisfied.

As he began to respond, I silenced him with another kiss. This time it was slower, deeper, our lips exploring and wrestling for dominance.

"Please," I pleaded, "let me make love to you."

Richard looked at me. His blue-grey eyes traveled from my face to my body. That look was too familiar to me; it was when his desires were too intense. I gathered the hem of my nightgown, climbed on our bed, and straddled him. He pulled me into a tight embrace. I wanted nothing more than to be pinned against his arms as his lips pressed against my collarbone.

My nipples were already hard, and the flimsy fabric was unable to conceal them and the sheer lace of my pale blue panties. His hands began caressing my thighs before his fingers ran along my breast. As he began to trace a familiar erotic touch around my nipples, I gently intercepted his hands. Offering him a seductive smile, I carefully guided his hands to rest behind him. Maintaining our intense eye contact, I bound his wrists with my silk scarf. A smirk of surprise danced on Richard's lips; he was clearly taken aback by this new side of me. Once I was certain the scarf was secure, I reached for another.

* * *

Methodically folding the second scarf, I held it up for him to see before slowly lowering it over his eyes, effectively blindfolding him. As the world around him darkened, Richard's breath quickened in anticipation.

"Hope..." he began, but I silenced him with a gentle press of my finger against his lips.

A playful smirk danced on my lips as I leaned in closer to him. My heart pounded like a drum echoing through the silence of the room. Slowly, I traced the contours of his full lips with my tongue, a provocative invitation that sparked an electric tension between us. He attempted to capture the teasing intruder. But, in a playful diversion, I let his mouth land on the smooth expanse of my bare arm instead.

A soft gasp escaped my lips as he accepted the invitation, exploring the uncharted landscape of my skin with his own tongue. His teeth grazed gently against my soft, sensitive skin, a delicate dance between pain and pleasure that sent shivers down my spine.

Guiding his head with gentle fingers entwined in his hair, I reveled in the exquisite sensation that coursed through me. It was agonizingly erotic, a crescendo of desire that threatened to consume me. His exploration became more confident, more intimate, revealing layers of vulnerability and passion that lay beneath our playful banter.

"Is this what you wanted?" He murmured against my skin, his voice a husky whisper that stoked the embers of my desire into a roaring flame.

"Yes," I breathed out, lost in the labyrinth of sensations he was drawing out of me. "And much more."

My fingers found their way to his chiseled jaw, tracing its outline slowly and deliberately. The anticipation was unmistakable between us, a tangible force that seemed to electrify the air. With a gentle nudge, I guided his mouth to my left nipple, already hard and waiting for his touch.

* * *

"It's frustrating not to be able to see you now, darling," he said as he bit and sucked it with the thin fabric.

"Richard, if you only knew how this one feels like," I cried. Each lingering kiss ignited a spark within me. Our actions were slow, deliberate — a dance of desire that left us both breathless with anticipation.

I tried to pull out my nipple from his mouth, but his lips and his teeth closed around it even more, not wanting to let go. I gradually rose from the bed, his touch reluctantly releasing my body. Slowly, I hitched up the hem of my dress, exposing the smooth expanse of my thighs. Sensing my movement, Richard instinctively turned his head, seeking a way to continue our intimate exchange. "Your scent is driving me crazy," he said.

Gently, I pressed my inner thigh against his eager lips. He didn't merely kiss my skin, he savored it — his teeth and lips leaving a trail of passion that would inevitably bloom into bruises by morning. I offered him parts of me that I knew would stoke his desire further. The veins in his neck and forehead stood out, indicating the intensity of his arousal.

The room was thick with anticipation, each moment building upon the last. His restrained position added an element of power to our dynamic, an intoxicating mix of control and surrender. It was a dance we were learning together, each step leading us deeper into unexplored territory.

I positioned myself in front of him, squatting down to his level. Guiding his head towards the warmth between my legs, I gasped out his name. With a sudden surge of strength, Richard managed to free himself from his bindings, and his arms found their way around my waist.

Gently, I removed his blindfold, revealing his wild, passionate gaze. The desire in his eyes was unmistakable, an indication of our shared yearning. In a swift move, Richard tore away my nightgown and my flimsy underwear, leaving me completely bare under his heated gaze.

* * *

Now freed from his binds, he took control. His strong arms held me close as he navigated the rhythm and pace of our lovemaking. The roles had now reversed — he was in charge, and I was more than willing to surrender to his lead.

"Richard, please..." I cried. Our bodies moved in harmony, each touch and sigh deepening the connection we shared.

The tease brought my body to the edge, but I craved something more... for him to take me completely. There were so many nights I longed for this moment. I watched while his touch focused on the area between my legs, rubbing, circling, teasing, and edging as his eyes gazed at my eyes.

I yearned for the intimacy between us to linger. With a surge of determination, I wriggled free from his hold, eager to reclaim control. I positioned myself on his lap, my body aching with a need that only he could satisfy.

He responded instantly, his lips peppered kisses against my neck before capturing my nipple in his mouth, bringing me to the edge. The sensation of his warm tongue against my nipple sent my need for him into overdrive. I unbuttoned his pajama top and hurriedly took them off. His body never changed. They were toned like he was working out regularly. I took my time and admired his body as I ran my fingers across his chest and down to his stomach. My lips followed my fingers and lingered around his nipples as my tongue circled them before gently sucking each. Richard moaned heavily and gripped my head with his left hand as he put his finger inside me. He knew my body, what button to press that would drive me to the edge.

Knowing he couldn't likely glide his manhood into me, I decided I would need to have it inside me in another way. I slid my body downward, disconnecting his fingers from me. I trailed kisses until I reached his pajama bottom. I held my breath in anticipation as I tugged at his pajama bottom like a woman possessed. I closed my eyes and kissed his intimate part — my mouth enveloped him. I made him feel my kisses. I used my hands and tongue, and he started to moan, his hips bucking with the desire for more. Then, his manhood came alive. It pulsed within my hands and mouth. He was feeling it! His hands gripped my head tightly. His fingers dug into my skull with his growing arousal. It was a dance of desire and dominance, a shared rhythm that coursed through our bodies. Our connection was intense, an intoxicating blend of passion and power that left us both breathless yet craving more. I continued pleasing him until he couldn't stand it anymore.

"Ride me now, darling," he commanded. "Ride me hard."

Excitement coursed through my body. This was it. After months of waiting, I would finally feel him inside me again. He was hard as a rock as I straddled his muscular, solid thighs and helped him push inside me. We found that perfect rhythm as my body bounced and ground against him. I wanted him to feel the way I do as he showed me how amazing it is for him to take pleasure from me as he moved in and out of my body. He sat with his back against the headboard as I mounted him. I've never enjoyed this before, being on top, being in control, but he made it so easy, so addictive. As his eyes widened, he grinned as he drank me in.

Sensing my goal to push us both over the edge, he gripped my waist as he controlled the movement of my hips. I was losing myself in this moment — touching him, hearing him, inhaling him. These swept me into a state of being that I cannot reach alone.

His mouth brushed against my flesh, my torso twisting in such a way that he could capture my nipple briefly before it was snatched away from him as I bounced up, attempting to trap it beneath his lips once more when I lowered myself down on his erection. When he missed, his lips and tongue caressed my skin, his hot breath tickling my flesh.

His fingers arched tighter against my hips as he thrust hard into me for the final time before his body was stunned by his pleasure, cried out my name, and spilled his climax deep inside me.

Our bodies were covered with sweat as I curled against him. His kisses were tender and sweet, his arms enveloping me in a warm embrace.

"Happy birthday, my love," I murmured, giving him my sweetest smile before I pressed another kiss against his lips.

"Thank you, darling. You're truly a miracle worker," he responded with a chuckle, his joy infectious. We settled into a comfortable silence, basking in the radiant afterglow of making love.

27

The morning sun, a radiant orb of fiery gold, timidly peered through the vast expanse of my office's floor-to-ceiling glass wall. Its gentle rays pirouetted across the room, casting long, dramatic shadows over the seemingly insurmountable stacks of papers and manuscripts scattered haphazardly across my sleek glass desk. This scene of organized chaos is proof of the numerous tasks vying for my attention. Despite its intimidating appearance, I found an unusual solace in it.

As Richard became more busy in his rehabilitation programs, I was back in my element, surrounded by the familiar frenzy of pending deadlines and unattended work. The decision to temporarily step away from all these that had been necessitated by Richard's accident made me realize no matter how I kept reminding myself that I was an independent woman, I was family-centric, too. I had willingly traded the adrenaline-pumping rush of the corporate world for the quiet, albeit emotionally draining, solitude of home care. But now, I was stepping back into my heels, ready to embrace the challenges that awaited me.

Earlier, as I stepped into the room, a wave of anticipation tinged with anxiety washed over me. The comforting scent of freshly brewed coffee permeated the air from the corner table, serving as a subtle reminder of the routine I had momentarily left behind. I had yearned for this feeling — the electrifying surge of responsibility, the exhilarating thrill of making pivotal decisions, and the quiet gratification that followed the successful completion of a task.

* * *

Just as I was about to dive headfirst into the first towering pile, the door creaked open, stealing my attention. In walked Yumi, her face a well-practiced mask of calm. However, her eyes, sharp and alert, betrayed an underlying current of apprehension.

"Good morning, Hope," she greeted, her voice steady as she gently closed the door behind her. "I trust you're settling back into the groove of things comfortably?" Her choice of words reflected her understanding of the emotional whirlwind I was experiencing. She knew, better than anyone, how much this return meant to me — not just as a professional but also as a woman trying to regain control over her life in the wake of a personal crisis.

"I'm on the path," I responded, my voice a soothing lullaby in the midst of an impending storm. A small, reassuring smile made its way across my face as I gestured towards the mahogany chair opposite my desk. "What's the latest from the corridors of power?"

Yumi inhaled deeply, her slender fingers adorned with a striking coat of black nail polish, rhythmically tapping against the leather-bound folder she clutched. "There are... murmurs," she voiced out cautiously, her words hanging heavy in the air. "Several board members have voiced their disapproval of your father's decision to sideline Edwin and appoint Richard to the board. They're apprehensive about the company's future trajectory."

The news hit me like a wave, causing my pulse to race and my hands to grip the edges of my desk involuntarily. My heart pounded against my ribcage like a frantic drummer. "Who?" I demanded, my voice straining to maintain its calm façade. "Who seeks to unseat him? They can't possibly do that. My father holds majority shares, after all."

Yumi hesitated, her gaze momentarily drifting away before realigning with mine. The silence between us was almost tangible. "It's all hushed talks for now, Hope," she spoke softly, her voice barely above a whisper. "But we must be ready to face the storm. While they can't strip him of his board position, they can certainly edge him out of the management team." Yumi locked eyes with me, her gaze unwavering as she reminded me, "Hope, this isn't just a family business anymore. We have external investors and public shareholders to answer to."

* * *

The news struck me like a sucker punch, leaving me winded and gasping for breath. My father, the man who had painstakingly built this company from nothing more than a dream and sheer determination, was under threat. His life's work, a legacy passed down from his own father, was on the brink of being snatched away. "They want to take all that he's worked for? Over my dead body!" I exclaimed, my voice echoing off the austere walls of my office.

Yumi paused, her usually calm demeanor replaced with a hint of concern. "Hope, we hold substantial sway with your father and Richard's votes, but we need Frank from finance on our side. His wife adores Richard; perhaps an invitation for dinner at your place might help. Then, shifting gears, she asked, "Speaking of Richard, how's he holding up?"

"He's progressing well," I replied, my thoughts drifting to my father. "He's working on transitioning from the wheelchair to a walker or cane. He's determined to be ready for The Getaway's dubbing in three weeks, just in time for its fall release."

"That's excellent news," Yumi responded, a glimmer of relief flickering in her eyes. "Richard's presence at the next board meeting would send a strong message. His charm and charisma might even sway some undecided board members."

"How about Michael?" I asked. "Do you think we need to keep him in the loop?

"Hope, let's keep this between us for the meantime."

I swallowed hard, my throat constricting as I battled the surge of anger and betrayal threatening to consume me. "Alright," I said, straightening up in my chair, my resolve steeling. "Let's get to work. Yumi, I want to know who these traitors are."

That night, I relayed everything to Richard. His face hardened as he listened, but he agreed to attend the board meeting after his doctor's appointment.

———

The chill of the boardroom was in stark contrast to the fiery debate that had been smoldering in this room for days. Michael hastily summoned an emergency executive meeting, pulling in all heads of subsidiaries under the umbrella of Ortega's Holdings. His move left me puzzled; his jurisdiction was supposed to be limited to the New York office, spearheading the expansion into US and European territories. My publishing firm, nestled comfortably within the folds of Ortega's Holdings, had continuously operated independently.

Clad in a tailored suit that seemed as sharp as his piercing gaze, Michael presided at the head of the expansive mahogany table. His hands were neatly folded before him, a picture of poised control. I found myself placed directly opposite him, at the far end of the table, under his mysterious scrutiny.

A quick glance around the room revealed the faces of the other key players. Lydia Flemming, the formidable head of our legal team, was present, her eyes hidden behind a pair of glasses. Raymund Prince, the wizard of Mergers and Acquisitions, sat next to her, his face stoic. Beside me was Frank Underhill, the head of Communications. The rest of the subsidiary heads filled out the remaining seats, their expressions a mixture of curiosity and apprehension.

"Thank you all for making time for this urgent meeting," Michael began, his voice cutting through the heavy silence like a knife. There was no preamble, no unnecessary pleasantries. He was a man who went straight for the jugular.

"As you're all aware, our expansion programs are proving to be quite the financial sinkhole. We must accelerate these projects to usher them into the profitability stage as soon as possible," he continued, laying bare the purpose of this gathering.

His words hung in the air, a challenge and a warning wrapped in corporate jargon. The power play was precise, and the game was on.

"Has the chairman been informed about this meeting?" Raymund, a seasoned veteran who had served my father faithfully for 22 years, interjected before Michael could proceed with his monologue. His snowy hair stood out against his immaculate white silk shirt and navy suit. Known throughout the company as 'The Watchdog,' Raymund was renowned for his omniscience regarding all the subsidiaries worldwide. "Knowing Oliver," he mused, "he has a knack for investing in projects with long-term vision, patiently biding his time until the ideal moment to reveal their full potential."

Alongside him was Frank, but more popularly known within his department as 'Jesus Almighty' due to his uncanny ability to make the impossible possible. Together, they were affectionately — or perhaps fearfully — referred to as the 'Demolition Twins' within the organization. They were the ones who dismantled departments, shut down subsidiaries, and even terminated executives. Any task my father was reluctant to carry out, they executed without hesitation.

Michael's face remained impassive, but I could see a flicker of annoyance in his eyes. "I appreciate your concerns, Raymund. Oliver has given me carte blanche to steer this ship, including calling executive meetings. Our focus should be on picking the low-hanging fruits to expedite savings and accelerate profits," he responded, his tone measured.

Raymund's eyes narrowed slightly. "Be more specific, Michael. Which projects are you planning to wrestle with?" he asked, his voice carrying a note of challenge.

Michael turned his gaze towards me, a predatory smile playing on his lips. "Let's start with the media and publishing firm. It doesn't align with our core business," he said, his words hanging heavily in the room.

I felt a surge of defiance. Before I could challenge him, Frank came to the rescue, "And which particular programs within Hope's company are you referring to, Michael?" he retorted, his voice steady. "As far as everybody is concerned, Hope's subsidiary is meeting the targets in terms of both revenue and profits."

The room fell silent, everyone waiting for Michael's response. The power play was now out in the open, and the actual game was just beginning.

"Yes, she's been meeting targets. But her TV series is currently on indefinite hold due to Richard's current situation. We have two films in the pipeline which were already budgeted, with part of the funds already allocated to various outfits," Michael stated matter-of-factly.

I bristled at his words. "Are you aware how much *Back In Time* grossed this year and continues to make money? The two films temporarily on hold are sound investments." I shot back, my voice laced with frustration.

"I understand your perspective, Hope," he began, his tone smooth, attempting to alleviate. "However, we must prioritize the company's best interests. At this point, Richard's projects pose a financial risk. His return to filming remains uncertain."

His words struck a nerve within me, igniting a spark of indignation. It felt as though he was trivializing my husband's aspirations, treating them like mere trinkets to be bartered or discarded without a second thought. I took a deep breath, striving to maintain composure amidst the rising tide of emotions.

"Michael, Richard's projects are not just numbers on a financial statement," I retorted, my voice steady despite the inner tumult. "They embody his passion, his lifelong pursuit. I shan't stand idly by while you dismiss them with such casual disregard."

"Michael, why cause a ruckus when it's in calm waters?" Raymund interjected, glancing at me as if to silently reassure me that he had my back.

The boardroom descended into an uneasy silence, the air thick with tension. The executive officers sat in their seats, observing the unfolding drama with a blend of anxiety and fascination. They were unwitting spectators to a power play that would indubitably influence the company's trajectory.

"I'm not suggesting we abandon them, Hope," Michael responded, his voice placating. "Merely that we consider recasting and then revisit these projects when Richard is back on his feet."

His words felt insincere. My father had entrusted him with our business expansion in the US and Europe, yet he seemed to forget his role was temporary stewardship of my family's legacy.

"Michael," I said, my voice icy, mirroring the frost-kissed boardroom windows. "You seem to forget your position. You're here because of my father's decision, not by your merit. Let's not lose sight of who the captain of these holding companies is. And, don't forget who's in front of you, right now."

A sharp, collective intake of breath echoed around the room. The executives squirmed in their seats, their eyes flicking nervously between Michael and me. The power dynamics had profoundly shifted.

A steely determination swiftly replaced Michael's initial surprise. "Yes, Hope, your name matches every corporate stationery," he acknowledged, his voice firm. "But at this moment, I'm the CEO. I am responsible for making decisions in the company's best interest."

"My firm operates independently!" I retorted, my voice escalating. My gaze turned towards our legal head. "Lydia, clarify this for us. As the CEO, can Michael interfere with its operations?" I held Michael's gaze, unflinching. This wasn't just about business anymore. It was about loyalty, respect, and defending what mattered most. I was prepared for battle.

Lydia cleared her throat, her glasses beginning to fog from the escalating tension. "Hope, while your firm is technically independent, it remains part of Ortega's conglomerate and is involved in the US expansion."

"Hope, this isn't a casual discussion in your father's living room where your status as his daughter holds sway," Michael retorted, his gaze locked on me.

"I won't let you dismantle those film projects, Michael!" I rose to my feet, slamming my fist on the table for emphasis.

"It's not about your preferences or decisions, Hope. Those projects will be liquidated whether you approve or not!" Michael shot back, rising to his feet and matching my intensity.

The tension in the room was suffocating when an unexpected voice cut through the charged atmosphere. "Raise your voice at my wife once more, Michael, and I'll personally escort you out the door."

I whirled around to find Richard standing in the doorway, suited up and leaning on a cane. There was no wheelchair, and no support team —just him.

Overwhelmed, I rushed towards him, throwing my arms around him without regard for the audience around us. Our lips met in a passionate kiss. Pulling away, he shot Michael a warning look. "I hope I made myself clear, Michael." Then, turning to me, he said, "Finish your meeting, darling. I'll be waiting in your office." He kissed me once more before exiting, leaving the room in stunned silence.

Returning to my seat, I kept my gaze firmly on Michael, a silent challenge in my eyes. The room was fraught with tension, the air thick with unsaid words and unmade decisions. The corporate power play had taken an unforeseen turn with Richard's appearance, and the boardroom was buzzing with unmistakable unease.

Raymund, ever the mediator, cleared his throat, breaking the heavy silence in the room. "Perhaps it would be wise to refer this matter back to the chairman," he suggested, his voice steady.

Michael's gaze flickered to Raymund, his eyebrows furrowing slightly. "That may not be necessary, Raymund," he said, attempting to regain control of the situation. "We were appointed to make these decisions."

Lydia chimed in, adjusting her glasses nervously. "With all due respect, Michael, considering the sensitivity of the subject and the potential repercussions, it is prudent to involve Mr. Ortega."

I seized the opportunity. "Lydia is right, Michael. You may be the acting CEO, but you don't own these companies. You can't make unilateral decisions that affect us all, especially when they involve personal investments."

The room fell silent again, all eyes on Michael. He looked around the table, at the faces of the executive officers, each echoing the same sentiment. It was clear. This was no longer just about business. It was about respect, loyalty, and the recognition of boundaries.

Finally, Michael nodded, albeit reluctantly. "Very well," he conceded, "We'll refer this to Oliver."

A collective sigh swept through the room. The storm hadn't passed, but there was a respite for now. As for me, I knew the real battle was just beginning.

———

As I rushed into my office, the sight that greeted me was one that tugged at my heartstrings. Richard was sitting at my desk, his fingers gently tracing the edges of the photos displayed there — snapshots of us, our smiles frozen in time. Seeing him up and moving around after months of being confined to a wheelchair was nothing short of a miracle.

Tears welled up in my eyes, threatening to spill over. The emotional roller coaster of the past few months had been grueling, and seeing Richard's progress felt almost surreal. I walked over to him, my heart pounding with a mixture of surprise, relief, and a twinge of hurt.

"Richard," I choked out, my voice barely above a whisper. "When did this happen? Why didn't you tell me?"

He turned to look at me, his eyes full of warmth and a hint of mischief. "It was meant to be a surprise, darling," he said softly. "We've been working on my recovery for weeks. I kept playing the part, pretending to need the wheelchair when I was actually starting to walk again."

Tears streamed down my face, not sadness but overwhelming joy and relief. I wrapped my arms around him, burying my face in his chest as

I let the tears flow freely.

"Oh, Richard," I sobbed. "You have no idea how happy this makes me."

He held me close, his hand gently stroking my hair. "I wanted to give you something to smile about today, darling," he murmured into my hair. "I didn't expect that scene in the boardroom, though."

Pulling back slightly, I looked up at him, our faces inches apart. I could see the love in his eyes, the same love that had carried us through all these turbulent times. Leaning in, our lips met in a tender kiss, a promise of better days to come.

"I love you, Richard," I whispered against his lips.

"I love you too, Hope," he murmured back, pulling me closer as we lost ourselves in the moment, leaving the world outside the door.

28

The grandeur of the boardroom was almost suffocating, an imposing testament to the power and prestige that resided within its walls. It has been three weeks since the unfortunate incident in this same room. Now, Richard and I found our places among the plush leather chairs, facing the endless expanse of the polished mahogany table that gleamed under the harsh glare of the overhead lights. Around us, a low hum of hushed conversations filled the air, like the quiet murmurings of an impending storm.

At the head of this impressive table sat my father, his presence commanding the room with an unspoken authority that silenced the whispers and drew all eyes toward him. His weathered features were etched with years of wisdom and experience, a stalwart captain steering us through the stormy seas of business.

"Ladies and gentlemen," he began, his voice resonating through the room, demanding attention without raising its volume. "I have the pleasure of introducing a new face to our esteemed board, although, given his reputation, I suspect an introduction may be rather superfluous." A light chuckle rippled through the room at his jest. "Please welcome Richard Collins, joining us today for his inaugural board meeting."

A murmur of acknowledgment swept across the room like a wave, acknowledging the newcomer. Richard returned the gesture with a nod, his face an impenetrable mask of calm determination. I glanced at him, my heart swelling with pride. This was his battlefield now, a world away from the simplicity of the life we once knew.

Our head of communications, Frank Underhill, smartly dressed in a navy pinstripe suit, rose and offered his hand to Richard. His charming, curly hair and single earring stud provided a playful contrast to the formality of his attire.

"Richard, old chap, it's an absolute pleasure to finally make your acquaintance. My missus is quite fond of your films. Saw you opposite Julia Roberts in *My Best Friend's Wedding*. Brilliant performance, mate," he said, brimming with enthusiasm.

Richard chuckled, "As flattered as I am to receive such praise, Frank, I believe you've mistaken me for Rupert Everett. Though, I must say, we are both rather dashing. A common trait among us Brits, wouldn't you say?" Frank ran his fingers through his hair, a clear sign of embarrassment. Both he and Richard were British, after all.

I couldn't resist a giggle and leaned towards Frank, who was seated next to me. "That film was from 1997, Frank. Richard was still strutting his stuff on the catwalk then, not gracing the silver screen yet," I whispered. He shot me a glance that could freeze lava.

"Did I make a right muppet of myself?" he asked, mortified.

"It was a bit of a faux pas, Frank," I replied, trying to suppress a chuckle. He rolled his eyes in surrender, and I couldn't help but laugh.

Michael was next to rise; the rustling of his expensive suit was the only sound in the room's intense silence. As the US and European operations CEO, he held the floor to present a radical new strategy, one that proposed a drastic shift from our traditional stronghold of film production and book publishing to the acquisition of a tech company specializing in social media and market influence.

"Ladies and gentlemen," he began, his voice steady and assured. "We find ourselves on the brink of a new era. An era where the tangible is being rapidly supplanted by the virtual."

With a fluid gesture, he pointed towards the large screen behind him.

It flickered to life, displaying a slide of plummeting sales figures for books and films in the universal market. "As you can see in the data, traditional strengths in film production and book publishing are no longer viable as primary sources of malls and real estate communications and engagement for our own marketing and advertising," he argued, his finger tracing the downward trajectory of the graph.

"But," he continued, his eyes gleaming with an infectious enthusiasm, "we have the opportunity to pivot, to focus on where the future lies: technology." With a decisive click, the slide changed, revealing the logo of a promising tech startup. "This company has demonstrated remarkable growth in social media marketing. Acquiring them would give us a significant competitive advantage and position us at the forefront of an industry that shows no signs of slowing down."

As Michael spoke, more slides flashed onto the screen, each one showcasing the potential benefits of the acquisition: increased market share, access to cutting-edge technology, a younger demographic, and the power to control algorithms that could potentially revolutionize the retail brands, which were a significant source of revenue for our mall and real estate businesses.

"In conclusion," Michael said, his voice resonating in the silent room, "by shifting our focus to harnessing the power of social media and market influence, we're not just keeping up with the times, but positioning ourselves at the forefront of the industry. This is a bold step towards ensuring our company's survival and prosperity in the digital age."

His presentation ended with a slide that read, "Adapt or Perish." The message was clear: Embrace change or risk becoming obsolete. His words hung like a heavy cloud in the room, challenging the board members to reconsider their preconceived notions about the future of the company.

"Wait a minute," I found myself saying, my voice ringing in tense silence. "Our media and publishing company is delivering tremendous growth. Its core strength lies in films and books. Why would we want to abandon that?"

* * *

Michael locked eyes with me, his demeanor unruffled. "We're not abandoning it, we're restructuring. Hope, the future is digital. We need to adapt or risk being left behind."

"I know. That was my line in one of the earlier board meetings. That's the reason why we acquired Montclair Tech for The SkyPitch App for writers and publishers."

"Hope, listen. I know the media firm is doing well, but it's about time to think bigger, which will give a higher potential for our US and European expansion." His words were met with a chorus of agreement from some board members. My blood boiled. This wasn't progress. It was abandoning a ship that was smooth sailing. I was about to retort when a calm voice sliced through the mounting tension.

"If I may," Richard began, his gaze steady and unflinching. The room fell silent as he slowly rose to his feet. His chair scraped against the marble floor, the sound echoing in the serene atmosphere. He navigated his way around the imposing mahogany table and positioned himself in front of the screen, opposite my father. His tone was calm but firm, commanding respect without demanding it. "While I agree that the future is indeed digital, I don't believe that we should completely abandon what has brought us to where we are today... which, by the way, still yields significant returns. People still love books; they still enjoy films, despite the rising popularity of short videos on TikTok and other social apps. These are media that ignite the imagination and stir emotions. Isn't that what storytelling, and by extension, branding, is all about?"

Richard paused, sweeping his gaze over each board member, gauging their reactions before continuing. "Imagine this: films and books telling people that mall culture benefits mothers raising their children, where education is seamlessly integrated into the environment. Bookstores, indoor playgrounds, nursing stations, and sports clinics."

He didn't stop there. "Books and magazines... television... showcasing the lifestyle of condominium living. Celebrities dictate every trend through movies and television. And books, too, before it trickles down to micro-influencers and is adopted by the mass market through social media."

He paused again, allowing his words to permeate the silence. "Instead of discarding these working platforms, why don't we use them to enhance our digital presence? Each book and film can be leveraged to create engaging content and drive conversations on social media. This way, we're not just adapting to the digital world. We are creating the conversations, dictating the tastes, and curating what people think and say. We're harnessing our strengths and making them work for us."

The room fell silent once more as Richard concluded. I scanned the room, seeing contemplation reflected in many eyes. It was a bold move, challenging the proposed strategy. But it was also a necessary one. In the silence that followed, I could sense the shift, the possibility of a new direction that bridged our past and future.

Everyone was steeped in silence as my father's gaze found Richard. His lips curled into a smile, the kind that softened the lines on his weathered face and crinkled the corners of his eyes. "Thank you, Richard," he said, his voice resonating with gratitude. "Your insights are valuable, and it's evident that we need to consider expanding our horizons."

He turned his attention back to the room, his aura commanding the undivided attention of everyone present. "I want everyone to consider broadening both our media and digital presence. Take Elon Musk, for instance. He acquired Twitter to serve his firm while simultaneously controlling communications and turning the platform profitable. It's about time we started thinking beyond traditional boundaries."

His focus shifted back to me, his penetrating gaze softening with paternal warmth. "Hope, I want you to collaborate with Yumi on the expansion into newscasting — both traditional and digital. I want our media company to stand autonomous and strong."

Then, he addressed Michael, "We will focus on the real estate and mall construction. The media and publishing, we'll leave that to Hope."

As the finance team presented the overall financial health of our US-Europe operations, a wave of satisfaction swept over the room. The figures painted a promising picture, making every board member beam with pride. Across the table, Richard and I exchanged a glance, a silent celebration of what we had accomplished today.

When the meeting finally adjourned, and I was beginning to gather my belongings, my father's voice stopped me in my tracks. "Richard, could you stay back a moment? There's something I'd like to discuss with you." His gaze flickered towards me, seeking my approval. With a nod, I moved towards them, kissing both cheeks before exiting, the door closing softly behind me.

———

The sensation of warmth seeped through the soles of my bare feet as they luxuriated on heated marble tiles. The once cool, elegant surface had transformed into a source of gentle warmth, a comforting contrast to the chilly evening air. A grand mirror held dominion over the room, its intricate frame gilded with real gold and embedded with tiny, twinkling LED lights that bathed the room in a soft, golden glow reminiscent of a setting sun.

Standing beside me was Richard, his reflection captured within the mirror's expansive surface. He was diligently brushing his teeth with a high-tech, battery-operated toothbrush, the device humming a low, rhythmic tune that added a soothing soundtrack to our nightly ritual. On the other hand, I was combing my hair, each stroke sliding easily through my silken strands that cascaded over the plush silk robe draped elegantly over my shoulders.

Richard's buzzing toothbrush went silent, abruptly ending its lullaby and replacing it with an intimate silence that echoed off the polished stone walls. He set the toothbrush down and met my gaze in the mirror, his blue-grey eyes reflecting the delicate light, adding an ethereal quality to his already handsome features.

"Why aren't you curious about what your father and I discussed after our meeting?" he asked, breaking the silence, his voice bouncing around the room, creating a soft echo that lingered in the air.

I continued to comb my hair, my reflection mirroring his in the grand mirror. "I was taught not to pry into matters that don't concern me or aren't meant for me," I replied calmly, my eyes meeting his through our reflections. "If Dad thought it was important for me to know, he would have kept me in the boardroom."

Each word hung in the air. A sign that the topic is off limits — one of the principles instilled in me since working with my father, and a subtle reminder of the boundaries we had in our relationship. Richard's expression remained unreadable, but a flicker of understanding passed through his eyes — a silent acknowledgment of the unspoken rules that governed our lives.

Richard inched closer, his reflection in the ornate mirror growing more prominent. The refreshing scent of his minty toothpaste wafted in the air, mingling subtly with the calming aroma of my lavender-infused hair oil. His robust arms, a symbol of his unyielding strength, encircled me, their touch a soothing balm to the harsh reality he was about to unveil.

"Your father was insistent on knowing about my full recovery," Richard admitted, his voice a low murmur against the silence of the room. "He was taken aback but expressed relief you stood your ground and challenged Michael's audacious proposal. Honestly, it frightened both of us."

My brows furrowed in confusion, "Why?" I queried.

"You've grown up too fast, Hope. You were supposed to be living a life full of carefree joy. Traveling with me, savoring the world, laughing at our shared escapades. Instead, here you are, burdened with a role that was thrust upon you without adequate preparation. Balancing that and looking after Samantha single-handedly." He gently disentangled himself from our embrace, spinning me around to face him. His eyes bore into mine, filled with regret. "I blame myself entirely," he confessed.

I silenced his self-reproach with a gentle finger on his lips. "It was my choice, Richard," I reassured him. My hands tenderly cradled his face. "I would love nothing more than to explore the world with you, to share every moment together. But that isn't our reality... that's not who we are."

Richard's gaze softened. "You don't need to carry these burdens, Hope. Oliver is still young. He can lead the holding companies for decades to come. You could defer your role in his company and pursue your passions. We could build this family together. I can take care of you. Money will never be a problem, with or without Ortega's Holding," he proposed.

I shook my head, my resolve unwavering. "Richard, we can't abandon Dad now, not until we uncover the identities of these traitors."

"Which brings me to another revelation. Someone tipped your father off that certain board members are plotting a coup to overthrow him," he confessed, his grip on me tightening involuntarily. His words echoed ominously in the confines of our luxurious bathroom, a stark contrast to the tranquil atmosphere. "We both wanted to shield you from the impending crossfire."

A floodgate of emotions threatened to consume me — fear, defiance, determination. I studied Richard, my rock, my confidante. "You can't push me aside. Ortega's Holdings is ours. It's the legacy for our children... and their children in the future. I can't bear the thought of someone out there plotting to steal it from them. My father's battle has become mine, too, and it's yours as well."

His hand enveloped mine, a symbol of our united front. "Then we'll confront this together," he vowed. As we caught sight of our reflections in the resplendent mirror, I knew we were prepared to stand against whatever storm loomed ahead.

———

The shrill ring of my phone was like an unexpected ice bath, jolting me awake from the warmth of sleep. I squinted against the harsh luminescence of the screen, the bold numbers 7:00 AM searing into my sleep-glazed eyes. Annoyance bubbled up within me, effervescent and sharp like a freshly uncorked bottle of champagne. Who on earth dared to shatter the sacred silence of dawn?

* * *

"Yumi?" I mumbled, my voice thick with sleep, recognizing the familiar sequence of digits.

"Don't rush to the office yet. Stay put. I'll meet you at home," she whispered. Her voice was a gentle flutter against my eardrum. Her words were cloaked in an air of secrecy as if the very walls of our corporate fortress had grown ears overnight.

"May I ask about the sudden change of plans?" I asked, curiosity piquing.

"No need for now. I'll fill you in later." Her response was curt and cryptic.

"Alright then, I'll have Leticia set an extra place for breakfast," I said, but the line was already dead, leaving only the hum of silence in its wake.

My gaze fell on the empty space beside me, Richard's imprint still etched in the sheets. Undoubtedly, he's having an early morning workout and therapy session. The rehab unit turned gym below our penthouse was probably echoing with his grunts and metal clanging. A fleeting pang of loneliness pierced through me, but I swiftly brushed it aside, the day awaiting my attention.

Trading the comforting embrace of my pajamas for the crisp lines of jeans and a pristine white shirt, I nestled into the morning routine with a new manuscript splayed open before me, its words dancing in the steam wafting from my coffee cup. Yumi's arrival punctuated the stillness, her leather portfolio bag swollen with clandestine contents. Her eyes bore the weight of unspoken storms, their depth stirring a sense of anticipation that drummed against my ribcage like a nervous heartbeat.

"Yumi, what's happening?" I asked, my voice barely more than a breath. She unfurled a bundle of documents onto the table, her fingers trembling like leaves caught in an unexpected breeze.

Before we could delve into the impending discussion, Samantha and

Henry emerged from their respective sanctuaries upstairs, their morning greetings slicing through the tension.

"Morning, Aunt Yumi!" Sam's voice was bright as morning sunlight, her quick peck on my cheek a familiar ritual.

"Good morning, Yumi. Hope, I've asked Jeffrey to chauffeur me to work after dropping Sam at school. I won't need my car today — I'm pressed for time," Henry said, his words tumbling out as he snatched a strip of bacon from the breakfast spread.

"If you're in such a rush, use Chen instead," I suggested, my tone light.

With a quick peck on my forehead and a grin that could outshine the sun, he replied, "You're the best!" His appreciation echoed in the quiet morning.

"Jeffrey is yours, but I'll have Chen and Arthur. I want to parade the two sentinels at school," Sam's voice chimed through the air, a playful negotiation with her brother, or perhaps more aptly, a skilled manipulation.

"If you want to show off, ask Dad to chauffeur you. I've trodden that path before, and it was as if the sun shone solely on me that day," Henry retorted, his tone laced with the wisdom of shared experience. Their voices ebbed into whispers as the elevator swallowed them, descending into the heart of the building.

As their banter receded, it left behind a trail of laughter and sibling rivalry that danced in the morning light, painting a vivid picture of their solidarity. Their words were laden with nuances of their personalities — Sam, ever the charmer, using her wits to get her way, and Henry, the older brother, using past experiences as a beacon for his younger sister. Their distinct yet harmonious voices echoed in the corners of the room, leaving a lingering sense of warmth and familiarity.

With the departure of Henry and Sam leaving a lingering silence in their wake, Yumi began to unfurl the mystery. "It's a board takeover, Hope," her voice was but a whisper, a phantom of its usual buoyancy.

"Michael Yang… and some others."

The name struck like a gust of frigid wind, chilling me to the bone. Michael. My father's trusted allies. Now a treacherous serpent in our Eden. Betrayal sliced through me, shattering my trust like fine porcelain dashed upon stone. A flood of emotions swept over me: anger that roared like wildfire, confusion swirling like a storm, but above all, a deep-seated hurt that gnawed in me.

"But why?" I managed to mutter out, my voice strained with disbelief.

Yumi responded with a solemn shake of her head, "Overambitious… and foolish. He's jealous of Richard and the sudden attention he's receiving from your father."

"Richard is family!" My exclamation echoed in the room, the absurdity of the coup's motive ringing loud and clear. "Richard had no desire for corporate power or management roles. His presence is to bolster our business' reputation using his celebrity status."

"That's precisely what fuels Michael's envy. He held some sway within the board, but then Richard stepped into the spotlight." Yumi paused, her gaze meeting mine, "Have you and Richard dined with Lydia as I suggested?" She asked.

"We have. Lydia is firmly with us. Richard ensured that," I replied, a faint smile tugging at my lips.

Yumi unfurled the enemy's strategy, "In the upcoming board meeting, Michael will call for Oliver to step down as chairman, citing a lack of confidence from the board and shareholders in his leadership. As it stands, we're outnumbered five to seven. But, I can sway Frank to our side. Joseph Sy is on the fence, but a quick trip to Manila might just tip the scales in our favor." Her words sketched out a battlefield, the stakes higher than ever.

"I want an eleven-to-one victory, Yumi. I wish to see Michael standing alone, the sting of defeat etched on his face," I declared, my resolve echoing in the room.

* * *

"If that's your aim, let Richard engage with George Lucca. Their shared British roots might just be the key. Oliver can work his charm on the remaining board members." Yumi paused, her mind a chess board of strategies and countermeasures. "Now, we move on to the next item on our agenda. After Michael's exit, I envision you stepping up as the new CEO for our US and Europe expansion."

"Yumi, it's too early. I'm not sure if I'm ready to shoulder such responsibility," I pleaded, feeling the weight of her words.

"Hope, no one is ever truly ready. Even your father wasn't when he first took the reins. But you have a strong board backing you. Waiting for the 'right time' is an illusion. You need to seize this moment and grow into it," Yumi urged.

"May I bare my soul to you, just this once?" I asked, my heart heavy. "I've recently entered married life and have weathered numerous life-altering storms. When Richard was in the hospital, and our future seemed shadowed by uncertainty, I blamed myself for not being there for him. I yearn for the simple joys of life… of motherhood. I want to start a family, or embark on spontaneous adventures with Richard."

Yumi sighed, "Oliver partly blames himself for thrusting you into this so early. He hails from a generation where children were groomed for leadership from a young age. He wants you to savor life with Richard. However, we can't halt the momentum you've built. At some point, you must take the leap."

"I still wish to oversee the media and publishing house. But I also crave time to write, to travel when inspiration strikes. Richard and his children have sacrificed so much, uprooting their lives to be here in New York. I want to tend to our home in London as well. Give me five years, Yumi, to embrace the roles of wife and mother," I begged.

"I understand. We need to find a suitable replacement for Michael," Yumi began, but halted when she saw my knowing smile. "Hope, I can't fill that role. Oliver needs me by his side."

"Could we find a substitute for you?" I asked earnestly.

* * *

"Your father is a visionary. He needs someone to bring those visions to life. My rightful place is beside him. What are your thoughts on Lydia?" She queried.

"Lydia seems a prudent choice. Her expertise in international law could prove invaluable," I pointed out. "Yumi, my father was aware of this meeting, wasn't he? This outcome aligns with his plans, doesn't it?" I asked, my eyebrows furrowing in suspicion.

A knowing smile graced Yumi's lips, "Let's say he insisted on you undergoing management training with Lydia and me over the next years. To learn the ropes, but still participate in pivotal decisions."

"I suspect Richard was also privy to this plan," I mused.

Her smile held a hint of mischief, "Perhaps?"

We sank into a comfortable silence, punctuated only by the rhythmic ticking of the clock. My world was morphing, the puzzle pieces slowly falling into place. The morning sun poured through the windows, painting elongated shadows on the floor. A new day had dawned, bringing with it the promise of a future I was ready to shape.

29

The sun's rays embraced me like a warm, tender kiss as I relaxed on a bench in the heart of Central Park. Methodically, I tied my shoelaces, my gaze drifting towards the expansive cerulean canvas above. The calm breeze playfully tousled my hair, seemingly carrying away the residual fragments of my worries.

I spotted a familiar figure jogging towards me from the corner of my eye. His silhouette, elongated by the early morning light, danced across my feet. As he came closer, my heart executed an excited flutter. It was Richard, donning his high-end athletic gear, which accentuated his well-toned physique. The sight of him, radiant and full of life under the morning sun, ignited a profound sense of gratitude within me.

Observing Richard, my heart burgeoned with a cocktail of pride and relief. His posture, upright and confident, bore no semblance to the man who had been shackled by a wheelchair for months. Witnessing him standing tall felt akin to watching a phoenix rise from its ashes, rejuvenated and prepared to reclaim its dominion over the world.

"Ready for our run, Hope?" Richard's voice rang out, echoing the infectious enthusiasm I yearned for during his recovery.

Rising to my feet, I allowed myself a moment to soak in his presence. His once pallid cheeks now bloomed with color, his eyes twinkling with newfound vitality. He had returned stronger and more determined than ever. My heart swelled with love, pride, and a wave of relief so strong it left my knees trembling slightly.

The park hummed with the melodic chatter of birds, the gleeful laughter of children engaged in play nearby, and the city's distant murmur. However, all of it faded into insignificance as Richard drew me into his embrace. His arms enveloped me firmly, his body radiating a warmth that seeped into my very core, grounding me in the moment.

"I love you, darling," he whispered, his breath caressing my skin. His words, though simple, reverberated with genuine emotion, sending delightful shivers cascading down my spine.

"Hmm... you're unusually affectionate today. Should I be worried? Are you planning a return to filming thousands of miles away from home?" I teased, trying to mask the slight edge of anxiety in my voice.

Richard's laughter echoed through the park, a sound I cherished dearly. "Of course not; you're beginning to sound like Sam." Brushing a stray lock of hair from my face, he continued, "I just want to take a moment to appreciate my luck for having such a beautiful and supportive wife who never let me surrender when I was on the brink."

Looking into his eyes, I saw my emotions mirrored back at me. Unable to resist, I leaned in, pressing my lips against his in a kiss that spoke volumes of our shared love and triumph.

The paparazzi descended like a flock of birds, their cameras flashing relentlessly, each shutter click punctuating the morning's tranquility. Reporters surged forward, their eager voices intertwining into a chaotic symphony of curiosity and admiration. Ever the professional, Richard navigated their inquiries with his trademark charm and poise. I watched him, amazed by his resilience. The limelight had always been Richard's second home, and seeing how effortlessly he returned to it was astounding.

"Richard, it's truly a pleasure to see you back on your feet," one reporter began, his voice carrying a hint of genuine concern. "Does this mean you'll be returning to the film set?"

A second one quickly jumped in, her voice eager, "And what's the status of *The Getaway*? Will the initial airing date still hold?"

"The film is progressing as planned," Richard responded smoothly, the British lilt in his voice adding a touch of charm. "We completed the dubbing weeks ago. There will be a press conference soon to share more details."

A third reporter cut through the chatter, his question sharp, "You've had a close brush with death. How do you feel about that?"

Richard's eyes found mine amidst the sea of faces. A warmth in his gaze enveloped me, acting as an invisible shield against the chaos around us. He extended his arm, pulling me closer to him. His touch was unexpected yet comforting, his arm around my waist a silent promise that we were a united front amid the frenzy.

"My Hope," Richard began, his voice soft yet resonating above the clamor. "She has been my rock throughout this journey." He paused, searching for the right words. "Every step I took towards recovery, she was there - cheering me on, pushing me to strive harder. She is the reason I am standing here today, ready to resume my place in the world I love."

His heartfelt confession stirred a wave of emotion within me. But I had learned to keep my composure in front of the press, a lesson Richard had drilled into me. Hearing him articulate his appreciation so publicly was deeply moving. His words were a soothing balm to the anxiety that had been my constant companion these past weeks.

A reporter's question snapped me out of my trance. "Richard, how does it feel to be back in action?" she probed, notepad at the ready.

"It feels like I've been given a second chance," Richard replied, his gaze firmly locked with mine. "This experience has taught me the importance of family. Never take it for granted. When everything else fails, family remains the only constant." His smile widened as he prepared to make his exit, "Thank you all, but I must be off now. I promised my wife a run and a visit to feed the ducks." With a final wave and a charming smile, he turned to leave.

* * *

As we began our run, the world around us blurred into insignificance. Paparazzi continued their photo assault, and reporters hurled questions, but none of it mattered. Richard was back, and we were stronger than ever.

Running under the canopy of trees, the wind playfully tugging at our hair, the ground firm beneath our feet, I knew we had weathered the storm. Our bond had emerged stronger, unbreakable. I blinked away the tears clouding my vision, not wanting to miss a single moment of this triumph. Richard was here with me; together, we were ready to face whatever the world threw at us. He was my beacon of hope, my rock, and seeing him stand tall filled me with indescribable joy.

30

The comforting hum of conversation and the rich, heady aroma of freshly brewed coffee enveloped Jenna and me as we nestled into a cozy corner booth at Lafayette. The Manhattan restaurant was an exquisite blend of rustic charm and modern elegance. Exposed brick walls juxtaposed against sleek black tables, and the soft glow of ambient lighting lent an intimate warmth to the space.

Our brunch spread was a feast for the senses. Towering croissants, their golden crusts flaky and buttery, sat next to a vibrant medley of fresh fruits. The star of our meal was undoubtedly the eggs benedict, poached eggs perched atop toasted English muffins, their deep sunset yellow yolks ready to spill over at the slightest touch.

I had chosen to wear a casual yet chic emerald green jumpsuit that morning. The fabric clung to my curves in all the right places, accentuating my figure. My dark hair was pulled back into a loose ponytail, with stray tendrils framing my face. Gold hoops dangled from my ears, catching the light and adding a touch of sparkle. Jenna, more fashion-conscious than me, sported a trendy floral print dress. The fabric was cinched with a thin belt at her waist, highlighting her slender figure. Her auburn curls bounced with every movement, a fiery halo around her head.

Jenna broke the companionable silence, her voice slicing through the restaurant's ambient noise. "Esperanza," she began, her tone serious, "we need to finalize the filming and production plan for *Back In Time*'s second season. I've read the script, and it's intense... and absolutely brilliant!"

A warm glow of satisfaction spread through me at her words. "Thank you, Jenna. Our team is really good," I replied, cutting into my egg benedict. The yolk oozed out, spilling over the bread in a golden river. I savored the rich flavors, the creamy yolk mingling perfectly with the tangy hollandaise sauce. "I'm still waiting on the final budget and the new castings," I added, my mind already whirring with the logistical challenges ahead.

"Brittany and, naturally, Richard are both signed on until the third season. We're also adding four new supporting roles, and casting is currently working out the contracts," Jenna shared, setting her silverware down with a thoughtful expression.

A sense of surrealism washed over me. "It's strange, isn't it?" I mused, my gaze drifting outside, where the city was alive with its usual hustle and bustle. "Just a year ago, my only role in this endeavor was writing the script. Now, I'm reviewing budgets and filming schedules and giving approvals."

Jenna chuckled, her eyes twinkling with amusement. "In less than two years, the tide has indeed turned. Even I need your approval now," she pointed out, her tone light-hearted yet sincere.

I laughed along with her, shaking my head. "Don't be ridiculous, Jenna. Nothing's really changed. *Back In Time* is incredibly dear to me. This is where everything started, where I met Richard. As long as you continue to weave your magic with the book series, we'll bring them to life on screen," I assured her, a promise from my heart.

The conversation flowed effortlessly between us, interspersed with laughter and shared memories. We knew all too well the hurdles that lay ahead. Yet, we acknowledged that no obstacle was insurmountable as long as we stood side by side. We were more than just colleagues navigating the choppy waters of our chosen industry, bound by our shared passion for storytelling and our unwavering belief in *Back In Time*.

"We've got five episodes left to deliver to ABC. After that, we'll negotiate with Netflix. Then we're faced with a few months' season break. I honestly don't know how in the world we're going to pull off airing season 2 on schedule!" Jenna exclaimed, her frustration evident.

I leaned back into the plush booth, cradling my latte between my hands. The warmth seeping through the ceramic mug was comforting. "We're built for this, Jenna. We thrive under pressure, remember?" I reminded her, a determined sparkle in my eyes.

Jenna's lips curled into a knowing smirk as she pulled out her phone. "Speaking of pressure," she began, her voice laced with an edge of intrigue as she showed me an interview of Ingrid Simon promoting *The Getaway* from her iPhone.

My eyes skimmed over the screen, taking in Ingrid's radiant beauty. "God, she's stunning," I admitted, a pang of jealousy twinging in my chest.

"But not nearly as captivating as you, my dear!" Jenna countered, her words bringing a small smile to my lips.

In the video, Ingrid claimed that she and Richard had maintained constant communication during his recovery from the accident, implying they had grown closer than ever.

A bitter laugh slipped past my lips. "That's quite the story. Ingrid didn't so much as send a get-well card to Richard, let alone visit him. She's simply spinning tales for publicity."

"Ah, but the media love a good drama. The tale of the ex-girlfriend who mourned the accident and swooped in to help with his recovery is just too juicy to resist," Jenna scoffed, rolling her eyes for emphasis.

"And since Richard isn't one for social media, he'll likely let it slide. I've seen this play out before with his ex-wife," I added, my annoyance evident.

Jenna reached across the table, placing a reassuring hand over mine. "This time, you don't have to play their game. Richard loves you, and in his own way, he'll debunk these rumors without engaging in a public spat," she comforted.

"I know, but it still irks me," I admitted, my gaze drifting to the half-empty coffee cup before me, my thoughts lost in the whirlwind of emotions.

"Something bothering you?" Jenna's voice broke through my reverie, her concern evident.

I found myself stirring my latte absentmindedly, the frothy milk swirling into a whirlpool of coffee and cream. "I'm not complaining about where life has taken me. It's been a whirlwind, yes, but it's also brought me so much happiness. I just... sometimes miss the simplicity of the life I used to have."

"Do you mean you miss writing?" she asked, her gaze holding mine.

I nodded, a small sigh escaping my lips. "Yeah," I admitted.

Jenna reached across the table, her grip warm and comforting. "Esperanza, writing is a part of who you are. Your career and family shouldn't stifle your passion. Writing is your lifeline, your escape. Amidst all the chaos in your life, find time for it. Make time for it. Your second book is due, remember?" Her words were a gentle push, a much-needed reminder.

Looking into Jenna's earnest eyes, I knew she was right. She wasn't just a friend to me; she was my mentor, my confidante. She had always been my protector, shielding me from the Ingrid Simons of the world, and even, at times, from Richard. But most importantly, she guarded me from myself, from my tendency to put others before my own needs and desires.

Before I could voice my thoughts, she cut me off. "You can't fully love Richard, Sam, or your parents if you do not love yourself first. And loving them doesn't mean you have to give up what you love most. Neither Richard nor your father would want that for you."

"I'm juggling too many roles, Jenna. I'm scared that one day, I'll drop one of them," I confessed, my voice barely more than a whisper.

* * *

Jenna smiled, her eyes twinkling with determination. "Remember your old mantra? 'Begin badly, but begin.' Grab your pen and notebook again. Set aside a specific time each week to write. Don't wait for spare moments when the work is done or after Richard falls asleep. Write on your own time."

I couldn't help but smile back at her. "That's why I love you, Jenna," I said.

"I know," she replied, her smile broadening. "Also, don't forget to figure out a way to make it clear to Ingrid that your husband isn't interested in her anymore."

At this, we both burst into laughter, our shared joy echoing through the restaurant until our stomachs ached.

———

Saturday nights at home were a cherished tradition in our family. Richard, Samantha, and I would carve out this time just for us, cocooned in the warmth of our den. There were movies to watch, board games to play, and stories to share. Our laughter would echo through the house, intertwining with the love that filled our hearts. Henry would occasionally join us when his schedule allowed and his presence added an extra layer of joy to our familial bond.

Tonight was no exception. The Monopoly board took center stage on the coffee table, awaiting a serious match between Samantha and Richard. As I emerged from the kitchen, my arms laden with steaming buckets of freshly popped popcorn and frosty cans of soda, the comforting aroma of buttery popcorn wafted through the room, mingling effortlessly with the familiar scent of our home. The soft, inviting glow from the night lamps bathed the room in a warm hue, casting dancing shadows that further amplified the cozy ambiance.

"Alright, who's ready to lose?" Richard teased Samantha, a playful glint in his eyes that mirrored the twinkle of the night lamps.

"In your dreams, Dad," Samantha retorted, her voice brimming with youthful competitiveness. Their light-hearted banter was the perfect symphony to my ears, coaxing an affectionate chuckle from me.

Suddenly, the harmonious atmosphere was punctuated by the buzz of Samantha's phone. "Oh, look! It's a reminder about Dad's interview with the full cast of *The Getaway*. It's about to start!"

Richard's gaze met mine, a silent plea flickering in his eyes. "Sweetheart, you don't have to watch it," he gently tried to dissuade her.

However, I returned his gaze with a reassuring smile, a silent promise to be okay. "It's alright, Richard. I want to watch it, too." Despite the unease creeping into my heart, I wanted to stand strong, not just for myself, but for my family as well. After all, we were just having fun together on a weekend night — with board games, and, yes, even the televised interviews.

Samantha rose from her seat, her youthful energy driving her towards the wide television screen that took pride of place on our living room wall. She fiddled with it for a moment before returning to perch herself on Richard's lap, her soft pajamas crinkling against the fabric of his worn-out jogging pants.

"Good heavens, Samantha! You're a ton!" Richard exclaimed, feigning surprise as he wrapped his arms around her.

"Daddy, I'm 11 now. Of course, I've grown heavier," Samantha retorted, her giggles intertwining with Richard's hearty laughter. As I passed the popcorn bucket to Samantha, I slid beside Richard, nestling into the curve of his arm. With one hand resting protectively around our daughter, he freed the other to delve into the popcorn I held for him. We waited with delight, our eyes fixed on the screen as the show began.

The interview started with a flourish, the screen bursting to life with the vibrant cast of *The Getaway*. Richard, looking every bit the dashing movie star in his sleek suit, was seated next to Ingrid Simon. Her flirtatious smile seemed plastered onto her face, and she appeared to find every excuse to touch Richard, laughing at his jokes and hinting at an off-screen camaraderie.

The hosts, ever so eager for juicy details, prodded them about their on-set relationship. "We've got each other's back. We've become each other's person," Ingrid responded, her fingers tracing a path along Richard's arm as if staking a claim.

The female host then steered the conversation about Richard's accident during filming. Ingrid latched onto the opportunity to play the concerned co-star. "Oh my, I was a complete mess! My world turned upside down. I wasn't on set when it happened, and no one was updating me about where they'd taken him!" Her dramatic display was almost convincing.

The rest of the interview blurred into a whirlwind of coy smiles, flirtatious comments, and subtle touches. Ever the professional, Richard tried to steer the conversation back to the film production and its expectations. Yet, there was no denying the unmistakable tension that had settled in our cozy den, turning our lovely family night into a test of patience and endurance.

Every touch, every shared laugh, every lingering look Ingrid bestowed upon Richard felt like a serrated knife slicing through my heart. A knot of unease twisted in my stomach, while a cold sweat slicked my palms, and a bitter taste tainted my tongue. Jealousy, an unaccustomed emotion, had begun its corrosive feast on my peace.

Feeling my tension, Richard slid his arm around me, his lips planting a soft kiss behind my ear. It was a familiar gesture, one that usually brought comfort. However, tonight, it fell short against the onslaught of my troubled emotions.

"Mum, are you okay?" Samantha's voice cut through my tumultuous thoughts. Her innocent eyes filled with worry.

I forced a smile onto my face, not wanting our family night to be marred by my insecurities. "Yes, sweetie. Just remember, you can't believe everything you see about your dad on TV or the internet."

"Yeah, I know, Mum. Dad's just playing along. They need to sell the film," she said sagely. Her wisdom sometimes belied her tender age, making her seem more grounded than me.

Richard chimed in, his voice soothing. "Darling, Ingrid is just playing up for the cameras. She's been instructed to drum up interest. Everyone knows my heart belongs to someone else." With that, he leaned in, kissing my lips tenderly. Yet, his words failed to quell the storm brewing within me entirely.

As the brief interlude arrived during the interview, they decided to air the trailer of *The Getaway*. Among the action-packed sequences and dramatic dialogues, it also featured the steamy scene between Richard and Ingrid. A wave of discomfort washed over me.

"Sam, don't watch this part," I advised quickly, my voice more strained than intended.

Obediently, Samantha squeezed her eyes shut and clamped her hands over her ears. She resembled a child playing peek-a-boo, yet the situation was far from playful. The sight of her innocence contrasted sharply with the mature content flashing on the screen.

Meanwhile, Richard reacted swiftly. His hand shot out, grabbing the television remote from the coffee table. With a quick button press, the screen went blank, cutting off the provocative scene mid-frame.

"I'm sorry, Sam," Richard apologized, his voice tinged with regret. "I should have remembered that scene was in the trailer."

"It's okay, Daddy," Samantha replied, her voice muffled as she kept her hands firmly over her ears. "Just tell me when it's safe to look again."

I glanced at Richard, our eyes meeting in silent agreement. We had always tried to protect Samantha from the more adult aspects of Richard's acting career. But sometimes, like tonight, we were caught off guard.

"Alright, sweetheart," I gently reassured Samantha, patting her arm. "You can look now. The scene is over."

* * *

Slowly, Samantha lowered her hands and cautiously opened her eyes, glancing first at me and then at Richard for confirmation. Seeing our reassuring nods, she relaxed and snuggled back into her father's arms. Sensing my continued distress, she shifted from Richard's lap to mine, wrapping her arms around my neck. "Mummy, we love you very, very much!"

"I know, sweetheart. I love you too." I hugged her fiercely, feeling a sense of calm settle over me as Richard enveloped us both in his arms.

Yet, beneath the familial warmth, my resolve hardened. The sight of Ingrid Simon attempting to stake a claim on what was rightfully mine — Richard, was unacceptable. And I wasn't about to let that pass without a fight.

31

The carpet beneath my pearl-embellished white Jimmy Choo pumps was a stark contrast to the purple wool and silk Dior mid-length bustier dress I had carefully selected for the night. The dress, hugging my form just right, revealed an elegantly structured corset bodice with delicate pleats and tonal laces that tied at the back, accentuating my waist.

A necklace of white gold and diamonds graced my neck, its large pearl pendant resting just above my collarbone. Its matching pearl earrings added a touch of sophistication, their weight a comforting presence. My usually loose, wavy hair was now swept into a chic updo, a departure from my usual style. My makeup was understated, enhancing rather than overshadowing my features.

Beside me, Richard stood tall and handsome in his black tuxedo. His tie, a perfect match to my dress, a small detail that didn't go unnoticed, added a harmonious note to our appearance. His hair slicked back neatly, framed his sharp features. A genuine smile lit up his face, reaching his mesmerizing blue-grey eyes — the same eyes I had helplessly fallen for.

We stood before the photo wall, the movie title emblazoned boldly behind us. The relentless flashes from the cameras created a dazzling spectacle, the bright lights persistently flickering at the edge of my vision. A wave of anxiety stirred within me, threatening to engulf me. But Richard, ever my rock, held my waist reassuringly and leaned in close.

* * *

"Easy, darling," he murmured, his warm breath sending a shiver down my spine. "Just breathe."

His soothing words worked like magic, instantly calming my frayed nerves. I had thought I would get used to this — the glitz, the glamour, the spotlight that accompanied Richard's life. Yet, it still felt overwhelming, almost suffocating. Taking a deep breath, I let the noise of the crowd fade into a distant hum, focusing solely on Richard and the sanctuary his presence provided.

As we navigated our way further down the plush red carpet of Regency Theatres on Broxton Avenue in Westwood Village in Los Angeles, I allowed my thoughts to drift back to the warmth of our home. I could almost taste the rich aroma of Richard's meticulously brewed morning coffee, the faint hint of our favorite vanilla-scented candles still clinging to its corners. It was a world far removed from this film premiere's sparkling glitz and unrestrained glamour, yet it was our sanctuary — our tranquil haven.

The sensory overload of the premiere was a stark contrast to our quiet life. The relentless flash of cameras, the cacophony of excited voices, the intoxicating blend of expensive perfumes — all seemed like an alien world. Yet amidst the chaos, a sense of surreal beauty was hard to ignore.

The emotional apex of the evening wasn't our grand entrance or the endless walk down the red carpet; instead, it was the swelling tide of pride I felt for Richard. This film, a highly anticipated remake of the classic *The Getaway*, had been a coveted role that had seen auditions from numerous seasoned actors. And now, as I watched Richard bask in the appreciation he so rightfully earned, I struggled to encapsulate my feelings into coherent words.

"Are you proud of me?" He asked, pulling me out of my musing.

"More than you'll ever know," I replied, leaning into him. Our eyes met, and just like that, everything else ceased to exist — it was just Richard and me. Then came the time for one final photograph, one last picture, our smiles radiant and genuine — a perfect snapshot of the night.

The VIP section's luxurious, plush velvet seats embraced us like a comforting hug as Richard and I eased into our assigned places. To Richard's left was the effervescent Ingrid Simon, his charismatic co-star. She was resplendent in a gown of silver sequins that danced and flickered with her every graceful move. Her companion for the evening, a renowned director known for his groundbreaking films, was engrossed in a fervent conversation with a high-profile producer seated a few chairs away.

The night's host, a magnetic television personality known for his quick wit and charming demeanor, strolled onto the stage. His voice, a resonant baritone, echoed through the grand auditorium, commanding the attention of everyone present. "Ladies and Gentlemen, I present to you the shining stars of the evening, Richard and Ingrid!" His announcement was met with a thunderous applause that seemed to shake the very foundations of the building.

Richard and Ingrid rose from their seats as if on cue, their faces adorned with radiant smiles. They waved graciously at the sea of faces before them, basking in the adulation. The duo then struck an elegant pose for the voracious cameras, their images instantly immortalized in countless photographs.

The atmosphere was electric, pulsating with the energy of the media frenzy and the anticipation of the elite few who had been granted access to this coveted event. It was a night that promised grandeur, glamour, and an exclusive glimpse into a world that was usually veiled behind the silver screen.

The Getaway is a classic American heist thriller film. First gracing silver screens in 1972, this riveting cinematic experience was the brainchild of director Sam Peckinpah and screenwriter Walter Hill. The storyline, plucked from the pages of Jim Thompson's 1958 novel bearing the same title, spins an intricate web of deceit, danger, and desperation.

The film's protagonists are Doc McCoy, an ex-convict who recently sprung from prison, and Carol, his wife whose loyalty knows no bounds. Their lives intertwine with the seedy underbelly of crime when a bank heist they orchestrate spirals out of control. To secure McCoy's freedom from the cold, rigid prison walls, Carol finds herself striking a deal with a corrupt Texan politician. However, the conditions of this dubious agreement soon propel them into a whirlwind of peril, forcing them to flee with their lives hanging in the balance.

The Getaway is widely acclaimed for its heart-stopping action sequences and adrenaline-fueled chase scenes, which are lauded for their refreshing adherence to reality, a stark contrast to the often overblown spectacles of modern cinema.

Over the years, the film has seen numerous adaptations, each leaving an indelible mark on cinematic history. The role of Doc McCoy was first immortalized by the legendary Steve McQueen, then later reimagined by Alec Baldwin. Now, Richard was stepping into those legendary shoes, bringing his unique charm to the iconic role. I couldn't help but feel an indescribable pride.

As the theater lights dimmed and the opening credits rolled, I felt Richard's hand find mine. His grip was reassuring, grounding me amidst the sensory overload of the night.

Halfway through the film, my heart stuttered as the scenes that had been infiltrating my thoughts for weeks appeared. These were the moments everybody had spoken about, the ones I'd glimpsed in promotional trailers and read about in articles. The intimate encounters between Richard and his co-star, Ingrid, were beautifully shot, but they made my stomach churn. I closed my eyes, my mind racing with irrational thoughts. "This isn't reality, Hope. It's just a movie," I chanted silently to myself, trying to quell the unease.

Sensing my discomfort, Richard pulled away from the screen. He turned towards me, his eyes soft with understanding. "Darling," he said gently, cupping my face in his hands. His thumb traced circles on my cheek, calming my racing heart. "Look at me."

I opened my eyes to meet his gaze, and before I could say anything, he closed the distance between us, his lips meeting mine in a passionate kiss that erased all my insecurities. The movie continued to play on the big screen, but at that moment, it was just Richard and me. The rest of the world dissolved into insignificance as I surrendered myself to the warmth and familiarity of his kiss, the silent reassurance that regardless of what transpired on the silver screen, I was the woman who held Richard's heart in the real world.

———

The Regency Theatres premiere unfolded as a grand tableau of glitz and glamour. As the evening rolled into night, the after-party began at one of the upscale clubs in the vibrant Westwood area. The venue was a testament to luxury, with vaulted ceilings graced by intricate chandeliers that cast a warm, inviting glow. Polished mahogany walls, dotted with art pieces, reflected the ambient light, and plush velvet couches added a touch of decadence.

The atmosphere buzzed with anticipation, a heady cocktail of expensive perfumes and the clink of crystal glasses filled with effervescent champagne. The room swarmed with celebrities, press, and production crews, their laughter and chatter creating an intoxicating symphony of excitement.

Richard paraded me around the room like a proud husband, yet Ingrid Simon, his leading lady, fluttered around us like a moth drawn to a flame, her eyes constantly seeking Richard.

I was a silent observer amidst the revelry, a storm of unease and irritation brewing within me. Every time Ingrid managed to pull Richard away for a photo op, my heart clenched. Outwardly, I maintained a calm smile, but inside, I seethed.

I leaned towards Richard and whispered, "I can't wait to get out of here, drive us straight to the tarmac, and fly home to New York. LA is starting to get under my skin."

He chuckled, a soft sound that warmed me. Gently, he tilted my chin upward, forcing me to meet his gaze. His eyes twinkled with delight. "You're adorable when you're mad," he said, a teasing lilt in his voice. "And jealousy? It only makes you more irresistible, darling."

Without warning, he leaned in, pressing a featherlight kiss onto my lips. The world seemed to pause around us. "I swear, Hope, I wish for nothing more than to whisk you away, so I can explore what's beneath this gown," he murmured, his voice dripping with passion. The promise he offered was a balm, easing the tension that had tied me in knots all evening.

As I succumbed to Richard's magnetic pull, a voice sliced through our intimate bubble. "Richard, darling, we must get a picture together," Ingrid purred, her fingers trailing down Richard's arm with an intimacy that made my skin crawl.

"Hope won't mind, will you, dear?" she asked, swiveling towards me with a predatory grin. Her question was a dagger cloaked in honeyed words, more of a declaration than an inquiry.

Before I could muster a response, the party hosts intervened, calling Richard and Ingrid onto the platform made for interviews and entertainment. The crowd fell into a hushed silence, their gazes riveted on the pair. The female host, her voice ringing clear and loud, showered praises on them. "Congratulations, Richard and Ingrid. Your performance was electrifying. Those love scenes had us all on tenterhooks!" Applause erupted from the audience, a wave of agreement sweeping through the room.

A male host, basking in the crowd's enthusiasm, threw out a suggestion. "How about recreating that famous kiss from *The Getaway*?" His words were met with an onslaught of cheers, the audience eagerly anticipating the spectacle.

Richard faltered, taken aback by the request. "I don't think..." he began, but his words were cut short by Ingrid's audacity. With a swift movement, she snatched his face, hoisted herself onto her tiptoes, and sealed his lips with a passionate kiss. The room exploded into applause; camera flashes illuminated the scene like a paparazzi frenzy, immortalizing the moment for all to see.

My heart hammered against my rib cage, a potent cocktail of anger and humiliation coursing through my veins. Yet, I remained frozen, unable to react amidst the sea of onlookers. Richard's face was a picture of surprise as he broke away from Ingrid's grip. He descended the platform, leaving Ingrid bathed in the spotlight, and made his way back to me.

"Hope, I..." he began, his eyes mirroring his apologetic tone. But his words were a mere whisper against the deafening echo of the audience's cheer and the searing image of Ingrid's lips locked with his. I merely nodded, swallowing the lump of betrayal that had lodged itself in my throat. This was just another scene in the drama that was our showbiz life, but tonight, it felt like a punch to the gut.

A familiar face emerged from the crowd — a friendly media contact from Yumi's network. As he approached us, his question cut through the cacophony, "Richard, why did you leave the hosts and Ingrid on stage?" Before Richard could respond, we were swarmed by the rest of the press. Camera flashes created a blinding halo around us. I pushed my feelings aside, forcing a smile and slipping my arm around Richard's waist as he pulled me closer.

He cleared his throat, a signal that he was ready to tackle the questions. "As everyone knows, actors perform as the script dictates. *The Getaway* is a romantic adventure film, and passionate scenes are part of the narrative. Ingrid and I are committed professionals." His smile was charming, disarming even as he navigated each query deftly. "But tonight, let's not play out our on-screen roles off-screen," he added, punctuating his statement with a quick peck on my lips.

Seizing the moment, a reporter turned to me, "Hope, how did you feel about Richard and Ingrid's intimate scenes?"

Feeling a surge of confidence, with Richard by my side, I responded, "As a producer myself and a writer by profession, I completely understand the demands of storytelling. Richard and Ingrid's chemistry on screen is undeniable, so much so that it sometimes felt almost real!" My laughter rang out, joined by Richard's and the press's.

One of the reporters threw in a playful question, "Is that why Richard was caught kissing you during one of the scenes?" The crowd erupted into laughter. I could feel my cheeks burning. Sensing my discomfort, Richard squeezed my hand gently, his warm eyes meeting mine. His smile was reassuring, a silent promise that spoke volumes.

* * *

"Well," Richard chimed in, "I did that intentionally. I wanted to make sure I still have a bed to sleep in tonight," he quipped, his humor diffusing the tension and earning more laughter from the crowd.

The stage was bathed in a softer, forgiving light to dissipate the lingering awkwardness. The DJ seized the moment, cueing up a dance track reverberating through the club, transforming the atmosphere.

"May I have this dance, darling?" Richard asked, his voice barely a murmur yet distinct amidst the clamor. The world around us seemed to pause, as if we were wrapped in our own serene bubble amid the flurry of the party.

I nodded, allowing him to steer me through the sea of people toward the beckoning dance floor. The thumping music, the strobe lights, the bustling crowd — all faded into insignificance as he guided me with an assured elegance unique to him.

Upon reaching the heart of the dance floor, he drew me in close. His hand settled on the small of my back, anchoring me to him, while our other hands were held aloft. My free hand rested on his shoulder, feeling the solid contours of his muscles beneath the delicate fabric of his suit. For a fleeting moment, it felt like we were the only two souls in the room.

The music morphed into a slower rhythm, the lights dimming further, casting an intimate aura around us. Richard steered us gracefully across the dance floor, each step a symphony in sync with the beat. His gaze was untiring, locked onto mine, making my heart flutter despite the whirlwind of emotions within me.

We swayed in harmony, lost in our shared rhythm. His hold on my waist tightened, pulling me closer. His signature scent enveloped me. It was a comforting contrast to the evening's tension.

As we moved together, I could sense the curious gazes of the party-goers. But their scrutiny was inconsequential. All my fears and insecurities seemed to dissolve in Richard's embrace. For those few precious moments, it was just us — a wife and her husband, finding refuge in their love amidst the storm.

32

For someone who had spent a solitary existence, my days filled with meals from bustling New York food carts and coffee shops, I was suddenly discovering an unexpected pleasure in the simple act of setting a dinner table. Tonight, the table was a visual symphony of our finest china and gleaming silverware, each piece dancing in the flickering candlelight. I stood back to admire the culinary masterpiece prepared by one of Manhattan's most celebrated chefs, a suggestion from Jenna.

Despite several hands-on tutorials from Erin and occasionally Leticia, my kitchen skills remained in a disaster zone. Yet, the tantalizing aroma of herbed lamb, the exotic allure of saffron-infused risotto, and the rich, decadent scent of lobster bisque wafting through the room made my stomach rumble with anticipation.

A sudden flurry of noise from the living room pulled me from my musing. Our guests had arrived. I shot one last approving glance at the impeccably laid table, smoothed out my navy blue dress, flashed a thumbs-up to Leticia, and hurried towards the sound of laughter where Richard and Samantha were welcoming our visitors.

"Agnes! It's wonderful to see you again," I greeted her, planting a kiss on each of her cheeks.

"Hope, you look absolutely stunning. Your home is beautiful," she replied, her hair elegantly swept into a bun accentuating her long, graceful neck. Her pink dress complemented beautifully with her complexion. Agnes and I shared the same number of years, making her four years Henry's senior. And speaking of Henry, he looked every bit as handsome as his father, both of them dashing in light blue shirts and dark grey pants.

"My mother always told me never to arrive at a dinner party empty-handed. I thought this Bordeaux might do the trick," Agnes said, offering me a bottle of wine with a humble smile.

"Well, isn't that thoughtful! We have a certain someone in the family who considers himself quite the sommelier," I said, my eyes sparkling with amusement as I handed the bottle to Richard.

Richard held the bottle up to the light, reading the label with an appreciative nod. "Impressive indeed," he quipped, his gaze shifting to Henry. "I'm beginning to like your choice, son," he teased, the corners of his mouth curving into a playful smirk.

"Daddy, I've made a mental note. My future boyfriend will definitely be required to bring wine, too," Samantha chimed in, her youthful enthusiasm cutting through the adult banter.

Richard turned to look at his daughter, his expression turning stern. "Young lady, that's a conversation we'll be having fifteen years from now," he said, his tone firm yet laced with fatherly affection.

Samantha rolled her eyes dramatically, "You're such a buzzkill, Dad," she retorted, causing a ripple of laughter to spread through the room.

As we settled into our seats for dinner, I couldn't help but glance at my family and Agnes, their expressions lighting up with pleasure as they savored the first mouthfuls of food. Samantha's eyes sparkled with delight as she bit into the herb-crusted lamb, and Richard's contented sigh echoed through the room as he relished the rich flavor of the lobster bisque.

The playful banter between Henry and Samantha began in earnest, their jovial tones infusing the room with a burst of infectious laughter. "Sammidoo, you've managed to decorate your face with sauce," Henry teased, a twinkle of mischief in his eyes. Samantha shot back with a feigned eye roll, "Well, Henrquedoo, at least I know how to savor my meal truly."

Agnes, who had been observing their exchange with an amused smile, turned to me. "Hope, this meal is nothing short of divine." Her compliment warmed my heart. She had integrated so effortlessly into our family dynamic, that it was difficult to recall when she wasn't part of these familial gatherings.

"I wish I could claim the credit," I confessed, "but a talented chef from Manhattan conjured the culinary magic."

Agnes laughed, her eyes sparkling with humor, "Well, they say women who cook at home tend to have healthier children, right? That must be why so many kids are obese now — mothers juggling work and home hardly have time to cook! Considering my non-existent cooking skills, I shudder to think how overweight my future kids might be!"

"Thank goodness for Leticia, and Richard's foresight in finding her before me!" I joined in her laughter.

Richard chimed in, "Darling, don't sell yourself short. The pasta you made at our Chelsea home that weekend was among the best I've had in years."

I chuckled, "That's very generous of you, Richard. But to be honest, Erin had to endure weeks of training me to perfect that dish."

"Mummy, you prepare my school lunches. You slice those apples and remove the seeds — they're delicious," Samantha interjected, causing a fresh wave of laughter to wash over us.

Suddenly, the pleasant chatter subsided as Richard cleared his throat, commanding attention from everyone around the table. He raised his glass, the crystal catching the candlelight. "To the family and our lovely guest, Agnes," he began, his voice resonating with warmth and authority. "And let's not forget the talented chef in Manhattan who has graced us with this exceptional meal."

As I lifted my glass to join the toast, a wave of dizziness washed over me. My stomach churned and performed a violent somersault — protesting against the decadent fare I'd been indulging in for the past few hours. Clapping a hand over my mouth, I made a mad dash towards the nearest powder room, barely making it before surrendering to the nauseating urge.

Richard was hot on my heels, his face etched with concern. He tenderly tucked away stray strands behind my ear and handed me a fresh towel. "Are you all right, darling?" he asked, his voice laced with worry.

Before I could respond, another bout of nausea swept over me. Cold sweat trickled down my face as I braced myself against the cold porcelain bowl.

"Richard, let me handle this," Agnes interjected, her serene demeanor slicing through the thick tension. She held Henry's stethoscope, which he had rushed to retrieve amidst the chaos. With a reassuring smile plastered on her face, she said, "Let's check your vitals, Hope."

Kneeling beside me, Agnes scrutinized my eyes with a small flashlight, then grasped my wrist to measure my pulse. Richard moved to sit behind me, offering his chest as a makeshift backrest.

"When did you last have your period?" Agnes asked nonchalantly, flashing a knowing smile at Richard.

"Oh God! I don't remember. But it should be due this week," I mumbled, despite my discomfort.

"You might find this strange, but I always carry a few essentials for medical emergencies. Henry, could you fetch my bag, please? And Richard, I need everyone out of the room," she instructed, her tone firm yet gentle, as she geared up to take control of the situation.

Henry returned with Agnes' bag just as the rest of my family vacated the powder room. As soon as the door clicked shut, Agnes unzipped her bag and retrieved a small box. Recognition dawned on me — a pregnancy test kit. She met my startled gaze with a comforting smile. "I'll leave you alone for three minutes. You know what to do," she stated, her voice a soothing whisper.

A flutter of nervous anticipation danced in my stomach. Fear had been my unwelcome companion the last time I navigated these waters. This time, a different type of fear gripped me — the fear that this might just be a false alarm. After meticulously following the instructions on the box, I closed my eyes and waited, each second stretching into an eternity.

The door creaked open, breaking the silence. Agnes stepped in, her presence radiating calmness. She gently pried the kit from my trembling hands. Her face lit up with a radiant smile as she glanced at the result. She turned the kit towards me, unveiling the two pink lines. "My suspicions were correct. You're pregnant! Congratulations, Hope!" she exclaimed, wrapping me in a warm embrace. Overwhelmed by a surge of joy, I found it hard to catch my breath. I took the kit back from her, gazing at the double strip in disbelief.

"Let's conduct a quick check-up to confirm," Agnes suggested, pulling out her stethoscope and running through a series of checks. Finally, after what felt like an eternity, she nodded, a satisfied smile playing on her lips. "First things first, you need to see your gynecologist as soon as possible for a series of tests and to formulate your prenatal plan," she advised, squeezing my hand reassuringly. "I can tell you've been yearning for this moment, and I couldn't be happier for you and Richard."

"Thank you so much, Agnes!" I exclaimed, throwing my arms around her in a tight hug. The joy welling up within me was too immense to contain. I was going to be a mother!

"Shall we share the good news?"

Together, we stepped out of the powder room, facing our anxiously waiting family. The moment my eyes met Richard's, brimming with hope and concern, I couldn't hold back my joy any longer. I dashed towards him; the pregnancy test clutched tightly in my hand.

Agnes turned to face Richard, her warm smile lighting up her face as she said, "Congratulations, Richard."

* * *

Henry glanced at the test, then at me, his eyes growing wide as he grasped the magnitude of this moment. He had been there when I lost my first pregnancy. He understood the significance of this moment.

Richard's eyes glistened with unshed tears as he gazed into mine. Enveloping me in his strong arms, he pulled me close and planted a passionate, life-affirming kiss on my lips that stirred my very soul. As he broke away, his gaze locked onto mine, filled with raw emotion. "I love you, darling," he murmured, his voice choked with emotion. His eyes, brimming with love and adoration, held mine until I could no longer hold back the tears welling up in my eyes. Overwhelmed by the enormity of it all, I flung my arms around him, clinging to him as if my life hinged on it.

"Mum, are you alright?" The small, worried voice of Samantha punctuated our intimate moment. Her wide, innocent eyes shimmered with unshed tears. My heart tightened in my chest. In the whirlwind of our joy, I had momentarily overlooked her.

Dropping to my knees, I swept her into my arms, drawing her near. Taking her petite hands into mine, I gently placed them on my stomach. "Darling, Mummy has some wonderful news to share. I'm pregnant. You're going to become a big sister," I told her, my voice thick with emotion.

Her eyes grew wide with surprise before a cloud of uncertainty moved into them. "Will you still love me the same, Mummy?" she asked, her voice barely a whisper.

I pulled her closer, nestling her small frame against mine. "My love for you and Henry will never waver, Sam. You're my little girl, my ray of sunshine. Never forget that," I reassured her, my tone firm yet gentle. She wound her arms tightly around me, her small body quivering with relief.

Just then, Richard joined us and put his arms around us. Then he scooped her into his arms like she was the most precious treasure in the world. "Hey there, you're still Daddy's little princess," he said, his voice filled with warmth and love. The sight of them together, their faces mirroring pure joy, was a perfect end to an unforgettable evening.

A wave of relief and happiness washed over me, leaving me breathless. Richard, his eyes gleaming with joy mirrored my own, pulled me up and into the shelter of his arm, holding me close. The warmth of his embrace was a comforting anchor amidst the whirlwind of emotions.

Henry, who had been observing the scene quietly from the sidelines, stepped forward. His usually stoic face was transformed by a broad, genuine smile that reached his eyes. "Congratulations, Hope, Dad," he said, his voice choked with emotion. "I can't wait to be a big brother again."

His words triggered a fresh surge of happiness within me. I extricated myself gently from Richard's protective hold and opened my arms to Henry. He moved towards me without hesitation, wrapping his arms around me in a gentle hug.

"Henry, thank you," I whispered into his ear, my voice shaky with emotion. "You've always been there for me, through all the highs and lows of my previous pregnancy. I couldn't have asked for a better friend."

He pulled back slightly, his eyes meeting mine. "And I couldn't have asked for a better one," he replied, his voice steady and sincere. "I promise to be the best big brother this baby could ever wish for."

Tears pricked at the corners of my eyes at his heartfelt words as I held him close.

33

The cozy warmth of the living room enveloped me like a comforting embrace as I nestled into the plush cushions of the sofa. Salem purred contentedly on my lap, his inky fur stark against the crisp white of my pajamas and the festive red of my Santa-themed socks. I savored the crunch of cinnamon-spiced berries, their tart sweetness harmonizing perfectly with the rich creaminess of Greek yogurt.

A soft, ethereal glow emanated from the towering Christmas tree in the corner, casting playful, dancing shadows across Richard's youthful face. He lifted our daughter Samantha high above his head, allowing her to place the shining star at the very peak of the tree. Her vibrant red onesie mirrored the bold hues of the ornaments that adorned the green tree, making her look like a living, breathing decoration herself.

The scent of fresh pine needles, mingled with the faint, tantalizing aroma of gingerbread baking in the oven, filled the air. Leticia was whipping up this batch of holiday magic in the kitchen. The combined scents wrapped us all in an invisible blanket of holiday cheer — it was a week before Christmas, after all.

The merry laughter of Richard and Sam reverberated throughout the room, creating a sweet symphony with the classic Christmas tunes spinning on our vintage vinyl player. Outside, delicate snowflakes danced and twirled in the crisp Sunday morning air, but inside our home was a world steeped in warmth.

Yet, beneath the joyous exterior, Samantha's laughter reflected a hint of melancholy as she recounted tales of Christmases past in London. Her voice, filled with longing, cut through the music, "Dad, do you remember what your Christmases were like in London? My friends and I used to go caroling and visit the huge Christmas markets."

Richard chuckled, his eyes distant as he delved into his own memories, "I vaguely remember my own experiences since my job had me partying on different continents every year. But yes, I recollect the good times from my childhood, the bustling markets, and the joy of caroling."

I felt a pang of guilt twist in my heart. It was because of my haunting nightmares that we had distanced ourselves from that city. Now, they missed a part of their cherished holiday traditions. Henry, too, was grappling with the challenges of a long-distance relationship with Agnes — and I had been the one to take it all away.

I tenderly placed both hands on my belly, not yet showing but already a haven for the new life within. This baby signified more than just an addition to our family; it was a beacon of hope, a symbol of new beginnings. A gentle reminder that I needed to forgive... and let go of the terrible event that had once marred my life. After all, everything I could ever want and need was right here in front of me.

Thoughts of splitting our time between the bustling metropolis of New York, the historic allure of London, and my culturally rich hometown of Manila started swirling in my mind. Could we handle it? Could we introduce our children to their varied heritage and navigate them through these three distinctive worlds?

With Salem still nestled contentedly in my lap, I slowly rose and ambled over to Richard. From behind, I wrapped my arms around his waist, resting my head against the reassuring firmness of his back. "How would you feel about spending some time in London after the holidays?" I asked softly, curiosity weaved into my words.

He turned within my embrace, surprise etched on his face, swiftly morphing into a blend of excitement and concern. "London? Really?" His voice was laced with anticipation, yet tinged with a note of worry.

* * *

Samantha, who had been meticulously arranging ornaments in her own little world, froze at the sound of our conversation. "Really, Mum? Can we really go back to London?" Her voice was eager, hopeful, her eyes lighting up like the twinkling fairy lights adorning our Christmas tree.

"Yes," I confirmed, a warm smile spreading across my face.

"Darling, let's not rush into this decision. I know that wound is still raw, and we can afford to wait," he said gently, brushing his thumb tenderly against my lips.

"This wound won't heal itself," I countered softly, meeting his gaze squarely. "At some point, I need to confront it head-on, and with Sam and our little bean here," I patted my stomach lightly, "I know it won't be as daunting. Besides, I want them to embrace their roots. But it's too late to do it this holiday as our home in Chelsea isn't prepared for our arrival. Besides, I want you, Sam, and Henry to experience the holidays in New York, especially New Year's Eve." Richard's smile widened unmistakably when I mentioned 'our home.'

A wave of pure, unadulterated joy swept through the room as Samantha's excited squeal filled the air, her small feet tapping a rhythmic dance to Santa's jolly tune. "Yippee! I'm so thrilled!" she exclaimed, her eyes sparkling with childish delight.

My heart swelled at her innocent enthusiasm, and I found myself nodding in agreement, a warm smile turning up the corners of my mouth. "Yes, really," I confirmed. I watched as her face lit up even more, if that were possible. "We can split our time between London and New York. We can start building new memories there." I paused, turning my gaze towards Richard. "And maybe," I suggested, "we could spend some time in Manila too. I have a feeling you'll adore it, Sam."

Her response was immediate and vehement. "Of course, I would! Summers with Grandpa Oliver are the absolute best!"

Richard's grin broadened, his blue eyes twinkling with anticipation. "I think that sounds like an excellent plan," he agreed, wrapping an arm around me.

"But we must remember, school is still in New York," I cautioned, my tone turning serious. "Mummy is taking her management training program with Yumi here. However, I can manage some work from the London office when we're there for the holidays and vacations." I added, hoping to reassure them that this new arrangement would not disrupt their lives too much.

The front door creaked open, and Henry stepped inside, shrugging off his winter jacket with a shiver. "What did I miss?" He asked, his voice echoing in the festive living room.

Samantha, bubbling over with excitement, rushed to him, her voice tripping over the words as she relayed the news. "Mummy said we could go to London after the holiday! And that's not all, we might even live there sometimes. Plus, we're going to Manila in the summer," she gushed, her eyes sparkling with anticipation.

Henry's smile widened at the news, then faltered slightly as he remembered my ordeal from the previous year. "That does sound nice, but let's not rush into anything," he cautioned, just like his father, his protective instincts kicking in.

I unwound my arms from around Richard and reached for Henry, pulling him into a comforting embrace. "I'm ready, Henry. It's about time," I reassured him, kissing his cheek gently.

"She's probably also considering your long-distance situation with Agnes," Richard said, his arms snaking around my waist from behind.

"That, too," I admitted, resting the back of my head against the firmness of Richard's chest. "I know how difficult it is being away from those you love."

Richard sighed, his voice tinged with regret. "I'm sorry, darling. But as I promised you, moving forward, I will only choose projects that are truly worthwhile."

A warm, knowing smile spread across Henry's face at our discussion.

"I'd better inform Agnes," he said, his voice tinged with a mixture of relief and excitement. The prospect of spending more time in London meant fewer miles between him and his long-distance love.

Their joy warmed me and eased some of the guilt. Perhaps we could make it work, live in all three places. The thought was daunting but also thrilling. It felt like a step towards healing, towards a new chapter for our family.

34

The following morning, under the harsh glare of fluorescent lights, I sat in the executive boardroom. The room was filled with the conglomerate's most influential figures, their collective power almost tangible. The air buzzed with anticipation as we awaited the arrival of Michael Yang, our usually charismatic CEO. His entrance today, however, was swift and silent, a stark contrast to his typical grandeur.

"Ladies and gentlemen," he began, his voice echoing through the cavernous room, "I have an important announcement to make." A hush fell over the room, the silence so profound that even the soft hum of the ventilation system seemed intrusive. "I've tendered my resignation as CEO, effective immediately."

His words hung like a heavy fog, casting a pall over the room. The shock was evident, as if the air had been sucked out of the room. The initial shock, however, gradually gave way to a stunned silence.

"I've made my decision," he continued, his voice steady despite the gravity of his words. "And I'm pleased to announce that Lydia Miller will be stepping up as my replacement." He gestured towards Lydia, who sat across the table from me. Her face was a mask of composure amidst the upheaval, her eyes reflecting a calm determination.

As his words sank in, the room erupted in applause. The sudden burst of noise was startling, shattering the earlier quietude. The atmosphere shifted from somber to celebratory as executives rose from their seats to congratulate Lydia. The mood was contagious, and despite the shock of the news, I couldn't help but share the excitement for Lydia. She had always been a force within the company, her unwavering dedication and relentless drive inspiring us all.

Michael, usually the picture of charisma with his handsome features and chiseled jaw, seemed diminished. His smile was strained, his jaw clenched as he looked at me. He bowed his head in a silent goodbye, his eyes betraying a hint of sadness. I acknowledged him with a nod, a soft smile, and a silent show of respect. Then, with a final glance around the boardroom, he exited quietly, leaving behind a room full of bewildered executives.

As the applause receded, Lydia navigated her way through the sea of congratulatory executives to stand by my side. She was a figure of calm amidst the whirlwind of activity around us.

"Hope," she said, her voice steady and reassuring amidst the clamor, "Thank you. Although you wouldn't confirm this, I know you have a hand in this." She locked eyes with me, her gaze unwavering and filled with determination. "I promise you, I will do everything I can to expand our presence in the US and European markets."

The sincerity in her voice was palpable, her commitment unquestionable. "Furthermore," she continued, "I'm committed to mentoring you, preparing you for a leadership role in your father's conglomerate. Together, we'll ensure that when the time comes for you to take up the mantle, you will be ready."

Her words washed over me, igniting a rush of gratitude. "Thank you, Lydia," I responded, my voice subdued yet filled with sincerity. "I'm eager to learn from you, to follow in your footsteps."

As the boardroom slowly returned to its usual rhythm, the executive committee convened for another meeting. This time, it was Lydia at the helm, commanding the room with an air of authority that was both new and familiar. Despite the excitement of the day, a pang of sadness tugged at me as I thought of Michael. He had once been a loyal confidant to my father, his dedication unwavering until his rivalry with Richard consumed him. Now, he was a ghost of his former self, a stark reminder of the price of ambition.

* * *

After the meeting, my father beckoned me into his office. It was a room that always hummed with an undercurrent of power and authority, its silence now almost unsettling. Outside his window, the cityscape stretched out, a vibrant tableau of life in stark contrast to the intensity of our impending conversation.

"Hope," he began, his voice softer than usual, "I apologize if I've been rushing you into different roles." His smile was calculated and practiced, but I could see the glimmer of excitement beneath it. He was eager to embrace his role as a grandfather again, the news of my pregnancy bringing him joy amidst the chaos. "I seem to have forgotten that you just got married and now have a child on the way."

"Daddy," I replied, my hands instinctively moving toward the collection of photos displayed on his desk. Each frame held a memory — a black-and-white photo of a seven-year-old me, my radiant smile on my wedding day, a family portrait with Richard, Henry, Sam, my parents, and myself. "I've learned so much these past few months, and I'm prepared for the challenges that lie ahead. But right now, I want to savor this time — my pregnancy, my family."

He nodded, his eyes softening. "Enjoy life, sweetheart," he said, his tone affectionate. "Do you think hiring an executive manager to take over some of your work would be helpful?"

I considered his proposal, my mind weighing the pros and cons. "I believe it's still manageable. My team is excellent, and I just need to learn how to delegate effectively. That way, I can also find time to write my next book."

His laughter filled the room, a sound that was both warm and familiar. "Delegation has never been the Ortegas' strong suit."

"I know, Daddy," I replied, matching his chuckle with my own. "But we must learn. When I almost lost Richard, I blamed myself for not being there for him." My smile faltered as I remembered the pain of those days. "This is our second chance at life, and we've promised to devote more time to the roles you've entrusted us with. We're going to make the most out of every moment."

* * *

"Oh, before I forget," my father interjected, a twinkle in his eye, "we've just acquired another private jet. I don't want you and your family shuttling on commercial airlines between New York, Manila, and London." He winked at me, the corners of his mouth turning up in a playful smirk.

"Daddy! That's excessively generous," I protested, a hint of laughter seeping into my voice. "You know Richard can acquire one if needed."

"I'm aware," he responded, his tone light but firm. "He offered as much. But I convinced him it would be more practical to have it under the corporation for operational expenses and service management." He paused, a satisfied smile playing on his lips. "In return, I asked him to commit to attending all board meetings, to which he readily agreed."

"Thanks, Dad," I said, my voice filled with gratitude. I walked over to him, wrapping my arms around his shoulders from behind. As I rested my chin atop his head, I was no longer the executive in the room; I was his little girl again, basking in the warmth of his paternal love.

The remainder of the day was spent in deep conversation, discussing plans, strategies, and my impending management training. But above all, we spoke of the future. A future that, for the first time in a long while, seemed less daunting and more inviting. I felt ready to embrace whatever lay ahead, secure in the knowledge that I had my father's unwavering support and belief in me.

35

As twilight began to drape its gentle shroud over the day, I was perched on the edge of a tranquil pond in Central Park. A paper bag filled with breadcrumbs nestled beside me, its contents slowly diminishing as I fed the resident ducks. The avian crowd was diverse in hues and sizes, their beady eyes gleaming with anticipation each time my hand moved toward the bag.

The frigid wind of winter whipped around me, its icy tendrils seeping through my clothing despite the lingering warmth of the day. The snow that had blanketed New York was finally starting to melt, leaving behind a chill that seemed to penetrate everything. I hugged my winter jacket closer to myself, the slight bulge of my growing pregnancy just barely noticeable beneath the layers of my outfit. My comfortable yoga pants and thermal heater pantsuit kept me reasonably warm, both neatly tucked into my trusty Uggs boots.

A particular duck on the pond caught my eye, its familiar waddle triggering a rush of memories. This park, this very spot, was where Henry and I first crossed paths— a time before Richard had become part of my life's narrative. The serenity of this urban oasis had drawn us both in, providing a respite from the city's relentless hustle. Our bond formed effortlessly as we shared laughter, stories, and breadcrumbs with the ducks, creating memories that warmed my heart.

From the corner of my eye, I noticed Chen and Arthur, my ever-watchful bodyguards. They stood at a respectful distance, their sharp eyes ceaselessly scanning the surroundings for potential threats. Their presence was a comforting constant, yet they managed to blend seamlessly into the park's backdrop, as unobtrusive as the shadows cast by the setting sun.

Tossing another handful of crumbs into the rippling water, I was swept up in a wave of nostalgia. With its towering skyline and ceaseless energy, New York had been my home, my sanctuary. It was here that I'd navigated the labyrinth of adolescence, transitioned into adulthood, and now, I was on the precipice of leaving it all behind... albeit temporarily.

A London sojourn beckoned me, an opportunity for Richard, Henry, and Samantha to delve back into their roots while I sought to redefine mine. The prospect was daunting. The thought of living on different continents, juggling the demands of work, family, and my insatiable passion for writing seemed like a Herculean task.

The city of London held a paradoxical place in my heart; it was a tapestry of joyous memories interwoven with moments of intense pain and fear. Could I ever truly be ready to embrace that city again? To forgive those who had caused me such deep anguish?

Richard had been patient, suggesting I take time before returning, until I felt ready. Yet, I couldn't shake off the guilt that gnawed at me. My reluctance was unfair to Henry, who was caught in a long-distance romance with Agnes. I was acutely aware of the sacrifices he was making for me. And then there was Samantha. I couldn't, in good conscience, deprive her of connecting with her roots, and her family from her biological mother's side.

I found myself torn between self-preservation and the needs of those I loved dearly. It was a delicate balancing act, one that would require all the strength and courage I could muster.

I was certain of one thing: Richard would follow me to the ends of the earth. And I was prepared to do the same for him.

Perhaps a change of scenery wasn't such a bad idea. My latest book wasn't evolving as I'd envisioned, the storyline stubbornly refusing to fit into the structure I had in my mind. Inspiration for my next novel felt like a shy creature, lurking just out of sight but never fully revealing itself. Ideas were swirling in my head, vague and shapeless, like wisps of smoke waiting for a gust of wind to give them direction.

Who knew? Maybe London held the key to unlocking that elusive muse.

Our new plan seemed like a promising compromise. Henry was set to return to his medical internship program in London. On the other hand, Samantha was preparing for a transatlantic education, shuttling between her current school in New York and a new one in London. Initially, I had concerns about how she would handle this transition, and the impact on her friendships. Yet, Samantha was brimming with excitement, eager for this fresh chapter in her life.

"Good luck to me, right, duckies?" I whispered softly, breaking the silence. Their responding quacks seemed to echo my sentiments. "I'm going to miss you guys," I added, a melancholy smile tugging at my lips.

With a sigh, I rose from the bench, brushing off the remnants of bread crumbs from my lap. I cast one last look at the tranquil pond, the ducks now drifting away, their curiosity sated. "Goodbye, New York," I whispered, my voice barely audible against the soft rustling of the leaves.

It wasn't a permanent farewell, merely a temporary separation, but it still tugged at my heartstrings. With all its noise, chaos, beauty, and ugliness, this city was a part of me. But for now, another adventure awaited. With a final, lingering glance at the park, I turned away, ready to face whatever lay beyond the horizon.

36

"Take your time, darling," Richard murmured, his warm blue-grey eyes meeting mine. His lips brushed against mine in a tender kiss, and I could taste the faint hint of mint from his toothpaste. The memory of it would linger, reassuring and grounding, as I braced myself to step out of the car. Chen held the door open with a sympathetic smile.

Hand in hand, Richard and I traversed the cobblestone path leading up to our home in Chelsea. Our Georgian house, with its elegant architecture and imposing stature, was usually a sight that filled me with warmth and comfort. But this time, it was different. The traumatic events of the past year had cast a long shadow, making the familiar feel strangely alien.

Inside, pressed against the window, I saw Samantha. Her blue eyes were wide with anticipation, her small nose squashed against the glass. She and Henry had flown back to London a day earlier than us, unable to contain their excitement about returning home.

As soon as she caught sight of us, Samantha bolted towards the door. It swung open with a bang, and she launched herself at me. "Mum!" she cried out, her arms wrapping tightly around me. Her voice was like a melody to my ears, a symphony of love and relief that melted the icy dread that had lodged within me since that dreadful encounter with Richard's ex-wife.

"Oh, sweetheart," I replied, my voice barely above a whisper. I held her close, her small body anchoring me to the present. The scent of her strawberry shampoo filled my senses, a familiar aroma that spoke of simpler times. It was a stark reminder of what was at stake, of what I had managed to hold onto despite everything.

She touched my stomach gently, "Oi, little bean, did you behave just like I told you during the flight? I hope you didn't give Mum any trouble."

"Well, little bean behaved quite well. It seems he listens to his big sister, I reckon," I replied.

My heart fluttered with a medley of emotions — relief, nostalgia, joy, and a tinge of sadness. The scent of lavender and warm spices permeated the air, as comforting as an old, familiar blanket.

Henry was next, his towering frame filling the doorway. The corners of his mouth were curled into a faint smile, his eyes twinkling with relief. "Welcome home, Hope," he greeted, his voice choked with a mixture of joy and relief. His medical internship in New York had taken him away from this home, but the worry for me had etched premature lines into his youthful face.

"Thank you, Henry," I responded, my voice barely above a whisper. I offered him a heartfelt smile, grateful for his steady support throughout my ordeal. "It's good to be back."

Stepping further inside, I was greeted by the familiar sight of our beautiful home. The polished wood floors gleamed under the soft lighting. The living room was tastefully adorned with plush furniture and carefully curated art pieces. The kitchen exuded a cozy charm, promising warmth and hearty meals. Each room was a testament to a home brimming with love and comfort. As I took it all in, I could feel the knots of tension within me slowly unraveling, replaced by a burgeoning sense of peace.

A new face appeared amidst the familiar surroundings—a stout woman in her fifties, wearing a cordial smile. "Madam Hope, I'm Priscilla, welcome back to London," she greeted warmly.

"Thank you, Priscilla. It's a pleasure to meet you," I replied, appreciating the kindness in her eyes.

Richard came up behind me, shrugging off his jacket. "Ahh, it's been a while," he murmured, his voice filled with quiet contentment. He gently helped me out of my own coat, handing them both to Priscilla.

My hands instinctively gravitated towards the gentle swell of my belly, a soft whisper of life burgeoning within. "Welcome home, little one," I murmured, my voice barely audible in the quiet room. Ever attuned to my emotions, Richard wrapped his arm around me, his hand coming to rest over mine on our unborn child. Leaning into him, I rested my head against his chest, his steady heartbeat a soothing lullaby that helped push away the dark memories that still lurked in the corners of my mind.

When I opened my eyes, it was to the sight of my family — my world. Henry and Samantha were engaged in playful banter, arguing about who would get the larger room in the west wing. Their laughter filled our home with a more comforting warmth than any fireplace.

Despite the American blood coursing through my veins, I wanted my children to have a connection to their English roots. To understand and appreciate the culture that was so integral to their father's identity. And so, we had made a deal to divide our time between New York and London, ensuring that our children grew up as citizens of both worlds.

"Our home needs a bit of love, darling," Richard joked, his eyes twinkling with mischief. "Little bean's nursery isn't going to set itself up. And I'm sure you'll find the perfect designers to bring your vision to life. My checkbook is already on your dresser, awaiting your magic touch."

I turned around in his arms, my fingers tracing the familiar contours of his face. His features were etched in my heart, proof of the love that had weathered storms and emerged stronger. Rising on my tiptoes, I pressed my lips against his, feeling his arms tighten around my waist as he deepened the kiss.

"Daddy, can you stop kissing Mummy now? We need to eat, hello?" Samantha's indignant voice broke through our bubble, causing us to pull apart with a start. Laughter bubbled up within me, a joyful sound that echoed around our home.

The evening unfolded like a beautiful dream. We gathered around the dining table, a feast of our favorite dishes spread out before us. The meal was hearty, each bite a comforting reminder of home. As we ate, we found ourselves slipping into familiar patterns, the conversation flowing as easily as wine. We reminisced about our life in London and New York, each memory a precious gem that we held close to our hearts.

––––––––

Later, as I made my way to our bedroom window, I looked outside — darkness had already descended. The last snowfall of the season began its gentle dance. The city was slowly blanketed in a layer of pristine white, transforming the landscape into a winter wonderland. Looking out the window, the falling flakes resembled tiny stars twinkling against the velvet night sky. It was a magical sight, one that added a touch of enchantment to the scene. To me, it felt symbolic, as if nature itself was acknowledging our fresh start, adding its own touch of beauty to our reunion.

Richard was already fast asleep. His chest rose and fell rhythmically; his face relaxed in the peaceful slumber. I couldn't help but smile at the sight, feeling a wave of affection for this man who had stood by me through thick and thin.

Approaching the bed, I reached out to cover his naked body with the soft duvet. His skin was warm to the touch, a stark contrast against the cold air seeping in from the window. I kissed his lips lightly — he smiled in his sleep as I was part of his beautiful dream. As I turned to leave, I noticed his bathrobe lying on the chair. Picking it up, I wrapped it around myself, its fabric still carrying his scent. It was a comforting aroma, blending his aftershave and the crisp winter air. With one last glance at Richard, I quietly left the room, leaving him to his dreams. My heart was full, brimming with love, and this moment.

With a newfound sense of inspiration, I quietly slipped away to Richard's study. The room was bathed in the soft glow of the evening light that filtered through the large windows. It was a sanctuary of sorts, filled with the comforting scent of old books and rich mahogany. Nestled atop Richard's grand desk was my laptop, patiently waiting for my return.

I settled into the plush leather chair, the cool material pressing against my skin through the thin fabric of Richard's robe. My fingers hovered over the keyboard, the anticipation sending a jolt of electricity through my veins. The blank screen stared back at me, its emptiness echoing the void I had felt a year ago. But now, I am different. I was stronger, braver, a survivor of my own personal hell.

As my fingers began to dance across the keys, each stroke felt like a heartbeat, echoing in the otherwise silent room. *"The Last Snowfall"* in bold font stared back at me. It seemed fitting, a tribute to the endings and beginnings that had shaped my life, a testament to the pain and healing that had marked my journey.

As I delved deeper into the narrative, it felt like I was threading a needle, stitching together the scattered fragments of my soul. Each word was a stitch, each sentence a seam, mending the wounds left by the chaos of the past year.

Bathed in the soft, warm glow of the desk lamp, I began to weave words into a tapestry of emotion. The keys beneath my fingers danced to a rhythm only I could hear, each one telling a tale of love and loss, resilience and rebirth.

I wrote about Samantha's infectious joy, a beacon of light in even the darkest times. I shared stories of her laughter echoing through our home, her wide-eyed wonder at the simplest of things, and her unwavering belief in the goodness of people. Her spirit, so full of life and love, was a constant reminder of what truly mattered.

Henry's strength, both physical and emotional, was next. His unwavering support during my ordeal, and his quiet determination to protect those he loved. He was my friend from the beginning, and his presence was always felt, his love a comforting blanket on cold winter nights.

I wrote of my father's constant encouragement, his faith in me never wavering even in the face of adversity. His gentle and firm words guided me through the storm, his wisdom serving as my compass when I lost my way. His love, deep and unconditional, was my safe harbor in the tumultuous sea of life.

Richard, my rock, my anchor, deserved chapters of his own. I wrote of his fall and triumphant return, his struggle mirroring my own. His journey back to us was marked with pain and struggle but also with hope and determination. His love for me, for Samantha and Henry, fueled his fight, his spirit refusing to surrender. His strength, resilience, and love were the foundation on which he built his recovery.

And then there was my story. A tumultuous journey marked by deep valleys and towering peaks. A journey of love, healing, and rediscovering myself in the aftermath of a tragedy. I detailed the pain, the loss, and the grief that threatened to consume me. But I also wrote of the healing, the acceptance, and the rebirth that followed. My journey wasn't just about survival; it was about finding hope amidst despair, about finding the strength to rise from the ashes.

As the words flowed out of me, filling the pages with my heart and soul, I felt a sense of release. Each sentence and paragraph helped stitch together the wounds of my past, transforming them into badges of honor, symbols of a battle fought and won.

As the final sentence fell into place, a wave of completion washed over me. I was home, not just within these familiar walls, but within myself. I was whole again, ready to face whatever life threw my way.

I closed my eyes. The house was silent, save for the soft ticking of the grandfather clock in the hallway. When I opened them, I looked through the window. Outside, the snow had stopped falling, leaving behind a pristine blanket of white. The first signs of spring were starting to peek through, a promise of new beginnings.

A profound sense of peace settled over me, a smile playing on my lips. The completion of my story, *The Last Snowfall*, was a metaphor for my own journey. I had weathered the storm, survived the winter, and now, I was ready to embrace the spring. I was complete, just like my story.

* * *

With a final flourish of the keys and a contented sigh, I clicked 'save' on the document. The glow of the laptop screen dimmed as I closed it, the hum of the machine falling silent. A smile tugged at my lips, my heart brimming with a profound sense of peace and accomplishment.

There it was. My story outline for *The Last Snowfall* was complete, each plot point carefully planned, ready to blossom into detailed chapters. It was like a roadmap of the journey I was about to embark on, filled with twists and turns, highs and lows, and characters who would come to feel like old friends.

And as I sat there in the quiet of our home, I realized that I, too, was ready. Ready to delve into this new story, ready to welcome our little bean into the world, ready to embrace whatever came our way. Because no matter what, I knew I wouldn't be facing it alone. I had Richard and our family by my side — their love, my guiding light.

Yes, we had weathered storms and faced dark days. But now, as the last snowfall of the season melted away, giving way to the promise of spring, I felt hopeful. Hopeful for our future, for the new life growing within me, and for the stories yet to be told. And with that hope in my heart, I knew we were ready to turn the page and start another chapter in our lives.

* * *

THE END
* * *

To Mila D. Aguilar.

In loving memory of a remarkable friend, whose spirit will forever
reside within these pages and in our hearts.

* * *

Dear Readers,

I wish to thank each one of you for embarking on the love journey of Hope and Richard. It is your unwavering support that motivates me to continue their story instantly. This book is a labor of love, and I'm grateful that you've chosen to accompany me on this adventure. Your engagement, curiosity, and passion for stories make every late night and early morning worthwhile.

To my meticulous book editor Frances Amper-Sales, who with her discerning eye and sharp wit, has transformed my thoughts into a story worth telling. My dear Frances, I love that you loved Hope and Richard, just the way I do.

To Cocoy, Mike and DW, your humor, wit, anecdotes and daily musings turned some of the characters relatable and fun. Your virtual companionship has also been a guiding light in my solitary writing journey, I can't thank you enough.

To Mike Dee, thank you for your remarkable fact-checking skills that have brought many scenes to life. Thank you for stepping in to rewrite certain scenes, in that way enhancing their credibility. I hope to see your name in your own book one day.

To Mila Aguilar, thank you for encouraging me to keep on writing and to write more.

To my beloved husband Carlos and our wonderful children, Luis and Julia, who have been my rock, my cheer squad, and my sanctuary amid a whirlwind of words.

With all my love. This book is dedicated to all of you.

Justine

ABOUT THE AUTHOR

Justine Castellon is a brand strategist with an innate ability to weave compelling narratives. She seamlessly blends her professional insight with her passion for literature. Her literary works include romantic drama novels—**Four Seasons** and **Gnight Sara / 'Night Heck**. With her ability to tell stories that linger long after the last word, Justine leaves a mark not only in the world of branding but also in the hearts of her readers.

www.justcastellon.com